NOT THAT KIND OF GOOD GUY

NOT THAT KIND OF GOOD GUY

JOHN RINGO

BAEN

A Baen Books Original

Baen Publishing Enterprises
P.O. Box 1403
Riverdale, NY 10471
www.baen.com

ISBN: 978-1-6680-7259-2

Cover art by Sam R. Kennedy

First printing, May 2025

Distributed by Simon & Schuster
1230 Avenue of the Americas
New York, NY 10020

Library of Congress Cataloging-in-Publication Data

Names: Ringo, John, 1963– author.
Title: Not that kind of good guy / John Ringo.
Description: Riverdale, NY : Baen Publishing Enterprises, 2025.
Identifiers: LCCN 2024059704 (print) | LCCN 2024059705 (ebook) | ISBN
   9781668072592 (hardcover) | ISBN 9781964856216 (ebook)
Subjects: LCGFT: Science fiction. | Novels.
Classification: LCC PS3568.I577 N68 2025 (print) | LCC PS3568.I577
   (ebook) | DDC 813/.54—dc23/eng/20241230
LC record available at https://lccn.loc.gov/2024059704
LC ebook record available at https://lccn.loc.gov/2024059705

Printed in the United States of America

10 9 8 7 6 5 4 3 2 1

As always
For Captain Tamara Long, USAF
Born: May 12, 1979
Died: March 23, 2003, Afghanistan
You fly with the angels now.

ACKNOWLEDGEMENTS

I hereby acknowledge that the main character of this book is an asshole and extremely politically incorrect. Give him a break, he was severely abused as a child, and he doesn't hate everyone. He hates you. Yes, you. Personally. And he hasn't even met you, yet. If you ever do meet, you should be extremely polite and back away slowly. Do not annoy the nuclear hand grenade with the pin half pulled.

I also sincerely doubt that Hawking Radiation has an effect on nucleosynthesis. All science in this book is entirely made-up handwavium and should be roundly ignored and even ridiculed.

IT'S ABOUT SUPERHEROES! DUH! THE SCIENCE IS MADE UP!

Although there is a theory that stars require a water layer to form. Which, if you're into cosmology, creates a chicken-and-egg problem.

A NOTE TO MY GENTLE READERS

Michael Edwards, aka various AKAs, is essentially a spiritual cousin of the character Oliver Chadwick Gardenier. If he'd been raised in a ghetto in the modern era in foster care and there weren't things that go bump in the night. He has Chad's smarts and smart ass as well as his redoubtable fighting skills, though he's a bit taller. So, you may see some resemblance.

This is a universe which very much mimics our own with the exception of a few changes, notably superheroes and some of the effects they've had. The Nebraska Killer killed Al Gore during the 2000 election, which just gave the Left another reason to hate Bush.

Everything else is real. The names have been changed to protect the innocent. The guilty can go to hell.

CHAPTER 1

"The Vengeful One" —Disturbed

"I shoulda just jacked a car."

Michael Edwards was in a crouch, laying down fire left-handed around a concrete column. Construction of the unfinished Jeffries Building was getting a pretty hard setback, what with the bullets tearing up every inch of drywall and exposed wiring. Michael was praising the maker that there was plenty of reinforced concrete for proper cover, but even that was getting chipped to hell.

His HK USP locked back just as the last round hit Little Brown Tattooed Fucker Twelve in the upper chest.

The five-foot, ten-inch thirteen-year-old with brown hair and blue eyes had left his SIG somewhere back in the warren and he was running out of mags for the HK. The bus station was only a block away, but a block might as well have been the moon. If he'd just *stolen a car* as soon as he heard MS-13 was looking for him, none of this would have happened. Or if he'd gotten fifteen minutes more warning from Gondola.

The only reason he hadn't was it would have left some poor person car-less. That decency, a reaction to the hell he'd been raised in, was going to get him killed. Damn him for having a sense of morality and decency. Why couldn't he just be like all the other kids raised in the ghetto and not give a *shit* about other people?

Michael reached under his sports coat for a reload just as LBTF

Thirteen came around the other corner. LBTF Thirteen was toting his AK with his left hand and carrying a machete in his right. He charged the teen, machete upraised.

The only real choice was to try to get inside the blade, so he sprang upward and twisted. The machete descended on his left ear instead of his head. Michael managed to get one hand on the MS-13 member's wrist, then another—losing his empty pistol—and then he was pushed onto his back. He was just trying to keep from being chopped to death, but the little brown tattooed fuck was strong as hell. Michael let go with his right hand and reached up to gouge an eyeball with a thumb. The blade cut across his face and cheek, and he realized none of this was working.

Taking the chance, he lifted his right knee, so his ankle was in reach, and made a desperation grab for his snubby. He managed to snag the Ruger .357 on the first try and brought it up to the El Salvadoran's side. One round in the ribs and one in the head and all Michael had to deal with was the dead weight and blood and brains in his face.

Generally, carrying three guns was for assholes and wannabes. Michael was perfectly willing to allow the terms since at this point, he'd used all three in this "active shooter" situation.

He was trying to push LBTF Thirteen off when LBTF *Fourteen* came around the corner. He'd dropped the machete in favor of carrying his AK properly.

Knowing the likelihood of it working, Michael nonetheless pointed the snubby at the guy and let loose with all three rounds one-handed while lying on his back with a body on top.

One miss, one shoulder graze, and the third by pure dumb luck hit LBTF Fourteen in the left eye.

"Thank you," Michael muttered, looking up at the ceiling of the unfinished commercial building.

He tossed the empty snubby, pushed the dead body off, and picked up his USP. He was starting his reload, again, when a Muertos Angelica popped his head out for a quick glance. A split second later, he rushed out sideways carrying an HK416 in tactical low.

The "elite assassins" of MS-13 were the real deal. Yes, Michael once before might have gotten the drop on three of them and killed them with chopsticks but that was a *completely* different situation. Generally, the heavily tattooed killers were extremely bad news.

Michael was dead. He knew he was dead. It didn't really bother him. Growing up in the ghetto in East Baltimore was sufficiently suck he didn't really care one way or the other. Hadn't for a very long time.

He just hated to lose. Dying felt a lot like losing. It had been his constant problem. If he'd just let one of the *many* people who had tried kill him do so, this absolutely suck existence would have been over long ago.

And if the doctors at Mercy Hospital would just quit bringing him *back from the dead*. All this was their fault, really. All of these bodies and bullets were a direct result of them constantly bringing him back to the hell that was 2025 Baltimore. They didn't even have to have a healer, just really amazing trauma care. If the Storm turned out to be a zombie apocalypse, it would probably start at Mercy Hospital.

Damn them and their advanced medical wizardry!

The only weapon immediately available was the machete dropped by LBTF Thirteen. Michael grabbed it and tossed it at the killer without looking. Maybe it would distract him. He had more important things to focus on.

It was one of those moments when time slows. He felt like he was moving in molasses as he reached back for one of his dwindling supplies of HK magazines. He got the magazine out and did the slowest reload of his life. At least it seemed that way. He was pushing his arm to just move faster, but it was still moving in molasses.

Be very careful about the reload. For some damned reason you're still alive. Wounded, but still alive. Seat the mag firmly.

Things were moving so slowly he could see the slide moving forward as he turned in a two-handed grip to shoot the assassin.

Who was standing there with an expression of "That did *not* just happen." The machete was stuck crosswise through his neck, deep enough that there was blood seeping around the blade.

"The fuck?" Michael said. That should *not* have worked.

The 416 slipped from the assassin's grip and fell to the ground, followed by the Muertos.

There was no time to waste. He was running out of bullets faster than he was running out of enemies, a not-uncommon occurrence in his short and pain-filled life.

He used the 416 to lever up the assassin's body and examined it briefly. It was magged for Colt and there were at least a couple of those that had been dropped.

He holstered the USP, then pulled out the two mags the assassin was carrying and stuck them in his own waistband.

"Sweet," he said, looking at the fine German craftsmanship of his newest acquisition.

With that, he put it in tactical front and kept trying to find a way out of this maze. From the blue lights reflecting in the interior, Baltimore PD had set up a perimeter. All he had to do was get out of the building, alive, and try to get through the perimeter, alive. The rest was what good attorneys were for—not that he could afford one.

He was moving down one of the prestressed concrete-lined corridors trying to find a way out that wasn't covered when he got hit. Hard.

As he fell, he caught just a glimpse of the camping asshole who'd shot him. It didn't really matter. He was hit hard.

He scooched to the wall as more AK rounds pocked it. He wasn't sure how many bullets had just passed into and through him, but it was *too* many. He was pumping out blood like a fire truck.

But he was going to get that camping asshole if it was the last thing he did. Which it was going to be.

He pushed on one of the worst wounds, but it didn't do much good as blood gushed through his fingers. Arterial. Well ...

There was a dead body and a dropped M4 with a Beta C one-hundred-round mag in it just out of reach. He had managed to hold onto the 416 and if he was going to be stupid enough to return fire on the camper, he should just use that. But the Beta C was sooo inviting. A hundred rounds was better than thirty.

He scooched along the wall as more rounds chipped it to pieces. The six-inch precast concrete barely slowed the rifle rounds, and they bounced around the open area. One hit him in the calf, and he barely noticed. He had multiple broken ribs, and his stomach wounds were flooding his abdomen with protein-eating enzymes. Compared to *that* pain, another flesh wound barely registered.

He managed to hook the M4 to him with his foot. That gave the guy an idea where he was, and another round grazed his arm. At this point, it was raindrops in a hurricane. He'd dealt with a lot of pain in his life, but this was reaching burn-ward levels, his previous standard for "this FUCKING HURTS!"

He got angry. Angry at the situation. At being left in an alleyway by his whore mother. At being left in this fucking hellhole by Baltimore social services. At MS-13 wannabes that thought jumping him at school was a good idea. Why couldn't he have been born in a suburb? No kid should be raised in foster care in the ghetto! Fuck social services! Fuck Baltimore PD for their cowardice in just setting up a perimeter! Fuck the doctors who kept bringing him back to this hell of an existence! And especially *fuck MS-13*!

So, I used chopsticks to kill three of your Muertos! IT WAS FUNNY! CAN'T YOU TAKE A JOKE?

The anger flooded his body with the last remnants of traumatic stress chemicals: norepinephrine, oxytocin, cortisol, endogenous opioids. The tightening of his vascular system slightly reduced blood loss. His hands shook from the cortisol but that was okay. He was dying so missing a little wasn't a big deal.

He got the M4 to him and scooched farther along the wall, going in the opposite direction he'd been going before, muttering about fucking doctors and fucking social services. He had two rifles, now, and the obvious answer was to just use the M4.

But he hadn't gotten to kill *anyone* with the 416. He was gonna kill that camping asshole and he was going to kill him with this sweet 416 or die trying. He was probably going to just pass out while attempting to switch mags and get chopped to death. He didn't care. He was going to do it anyway.

Blood loss and stress chemicals were a hell of a drug combination.

He fumbled out the Beta C, which felt like it weighed a ton, pushed the M4 aside, and got the mag seated. He could hear the camping asshole shouting to someone.

He'd gotten enough of a glimpse of the camper's position to have a fair idea where he was.

Michael scooched along the wall again then, groaning at the pain, pulled himself up to look over the wall.

The camper had been on an elevated walkway but wasn't currently in sight. Probably reloading. There was a section of vertical precast that was the only place to hide behind. It was nonstructural like the walls around him. Bullets would go right through it.

Michael propped the 416 with the hundred-round mag on the top of the wall, sighted as well as he could with graying eyesight, and cut loose.

The bullets sprayed all around the obstruction but through it as well and the camping fuck came into view. Another Muertos from the tattoos. Michael's vision was in zoom mode, another combat response, and he could see roses all over the fucker. Rapist fuck. He just held the trigger down, the bullets going everywhere but definitely into the rapist camping fuck who danced from the hits, blood splattering the wall behind him.

The mag locked back as the hundred rounds were expended and Michael dropped to the ground, leaning against the bullet-pocked concrete wall in a puddle of blood.

He knew he had to reload but his vision was going dim. He'd killed that bastard at least. He wasn't sure how many of the other little brown tattooed fucks he was taking with him to hell, but it was a bunch.

Three more piled in from a cross hallway. They were all carrying their guns and had machetes in sheaths.

Michael was too tired to try to draw his USP. He couldn't even lift his arms. So, it was going to be machetes. He'd had worse. It couldn't hurt as much as the burn ward 'cause it wasn't going to last as long. And at least his fucking life would finally be over. He'd see what was on the other side. It had to be better than this side.

Hell held no worries to a kid raised in East Baltimore.

He slid sideways on the wall to lie on the ground, leaving a smear of crimson. He'd really liked this sports coat. It was the nicest clothing he'd ever owned. Pity it was shot to hell.

His vision went black shot with a pattern in red, blue, and purple. It looked like lightning and was rather pretty.

Odd thing to see as your last vision.

A deep basso profundo voice suddenly reverberated in his head: *"THE STORM IS COMING!"*

Michael took a deep breath and looked around the all-too-familiar room in the Baltimore Mercy Emergency Department.

Dr. Miller was to his right and Nurse Betty standing by him, per usual, with a very strange look on her face. To his left was another doctor with the name HOWARD embroidered on her lab coat.

He looked at Dr. Miller and frowned. This was not where he'd expected to end up and he was not liking it.

"What, *exactly*, is so hard about the words 'Do Not Resuscitate'?" Michael asked angrily. "I was dead again, *wasn't* I?"

"Yes," Dr. Miller said, nodding.

"'Again'?" Dr. Howard said, frowning quizzically.

"He dies here a lot," Dr. Miller admitted.

"Who are you?" Michael said, sitting up. He was unusually lacking in "discomfort" for having been shot multiple times. He actually felt pretty good. Also, he should have been waking up in recovery from emergency surgery. Again. He pulled his right earlobe in thought. "You're new."

"I am Dr. Bethany Howard, the healer from Johns Hopkins," the short brunette said, smiling and holding up a handful of lead. "You had *quite a few* bullets in you, young man."

"Some of 'em were probably left over from one of the other times," Michael said, stretching. There was something weird about the lighting in the room—or he was still recovering? He was weak. That was blood loss, but he felt fine otherwise. What was with the flickering colors? "Why this time of all times did I get a healer? I was ready to go. Pushin' up daisies. Pinin' for the fjords..."

"What's the last thing you remember?" Dr. Miller said.

"Getting nailed by some camping asshole," Michael said. "Got that fucker, though. I made him *dance*. Then three little brown tattooed fucks coming around the corner with calculating expressions and machetes. Then... Oh..."

He held his arms up and realized that one of the reasons for the weird light was he was glowing in a pastel of colors, rippling up and down his arm.

"Oh..." he repeated, examining the distinctive aura emitted by a super. "You have *got* to be joking."

"Boogie Knight gots superpowers," Nurse Betty said, shaking her head. She turned to walk out the door. "Boogie Knight gots superpowers... What a world..."

"Welcome to the Super Corps, Mr. Edwards," the healer said with a smile.

"Oh, *fuck me.*"

CHAPTER 2

"Welcome to the Super Corps, Michael!"

Based on his nameplate, the speaker was a Mr. DiAngelo. Medium height with dark brown hair, a bulky, muscular build, and a distinct Staten Island accent, Michael was making a stab in the dark, coupled with the name, that he *might* be of Italian background. And since he had the build of a Flyer, that meant he was probably Italian Falcon. Or, as Michael had decided to tag him, Dago Duck.

Michael Robert Edwards, recent resident of Baltimore, had never been into Supers, but since Acquiring he'd been brushing up. His recovery had been expectedly rapid considering his newfound "gifts," yet they'd kept him in the hospital a few extra days anyway. He'd spent his time researching his new group of peers and had a whole list of insulting nicknames ready to go.

As the office chief, Mr. DiAngelo apparently rated a nice, though not altogether large, corner office on the sixteenth floor of the Jacob K. Javits Federal Building in New York City. The office had a lovely view of Tribeca, if such were possible. Also, the Hudson if it weren't for all the other buildings in the way. Decorations were fairly spartan but blended patriotic with "caring supervisor"—complete with a professional library of the latest trending books on leadership.

"I'm Anthony DiAngelo," Mr. DiAngelo continued, fulsomely. He stood posed by the window and seemed to be reading from an internal script written for a superhero movie. "Italian Falcon," he added, nodding confidently.

Damn, got it in one.

"You can call me Tony," he concluded.

"Okay," Michael said then: "Sir."

Don't call him Dago Duck. Do not even think the name... Damn, I thought it.

"I understand there were some... issues with your Acquisition," Tony said as he took his seat.

"Oh, no issues," Michael replied, shrugging. "Motherfuckers needed to die. They tried to kill me, I objected strenuously, they lost. Fair's fair. Besides, they were MS-13. That's a death penalty offense in any reasonable jurisdiction. I admit, I'm still looking for that reasonable jurisdiction but it's the journey, not the destination, right, D... Falcon?"

Michael was pissed. He'd *just* managed to establish enough street rep in Baltimore people generally knew to leave him alone. The minor little dustup with MS-13 that only resulted in ten or twelve dead. But now he'd been sentenced to join the Junior Space Eagles over some fucked-up bullshit gun charge.

It was not working out to be the greatest week ever.

He thought about his life up to this point and had to admit it wasn't the worst. Not by very long stretches of the imagination. Probably somewhere down in the hundredth worst. Though, the very real possibility that the Supers were controlled by The Society moved it up the list.

Having superpowers was nice, though the ability to throw dirt around wasn't exactly the coolest power on the block. Of course, the applications *were* intriguing...

"I was talking about the, uh, charges," Tony said, obviously trying to adjust.

"Fucking bullshit," Michael said, pulling his earlobe. "Yeah, *duh*, I was armed. Going 'Yeah, sure, all those *bodies* were self-defense, but you were carrying so you've gotta go to jail' where... lemme see, MS-13 would *kill* me! So, yeah, six months 'community service' in the Junior Fucking Super Corps was an improvement over, I dunno, come to think of it, being stuck in the slam with MS-13 with superpowers... Can I rethink this? *Was* this the right move...?"

He casually looked out the window. It really was a decent view. Better than any view he'd ever had, at least.

"But, hey, a move to New York City and out of God Damn Baltimore! Fantastic. I can hide out of town in a new... Oh, I *don't* get a new identity? But I'm going to be able to *lay low* in New York, right? Like in witness protection or something? No? I'm not a witness? But I've witnessed *lots of stuff.*"

Dago Duck raised a hand to try and regain control of the meeting, but Michael was just getting warmed up.

"Instead, I'm supposed to parade around Central Park in some costume, to be determined, that will 'disguise my identity.' Lessee, a thirteen-year-old Earther manifests in Baltimore and a few weeks later a thirteen-year-old Earther turns up in New York City. Fortunately, MS-13, who lost three of their little brown tattooed fuckers to an Earther Acquisition, are *never* going to put two and two together and, say, turn up in Central Park with a bunch of fully automatic weapons, again, and spray bullets everywhere, again, and hit a whole bunch of innocent bystanders trying to kill *me*, again, 'cause... lessee... *that shit's illegal!*"

Michael held his hands up, palms upward, and waved them back and forth.

"Right? Right? That shit's against the law! Unlike, I dunno, gang-raping twelve-year-old girls and pimping them out? Or, you know, chopping up people with machetes or... I dunno, just generally killing people? They're totally *not* going to try to gun me down in the park! Who would *dare?*"

"You done?" Falcon asked.

"I'm barely getting started!" Michael said. "Where was I? You realize that if they're trying to shoot me and I'm, you know, standing near the other junior Guardian Angel Vigilantes with really weak and shitty Superpowers and No Policing Authority, and whereas we of the super persuasion, unless invulnerables like, say, *you*, do not harden and become bullet resistant until we are eighteen, and whereas let it be known to all here gathered that all four members of the New York Branch of the Junior Super Cadets would presumably be standing together, maybe in a group, getting pictures taken, by like civilians who would be in the line of fire, where it be further known to all and sundry that *you* might have to stand up and tearfully explain to the general populace of the New York Metropolitan Area and indeed the citizenry of These United States how you lost three of the four members of

Junior Super Corps, New York Branch, and sixteen idiot tourists to one fucking 'active shooter incident.'"

"Three of four?" Falcon asked with a raised eyebrow.

"Amigo Podus is a hulk," Michael said. "Invulnerable. Duh again. You're a Flyer, you don't know you're invulnerable to bullets? Is this a new thing? Or did I miss that class?"

"'Hulk' is considered an offensive term," Falcon said, clearly trying not to sigh.

"I hear 'Pigeon Poop' isn't something to go with as well," Michael said. "I also hear tell where California Girl particularly objects to Tink—"

"Just stop there," Falcon said, holding up both hands. "Jesus, you've got a mouth on you, haven't you, kid? Have you ever even thought about *trying* to make friends?"

Michael looked out the window again and spotted a news helicopter hovering over Tribeca. He watched it for a moment while crafting his response.

"So, I'm eleven years old sitting in this abandoned chemical facility straight out of . . . well, a superhero movie," Michael said, tugging on his earlobe. "Figured it was going to take twenty years off my life from cancer so my newfound regenerative healing and well-nigh total resistance to disease or toxins is appreciated at least. The inability to get drunk is less so. I'm done cleaning the two guns I took off of the two full-grown male assassins who had kidnapped me and my social worker.

"I hold the guns up and look at 'em."

Michael made two gun-fingers in front of his face.

"'Michael,' I says to myself, 'You gots a superpower.' You ain't no good at makin' friends but you gots more people trying to kill you nor you gots bullets.' Then couple of days later, the gang found me. They was a mite offended I'd torched they Escalade but I was a mite offended about them trying to kill me over, honestly, a beef with another kid at school.

"Anyway, I objected strenuously to their offendedness, they raised counter objections, we objected back and forth for a bit in the court of lead and souls, and they lost. Fair's fair. Also, the reason I'm a firm supporter of the Second Amendment. Twelve adult males going to kill a 'leven-year-old, 'leven-year-old ain't got *no* chance 'cept he gots guns.

Same deal with a juvie Earther with a range about from here to the wall and a super-duper ability to maybe throw a pebble. And lemme guess: There ain't *no* way you're going to let me patrol with, say, a full SWAT rig and load-out, is there?"

"Okay, I see your issues," Falcon replied with an assuring nod and smile as if he had the solution. "They have been recognized, discussed, and considered. FBI informants say that MS-13 has dropped the hit against you since, you know, super."

"Ah, the FBI," Michael said. "The most competent police force on the face of the planet."

"The subject has been deemed *not an issue*, Michael," the office chief said, now with a frustrated grimace since the smile and nod didn't work.

Michael kept his peace. He was going to have to either figure out how to train his powers or find a piece. He hadn't been afraid of death since he was eleven. Honestly, with his life either way was fine. But he just hated to lose. And letting people kill him was pretty much the *definition* of losing.

There were still unexplored options. He hadn't had a chance to check in with Gondola since Acquiring.

"Junior Super Corps is, normally, entirely voluntary . . ."

Michael snorted while trying to keep a straight face.

"You disagree?" Falcon said, clearly trying to keep calm.

"Every Acquisition you go black, and you see a quantum vacuum energy pattern of plasma discharge . . ."

"A what?" Falcon asked.

"Quantum vacuum energy pattern of plasma discharge," Michael repeated. "You see black shot with blue and red and purple and what looks like those patterns you see when you close your eyes. You *are* a super, right? Or did I miss that? Some people say it looks like blue and red lightning. What you're seeing, though, is the QVE pattern of a plasma discharge. Trust me, I know for physics. What *you* saw when *you* Acquired slightly before the comet took out the dinosaurs."

"Oooo-kay," Falcon said dubiously.

"I didn't get recruited to Stanford at the tender age of ten for my boyish good looks and charming personality," Michael said. "And you hear the words 'The Storm is Coming.' Right?"

"It was . . . actually, it was while I was hunting a mammoth . . . He was coming right for me..." Tony said, shrugging. "Next thing I knew, I was flying. And shortly after that became the Great Hunter of the Warthog Tribe."

"My sincere apologies, sir, at misjudging your antiquity by between sixty and sixty-five million years," Michael said, nodding and giving the office chief a minor note for a sense of humor. "My bad. My point being, during the Acquisition Event, previously referred to as the now unacceptable 'Transition Event,' you have a lack of ego awareness. That is, *during* that event you have no rational control over your actions."

The news helicopter turned and disappeared behind a high rise.

"And the event, whatever you call it, is always while under some distress. Drowning. Bullying. Abuse. Four abdominal and three thoracic GSWs from some camping asshole are, I assure you, distressing in the extreme.

"Then your powers manifest and take care of the problem without conscious volition. Depending on the power, it may be kinetic or otherwise.

"Firestarters: all male, frequently due to wrestling around with somebody and, well, whoever they're wrestling with just went to the burn ward. Electros...hope whoever is distressing them lived, 'cause those have the highest rate of death in an event. Waters: always female—same as all Earthers are male—generally something directly water related, drowning or being dunked common, and rarely lead to deaths. When they do, it's exploding all the water in their attacker's body, and it gets...very messy. Et cetera."

Tony waved a hand again and shook his head. "This is great and very informative, but I know all this. How you know is worth circling back to, but—"

"In my case," Michal continued, undeterred, "the immediate problem that caused my Acquisition being nearly the last of the little brown tattooed fucks, three of them, finally had me dead to rights. But only because of that camping asshole and the abdominals and thoracics. I could have taken them if it wasn't for that."

"Earther Trans...Acquisitions rarely cause death," Tony said. "Especially filling three guys full of glass shards."

"Silica," Michael corrected. "Shaped silica shards drawn from the concrete walls. Which probably fucked up the concrete as well. I don't recall. I went straight from Acquisition to waking up in Mercy

Hospital, again, in the emergency department, again. At least it wasn't recovery from emergency surgery. Again.

"My point being that ninety percent of Acquisition Events involve the Acquirer doing harm to someone whether they deserve it or not—and I assure you, those three LBTFs *totally* deserved it. And despite a complete lack of ego awareness—which is technically labeled 'temporary insanity'—we get charged for any damage anyway."

Mr. DiAngelo tilted his head thoughtfully, as if he might be catching on to Michael's point.

"And even in rare cases where they *don't* do harm, the G Man from J. Edgar Vacuum-Brand and Sons gets all shirty if you *don't* join Junior Super Doofs and 'learn the proper way to be a Super.' 'Proper' being whatever is the Hot New Thing 'cause apparently the Secretary—who, have you ever noticed, looks *suspiciously* like California Girl—is a flaming progressive, no matter what administration, and no matter what administration, they're always into the Hot New Progressive Thing.

"Currently that would be transgender and I'm down with that," Michael finished, pointing two gun-fingers at the office chief. "'Cause I am a currently male-presenting female homosexual. *Rabidly* homosexual."

"Oh . . ." Falcon had opened his mouth to say something but paused and creased his forehead as he tried to parse it out.

"Lesbian in a man's body," Michael translated.

"Just . . ." Tony said, facepalming. "We are a department of the federal government," he continued, holding out both hands to forestall the inevitable reply. "A *department*. We have a member of the *Cabinet* in charge of three hundred and thirty-six individuals . . ."

"'Cause of the Supers Act," Michael said, nodding. "'The Secretary shall act to ensure the Civil Rights of America's smallest minority.' Which was an *incredibly* bad precedent in statutory law, in my humble opinion, and I am *always* amazingly and *magnificently* humble.

"Now there's got to be a Department of Asian Affairs, whose acronym wouldn't be too bad, Doh-Ah-Ah, Do-do-do-aaaaaap, Doh-AaaaaaaahAh-Ah-Ah-AH! But by the time you get to a Department of Persons of Color Affairs you get Doh-Pah-Cah, which sounds like the guy you get on the phone when you call Tech Support . . .

"'Hello, this is Dopaca, how can I help you with your computer today?'" Michael said in a bad Indian accent. "'Have you tried turning your computer off and back on again...? No? Okay, let's start with that...'"

"*Stooop!*" Tony screamed, grabbing his head and clearly trying to hold back laughter. "Just stooop! For the Love of God! Stop!"

He motioned for Michael's mouth to close.

Michael stopped, watching warily.

"You..." Tony said, very carefully. He jabbed a thumb out the window toward the city. "Are going to be out there...in public... representing the *entire* United States government—"

"In some stupid fucking costume that has no variation for the enormous temperature changes experienced by New York City..."

"Mggh! Mgggfh! Zip! Zip!" Tony snapped, making zipping and mouth-closing gestures.

Falcon drew in a calming breath and regarded Michael carefully, who innocently looked back. It wasn't, quite, a staring contest.

"Representing the Super Corps," Tony continued, quietly. "And the entire United States government. There are approximately sixteen bazillion cameras in people's hands in New York City..."

"The average person..." Michael said.

"Zip...!"

"...only has one and there are..."

"Zip it!"

"...only eight million people..."

"Just..."

"So, a better approximation would just be eight million, sir," Michael concluded rapidly and made a zipping motion across his lips, then folded his hands in his lap.

"There are approximately eight million cameras in people's hands in this city," Tony edited. "Plus some number of tourists..."

"New York City receives approximately sixty-five million visitors each year," Michael said. "Many, if not most, are business travelers..."

"Wait..." Tony said. His hands had balled into fists, but now they flattened onto his desk. "You actually know the numbers?"

"I was trying to figure out how many cameras would be pointed at me on an average day," Michael said. "The average Instagram account has only one hundred and five followers. So, with about one hundred thousand visitors to Central Park on, say, Saturday and we'll encounter about ten percent, let's say, at most that works out to ten thousand people. But everything they post will be seen by about one hundred people. So that's nearly a million impressions per visit."

"That tracks with our studies," Tony said, interested.

"So that means I get to piss off approximately thirty thousand of the most vocal crybabies on the face of the planet, Every! Single! Patrol!" Michael said, throwing his hands in the air. "The crybullies are going to be calling for me to apologize every single patrol! I'm sure to get protesters! People will be throwing horse manure and bottles of frozen water! I'll hide behind Amigo Podus..."

"Who...?" Tony said, grabbing his head again. "Who the hell is Amigo...?"

"What's his super name?" Michael asked. "Hombre! That's it! Hombre do POTUS...? No, that sounds a bit off... Hombre...?"

"Hombre de Poder?" Tony asked, grinding his teeth.

"That one. Anyway, the Secretary, who"—Michael stuck his finger into the back of his mouth and made vomiting noises—"actually posts fucking *selfies* on Instagram, is going to go absolutely *ballistic*!"

"Which is exactly what I'm *trying* to *avoid*!" Tony snarled.

"Anyone who posts selfies gets what they deserve," Michael said. "... Thus taking me *off* of patrol and preventing harm and death to *uncounted* people including my fellow Cadet Space Rangers!" he finished triumphantly. "Except Hombre Do the POTUS, who is, of course, invulnerable to even heavy machine-gun fire. Or has that changed? Did I oversleep and miss that class? Where is that classroom?"

Tony hung his head in his hands.

"If you call Hombre that to his face you won't have to worry about the Secretary," Tony said, not looking up. "'Cause he'll rip your arms off and beat you to death with them."

The office chief looked up with a not-yet-defeated expression.

"So, you're going to piss people off just to get out of patrol?" he asked.

"Jury's out," Michael said calmly.

"Jury's out?"

"You may find this hard to comprehend, Italian Falcon," Michael said seriously, "but most people don't pay too much attention to Super

Corps or supers in general. One in a million Acquire. Every super gets concentrated in New York or LA with a small team in D.C. 'Cause those cities, apparently, are the *only* cities that exist in These United States of America. Well-known fact. There really is no, say, Philly much less Boise. They're figments of the imagination. Boise being a really weird fantasy that involves red cloaks and bonnets for some damned reason.

"Ask anyone in, say, New York and they're not sure that Washington exists much less Peoria. Most people have at best a vague clue that the Spangly Tights Brigade exists despite your Secretary's apparent frenzy to get you into the news cycle at the *slightest* opportunity..."

"PR gets Congress to get us funding..." Tony said wearily. "'Spangly Tights Brigade'..." he added with a groan.

"Oh, got that," Michael said. "But it still means that hardly anyone really cares about supers. Which is one issue of funding. Sure, there are the cape fanatics. They're all over social media to the point they seem like bots. But they're actually a relative handful in the total population.

"*I* couldn't have cared less. You impinged not at all on my daily round of trying to survive East Baltimore. Even if there *was* a super in Baltimore, he'd be prancing around the Inner Harbor or Leakin Park, taking selfies with people or stopping the occasional purse snatcher. He wouldn't be stopping some foster dad from beating me half to death 'cause he just doesn't like me. He wouldn't be stopping some girl from getting gang-raped in the next room. He wouldn't open up a closet door to find two black kids dead of starvation and the sole white kid just barely alive..."

"That's a...?" Tony said cautiously.

"Read my fucking file," Michael said, his face hard. "He might have turned up when there was an 'active shooter' incident downtown. Probably just in time to fly me to the hospital to be 'saved' by the healer instead of, you know, being transported by ambulance.

"US supers are so weak our freaking Healers can only treat four or five people a day. That Dr. Howard's right there at Johns Hopkins. When she found out I'd been recruited to Stanford she asked why I hadn't gone to Johns Hopkins. I said I *had* been there. I didn't add *twice in the burn ward* when I was five. Two separate incidents. I didn't say the third was a month recovering from being deliberately starved to near-death and the other two kids died. But I had a question I didn't ask her about.

"I assume a healer can't do much for starvation. But where was she the two times I was in the burn ward when I was five? The second time there were even three little black kids, one female. So where was the healer?

"Ever been in the burn ward, Falc? Get burned before you Acquired? Forget the skin grafts which are, to be clear, peeling your skin off your body in small strips. Literally, a well-known torture. Skinning someone alive. Want real bad? That's debriding."

Tony straightened and his face softened. Give the guy credit, he knew when it was time to let a kid vent.

"See, the problem, Falc, is the class two and three burns, if they leave the burned meat, they get infected, and you die. So, it has to be removed. The burned skin and meat. On your body.

"So, what they do is five or ten nurses hold you down and say soothingly, 'We're doing this to *help* you . . .' while a doctor who is, and this is *not* an exaggeration, chosen *specifically* for his, her, or its sadism, it/he/they takes this thing like a cheese grater and scrapes the burned flesh off."

The office chief flinched a little. He was doing his best not to show his discomfort, but his left hand was fidgeting in and out of a fist.

"You remember burns, Falcon? Remember how you'd get a burn from some hot oil popping off the stove and how much it hurt? Now take that cheese grater in the drawer yo mama used for grating Parmesan and grate your skin and meat off in strips until you're so weak and literally *dying* from the pain that they take you back to the ward to rest and heal up for a couple of days until you're strong enough to . . . go back to being debrided.

"Over and over again.

"Five years old, Mr. DiAngelo. Twice. Forget the Spanish Inquisition. Just send campers to the burn ward."

Tony just nodded his head and bit his tongue for a second.

"So where was 'Dr. Bethany Howard,' Mr. Falcon?" Michael asked, his jaw working. "Where was this *amazing* Super Corps when me and three little black kids were being set on fire in a 'fiery but mostly peaceful protest'?! I mean, we were right there at Johns Hopkins, for fuck sake. I knew there was a healer there. It was all over the news, about how great Super Corps was and their *amazing* Healers! I literally *begged* them to please get me a healer. Both times. And you know what? Prayers and begging do as much good as crying—none."

Michael paused and looked the office chief in the eye.

"Most people don't *care* about the Super Corps," Michael said. "Supers don't matter to people on a day-to-day basis at all. My interest in supers died when the only people who would help four burned kids in a riot were some contractor mercenaries. Not the news crew they were guarding. For damned sure not the Super Corps or their precious Healers.

"More people care about the Kardashians than the Secretary— which, based on her ... everything is one of the things that pisses her off more than ... anything. But now I've got these powers. Which I'm supposed to keep weak? Because of some dude who went off the reservation literally before I was born."

Then again, Michael knew the truth behind the Nebraska Killer, and the part The Society played in his psychosis.

"Yeah," Tony said, nodding definitely. "Because it was before you were born, Michael. I was *there*. You weren't. NK was ... not easy to take down."

"Got it in one, Mr. DiAngelo," Michael said. "Got the memo—I'd say in school, but I dropped out when I was eight. But here's the thing, Mr. DiAngelo: The Storm is Coming."

"I do understand ..."

"I really don't ..."

"Stop," Tony said, making the close-mouth motions again. "When I heard those words, I knew, in my bones, right then, that I had to be ready for anything. I'm from here ..."

"Really?" Michael said, acting surprised. "Jeez, you sound *exactly* like you're from rural south Alabama! I figured you for a Lynyrd Skynyrd fan! I would *never* have *guessed* you for a paisan from Staten Island!" he added, shaking his head in wonder. "What a world ..."

"You ... effin' kid ..." Tony said, shaking his head and laughing. "But *as I was saying* ... I knew, right in that moment, that I had to protect my town, my country, I had to, yeah, protect the Island. I had to be *ready*. The Storm was coming. And"—he paused and looked out the window—"I did get some training, yeah? Cally ... Some other people ...

"But that was then, kid," Tony said, sighing. "That was before J . . . the Nebraska Killer . . . That was before a lot of things. My transition was . . . jeez, is it thirty years already . . . ?"

"'Twenty years now, where'd they go?'" Michael sang. He had a pretty good singing voice courtesy of years of training in ABE choruses and a fortunate puberty voice change. He took in the view again for drama's sake. "'Twenty years, I dunno. I sit and I wonder sometimes . . . where they've gone . . .' You don't look a day over . . . twenty-five, give or take? Pretty good for a guy who was hunting mastodons . . ."

"Mammoths, kid, mammoths," Tony said. "Great Hunter. Also, we've got regenerative healing, which looks like it might, yeah, add some years onto our maximum lifespan. My wife is *not* happy she looks twice my age. Point being . . . Storm never comes. It's like that play . . . *Waiting for* somebody . . ."

"Godot," Michael said, tugging his ear. "*Waiting for Godot.*"

"You know it," Tony said.

"Lucky guess."

"Point being, again . . . Storm never comes," Tony repeated. "Right now, here, today, we've got people to save. People to help . . ."

"Selfies to take," Michael said.

Tony got that look again and puffed out his cheeks, at which Michael did the mouth-shut motion.

"Oh, you think . . . ?"

"Muff!" Michael said. "My turn. I have the talking stick."

"There is no talking stick," Tony said.

"Do not make me pull it out and disprove that statement," Michael said, reaching for his zipper.

"You have the talking stick," Tony said, holding up his hand and turning his head to the side.

"My point being . . ." Michael said, then paused. "Was your dad a cop?"

"Yeah," Tony said, nodding. "Retired as a sergeant in the NYPD. Still lives out in Staten."

"We come from different viewpoints," Michael said. "Staten Island is sort of tough from what I've heard . . ."

"*Very,*" Tony assured him.

"Sort of place where you get hit by a bouncer in the leg when you're six playing 'Let's Do a Drug Deal,'" Michael said. "Which was ironic 'cause as the white kid I was the one who *always* got shot anyway. That sort of place?"

"Not..." Tony's brow furrowed. "...often...? Let's do a drug deal?"

"Kids mimic what's going on around them," Michael said. "Let's Do a Drug Deal, somebody's getting shot, Pimpin' Out Yo Ho, somebody's getting knifed, Jackin' a Cah, there will be a chase. Runnin' from the Poh-leese, that's 'Tag' to people from, say, the Hamptons. Bangin' wit' the Poh-leese, that's Cops and Robbers, but the Cops are *always* the ones who get shot; I was *always* the cop. Jackin' a Licker Stoh, *everybody* gets shot..."

Tony's jaw dropped and his eyes went wide.

"You probably got beat down to the point of being put in the hospital nine times, minimum, right, Mr. DiAngelo? At least sixteen in total, what with the all the times you were in the burn ward and the starvation? Oh, and the getting shot over and over again. You've had your heart stop in the ambulance, right? And in the ED? And on the table? That's a thing when you were a kid, right? Thrown across the room into a wall by your foster mom's boyfriend when you were two? Beaten for putting the toilet lid down—note I said *lid* down—instead of leaving it up, when you were four, back in the hospital, broken clavicle, assaulted every single way, yes, that way, thank you for not asking."

Now the office chief looked away again in discomfort.

"Staten Island is *definitely* a place where you trip and sprawl face-first running to the school bus, all the kids laughing at you, 'cause you didn't *quite* clear the hurdle of the dead and starting-to-bloat body... I mean, that *was* a thing when you were growing up, right, Mr. DiAngelo? Tripping over dead bodies on the way to the school bus and the part that was *bad* about it was the kids laughing at you? In 'very tough' Staten Island...?"

"Not...so much...?" Tony said, shrugging defensively. "Is there a point?"

"You come from a really tough place, obviously," Michael said. "So, you know, coming from a tough place, that you *cannot* let your guard down. It's literally impossible for you to not be on alert one hundred percent of the time. It's a PTSD thing. Forget 'the Storm is Coming.' The Storm was here before I ever cared about supers. It's around every corner. Behind you. In every nook and cranny. There is *no* place that is safe—not your bed, not your home, not anywhere for sure on the street."

Falcon raised an eyebrow and looked lost.

"I'm sure that in Staten Island you'd grab any electronics that hadn't been stolen from you and sneak into a coffee shop somewhere, dressed like a homeless kid, complete with stink, and hide in the corner on the floor with your back to the wall so you could put on headphones and watch two college lectures at a time, sped up to triple speed, rocking back and forth like a drug fiend waiting for his next hit..."

"Why *didn't* you go to Stanford?" Tony asked, shaking his head. "I was told you had a full ride; they'd fly you out there, put you up...?"

"'Cause I'd never have gotten there...Tony," Michael said.

"That's kind of defeatist don't you think?" Tony said.

"Here's how it would have played out," Michael said, matter of factly. "'Hi, Baltimore City Department of Social Services? This is Stanford University! We would like to offer one of your foster children a free ride to Stanford! He's white, which sucks, but we'll take him anyway!' 'That little motherfucker Michael Edwards is getting recruited to college! That's white privilege for you!' 'Where?' 'Somewheres in California!' 'Man, he don't need to go to California! There's a college right here, ain't they?' 'That right, John something!' 'That way we can keep his ass in the ghetto and keep them fat stacks rollin' in! Call them perfessers over at John Something, tell them we got a ghetto kid gettin' recruited by some university in California but they get him! Long he stay the ghetto an' we keeps getting' the mohney. Tell 'em, 'Sorry he ain't black...'

"Then I'd be *noticeable*. Then I wouldn't have the *freedom* to break into those abandoned houses to just have somewhere halfway safe to think. Then I couldn't curl up on the floor of a coffee shop and listen to lectures.

"The one good thing about anarchy is it does represent a certain form of freedom."

"That's sort of..." Tony said uncomfortably.

"You really think they were going to let me go, Mr. DiAngelo?" Michael asked. "The only way they were letting me go was if the federal government came along and said 'Yeah, that kid? He's moving to New York.'"

He wistfully looked across to the adjacent building, where there was a gym a few floors down. Sadly, it wasn't close enough to get a good look at any of the women working out. Michael closed his eyes and sighed.

"I got found in an alleyway with my umbilical cord attached and they *left* me there. In the fucking ghetto. Because 'children should be raised in their native culture.' Since my whore mother was probably ... a whore, I guess that might count for my 'native culture.' *No* child should be in the ghetto, and for sure and certain no foster child! The state could have put any of the children I was fostered with anywhere in the damned *state*. The state was responsible for our care. Every single horror I've lived through and witnessed, the precious state could have avoided.

"The state is my mother, the state is my father, and my mother is a whore and my father is as much of a bastard as I am. The ghetto has a massively higher rate of CPS cases just like it has a massively higher rate of every other offense against God and man. So why leave kids there? When you can put them anywhere?"

"Because ..."

"Money," Michael snapped, locking eyes with DiAngelo. "Filthy lucre. Fat stacks. Because every child in foster care represents a little pile of green. The more children, the more green. The more children, the more social workers, which means more promotions and more green. If they could just get the green without the pain-in-the-ass kids, they'd be happier.

"And if anyone so much as mutters 'Is it really wise to put children in a place with so much violence, hell, and anarchy?' they're called 'racists' and 'white supremacists' and people who want to 'take money out of the mouths of poor children' and 'people who want to destroy urban black culture' who are, let me make sure everyone hears in the back, 'RAAACISTS!'"

"Okay ..." Tony said, wagging his head from side to side.

"Want to know how bad foster care is, Signor DiAngelo?" Michael asked. "Not just Baltimore in the ghetto. Everywhere. There are very few things that are one hundred percent with *Homo sapiens*, Signor DiAngelo. We are, automatically, without considering race at all, a very diverse bunch. One hundred percent are not heterosexual. One hundred percent cannot spell or count. One hundred percent are not born with all their limbs.

"One hundred percent of females in foster care are raped by someone in or associated with foster care by the age of sixteen."

Tony froze and looked horrified. "*All* of them?"

"All. Of. Them," Michael replied. "The average national age of first rape in foster care is *nine*. Right here in These United States and, I quote, 'Greatest Country in the World.' That's the average. Want to know the average in East Baltimore?"

"My dad was a cop," Tony said, nodding. "Young."

"Eight," Michael said. "Oh, sorry, that's the average *overall* in East Baltimore. Overall, the average age that a girl is raped in the ghetto is *eight*. The average. And, again, very few make it to sixteen."

"Jeez..." Tony said, shaking his head. "I thought Crown Heights was bad."

"Pussies," Michael replied. "The point to yet another diatribe, Mr. DiAngelo, is that I didn't grow up somewhere 'tough.' I grew up in anarchy and blood and pain and death and hell..."

Michael stopped, sighed, and looked back at the gym across the way. Even if he couldn't see too well from here, he could make out women in tight spandex and imagine what they'd look like closer up.

"The only thing I've ever wanted in my life was the things I only saw on Tee-Vee," he said sadly. "A clean house. Clean cars, clean yards, clean people... A wife who loved me, some kids, maybe a dog. That stuff was as far away as Mars in East Baltimore, but I was going to make it. I was going to escape gangster's paradise. Assuming I survived. I was going to succeed and escape and never go back again... All I've ever wanted was some gentle Eden..."

He looked at Falcon and shook his head.

"Don't feel sorry for me," Michael said, grinning ferally. "If what doesn't kill you makes you stronger, I be *diamond*, Mr. Falcone. I am a katana, folded, spindled, and mutilated a thousand times, sharpened to a nanometric edge..."

"Wait, wait..." Tony said, his brow furrowing. "Isn't Falcone one of the bad guys in Batman?"

"Yes," Michael said, looking at him side-eye. "And it literally is Italian for *falcon*. You named yourself Italian Falcon. I assumed you knew that."

"No," Tony said, shrugging. "My family hasn't spoken Italian in a couple of generations. I think my granddad spoke it and he's dead."

"*Questo spiega alcune cose,*" Michael said, tugging his ear.

"*Que?*" Tony said, brow furrowing again.

"Moving on," Michael replied. "The Vishnu—the Indian supers—and the Chinese Super Force are dialed up to the point that is—I hate to say it as a Believer in the One God—very much *god*-like . . .

"The Vishnu are human nuclear weapons. Which presupposes that whatever we are going to face will *require* that sort of power to defeat. That magnitude. I'm hoping for Mechagodzilla and if it's *A Quiet Place* I'm going to be *so* totally annoyed."

"What?" Tony said, trying desperately to keep up.

"Did you even see the *trailers* for Two? They started in a small town in the South. Right 'chere in the land of the Free and the home of the Second Amendment. And those things came out of nowhere, right? And everybody died from them, right? Got killed and eaten . . . Are you fucking *kidding* me? That's the plot? *That's* how the world ends? That's Armageddon?

"Those 'we can't see so we depend on sound so stay really quiiiet' dragon whatchamahoozits could eat people so presumably they could *be* eaten. There are *four hundred million* guns in private hands in These United States. And those idiot bird/lizard/whatever cannot hear you beyond *pistol* range!

"If the Storm is anything like *A Quiet Place*, it might be bad in Manhattan—like in that later movie—but not Brooklyn or Queens, and I have a hard time imagining there are enough suddenly appearing to affect the population numbers in a megacity. It'd be like a salmon run but the bears are all lizard dragon whatsits that don't have any eyes. People'd still be going to work.

"'Where's Bob? Out sick?' 'Dragon whatsit got him, poor guy.' 'Eh, better than the muggers, there's more of those. Does our insurance cover dragon whatsits or is it under "Acts of a Humorous God"?' *New York Post*: 'Last Dragon-bird-whatever killed by mugger in Times Square' and that's the end of the dragon whatsits. Muggers got 'em. Pissed-off muggers 'cause dragon whatsits *never* have any cash on 'em. Fucking cashless society.

"But the place to be is somewhere in Louisiana. Bet they make *spectacular* jambalaya," Michael concluded.

"Eh . . . uh . . ." Tony said, shaking his head. "WHAT?"

"You can say 'The storm never comes', Mr. DiAngelo but when it comes, and it will come, and when people are calling upon the Lord for a Savior, I might just ask them, 'Does a white one count or would you prefer that I go find someone from DoPoCA?'

"'Hello, this is Dopaca, how can I help you with your Armageddon today? Have you tried turning your country on and off? Oh, you're just turning it off? That's a method, I suppose...'"

"God, God, God..." Tony said, very carefully banging his head on his desk.

"If nobody *else* is going to be prepared, I am too paranoid, too terrified of all the giant monsters that have *already* populated my fucked-up existence, too beaten, too abused, too familiar with hell to *not* find a way to become the most powerful super the US has ever seen. So that if no one else in this country survives, I will. And maybe, maybe, I'll help some people as well as I can. Assuming they're also willing to accept me as the screwed-up alien from Antares I am and help as much as *they* can.

"No serial-killer super-terrorist boogieman from before I was born, or a Cabinet secretary for that matter, is going to *stop* me."

Tony just held his head in his hands and shook it back and forth. Due to concerns about Society control over the supers, Michael had been torn over whether or not to be honest with Dago Duck about his intention to develop his powers. But he seemed genuine, and Michael had spent most of his life developing a sixth sense for evil people—of whom he'd encountered far too many. Tony wasn't one of them, and he'd handled everything Michael had said remarkably well. So, despite Michael's extensive trust issues...

"But your question, if you recall, was about my being in the Corps," Michael said. "I said 'jury's out,' which you were surprised by. And the answer is yes. And I'm even going to try *not* to cause a stir."

"What?" Tony said, raising his head and looking at him skeptically.

"I'm smart," Michael said. "When the Storm comes there may or may not be a federal government. But if there *is*, having it as an enemy would just mean one person having to fight a two-front war."

Especially as whether or not the Society controls the supers, they most definitely control most of the federal government.

"I am the humblest person in the world, without question," Michael said, then paused and looked up at the ceiling in a heroic pose and nodded. "My greatest strength is my humility. That and my fanatical devotion to the pope. My two great strengths are ... Never mind. But I must relate that, humbly, fighting the Storm and feds simultaneously *is* potentially doable. Oftimes when you have two problems, they cancel each other out. So I could, for ex, let the federal government— if it survives at all—fight it out with the Storm, whatever it is, and take on the loser ..."

He paused for a moment and nodded in thought, rubbing his chin.

"Not that I would ever contemplate anything like taking over the United States and ruling it with a firm but—mostly—benevolent hand with the exception of the compulsory harem duty, which is why the capital *shall* be moved to Boise," Michael said. "If you do any investing, you might want to go long on red and white cloth."

Tony set his forehead on his hand and just started laughing, softly.

"The freaking *Handmaiden* reference was what finally got you?" Michael asked. "Interesting."

"I'm just trying to keep up," Tony admitted. "You were saying about being in the Corps?"

"Having a marginally civil relationship with the federal government has a potential value and is not at all luring them into a false sense of security about my true intentions, which do not at all involve taking over this fucked-up country and fixing some of the many issues by, for example, killing a bunch of bureaucrats and whipping the rest. Not into shape. Just public floggings at random so they get the idea that reaching for something mildly resembling competence should be their one true goal—not just screwing people over and drinking coffee."

Tony chuckled. Apparently Michael had found the proper balance of absurd so as to make Dago Duck think he was *mostly* joking.

"Ergo: Try to get along in Junior Spangly Tights Brigade. I do not intend to cause a stir or a scene that will bring the Secretary down upon you like some enraged banshee. I intend, to the best of my ability, to just answer the questions from stupid tourists as if they are not, in fact, stupid and to generally act as if I'm from ... say ... Tennessee as opposed to New York. Or Baltimore, for that matter. Politeness and courtesy is the order of the day. Are the order? Politeness and ... Politeness and courtesy *are* the order of the day. Orders ...? I growed up the ghetto. My grammar ain't all that."

"So, what was"—Tony waved his hands vaguely in the air—"that?"

"*That* was me getting off my chest just how *stupid* this is," Michael said, throwing his hands in the air again. "Always has been. Kids wandering around in the dark in Central Park with the law enforcement training of ... *What* law enforcement training? In spangly tights that have no real functionality at all when one of them is being hunted by a transnational gang whose motto is literally 'kill, rape, intimidate'?

"It's not that little brown tattooed fuckers are hard to kill, but there's thirty-five thousand of them and it's just work, work, work all day long, Falcone."

"This is gonna ..." Falcon said, holding his head in his hands and shaking it back and forth.

"That forty-five-minute diatribe when you were expecting and scheduled for a five-minute meet-and-greet was me *venting*. I am smart. An entire department of the federal government complete with Cabinet secretary based on *comic books* is ... Words fail."

"Finally," Mr. DiAngelo said, rolling his eyes.

"I can find more," Michael said, pointing a finger. "I have words."

Tony held up his hands and shook his head.

"Lemme, okay?" the office chief said. "We're ... glad you're here. Just ..."

He grimaced.

"No doing the Dopaca routine in front of cameras," Michael said. "Do not reference horror movies as training for the Storm ...?"

"Just ..."

"No greeting German tourists with a Nazi salute ...?"

"No ... what?" Tony said.

"Ever read the Skippy's List?" Michael asked. "I have. I have it memorized. You should brush up. Is there a Super Corps anti-mime campaign? There should be. Those guys are creepy ... THERE IS NO WALL, YOU MORON! THERE IS *NO* FUCKING *WALL*! JUST KEEP WALKING!"

"Oh, God!" Tony snorted, finally breaking down in howling laughter. He was laughing so hard he hit the top of his desk—which promptly broke in two. "GOD DAMNIT, NOT AGAIN!"

"Not again?" Michael said, belly laughing. "Not *again*?"

"Well, God damnit ..." Tony said, shaking his head. "MIRRRRI!"

"You rang, boss ...?" the forty-something brunette office manager said, sticking her head in the door. "Oh, not *again* ..."

"NOT AGAIN!" Michael said, still howling.

"Can you get this...this out of here?" Tony said, pointing at Michael. "Alexander will be showing you around. Be nice!"

"Like rice," Michael said.

Miri walked up beside Michael, smiled, and politely waved a hand toward the door.

"Okay..." Tony said, standing up from his desk and shaking off bits from the desktop. "I know I'm going to regret this: How is rice nice?"

"It doesn't have lice?"

"OUT!"

CHAPTER 3

"You *were* scheduled for a three-hour IQ test," Alexander said diffidently.

Alexander Thompson turned out to be a six-foot-four or so slender black man in his twenties in dress slacks, neatly cropped hair, and a Super Corps polo shirt. While his actual position wasn't clear, he obviously wasn't a super. Mentally labeling him "lackey" felt unkind, so Michael decided to go with "aspiring suit."

Michael could tell right away that the guy was unsure where Compton *was* much less had ever been there. This guy was straight out of Long Island. He decided to take it easy on the guy—at least at first.

"You been waiting this whole time?" Michael asked. "My bad."

"It's alright," Alexander said, holding up his phone to indicate how he'd passed the time. "The problem being if you start now it would run into lunch. I'm fine with that but I was told you have . . . food insecurity issues?"

"Being starved nearly to death does that," Michael said, shrugging. "But I also have skipped more lunches than I've had. Also, it won't take three hours, so let's go. Where?" he added, gesturing around the office lobby.

The lobby of the Super Corps New York offices was a little nicer than most such government buildings. Two stories in height, it was about four thousand square feet with decorative marble pillars, a marble floor with the Super Corps emblem on it, wood-paneled walls, and potted plants in selective corners. Directly opposite the entrance was the "Flyer exit," a sliding glass door that led to a small runway for Flyers to take off on their patrols.

Pretty much the entire sixteenth and seventeenth floors of the Javits Building were devoted to the Corps despite the fact that there were only about a hundred total supers who worked there, and most were out on patrols.

"This way," Alexander said, gesturing down one of the side corridors.

"Thing about IQ tests is the more time you take, the lower your IQ gets graded," Michael said. "IQ is about speed of thought as much as anything. So, the faster you answer the questions, the higher your IQ is scored as long as you get the answers *right*. You're graded on speed, yes, but get a double-down on wrong answers. So, skip any that you're unsure. Better to skip than get one wrong."

"I wasn't aware of that," Alexander said. "I usually go back and check and recheck on a test if I have time."

"Thing is, not only is it weighted to score higher the younger the person is, depending on how it's structured you can get various answers," Michael said. "This a computer test where you hit the correct circle on multiple choice?"

"I think so," Alexander said, puzzled. "It's on a computer."

"So, a person who hasn't used a computer to take tests very much is going to be slower," Michael said, shrugging. "That's one reason that blacks tend to score lower—less experience with computers and computerized tests growing up. Even today. Also, how's your hand-eye coordination? How's your eyesight? So, unintentionally, it's also testing what's called kinesthetics."

"Well," Alexander said, gesturing at a door marked Briefing Four, "we're about to find out how you do. You've taken a couple, obviously."

The door had a card-and-code lock on it and Alexander inserted his Common Access Card then entered a code.

Michael pretended not to notice the code and considered the sixteen ways he'd already come up with to swipe a CAC.

"Once managed to score an IQ of four on one," Michael said, entering the room.

The briefing room was, again, well fitted out for a government office. The walls looked as if they'd been painted yesterday in the same blue-white color as the corridors while a massive, high-end, plasma screen practically filled the far wall. There was a laptop set up on the fine-grained wood conference table and, incongruously, there was a mound of backpacks piled under the plasma screen. Each was marked with the Super Corps logo, and they were the only thing that was dusty.

"Four?" Alexander said, opening up the computer. Michael had been hoping for a chuckle, but Alexander was standing strong. It was only a matter of time. Michael would break him.

"That's about the IQ of a planaria worm," Michael said, walking over to the bags. "If a human was actually a four, they'd have to be on a ventilator that you might as well unplug."

The bags weren't flat and empty, like they were giveaways or something. They were full. He opened one up, curious, and, yep, it was full of "bug-out" stuff: water bottles, survival rations, medical materials, bandages. Everything in the bags was about six months before expiration.

Some federal contractor had been paid to fill up Super Corps logo bags with bug-out supplies. They had to be regularly replaced, at least every five years, to keep in expiration dates. And if there ever *was* a bug-out, five got you ten that nobody would even remember they were here. They'd been ordered because somebody said "we need bug-out bags" and tossed in a corner and forgotten. Hell, they'd probably been ordered because some other department was ordering some for their people and Super Corps wasn't about to lose a Budget Snuffling Contest like that one!

The federal government didn't just waste money, it burned it like the RAF had burned Dresden.

"All set up," Alexander said as Michael walked back with a water bottle. "I don't think you should . . . I can get you a water."

"I am sure that taking this bottle out of an unused bug-out bag will *ensure* that some member of the Super Corps or their mortal minions will *definitely* die of thirst in the event of a bug-out," Michael said, sitting down at the computer. "By taking this bottle of water, Alexander, I am literally condemning some poor soul, possibly you, to a long, lingering death by dehydration." Michael took a sip of the water and set the bottle down.

"It is my entire intent, Alexander. I am death by proxy to all around me."

"I see," Alexander replied, shaking his head.

"On the other hand, this water will expire in six months and everyone knows that if you drink expired water, it is a *literal* death sentence. Water becomes exceedingly and exotically toxic after five years, known fact. So, by taking this bottle of water, I am instead saving some poor soul a nasty death by old water in the event they find it in the aftermath of whatever apocalypse finally and thankfully *consumes* this fetid hellhole called New York."

"So . . . are you trying to kill someone or trying to save someone?" Alexander asked, puzzled.

"Win some, lose some, it all evens out in the end, Alexander," Michael said, examining the test program. "Alexander, I grew up a poor foster child in the ghetto. If there is free shit sitting around, I don't just let it go to waste, okay? The fact that a pile of bags full of video-game loot is simply sitting there with dust on them boggles my fucking mind. Where I'm from, drug fiends dig into concrete to dig out the rebar to sell for scrap to buy drugs. Got any idea how little money you get for rebar scrap? Just *sitting* there. Dusty. Fucking unreal, my man."

Alexander glanced at the computer, then his watch, and shrugged before politely returning his attention to Michael.

"Then there's the fact that someone is going to *throw all that stuff away* in six months. In six months, some hourly wage employee of a federal contractor is going to pour out a perfectly good bottle of water that is made of really expensive plastic that doesn't even leave a bad taste to it. Checked. The likelihood that there will be an apocalypse requiring everyone be issued one of those bug-out bags so they can make for the hills of Vermont in the next six months is extremely low. Very close to zero statistically.

"So, you can waste your time going and getting me an absolutely *fresh* bottle of water supplied by the General Services Administration from probably the exact same approved, probably 'minority,' contractor and I can drink *that* one or the one that's almost certainly going to be discarded in six months. Which one makes more sense when you think it through, Alexander? Which one will cost the federal taxpayers—of which I assume you are one—the least?"

"The bottle of water from the bug-out bag?" Alexander asked.

Michael simply put his finger on his nose then took another sip.

"Watch the Storm hit as I'm taking this test and you grab the one I stole the water from," Michael said. "Two weeks later you're lying by the side of the road as part of a stream of terrified refugees, croaking out your last words as you die of thirst:

"'Curse Michael Edwards! Curse that murdering fuck! If only he hadn't taken that bottle of water, I *surely* would have made it to the refuge! So close! So close! I only needed *one* more bottle of water! Curse him, Lord! I curse thee with my last breath, Michael Edwards! *Maledicta, maledicta, maledicta!* Cuuuurse theeeee...' Gack."

"Are you always like this?" Alexander asked, still expressionless but checking his watch again.

"Pretty much," Michael said. The navigation would let you go to the end of the test, which was nice. He hated the ones that forced you to go one question at a time from the beginning.

"I don't have an inside voice. But when we meet in Hell, remind me to tell you of the horror of death by...*expired water!*"

He looked at Alexander, who, for a moment, just looked back.

"I don't actually get to see your psych test," Alexander said after a moment. "And I'm wondering if I want to..."

"You don't," Michael said firmly. "The eldritch horror of the Stygian depths of my mind would shatter your very soul."

He looked at the computer and cracked his knuckles.

"Okay, let's get this party started. I'll be a little less than an hour by the look of this thing. What are you gonna do?"

"I'll be right...here..." Alexander said, pointing to one of the chairs. He held up his phone again. "I'm supposed to keep an eye on you."

"Who did *you* piss off?" Michael asked as he started the test.

After a bit of fiddling on his phone Alexander looked around then, sheepishly, went to the pile of bags, and pulled out a bottle of water as surreptitiously as possible.

Michael successfully suppressed the chuckle and pretended not to notice.

One more soul for your pit, Lord Satan!

"Done," Michael said forty-six minutes later. He'd briefly considered taking an extra minute trying to reach Gondola, at least to send a message since he was getting *really* itchy to contact them. Ultimately, he'd decided against doing so on a government computer, even though he knew several good workarounds. The risk didn't exceed the benefit, especially since the Society might have eyes everywhere in the super building. He could be patient a little longer.

"Already?" Alexander said, startled.

"Some of the third-order polynomials were a bit tricky," Michael admitted. "Hate having to use Newtonian calculus. It's so cumbersome. Done."

"Okay," Alexander said, looking at his phone. "It's a little early for lunch . . ."

"It is never too early for lunch," Michael said. "I eat to live, not live to eat, but I'm also a growing teenage male and I'm pretty sure the super-metabolism is doing something in that regard . . ."

"We could break for lunch," Alexander said and then brightened up. "Or I could see if The Designer is available?" He was clearly excited by the prospect and the Capital Letters were clear. It was the most emotion Michael had seen yet from him.

"The costume designer?" Michael asked.

"Yes!"

Alexander was clearly *really* into the costumes. Which meant . . .

"You have a comic book collection, don't you?" Michael said carefully. He was holding his ground. He refused to back away. He would *not* back down.

"A small one," Alexander said with a defensive shrug. "I mean, I'm not obsessive or anything. It's a hobby."

Hold your ground, Michael. He's probably harmless and you have superpowers.

"You don't own *Red Horse Surfer Girl* seventeen, do you?" Michael asked cautiously.

Alexander looked shocked and shook his head.

"No, no," he said, making a disgusted face. "I don't get into that sort of stuff. And that one was just disgusting! They never should have shown Calif—*Surfer* Girl like that!"

"Not even under your mattress?" Michael asked archly.

"*That's* crossing a line, Michael," Alexander said, blushing enough it was noticeable with dark skin.

"You know it actually happened, right?" Michael said. "Almost assuredly."

"It didn't happen," Alexander said definitively.

"You understand the physics of going supersonic, right?" Michael said.

"Does it matter?" Alexander asked.

"When an object moves through air, it sets up harmonic disturbances we perceive as sound," Michael said. "When a Flyer is moving really fast down the street there's probably this sort of 'booga-booga-booga' sound as they go by, right? Ever heard something like that?"

"Yes," Alexander said, looking interested.

"It's like moon-roof effect," Michael said, trying to figure out how to explain in not-physicist terms. "It's what's called the Bernoulli effect and it's why flags flap in the wind instead of just flying straight, okay?"

"Okay," Alexander said, nodding. "That kind of makes sense."

"What gets me is why that little cheerleader skirt on California Girl didn't tear apart when she was flying fast," Michael said musingly. "It really should have. The real reason for 'no capes!' But with Surfer Girl, she wore hot pants and a tight midriff top and went barefoot—'cause 'Surfer Girl,' right?"

"Yes," Alexander said. "I do have a *couple* of Surfer Girl comics, I'll admit."

He has the complete *set. Even seventeen, which is hard as hell to acquire these days. Most of them are listed as "slightly dog-eared, pages stuck together tightly."*

"The booga-booga is caused by intermittent areas of high pressure and low pressure, which is what sound is, by the way."

"Okay?" Alexander said, frowning.

Danger, Will Robinson! Danger! You're losing him!

"Hang in there," Michael said, holding up his hands. "It's about to get tricky. When you pass the sound barrier, you pass *through* the intermittent pressure waves because they *can't* move as fast as you move. They are, literally, *sound*. And you have passed the speed of sound."

"Oh," Alexander said, furrowing his brow. "But the air is still there."

"Yes," Michael said. "But it suddenly reshapes into a cone ahead of the Flyer and a trailing edge where the intermittent pressure zone, the sound waves, reshape. Got it?"

"Yes. Sort of."

"When you pass *through* the intermittent pressure zones, they get high. *Really* high. Very high pressure in one area, very low pressure in the next, and extremely close together. High-pressure zone, low-pressure zone, bunch of them close together. Still with me?"

"Yes. That I get."

"So, what does that do to fabric?" Michael said, taking a pinch of Alexander's shirt and pulling on it slightly. "You push air under the fabric with high pressure. You then pull it out with low pressure, very low, nearly vacuum. Repeat those five hundred times or so in less than a second. What happens?"

"Oh..." Alexander said, nodding. "But they didn't have to make it a thing, you know? I mean, everybody knows it's about...the Madame Secretary."

"You know comic book nerds," Michael said. "There was one part of the writers going 'So this is totally going to happen, did happen, so we should really show the effects of sonic boom on clothing. It's science.' And there was the *other* side of them going 'It's going to be drawing a fourteen-year-old smoking hot chick totally stark naked as she flies around Los Angeles, trying desperately to stay unnoticed in broad daylight!' And 'This is going to sell like hotcakes! I'm keeping my personal copy under my mattress!' It's misogynistic, it's wrong, but it's also very human," Michael ended with a shrug.

"Very human like racism and white supremacy," Alexander said.

"As long as we are human, we will never be entirely rid of them," Michael said, trying not to flinch. He had hot buttons related to those two terms. Serious ones. "Tribalism, attraction by males to younger women, and aspects of what we call misogyny were *survival traits* for too long in our evolution. I could get into a long discussion of why we're wired that way. It's very innate.

"The gene is selfish; it just wants to propagate. It's the reason for almost everything that human beings do, good and bad. The gene is selfish is the reason for altruism and greed, for vanity and shame, for heroism and villainy. It is what drives us to greatness and to horror, to courage and genocide, Alexander. We are sinners and we are saved. It's quantum."

Explains the Society pretty damn well: People crafting a world where they're unfettered while making themselves appear altruistic.

"You're not actually from this planet, are you?" Alexander said carefully.

"You've divined my secret, mortal!" Michael said dramatically. "I must wreak my doom upon you!"

"This is a great discussion," Alexander said. "But I should probably get ahold of The Designer."

"Does The Designer have a name or simply a title with capital letters?" Michael asked.

"Kevin," Alexander said. "Kevin Winchard."

"So, let us go see"—Michael paused dramatically—"The Designer!"

"I'll text him and see if he's available," Alex said, tapping at his phone.

"So . . . we meet him here?" Michael asked.

"I'm checking . . ."

"I'll just sit here and wait, then," Michael said, eyeing the computer. "Do I get to keep this?"

A kid could hope.

"Uh, no?" Alex said, still examining his phone.

"Would anyone notice if, you know, it got lost in inventory or if someone—not me—were to Strategically Transfer Equipment to an Alternate Location?"

"Since it's my work computer, probably yeah, someone would notice," Alexander said, giving him the Spock Eyebrow. "And Strategically . . . what?"

"Strategically Transfer Equipment to an Alternate Location," Michael repeated.

Alexander's lips moved for a moment, and he looked at the ceiling muttering, then frowned.

"Don't S.T.E.A.L. my computer," Alexander said, returning to his characteristic deadpan.

"Wouldn't think of it," Michael said, pushing the laptop over. "It's not *nearly* powerful enough to compute the variables of water compression in various stellar configurations."

Alexander started to open his mouth, shook his head, and went back to fiddling with his phone.

Michael put in a pair of earbuds, chose a heavy metal soundtrack on his phone, then leaned back and steepled his fingers, eyes closed.

The chicken-and-egg problem wasn't going to sort itself out.

CHAPTER 4

"Sharp Dressed Man" —ZZ Top

Kevin was one of those people who Make an Entrance.

Fortunately, Michael had been alerted that The Designer was about to arrive, so he didn't immediately go into combat mode and kill everyone in the room when the door of the briefing room was flung aside and The Designer entered the room with a flourish, hands outstretched to the side, butt cheeks clearly pressed together like squeezing steel into neutronium and with a distinct twist to the hips.

Kevin Winchard was about five foot six with a sandy blond coif that cascaded to his shoulders and a well-preserved fifty or so courtesy of extensive but well-done plastic surgery. He was dressed so tastefully, Michael immediately regretted wearing jeans and a T-shirt. Coming from a black cultural background, Michael preferred to dress well when the situation called for it. And the situation *always* called for it when in the room with The Designer.

Crocodiles perished when The Designer came within a hundred miles of their location.

The Designer examined his newest client with due regard, his hands working about as if to frame the picture, then clasped them together and exclaimed:

"OH, YOU'RE LIKE A LITTLE MICHAELANGELO'S *DAVID!*"

"And you got the Bunsen burner turned *all* the way up, don't you?" Michael replied. "Also, I am quite offended by that comparison."

"I didn't mean to give offense," Kevin said, clasping a hand dramatically to exactly where a pearl necklace would rest.

"I am not only better looking than Michelangelo's model, but I also humbly admit my dick is bigger," Michael said, nodding sagely. "He ain't exactly hung if you know what I mean."

"Oh, you are *naughty*!" Kevin said, touching his fingers to his lips.

"And you are just about the gayest gay guy ever," Michael said, chuckling.

"I hope you're not . . ." Kevin said, clearing his throat.

"Homophobia is very common in the ghetto," Michael replied. "But, nah, I ain't. You ain't no ped, neither. Don't give off the vibe. You the reason gay called *gay*. It's a synonym for *happy*. Just flame on all the time. But Asian people must be terrified when you walk down the street."

"Excuse me?" Kevin asked, confused. "I get along *extremely* well with Asian persons."

"Man, with that flamethrower going *all* the time?" Michael said. "Japanese be like 'He's coming! The flaming man! He comes! The caves will not save us this time!'"

"Michael!" Alexander said, grimacing.

"Oh, my!" Kevin said, putting a fist to his mouth and trying not to laugh.

"Napalm at your decibel is a *terror* to the gooks," Michael continued. "Naked Asian kids be runnin' down the street screaming. 'He is destroy the village to save it! Run for your lives! Kevin is coming!'"

"Oh, that's terrible!" Kevin exclaimed, but he was laughing as he said it. "I am so embarrassed to laugh at something so terrible."

"All comedy comes from pain," Michael said. "Which is why I am *very* funny. Nah, I ain't no homophobe. My Mama's trans."

"Your . . . mother?" Kevin asked.

"Nah," Michael said. "My mother left me in a alleyway as a newborn. My Mama be Miss Cherise. She the lady found me. She wanted to 'dopt me but they wouldn't let her. Wasn't 'cause she was black—all my foster moms pretty much was. Probably wasn't 'cause she was six foot four in her fishnet stocking feet and"—Michael deepened his voice to a baritone—"talked like this. Probably 'cause she's a drug fiend and a street ho. But that my Mama."

They'd only been in touch once since his Acquiring, when Michael had called to let her know he was alive and safe. They didn't talk often, but his Mama had always been one of the few bright spots in an otherwise miserable life.

"Oh," Kevin said, his face taking on the exact expression of a Labrador puppy looking out the window at his departing family. "That must have been a *terrible* childhood!"

"If what don't kill you make you stronger, I be diamond," Michael said. "So, what's up with the costume stuff?"

"Well, I need to think on this," Kevin said, walking around the juvenile super and regarding him professionally. "It has to be *just* the right look. Something that expresses who you *are* while being fashionable and presentable. Also, wearable. You'll have several; they will be washable or at least can be dry-cleaned."

"And no capes," Michael said.

"Absolutely not," Kevin replied. "Well, we need to get you measured."

"Joy," Michael replied.

"It's entirely hands off," Kevin said with a friendly smile. "We're *very* high tech around here!"

Michael stepped up on the dais in the Costume Department and turned around.

"Sooo...?"

He'd changed into a skintight body suit that left very little to the imagination. He was okay with being eye candy. It was better than some things that had happened in his life. But the body suit was pretty revealing. The polypropylene fabric was so thin as to warrant the term "sheer."

"Just stand with your hands to the side, fingers spread, feet shoulder-width apart," Kevin said, standing by the technician. "The lasers will create a three-D picture of you and then we three-D print a replica. We fit the suit on the replica. After I have ... Designed it."

"Got it," Michael said. The federal government burned money like a California wildfire.

"Please hold still for ten seconds," the tech said. "In three, two, one, close your eyes ..."

Michael closed his eyes and listened to the buzzing. The ten seconds were enough to get through the quantum bindings of a series of water layers in meta-solid state.

"And we're done," the technician said.

Michael kept his eyes closed for a moment longer.

"Done?" the tech repeated.

"Got it," Michael said. "Sorry, I was thinking. I do on occasion."

"And as soon as you're changed, time for lunch," Alexander said.

"Hot diggity," Michael said, hopping off the dais. "Anyplace around 'cher gots shrimp tacos?"

"This ain't half bad," Michael said, munching on a shrimp taco. "Not as good as Mama Cabrera but ain't much as good as Mama Cabrera."

A Mexican place that had a menu online that included shrimp taco was up in Gramercy Park. After some thought they'd taken an Uber as the best alternative. Michael had ridden in silence, contemplating the mysteries of the stars.

The restaurant was more cozy than large and had a rustic feel without being too dirty.

"You either don't talk at all or talk a mile a minute," Alexander said. "You didn't talk at all on the ride. Just sat there with your eyes closed."

"I don't talk when I'm thinkin' real hard," Michael said. "When I'm not thinkin' real hard, my mouth is on autopilot."

"What are you thinking about?" Alexander asked.

How soon can I contact Gondola?

How deep is The Society into the Supers Department?

How soon is MS-13 going to find me?

How incredibly cheesy/fruity an outfit is The Designer going to make me?

"Know much about astrophysics?" Michael asked.

"I heard you'd been recruited by Stanford in that," Alexander said. "Seriously?"

Michael paused to take another bite before answering.

"There's this company online," Michael said. "It's an online university but not like Phoenix or whatever. You can get a couple of degrees from it—economics, finance, programming, stuff don't need no science labs. But it doesn't have its *own* courses. It sort of aggregates courses from other universities. It's got contracts with all sorts of universities—Stanford, Wharton, London School of Economics. Southern New Hampshire University is big.

"If you pay for the course, and you've got to pay full rate, you can get credit, ya dig?"

"I dig," Alexander said.

"But if you ain't got no money and don't need the credit, you can audit the courses for free."

"From Stanford?" Alexander asked.

"All of 'em," Michael said. "I learned about it when I was eight. See, I'd been looking at YouTube videos since I was a kid. All sorts of lectures are online. I was studying calculus before most kids were learning one plus one equals a transgender. But sometimes you get more from actual courses. Even I, I must humbly admit, occasionally need to ask a question. So, I started taking those courses. Mostly to get away from school."

Michael noted the door swinging open, and a pair of Hispanic men headed to the counter to order. From habit born of a life spent watching his back, Michael tracked them until he judged them to be harmless.

"I got this real bad beatdown, nearly kilt me when I was eight," Michael said, shrugging. "My face be all reconstructed. Older brother of this kid name of Trayvon. Trayvon always startin' shit. All mouth no trousers, little pussy mama's boy with a mouth cashin' checks he couldn't back up. But his brother, Ahrmos, he was the opposite. Ahrmos all rage and anger and animal violent. Ahrmos one of the heads of Fifth Street Kings, ya dig? Same mama, different daddies.

"Trayvon start some shit with me at school and I don't think nothin' of it, just knock him down, move on," Michael continued. "Walkin' back to the home, mindin' my own bidnett, beat-up little sedan pull up, Trayvon and some dude I don't know get out. I don't pay no mind. Trayvon just an irritant. A flea. Like that bit of spring up in your bed you can't quite avoid when you're sleeping, ya dig?"

The two men finished ordering and grabbed a table on the far side of the restaurant.

"Turns out his big brother just got out the slam," Michael said, munching taco. He'd perfected the art of putting a bit of food in the corner of his mouth so he could talk and not spew food everywhere. "Five-to-ten felony drug trafficking, time off for good behavior—but it being Ahrmos, no way there was good behavior. Anyway, Trayvon pointing at me, dude just walk over, kick me in the stomach, start beatin' me down. Last thing I remember was his fist headed for my face. Next thing after that waking up in recovery from emergency surgery in Mercy Hospital."

"Seriously?" Alexander said.

Michael just gave him a look.

"Broke collarbone, broke ribs, broke arms, skull fracture. Face all smashed up. Ahrmos had flat stomped me near to death. Stomped an eight-year-old. Later kilt a eleven-year-old. Same thing. Most deaths from violence are due to something like that or blunt instruments rather than guns, 'case you didn't know. Why sort of the question, right?"

"Yes," Alexander said.

"See, Trayvon start some shit, all mouth no trousers, get his ass kicked, then run home to his mama cryin'. Then his mama be visitin' Ahrmos upstate and giving him a load of shit about all the kids 'picking' on Trayvon—who always, and take my word for this, *always* started it. Every damned time."

Now a young couple came through the door, hanging off each other. Alexander, to his credit, also had his head on a swivel, hawkish eyes casually assessing everyone who came in. Maybe he wasn't just a wannabe suit.

"Mama, Lucea, she the real problem. She wanted Trayvon to be *like* Ahrmos. Always beat the other kids down. Always on him to be the toughest and the strongest and grow up to run his own gang. That biggest part of the problem inner city schools, mamas like Lucea.

"Thing is, he ain't got it. He a mama's boy. You don't suddenly get whatever Ahrmos has, hell, what *I've* got. Think it's something you're born with, truth. Can talk about the neurology. But Trayvon ain't got it.

"After that, seein' as Trayvon would *always* be startin' some shit, figured it best to avoid school entirely. When you got what Ahrmos got, what I got, you *cain't* back down. There a bit of back-down in you, you ain't got that. You can try to deconflict. I've deconflicted before. But most wise, in the ghetto, ain't gonna work and often the wrong choice. Most times, one who gets there first with the most the one who's gonna walk away from it.

"Let me give you one piece of advice, Alexander," Michael said seriously. "You older nor me but this about survivin'. Someday, Storm, somethin', find yourself in a bad place, you might need to know how to survive."

He glanced around to see if anyone was listening in, leaned forward, and lowered his voice.

"I lived, grow'd up, in that movie *The Purge*. People thinkin' that would be fun and stuff. Why don't you just go live in the ghetto? It's *The Purge* every single day. Ain't no law. Ain't no justice. Ain't no rules. Gangsta Paradise. You think that's fun? Go *live* it. All you gots to do is cross that line into the ghetto and you're there.

"Rape if you want, ain't no rule. Kill if you want. You'll get away with it. Ain't nobody gonna talk to the poh-leese. But be aware, you're the one who's probably going to be doing the dying, be the one that gets raped. Man or woman. 'Cause if you think *The Purge* looks like *fun*? You ain't got it."

Expression as stony as ever, Alexander nonetheless stopped eating to take in what Michael was saying. Minor shifting indicated he was uncomfortable with the conversation topic.

"The advice is this, Alexander," Michael said. "When you're in a situation that's going to end in violence, don't do *no* talkin'. If the inevitable end state is violence, just go *straight to it*. Don't talk to people when you're killin' 'em. Ain't no point. Maybe there's a heaven or a hell they're going to. Maybe there's an eternity they can think on what you said. But it's pointless. They're dead. Never talk to people when you're killin' 'em.

"That's not exactly..." Alexander said, frowning.

"Sporting?" Michael asked. "Fair? Proper? There's no 'fair' in the quick and the dead, Alexander. I don't mean if you're having a beef with a coworker at work. You deconflict that shit. I'm talking about if you're in the depths, in hell, in whatever apocalypse takes you. Hell, in the streets of New York these days. You can take the advice or not. But if you're in the shit and you don't... well, you won't last two days. Less."

Michael picked at the last of the rice on his plate, getting every last crumb. Alexander was barely halfway through his burrito.

"I'll keep that in mind," Alexander said. "If I'm ever... in that situation."

"Only would in anarchy." Michael gestured out the door of the restaurant. "Which is what New York is rapidly becoming. And it don't have to be this way. It's all because of lack of contract enforcement. The weak point of *any* anarchic system is the lack of an equitable contract resolution process with enforcement systems."

"Do you have any idea how hard it is to keep up with you?" Alexander said.

"Yes," Michael replied. "I grew up in the ghetto and being a thinker would wonder 'Why's it gots to be this way? Why's there always bodies littering the streets?' And the answer I arrived at it was lack of an equitable contract resolution process."

He looked at Alexander, who was clearly not processing.

"Think about a drug deal," Michael said. "So, you've probably bought drugs, at least in college."

"Maybe," Alexander said.

"And say the dealer sells you some...I dunno...with you it'd probably be Ecstasy or some shit, supposedly, but it turns out to only be candy. What do you do?"

"Don't use that dealer again?" Alexander said, taking another bite of his burrito.

"Some people are stupid enough to go to the cops," Michael said. "Meth heads usually. In the ghetto, you kill that motherfucker. What you *can't* do is take them to small-claims court. You can't have them arrested for fraud.

"The ghetto exists as a clearinghouse for physical transfer of restricted materials, whether that be drug trafficking, stolen materials trafficking, weapons trafficking, sexual trafficking, what have you. Along with government largesse it is the only real economics of the ghetto, and it is in the range of government largesse in most as an economic input."

The girl of the couple glanced his way with a disgusted look.

"Drugs come in wholesale quantities and concentration, are certainly repackaged to retail quantities and *hopefully* well-cut retail concentrations. They are then distributed to persons who want them with the moh-ney coming from elsewhere—such as the drug addict driving up to the nice corner drug dealer in a system that resembles in some ways a McDonald's drive-thru and which was taken from that in a BMW. Fellas goin' out the ghetto to rob a house or a store. Point being, materials come in, labor is added, materials are sold, and the money for them comes from elsewhere. That's straight up Adam Smith economics.

"Trade is the wealth of nations but it's also the wealth of cities, of neighborhoods, of people. The ghetto is the most Smithian economic system in history.

"The real issue is that there is no legal mechanism for contract resolution, other than just going straight to violence. And once the basic mechanism for either social or economic contract resolution becomes criminal action, killings and beatings over bad drug deals being high on the list, criminal action spirals out of control. Dude gets killed over a bad drug deal. Dude's friend kills the dude who killed him. That dude's brother kills the friend of the first dude who was killed and so on and so forth, day after day, world without end.

"A lack of equitable contract resolution mechanisms is why I'd trip over dead bodies on my way to the school bus. Make sense now?"

"Sort of," Alexander said. He shifted uncomfortably again.

"It's the weakness of any anarchic system," Michael repeated. "And the people who are trying to foist anarchy on These United States and the world are idiots. Don't care if they be libertarians or Antifa, they idjuts. Anarchy works reasonably well for some but not most. In shape, violent twentysomething males do just fine in anarchy to the extent there are any available resources. Mad Max. North Philly. East Baltimore. Southside Chicago."

Granted, that anarchy is actively created by The Society to keep the fabric of lower case "s" society weak, so they can use their useful, violent idiots to apply pressure where they need. But that's not a conversation I'm ready to have with you, if ever.

"Twentysomething in shape males can survive, even thrive. *Everyone* else suffers—elderly, children, women, the weak in general. Most of the campus 'radicals' pushing for anarchy wouldn't last a day in South Chicago. Everything you see in *The Purge* is a wet Thursday evening where I came from.

"Most of them were bullied by the jocks in school and are just itching for some payback. Guess again, scrawny anarchist dude: those jocks are going to do more than pants you and take your lunch money. They're going to take your money, your girl, and your *life*."

The server passed the couple a bag and they headed to the door. The girl shot Michael one last revolted look on the way out.

"Notice how Antifa got itself pantsed a few times by just general dudes, Kyle Rittenhouse comes to mind, there were all of a sudden articles about 'The White Supremacy Basis of Working Out'? That's 'cause the anarchists realized that the people who *weren't* anarchists tended to be more in shape than they were. And better at violence. Helps to eat meat.

"There is no nobility to savagery," Michael concluded. "Nobility is being *capable* of violence, while in the main refraining from it."

"I guess that being from ... there you probably don't like the idea of being a sort of super cop," Alexander said.

"Not sure where you're going there," Michael said. "My problem with being a super cop is that I think we should be more like the military. Just train for the Storm. But ... not sure what you mean."

"Well ..." Alexander said, ducking his head. "The cops are the oppressors, right?"

"Oh, Jesus wept," Michael said, shaking his head. "Ever seen a poll from the ghetto on feelings about police?"

"They're not well liked," Alexander said.

"You grew up in a suburb or something, didn't you?" Michael said.

"Alexandria," Alexander said.

"Well, let me clue you in on some things, Alexander of Alexandria," Michael said. "It's not true to say that most people in the ghetto love cops. More like adore them."

"Uhm ..."

"Alexandria a ghetto, Alexander of Alexandria?" Michael asked.

"No, but ..."

"But nothing," Michael said. "But shit. But get the shit that was crammed into your brain by your professors, who *also* did not grow up in the ghetto, *out* of your brain. The oppressors in the *ghetto*, Alexander of Alexandria, are the *criminals*. The cops are the *liberators*.

"Think I'm lying? The gang that tried to kill me was called the Fifth Street Kings. Ahrmos was the muscle. The brains was Davon Walker. Not that Davon wasn't violent, he was. But he mostly let Ahrmos or Two-Shy or Gun Face handle the killings. And there were lots of killings. Not just lack-of-equitable-contract-resolution killings. Just killing. Like a group of serial killers—which is what they were—had broken loose. In the history of violent and murderous gangs in

Baltimore, the Fifth Street Kings might not take the cake but they're in a run for the knife."

Michael noted the two men were done eating and departed. Alexander, meanwhile, was still nibbling away.

"At one point I had fairly good relations with them," Michael mused. "Won't get into why 'cause it was a federal violation with a *very* long statute of limitations. Wrong thing for the right reasons sort of thing. One time when I was pretty sure he wasn't going to kill me, I asked Davon: 'Davon, why you always going around killing people sometimes seems for no reason at all? Double Talk wasn't no snitch or nothing. Kin I ask and not get kilt? Please?'

"To which he replied: 'The purpose of terror *is* terror.' He quoted Vladimir Lenin, one of the most notable oppressors in history. Tell me he didn't understand that he was the oppressor.

"You seem like one of those good-hearted people, Alexander of Alexandria," Michael said. "But you're also a product of some of the biggest lies, or at least misstatements, in history. I'm sure you support criminal justice reform and giving people a second, third, and indeed hundredth chance."

"Is there a problem with that?" Alexander asked.

"The good people of the ghetto—and there *are* good people in the ghetto—are the biggest victims of crime, Alexander. The robbery, the assaults, the rapes, the murders. *They* are the ones who suffer the most. So, when you support letting criminals go free, cashless bond, no bail, reduced sentences, Alexander of Alexandria, you are saying 'Let free the wolves upon the sheep. *Let* them rape. *Let* them rob. *Let* them oppress those already suffering greatly! It makes me feel good about myself, so it *is* good!'

"Not your sheep, of course, Alexander of Alexandria. If you can catch an Uber, you'll probably make it home okay. You ensure the oppression and pain of those most vulnerable in our society. The poor. The truly oppressed. Almost all persons of color. And I don't know which is more evil: that you ensure harm comes to the weakest of our society, or that you turn yourself into a pretzel patting your own back for it.

"You may be a man of good heart, Alexander of Alexandria. But that does not mean you are a good man."

CHAPTER 5

"Secret Agent Man" —Johnny Rivers

Michael was being housed in a decent, if generic, midtown hotel while going through "evaluation." At the end of the workday Alexander, who had grown notably cooler, turned him over to two decent enough federal marshals who got him dinner, a good hamburger, conveyed him to the hotel, then parked outside his door.

"Your gear from Baltimore has already been delivered," Marshal Simpson said. "Anything we can get you before you tuck in?"

"A Razer 15 with i9 Twelve Nine Hundred H core, Nvidia RTX 3080 Ti, 32 gigabyte DDR5 and a one-terabyte optical drive?" Michael asked.

"I was thinking something more like a water," the marshal replied. "Ice?"

"A kid can hope," Michael said. "Nah, I'm fine. 'Night."

"'Night."

When he'd been shot in Baltimore, he was carrying both his pad and his phone. They'd ended up as riddled with bullets as he was.

The phone had been replaced with the latest Samsung, apparently courtesy of the federal government. The pad not so much.

He really, really hoped that it was just junked. No, that might not be good, either.

He considered the phone, looked at the door where two federal marshals were presumably standing, muttered "Fuck it," and dialed the emergency number, hoping against hope someone would pick up. He clicked the temperature down on the air conditioner. As hoped, it rattled obnoxiously. While the phone started ringing, he turned on the TV, cranked up the volume, and twisted it to face more toward the door.

"Four-one-four-five."

Michael hustled to the bathroom and left the door barely cracked open.

"Mountain Tiger. Code Aspirin Fly Trap Cigar 4144868 Delta. God is building an army."

There was a series of clicks.

"Mountain Tiger, Celsius Twenty-two. Welcome back. Glad you survived. Again."

Michael had no idea who Celsius 22 really was or why that code name.

Gondola didn't exist. Its physical presence was worldwide, covered by dozens of different front organizations. But the members, who also did not exist, were all online and shared three common features: they were the hacker elite, they were willing to volunteer their time, and they were willing to *die* to save others.

Michael was a Level 6, just barely above the paid contractors who were occasionally used for cybersecurity or hacking at Level 7. He'd been offered promotion a couple of times, but with his studies and the vagaries of the ghetto, he really couldn't put in enough time.

Despite that, he'd been in the network long enough that he knew most of the big bosses and they mostly knew him by code name. He'd even talked to the Faerie Queen. More than once.

"Is this clear?" Michael asked, glancing through the crack at the front door again.

"You'd have gotten a 'this number is not in service' if it wasn't," Celsius 22 replied.

"I was briefed," Michael said. Never paranoid enough, he searched the bathroom for any sign of monitoring devices. Gondola would probably know about them before he did, but he still wanted to do his due diligence. "I just never had to use it."

"It's good enough for a quick chat," Celsius said. "How are you doing, superhero? My man is a *superhero*! Whoot!"

"Regenerative healing is fucking awesome, I'll tell you that," Michael replied, opening the mirror. "I've got all my lung tissue back. But my teeth are starting to come back in and it's playing hell with my plate. Business first. I'm worried about my phone and pad. I don't know what they did with them."

"Evidence in your shooting," Celsius said. "According to Titanium, they briefly disappeared from the evidence locker and spent a few seconds in a microwave. Not long enough to be noticeable, long enough the codes are gone."

Michael breathed a sigh of relief. He glanced at the front door again and then sat on the closed toilet.

"In that case, so far I haven't met any of the other kids or even most of the supers," Michael said. "The supers come and go on patrol or whatever and the kids only come in for patrol, right? So, no inside scoops, yet."

"I'll give you one but it's not about Earthers," Celsius said. "Talked to one of the Vishnu Flyers doing an op. That thing you were talking about with your handler about clothes blowing off. It's a real thing."

Rather than being pissed that they had listened in on the conversation, he was warmed that they had. His only friends in the world still needed him and still cared.

When you worked for Gondola, you lived in a fishbowl. Gondola was secret. Anything above your clearance you didn't ask. *You* had no secrets and neither did the world. It wasn't the NSA that was watching; it was Michael and an unknown but large number of other hackers dedicated to preventing nuclear war, rescuing kids from trafficking, keeping The Society from destroying everything, keeping the often poorly maintained lash-up called the power grid and the internet running and generally making the world a better place.

Most of Gondola's members were not like Michael. They were not survivors. One member who was caught in an earthquake didn't even know how to use a manual can opener.

They were people, often very financially successful, who mostly worked a full-time job, often in IT, then went home at night, put on their cape, and went out on the internet to be superheroes in secret.

But most of them were lost without delivery service. Another reason to keep The Society from destroying the world.

"Thought so," Michael said. "I wish I'd delved into the super databases more. Except for what you needed to know for ops, didn't seem worth it. Vishnu are cool. Corps is about as fucked up as I expected. It's a Society op. It's going to be screwed up."

"Well, what files we have are there when you get some electronics again," Celsius said.

"You have my thanks," Michael said. "Is there anything on Vishnu training methods?"

Now that he'd finally gotten in touch with Gondola, his next biggest frustration was the inability to train with his powers in any meaningful way without risking nearby destruction or possibly injury to himself. The Department of Supers' releasable—even to him—knowledge of Earth powers essentially ended at "they move Earth and stuff."

"No," Celsius said. "I asked about that once. It's classified above our level."

"Damn," Michael said. "Freaking Nebraska Killer is general background, but how the Vishnu do it is *classified*? Figures. I'm hoping I can get cleared. I want to train these powers. But figures we'd at least have it."

"Obviously," Celsius said. "If there's a secret, we own it. Titanium's coming in. Maybe ask her?"

"Welcome back, Tiger," Titanium said.

"Heyo, Bossmang," Michael said.

Calling Titanium Asteroid, whose Tetum accent bespoke Indonesian background, "bossmang" was misgendering but he'd picked it up from one of his favorite sci-fi TV shows.

"You know how much we work with the Vishnu," Titanium said.

"Yes, ma'am."

"How they accrue powers you'd have probably learned if you'd taken some of the promotion offers."

"Busy, busy, ma'am."

"You're going to be on with the Queen as soon as she gets free," Titanium continued. "Discussion, whether we can read you in."

"Roger, ma'am," Michael said. "I'm in a moral quandary on it. It seems like using the network for personal benefit."

"Powers, used properly, benefit the world," Titanium said. "That's not the issue. The issue is that we didn't steal the information so it's not, technically, ours to give away. The Vishnu must clear it and you know how much they hate American supers and the Corps."

"Understood," Michael said. "I'm in Society Central here, ma'am. New York is ground zero in the US, and the Corps is literally one of their creations. Am I going to be able to continue to work with the network?"

"Once you get turned back over to foster care, you'll be clear enough," Titanium said. "Faerie Queen coming in."

"Welcome back, Mountain Tiger. Glad you survived."

The Faerie Queen's voice was distorted and deliberately had a Russian accent added to it.

Nobody below Level 3 even knew the Faerie Queen's real *nationality* much less identity. When you had more contracts on you than the POTUS, invisibility was your best option. The last running estimate Michael had seen of bounties on the Faerie Queen ran over a half a billion euros. Since most hits cost less than an inexpensive used car, that was a lot.

And nobody who knew about the Faerie Queen believed he was a she. Every world leader was sure, absolutely sure, that the leader of an organization like Gondola could *not* be a woman. Especially given how ruthless she was to enemies. Even female world leaders were *sure* "she" was a he. Angela Merkel had once told the Faerie Queen to "drop the act." She was constantly being "identified" as various males.

Over the time that Michael had been with Gondola, she had been variously "positively identified" as a ninety-year-old Russian in Siberia, a Chinese businessman, a wine farmer in Italy, and the prime minister of Great Britain.

Michael knew for a fact that last one was wrong. He'd been the Gondola on-call economics advisor to the prime minister for six miserable months at one point and that Society-installed moron could barely tie his own shoes.

Most of the rest were dead and as it turned out most were people who had come to the Faerie Queen's negative attention. Pedophiles and child traffickers mostly. Why pay for shooters when your enemies will do the job for you?

"Glad to be back, ma'am," Michael answered.

"I introduce Hayagriva, Lord of Time, to discuss Vishnu training," the Faerie Queen said.

"Mountain Tiger, namaste," Hayagriva said.

"Namaste, Lord of Time," Michael said, gulping.

Dr. Shyam Patel, Hayagriva, Lord of Time, was one of the oldest and most renowned supers on Earth. Leader of the Vishnu Council of Masters, calling him a "speedster" was a base insult. The man was known to be able to cross the planet in a few minutes, somehow using time dilation powers to do what only gaters could normally do.

The Vishnu did not, normally, speak to mortals. They might do so in human form with an often not-so-secret identity. Sometimes they just wanted to live life as a normal. Many were social media "influencers" and constantly in front of the cameras. There were Indian reality TV shows about the "lives of the Vishnu" and the constant internal squabbles of the gods. Those would sometimes deign to talk to "mortals." And they would talk to the members of Gondola, whom they regarded as a form of superheroes for their supernatural abilities in the electronic realm.

Otherwise, they only spoke to "mortals" through their priests.

Speaking to the Lord of Time, personally, wasn't something he thought he'd ever do. He didn't hero worship, but Dr. Shyam Patel was also a notable physicist, not too surprisingly one of the world's great experts on time in physics. Best of all was the implication he was about to receive the grade AAAA, quintuple-emerald standard of training methodology.

"I have read your papers, Lord of Time," Michael continued, trying not to fanboy. "They're amazing."

"And your paper on the effects of Hawking radiation on nucleosynthesis was of great merit," Hayagriva said. "I recommended it most heartily to the head of the Indian Fusion Project. I would talk with you more about physics, but we must discuss your ascension to the ranks of Vishnu."

"Yes, Lord," Michael said. He instinctively leaned forward and checked the door again. A loud drug commercial blasted on the television, and Michael fully closed the door in embarrassment. The Lord of Time, thankfully, didn't seem bothered.

"You are aware that Lord Brahma's invasion of the US Embassy was in retribution for the CIA's deliberate conversion of my personal friend, Lieutenant Colonel James King, into a god of chaos, yes?"

"Yes, Lord," Michael said.

He hadn't realized they were friends, but he knew that the CIA had deliberately turned Major Freedom—Lieutenant Colonel James

King—into the Nebraska Killer, a serial killer and super-terrorist. It was part of the required background brief on The Society. Just like The Society's hand in 9/11, which Colonel King had been trying to *stop* when he was brainwashed.

The 9/11 Commission had identified fourteen "mistakes," each of which done right could have stopped it. Since then, seven more had been declassified. Once is happenstance, twice is coincidence, three times is enemy action. What the hell is twenty-one?

Answer: An international criminal conspiracy so powerful it essentially *was* governments, that had come up with the idea in one of their think tanks, fed it to Atta, introduced him to UBL, supplied half the funding, guarded the plan through their control of the CIA, FBI, and Bill Clinton personally, then reaped the benefits in the Supers Act, the Patriot Act, the TSA, the so-called "Global War on Terror," not to mention making billions on one of the worst single days in American history.

The reasons to hate The Society were so numerous it would be work, work, work all day long just to build the list. World's largest child trafficking organization. Firm believers that there should only be slaves, overseers, and the elite, which didn't sit well with a super-genius raised on the streets. The organization ran half the world's governments on the basis of "never let a crisis go to waste; if you don't have a crisis create one, and if you do have a crisis make it worse." Gondola's Enemy Number One. The list went on and on.

"On a personal level, I occasionally feel sorry for Secretary Harris," Hayagriva continued. "She was forced to kill her fiancé, the only man she'd ever loved or trusted, by the machinations of The Society. Then she does something that reminds me that The Society's description of her as a 'failed cheerleader bimbo' has great accuracy.

"To make it simple: The Council of Masters' hate for the Super Corps is great. They allow themselves to be owned by evil mortals, even if it is through manipulation in most cases. Vishnu should *not* be controlled by mortals. Our powers are too great to be used as a boot of the oppressors. Nor should it in the main involve itself in mortal affairs. Our purpose is to defend the mortal realm against the Storm. That is the sole reason we are Avatars. All else is unimportant. Only the Storm is important.

"The Society, in their power-hungry madness, wish the Storm to succeed. They seek to be rulers of the Apocalypse. Powerful Vishnu may preclude their plans. And powerful Vishnu, were they to become aware of The Society and their machinations, might become a direct threat. As we are to them here in India.

"If you train and they are aware of it, they will attempt to find a reason to have their pet judges enact the great blasphemy. Do you understand?"

"The Great Blasphemy" was severance, taking the power of a super. It could be done by a surgeon with a knife or by a healer and was supposed to only be done when the FISA court had ruled the super was "a real and immediate threat" to the general public.

Since the FISA court was composed of Society judges, it meant that The Society could pull his powers at any time if they thought he was a threat. Not to the "public" but to The Society.

"Yes, Lord of Time," Michael said.

"There were some objections to training an American," Hayagriva added, "but it was a misunderstanding. The House of Earth, particularly, protested until I pointed out that you were a member of Gondola—at which point the Masters and Mistresses of the Houses were all in agreement. So, you will be given access to the secrets."

"Namaste, Lord of Time," Michael said, smiling. His capacity for excitement was maxed out and kept going. He had to forcibly remind himself to calm down and remain humble. "And namaste to the Masters and Mistresses. I shall not fail."

"Even in the Temples, the simple truth is that it is up to the individual Vishnu," Hayagriva said. "Fewer than ten percent of the Vishnu do the necessary work to become guru. You can be taught some of the basics, and there are some advanced practices that can be taught. But attaining the chakras, especially, is difficult, and building power and range is up to the individual. It takes patience, dedication, and time. The youngest Master, in terms of power and range, attained mastery at twenty.

"This is the simplest part of it: Use your chakras. Exercise them. They expend, like a battery. You must expend the battery every day. Your power will grow greatly as a young man, then it will level off until by the time you are twenty-five no more power can be attained. By then, if you are not a guru you never will be.

"The chakras must be sought in each Vishnu's mind. You will be given a guide, but *you* must find the chakras. This takes patience and young men are rarely patient.

"Of the chakras of Earth there are these:

"The Chakra of Light, which all Vishnu have. You call this an 'aura' but it is far more.

"The Chakra of Earth Sense, which all Lords of Earth feel.

"The Chakra of Earth Move, which all attain.

"The Chakra of Stone Shape, which most attain.

"The more difficult Chakras, which most Indian Vishnu attain are these:

"The Chakra of Thermal Earth, to heat and cool earth.

"The Chakra of Earth Sight, which *must* be attained to reach journeyman.

"The Chakras of Elemental Sense and Chemical Sense, which are almost *purely* Earth Lord abilities and are also required for journeyman or higher.

"To attain journeyman in all houses requires the Chakra of Light Shape, which is to project your aura and shape it.

"Chakras *must* be attained by the age of sixteen. At that point your brain stops growing, new neural connections slow, and if you have not attained the chakras by that age, you never will.

"The House of Earth also requires that for Senior Master and Grand Master, Guru Ji, that you have an extensive knowledge of rock and soil types and while not compulsory, they generally attain degrees related to civil engineering, geology, or mining."

The Indian and Chinese Earthers' ability to find mineral deposits was legendary.

"Indians have a reputation for hard work, but some Indian Vishnu never become journeyman. They do not put in the work to attain their chakras, preferring to revel in the earthly delights that are available to a Vishnu in India."

Hayagriva was, besides a physicist, a very notable ascetic who was still occasionally found in the markets wearing a dhoti, in a lotus position, his begging bowl in front of him. He was not into "earthly delights."

Michael, having chatted with Vishnu on ops, was aware of some of the "earthly delights" available. Besides living a life that was the envy of about half of India's still very poor population, there was the, ahem, love-life aspect.

A large majority of India's almost one and a half billion people were practicing Hindus, the largest sect of which is Vaishnavism. That worked out to a LOT of Vaishnavas.

Vaishnavism was like any religion—some people were really into it while for some it was just social. But India, generally, was much more moral in sexual aspects than the West. There were various reasons but actually having your gods right there, judging you, had an impact.

Premarital sex was, therefore, societally frowned upon. It was assumed that a lady going to her marriage bed was a virgin and if she was not, it was potentially scandalous. That even held in upper-class Indian families.

Unless, you know, her previous paramour was a god.

Extremely popular bands were referred to as "rock gods." To the Vaishnavas, the Vishnu were *literal* gods. It was like that.

Michael was a thirteen-year-old male. He could see where "earthly delights" could interfere in those circumstances, especially if you had to put in most of the work before you were *sixteen*.

"Hacking requires great patience," Michael said. "And I look forward to searching for my chakras, Lord of Time. And earthly delights for a Vishnu in the US are less... available. That sounds... fascinating."

"Your work ethic as well as personal ethics are well known, Mountain Tiger," Hayagriva said. "I am sure you will not abuse this power. Mountain Tiger would make a good Earth Lord name; pity you can't use it. That is all of it. I look forward to seeing your progress. Namaste."

"Namaste, Lord of Time," Michael said.

"We shall meet someday," the Lord of Time said. "Good luck."

CHAPTER 6

"We've put copies of everything we have on training methods on a gray server," Faerie Queen said as the Lord of Time left the circuit. "Titanium will direct you there. You can use the news feed app to read them. My call is that it's more important to the world for the United States to have at least *one* powerful super than one more hacker. You're a member but if you have to take the time to work on your powers, that is more important. Understood?"

"Yes, ma'am," Michael said.

Michael generally hated to take orders, mostly because the people giving them were morons.

He did not have a problem with orders from Gondola. The leadership was as smart as he was, far wiser, and had access to gobs of information. Often you weren't sure what you were working on was worth the time, then it turned out, yeah, it was.

If the Faerie Queen wanted him to concentrate on powers, he'd concentrate on powers.

"The rest of it is up to you," the Faerie Queen continued. "Your life. If The Society is going to sever you, we may interfere. Otherwise, you live your life—good, bad, hard, easy. You don't become strong in a hothouse, it's wind and weather that makes you strong. You certainly *haven't* been coddled, but like the Corps and all supers, we all have had 'stuff' in our lives that drives us to do this."

"If what doesn't kill you makes you stronger, ma'am, I be diamond," Michael said. "My life to make and survive."

"The MS-13 issue remains," Faerie Queen said and sighed. "On the one hand, it's your life and your problem. On the other hand, it's El Cannibale. He's been on my to-do list for being, well, El Cannibale. But it would require significant expenditure and he's been more or less 'if the opportunity presents' for a few years and the opportunity has never presented. Our resources on the ground in South America are less than in Europe, Asia, and Africa."

The Faerie Queen had the habit of referring to everything south of the US border as "South America." It annoyed the Central Americans in the group and was a source of regular humor.

"He has sworn eternal vengeance on you for killing his grandnephew. Given his relationship with his sister, Cara De Pene might have been Cannibale's grandson. We're awaiting DNA.

"Bottom stretch, he's not going to stop trying to kill you. FBI is, of course, saying the whole thing is over. Their informants lead them around by the nose. Cannibale is planning on coming to the United States to take care of the problem himself. We'll be monitoring."

It occurred to Michael his room was going to be freezing soon if he left the AC running strong, so he headed into the room and switched it off while listening.

"We've whispered in ears. You should be getting a new identity courtesy of our friends the marshals. That will reduce the likelihood of them coming after you in your secret identity. Unless, of course, they get their hands on the Supers List, which is likely.

"The damned thing is classified 'Top Secret, anyone who wants it.' Giving you a new identity to protect you, then telling every member of the press, every congressman and senator, every person with a net worth over a hundred million dollars, and, oh, by the way, every other country's embassy is the usual sort of 'we really didn't think that through' idiocy you see in any Society organization! But, right now, it's the best we can do. It should slow them down."

He returned to the bathroom and shut the door.

"Give me some time to study my powers and increase them and, well, they can bring it, ma'am," Michael said, his voice relatively low. "I'm mostly worried about them harming others. But if Cannibale is coming here to kill me, just get me in range. He'll be off your to-do list, ma'am. I usually don't talk to people when I'm killing them but if I get the chance, should I say hi for you, boss?"

"Please do," the Faerie Queen said. "Next item: We may involve you in an operation to take out a particularly intractable problem that's been an annoyance for some time.

"Electrobolt—Madeleine Cromarty—is an active and aggressive pedophile. She is also the 'youth outreach coordinator' for the New York Super Corps and in charge of the Junior Super Corps. She's one of those predators who uses her position to get close to disadvantaged youths, such as yourself, groom them, seduce them and sexually assault them. There are dozens of victims."

"That has the stench of The Society all over it, ma'am," Michael said.

"Which is why we haven't been able to take her out," Faerie Queen said. "We've only recently started doing operations in the US beyond tracking traffickers and child pornographers, and even then we work with law enforcement instead of handling the matter ourselves. With the FBI more or less completely corrupted by The Society, NYPD neutered by her position, and all the Society protection around her, we haven't been able to stop her depredations. There's a plan to use you to take her out, but it would require publicity and you *know* how much I *love* publicity."

"Yes, ma'am. About as much as I do."

"Keep your temper," Faerie Queen said. "Don't let her get to you. File written reports on every incident if any. She's been 'counseled' and probably will be again. But she also feels invulnerable and has *very* little self-control. You're going to have to be the one with self-control. She's trans, by the way."

"Sounds like the kind that makes Mama mad cause they make all trans look bad," Michael said.

"Yes," the Faerie Queen said. "Other than that, study your powers, keep your head down, and your profile low. Have you called your mama?"

"That was on the schedule after this call, ma'am."

"Call your mama. See you on the flip side."

"Okay, so much for old business," Secretary Harris said over the video conference.

Tony DiAngelo scanned her background and always marveled at how she'd carefully crafted her office so the wall behind her displayed accolades and pictures with prominent people. The other members of the videoconference all looked away as she addressed him, presumably to pull up and work on other tabs.

"New business. Tony: The new kid. Edwards. How's he settling in?"

Katherine Harris, aka California Girl, five feet four inches tall, Secretary of Super Affairs, was pushing sixty and looked twenty or so. She could have had the longest career in history as a supermodel. The heart-shaped face, aquiline nose, delicate though invulnerable chin, and crystal blue eyes were surrounded by a halo of golden hair. Anyone daring to comment on her torso area risked instant death.

She'd often quietly commented that if one more bastard just started babbling compliments at her and offering marriage she was going to make a knife hand, drive it into his chest, and rip out his still beating heart.

So far, she'd done exactly that three times to super-terrorists. It was not an idle threat.

Then there was that time when the ambassador from Ghana mistook "secretary" as meaning "executive assistant." And since EA in his culture translated as "mistress" . . .

Tony considered her a decent boss most of the time, but she'd also fully committed to drinking the progressive Kool-Aid. As such, it wasn't hard to guess what judgments Katherine had already passed on Michael, so he geared up to defend the kid.

Start with the obvious positives . . .

"Blowing through the tests," Tony said. "Stanford missed a bet. I didn't even know there *was* such a thing as an untestable IQ."

"Now you know," the Secretary said. "There's been some angst expressed."

"Okay?" Tony replied.

"His background is . . . somewhat difficult," Katherine said.

"He gave me a forty-five-minute diatribe that included that as part of it, yeah," Tony said. "Main thing I'm worried about is public image. He says he's going to try to just keep his mouth shut but I'll believe it when we see it. Kid's got a mouth on him. His foster moms clearly never washed it out with soap, and he does go on. Hate to put it this way, he's basically an apparently white Dave Chapelle except even Chapelle would go 'Kid, you need to dial it back a little.'"

"That's a real issue," Katherine said.

"Again, he *said* he was going to try to keep his mouth shut," Tony replied. "And be polite. Like, from Tennessee polite, not New York polite, which I didn't appreciate but I got what he meant. I think the kid's got a good heart, Katherine. He's worried about the MS-13 thing..."

"FBI analysis is that MS-13 is not going to target him," Katherine said. "It's more or less pointless targeting a super."

"The kids aren't hardened, Katherine," Tony said doggedly. "They're still growing. We're hardened from the beginning. Junior Supers have been lost before. Hell, the Vishnu have lost a few."

"Analysis is that he is no longer a target," Katherine said, cutting off that line of discussion. "The other analysis is that *he* is a potential threat. He tends to respond to pressure with extreme levels of violence. The MS-13 incident was not his first such incident. He does not do effective deconfliction."

"God, we're talking about a kid growing up in the ghetto, Katherine!" Tony said, waving his hands. "Show a time when *he* was the aggressor. Everything I've read—and, yeah, I know about the thing with the gang trying to kill him—it's when people attack *him*. Just the MS-13 thing, okay? When he talked about that, he was talking about the potential harm to the general public, okay? He was worried about the other junior supers, okay? He wasn't worried about *himself*. The kid's got a good heart, Katherine. To call him 'rough around the edges' is an understatement worthy of *framing*. But he's got a good heart. And I'm standing by that."

"The issue is he seems to have an issue with persons of *color*, Tony," Katherine said tightly.

"What issues?" Tony asked, puzzled. "He grew up in a black ghetto."

"Did you notice the race of the people he's killed?" the Secretary asked. "Michael Edwards has been repeatedly reported in the news as being a white supremacist. We can't have that in the Corps, Tony."

Everyone else in the videoconference froze awkwardly and looked back toward the screen. This card was inevitable, and he was surprised Katherine had taken this long to play it. But he couldn't exactly cut straight to the trump card. Michael deserved more defense than a surprise technicality.

"Oh, for the love of Pete, Katherine!" Tony said, exasperated. "Those people were trying to kill *him*! It's not *his* fault they were black or brown, Katherine!"

"And their motive?" the Secretary said.

"In both cases it started as a beef with some kids at school and you can say spiraled from there," Tony said. "I've talked with this kid. He's *not* a white supremacist, okay? He's supersmart, he's funny, he's irreverent, and politically so incorrect it's painful, he's PTSD and ADHD and every other kind of letters of the alphabet, but what he is *not*, Katherine, is a white supremacist. And even if you or your lunching friends disagree on that, what you haven't let me do is update you on some stuff about him that may *help!*"

"Which is . . . ?" the Secretary said.

"He's Native American," Tony replied.

Apparently mollified, the others returned to their distractions.

"Really," Katherine said. "He doesn't look it."

"Oh, who's being racist *now*, Madame Secretary?" Tony said. "What's a Native American look like, huh? Okay, I'll admit he doesn't look it. Genetics came back. One-quarter Lakota Sioux. Which makes him legally, by federal law, Native American."

"That's something to . . ." Katherine said, looking thoughtful.

"This is a good thing, Madame Secretary," Tony said. "The Corps is pretty much precisely as diverse as this great land of immigrants of ours. We've got Asian and black and brown and white and Italian and Greek more or less in such an exact mix, Harvard eat your heart out."

"Tony."

"But there's one percent of Native Americans in the US and we only had *one*," Tony continued, ignoring his oldest friend. "Lightning Eagle. We should have three and a half. Since he's a quarter, I'm not sure how that works out. Equity math. Not my strong suit. But the point is now we've got *two*, which is closer to three and a half. We approach perfection of diversity."

"Tony," Katherine said, shaking her head and closing her eyes.

"I don't make the rules, Katherine," Tony said. "I just have to live with them. This is a good thing. And it opens up some other possibilities."

"Which are . . . ?" the Secretary asked.

"I know what you and the FBI are saying about MS-13," Tony said, holding a hand to forestall a reply. "But. If there is an active shooting incident, it's on my watch. And I'd like to avoid that, as well as a potential school-shooting incident . . ."

"You think he'd shoot up a school?" Katherine asked. "Then we've got a real..."

"Oh, Christ, Katherine, no!" Tony said. Deep breath. In through the nose... "If Michael gets detected in his secret identity. Kids are going to be on social media going 'Oh, my God! Like, Michael Edwards, that horrible white supremacist from Baltimore is, like, totally *in my school!*'"

Secretary Katherine Harris, former teenage resident of Sherman Oaks, stuck her tongue in her cheek and rolled it around.

"Are you trying to imply something there, Tony?" she asked, a tad sharply.

"Yes, Madame Secretary," Tony said, steely but calm. "That kids are stupid, and MS-13 can use social media. Also, that I've known you since you were seventeen and I was thirteen. FBI may say they're not going to go after him if he's on patrol, but what about when they find out what school he's in? Do we *need* another shooting?"

"Not really," Katherine said.

"ACS—that's the Administration for Children's Services—hasn't placed him, yet," Tony said, "but it doesn't matter *what* school he's in. Do you want a school, which is the easiest place to find him, shot up by a transnational gang? His foster home? I think the answer to that is obvious."

"What's the answer?" the Secretary asked.

"Get him a new identity," Tony said. "We've got the marshals right here. They can literally press a couple of buttons. An email to the commandant would be nice but I could probably swing it with 'the Secretary would appreciate it.' I just need the Secretary to *say* she appreciates it. The white supremacy thing, with the exception of 'in the know,' goes away, the MS-13 problem goes away, and the white Dave Chapelle problem will hopefully never publicly surface."

"So that's that," Katherine said, nodding. "Good talk."

"Except there's one more problem and I cannot fix that, only you can," Tony said, trying not to grimace. This was, by far, his least favorite discussion point, but second most important after protecting Michael from MS-13.

"And that is...?"

"Bolt."

Now the other members carefully avoided any eye contact

whatsoever with the screen, though Tony saw eyes shifting around with anxiety. Katherine stiffened defensively and sighed.

"Tony, Madeleine is *incredibly* popular with certain senators," Katherine said. "I understand you have issues..."

"I do not have issues, Katherine," Tony said. "*Bolt* has issues. Bolt has more issues than *National Geographic*. I'm *not* the problem, Katherine. The fact that Bolt is in *my* office, running *my* kids and he...f...SHE feels like *she* can ignore me because *she* is so *incredibly popular* with certain senators we depend upon for funding is the issue! If *she* is so incredibly popular in Washington, why is she *my* problem, Katherine?!"

"We've been over this, Tony," Katherine said, getting angry. "Bolt has more public presence in New York. *She* is an iconic figure there and it is about presence rather than politics. So, this is *not* new business."

"The *new* business is twofold," Tony snapped. "One is old business that she's hitting on Jorge. Again. Since she's not listening to *me* anymore, you're going to have to call her. Today."

"I'll put it on my schedule..." Katherine said with a sigh.

"Oh, what, not going to ask me to ask the other members of the juniors if he's exaggerating?" Tony said. "Do an investigation? You starting to grasp that *she* has *no* control when it comes to pretty little boys?"

"Tony, Madeleine is not a *pedophile*, okay?" Katherine snapped. "She's very tactile, yes. Perhaps too much so. But that does not mean she engages in pedophilia. Just because you have some lingering... cultural issues..."

"Oh, do not go there, Katherine!" Tony replied. "You remember you jumped all over me one time when I said something *sort of* off-color to Windstorm?"

"It was more than off-color, Tony!" the Secretary replied. "You told her she had a nice ass!"

"She *does* have a nice ass," Tony said. "And that's kind of different than, you know, rubbing your hands all over somebody when they're trying to get changed into their costume and sexually propositioning them! And Windstorm was *eighteen* when I said that, and it was a *slip*! I didn't rub my hands all over her, whip my dick out, and suggest she suck it! I sure as hell didn't do that when she was *thirteen*!"

"Madeleine has been counseled on that," Katherine said tightly.

"I beg to disagree, Madame Secretary," Tony said archly.

"I wrote her a very specific counseling statement on that matter," Katherine pointed out.

"I again beg to disagree, Madame Secretary," Tony said. "You wrote one on Edgar. Not on Madeleine."

"That's splitting hairs, Tony," the Secretary replied.

"Again, disagree," Tony said. "When a person transitions, it's like them Baptists and being born again! They're new people, their sins cast off with their old names and genders! They are whole new people!"

"Tony," Katherine said warningly. "You need to stop making fun of the trans movement."

"I am not," Tony said. "That is exactly what they say. That they are new people. But here's the thing, Katherine. A leopard can change its gender, I suppose, but the spots don't change. And Bolt has not changed. Just clothes. And did you notice that Edgar suddenly became Madeleine right after you actually called him on the carpet? Finally. Back when he was a she . . . she was a he?"

"Tony," Katherine said, grabbing her head in her hands.

"And the second new business is, again, Michael Edwards," Tony said. "Specifically in relation to Bolt."

"Is he transphobic?" Katherine asked. "Not that, too."

"Katherine," Tony said, trying not to sigh again. "I love you like a sister. And sometimes, if it would do any good, I want to throw you out a window. But you can fly so it wouldn't do any good."

"And I guarantee you I wouldn't be the one going out the window," Katherine said. "Your point?"

"His . . . 'mama,'" Tony said. "The lady that really raised him, the one constant in his life, she's named Miss Cherise."

"Point?" Katherine said.

"Miss Cherise's 'dead name' is Thomas Carter," Tony replied. "Don't even think Michael knows her original name and she hasn't used it since she was nine. Six-foot-four black trans street hooker and drug addict who found him in the alleyway and has been his only real mother since. So, no, he's not transphobic. What he is is severely abused. Most of us have got stuff we acquire due to stress and trauma, right? Generally, that's not the first serious trauma. We've had stuff." He looked at her and waggled his head.

"Point?" Katherine said, her face hard. "You're covering stuff we discussed in the nineties, Tony. And I'm a busy person."

"Michelle called his social services file 'the *War and Peace* of child abuse but with more war instead of any peace,'" Tony said. "Take any ten of us that had . . . stuff, wouldn't add up to what Michael's been through. Not an exaggeration. Question is how he survived it all.

"He's a good kid," Tony repeated. "Got a good heart. If he goes Chapelle on patrol and gets us in the hot, that's on me. I'm vouching for him on that. What I'm *not* vouching for him on is Bolt. Because the kid is also a hand grenade with the pin mostly pulled. PTSD causes real anger management issues. So does TBI. Kid's got both and his PTSD, like his brains, is off the scale.

"Michelle brought it up," Tony said. "I don't got a problem with you asking her direct. Michael will talk very glibly about most of it. Burned, cut, shot . . ."

"Burned?" the Secretary asked.

"He gave me a really graphic description of being in the burn ward," Tony said. "Burned like that. Twice. When he was five."

Several people briefly glanced away at this and visibly shuddered.

"Oh," Katherine said, making a face.

"That stuff he can, kind of, talk about," Tony said. "Usually babble and he just ignores what he's saying. Michelle says he's not going to be able to really work with it for a while and only if he's not abused more. The one thing he *can't* talk about, mentions but just goes past, is the sexual stuff. Won't cover details at all. Michelle feels he hasn't been able to work with it the way he can the physical stuff. Not that it wasn't physical.

"So, thing is, Madame Secretary . . ." Tony thought about what to say for a second, then shrugged. "Kid's already killed twenty-four people. Madeleine goes after him the way she went after Jorge, don't be entirely surprised if it's twenty-five."

"Well, that would be a severance," Katherine said.

"Not if he can reasonably plead self-defense from a pedophile," Tony said. "And do we want that? Especially when his attorney brings up what was going on and even what had gone on in the past? You want *that* publicity, Katherine? Sure, nobody *you* know reads the *Post*, but people *I* know read the *Post*. You want the headline to be 'Pedobolt'?"

"I will speak to Madeleine, Tony," Katherine said. "Any major other new business? Because this has gone overtime."

"No," Tony said, shaking his head.

"I'll talk to her," Katherine repeated.

It was the best he was going to get.

"Roger, Madame Secretary."

"Oh, Pretty Woman" —Roy Orbison

Michael was waiting in the lobby for Alexander of Alexandria to escort him in, which was becoming downright tedious but that's the speed of government agencies. He hadn't been around when the junior super-teams were coming in for patrol. They only patrolled one "school night" a month and every other Saturday. They'd done a patrol this last Saturday from what he'd picked up. Saturdays weren't a workday. Michael had spent Saturday in his guarded hotel room doing equations, digging through the files Gondola and the Lord of Time had sent, and cautiously testing his powers.

So, it wasn't patrol-day but the gorgeous teenage brunette in the lobby just had to be a super. Either that or a teenage supermodel had stopped by to say hi. And since the location of "Super Headquarters" was technically secret, and even then required access cards to get in, not to mention being in the Federal Building, she was probably a super.

And his future wife if he had anything to do with it.

Michael hadn't spent much time studying supers before Acquiring but since then he *had* been studying and he had come to the—not new—conclusion that supers were supposed to be regarded by normals as gods or at least demigods, because they didn't *just* get superpowers, the powers changed their appearance as well.

First of all, when they Acquired, they exhibited an aura. Chakra of Light. Turning off your aura was the only thing easy with superpowers. Just a thought and it went away or returned. They also reflected the power of the super. With new Acquires, the aura was there but barely beyond their skin. For supers like California Girl, it would fill a room.

Michael had been unconscious after Acquiring and his aura had remained on. After talking to the Lord of Time and reading the instructions carefully, he'd tried it in the hotel room before he went to bed. It was about as useful in the dark as a glow-worm lantern but pretty cool. Turn off all the lights and you could still make your way around. That, so far, was as far as he'd gotten on trying powers.

So, they glowed, which, even in some primitive society, would tend to make the regular people consider them godlike. Which probably was designed, by whatever was sending superpowers to the Earth all of a sudden, as a survival trait. Most adults are not going to take on a kid who has just, for example, flamed someone he was fighting and was now glowing.

Of course, if it had happened in, say, sixteenth-century Germany, they'd probably be burned at the stake. Which was what had happened at first, and still occasionally, in Islamic countries. Though it leaned more to the kid being stoned to death. Afghanistan had a notable dearth of supers.

Then there was the personal appearance aspect.

Supers still bore some superficial resemblance to their parents but tended to exhibit much greater beauty. They were all as good-looking as the highest grade of male, female, or other models. People would pay millions in plastic surgery to even be *close* to the looks of supers. Women tended to be larger breasted than normal with A going to C and ratios on up. Female supers who would have been naturally large breasted were...extreme.

With men, instead of secondary sexual characteristics being enhanced, *primary* sexual characteristics were enhanced. And that, too, led in some cases to ludicrous extremes.

Michael hadn't been entirely joking about the Michelangelo's *David* comparisons.

Bottom line: He was a very good-looking guy with not only street smooth but scars. Ladies dug scars. She *would* be his bride and they would have many children.

He put on his best player mode and sashayed over.

"Hey, babe," he said, nodding in approval and clicking his tongue. "You be fine as Corinthian *leather*."

The girl wore her jet-black hair straight down her back to butt level. An aquiline perhaps too beautiful face was barely noticeable because of the emerald-green eyes. The eyes were the eyes of a Gorgon, so beautiful they could turn a man to stone.

"Is that supposed to be a pickup line?" the girl asked, shaking her head in disbelief.

"Michael Edwards," Michael said, sticking out his hand. "Your future husband."

"I'm considering shaking that hand," the girl replied. "But only because we have regenerative healing, and it would eventually grow back."

"Invul, huh?" Michael said, pulling his hand back. That might create some difficulty in the relationship. But as she'd said, he had regenerative healing, and he was willing to risk having to grow back something *much* more important than a hand to have this incredible woman. He'd go back to the burn ward for her. "That would make you Ivory Wing."

"Yep," Ivory Wing said. "Sasha Nikula. Chosen a super name, yet?"

"Nah," Michael said. "I usually make quick decisions but since it's a pain to change I'm thinking it through. Come here often?"

"You don't stop, do you?" Sasha asked.

"Rarely," Michael admitted. "Seriously, I'm here to eval. What's up with you being here? Not that I mind. At all. One bit."

"I have to get my uniform refitted," Sasha said. "We grow, right?"

"Absolutely," Michael said, trying not to look down. At a guess, Sasha would have naturally been a B. A spectacularly perfect B. "Been supersonic, yet?"

"Not yet," Sasha said. "I'm hoping to this month. It's *hard*. The air gets like solid rock the faster you go!"

Do not *do the physics lecture. Do not . . . Muuust suppressss Bernoulli equations . . . !*

"Can I let you in on a secret?" Michael asked, trying not to say that the problem of the atmosphere wasn't that it was getting harder, it was that the molecules were impacting on the surface at a higher speed so it was a momentum issue versus solidity . . .

"What secret would that be?" Sasha asked, bracing slightly. "Please don't let it be about your penis. I've heard it."

"Okay, given your age, that ain't right," Michael said, shaking his head angrily.

"You haven't met Electrobolt yet, have you?" Sasha asked.

"No," Michael said.

"I'll let you enjoy the experience for yourself," Sasha said, with a touch of ice. "What super-secret super info does the new kid on the block have?"

He motioned her toward a quieter part of the lobby and glanced around.

"It's about when you go supersonic," Michael said in a lower voice. "You're still in cloth flight gear, right?"

"Yeah," Sasha said. "You don't get fitted for your leather flight suit 'til you join the Corps. Too expensive while we're still growing to keep changing suits."

"That's not the only reason," Michael said darkly. "When you hit super, there's a sudden condition caused by..." Michael stopped before he almost made the classic nerd mistake and bored the pretty girl with a physics lecture. Alexander, sure. This goddess descended to a fallen Earth, not doing it. Close call there.

"Just...the physics. Trust me. When Cali was first flying, she finally hit supersonic, and her cheerleader costume blew off because of the effects. She had to fly around LA totally nude and somehow sneak home."

"Oh, my God," Sasha said, horrified and trying not to laugh. "You're kidding, right? The Madame Secretary?"

"Here's the thing, right?" Michael said carefully. "When you hit Mach One in that cloth suit, *same thing* is going to happen. You're going to end up wearing only your boots, helmet and pack. You might retain your bra if you stop fast enough."

"I have a hard time believing that," Sasha said. "They'd tell me... right? Warn me at least?"

"It's a rite of passage," Michael said, shrugging. "Happened to Cali so it's just...something they deliberately *don't* tell you about."

"That's hard to...?" Sasha said. "Patrick's not that way..."

"Rite of passage," Michael said. "Tight groups have ways of testing the new kids. Like in the Navy they'll send some new guy out to get a hundred yards of flightline."

"And the problem with that is...?" Sasha asked.

"The flightline is where they line up the planes," Michael said. "Grid squares, chemlight batteries, they're all things that don't exist is the point. And they'll let you make the mistakes they made just to see how you handle them. It's a normal thing in groups like Super Corps, cops, military, EMTs, though I think essentially stripping teenagers is probably over the line."

"Kind of," Sasha said, her expression a blend of disturbed and contemplative. Her superhero posture drooped defensively. "So . . . I just got to go through it, I guess?"

"Thing is this," Michael said. "If you spot it and do something to make it lesser, it shows you're on your toes. Makes you look better than it just happened. Suggestion?"

"Okay?"

"You're going to retain your commo pack," Michael said. "There's a personal effects compartment, right?"

"Yes."

"Throw some clothes in there," Michael said. "Surreptitiously. Could be just a pair of boy shorts and a sports bra. That's not much to fly back in but it's *something*. What you can fit and will stay on flying low speed. Then, when you go super and are suddenly nekkid, just stop, put on your spare clothes, and fly back to the support ship. It'll make you look supersmart and prepared. Sports bra and boy shorts is less embarrassing than 'Oh, God, I'm naked!' And it will impress them."

"Makes sense," Sasha said with a sigh. "I guess maybe that's why the locker room is coed. Just get used to it or something?"

Michael's mind normally sparkled and burst so fast that he had a hard time carrying on normal conversations. Despite talking with the most beautiful girl he'd ever seen, other tracks of his mind were, variously:

- Wondering that a water layer, which was made up of hydrogen and oxygen, was necessary for solar fusion which was necessary for nucleosynthesis of higher-level atoms than hydrogen, like oxygen, but the Big Bang Theory stated that the universe had been formed with only primordial hydrogen with a smidgeon of helium and lithium, none of which could be used to form water so there was a chicken and egg problem. Where had the water to induce fusion to induce nucleosynthesis to make oxygen to make water come from?
- Wondering how he could con Alexander of Alexandria into getting shrimp tacos again. He probably shouldn't have given the lecture on how people in the ghetto really felt about cops. Things were still a might chilly. Also, apparently "Michael is a white supremacist" had followed him to NYC. Joy.
- Working on the Chakra of Earth Sight, idly, not that he wanted to see what Sasha's bone structure was like or anything. It was obviously perfect.

- Wondering what Sasha would look like in red and white. The red might clash with her eyes.
- Wondering how to convince his future fiancée that even if the red clashed with her eyes, a sexy Handmaiden outfit made a perfect wedding dress...
- Wondering what a one-on-one between Kobe Bryant and Wilt Chamberlain would be like.
- Doing the physics of how fast a one-hundred-ton boulder would have to be to punch 2017 Godzilla hard enough in the jaw that it would cause him to be at least knocked around if not knocked out since his ability to take a punch was unclear depending on the various movies.
- Working out the mechanics of using Earth Move and Earth Shape to lift a fully loaded shipping container and throw it at a kaiju a la *Pacific Rim* but without the mecha.
- Wondering if you could use Earth Move and Earth Shape to make an Earth Mecha and ride it to fight kaiju.

And various other important subjects.

The moment that Sasha, who would be coming in and changing at the same time as the other Junior Super Corps, like Michael, said that the locker room was *coed*—

All of those thoughts ceased in an instant. His mind stopped completely for the first time in his life that did not involve severe head trauma.

So did his breathing.

That's it. She'd done it. She'd turned him into stone. He couldn't move. Couldn't breathe. Couldn't think. He was just going to die that way, standing in the lobby for all time as a stone statue.

"Are you okay?" Sasha asked, tilting her head to the side. "Hello!" she added, snapping her fingers in front of his face. "Earth to Michael!"

Michael suddenly took a deep breath as his CO_2 response kicked in.

"Yeah!" he said, rapid fire. "I'm fine! Never better! Just an epiphany! I was just thinking about this chicken-and-egg thing in stellar nucleosynthesis! Hahah! Nothing about the locker room at all! You need oxygen for water, right?!"

Inside Michael's head was a little voice going *"Stop! Stop! Stop!"* But he just couldn't stop.

"Dihydrogen monoxide poisoning, right?" he continued, tugging his ear furiously. "Hahahah! Like water in a shower...Never mind! Hahah. And it's only primordial hydrogen! Which can't fuse due to its high Coulomb barrier and that it forms hydrogen diamond—which, clearly, isn't going to fuse under gravity alone with that Coulomb barrier, obviously, right?"

"What?" Sasha asked.

"And so, there's totally going to have to be some nucleosynthesis in the expansion phase of the universe! Because otherwise the big bang theory is totally out the window, right? I mean, because obviously God didn't create the universe with some magic finger snap!"

Stop! Stop! Stop! Stop tugging your ear!

"So, what if, and this is just blue skying which also needs oxygen obviously, hahahah, because of the very high density and heat of the early expansion phase when all the universe's matter is squeezed into a very small space, comparatively, and that with quantum vacuum energy causing ninety percent of the matter into fifty percent of the space which you're even going to have in the early universe, obviously, 'cause you see it in high energy plasma discharge like what we see when we Acquire and there's lots of red do you like red?"

Stop! Stop! Stop! Quit mentioning red! Stop!

"What if and this is the important part there *was* nucleosynthesis but even *that* doesn't work because the pressures still aren't enough to overcome the Coulomb barrier so it would *have* to have some sort of *catalyst* and the other thing you've got is Hawking black holes, which, obviously, give off Hawking radiation 'cause of the matter-antimatter collisions, so what if Hawking radiation is the catalyst, right? I mean, it's just a hypothesis but it's better than nothing, right? Do you think red goes with your eyes? What did I say? Never mind! Hahahahah..."

He stood there grinning maniacally at her, tugging his ear and shifting from foot to foot, then cursed.

"Shit. I just totally blew my cover."

"What...was that...?" Sasha asked.

"I hereby confess to being a nerd," Michael said with a sigh. "I do astrophysics and economics papers as a way to relax. I like calculus. I'm a nerd. Need any help with your homework? I do *awesome* term papers!"

"You're the one that killed all those . . . people, though, right?" Sasha asked carefully.

"Well, yeah, that too," Michael admitted. "But I was *very* nerdy in doing so. Ballistics is nerdier than you think. It's like weaponized math. Though the whole thing with the machete was a total fluke."

"The. What?" Sasha said, her eyes going wide.

"Sasha," one of Kevin's assistants said, waving to the support area corridor. "Kevin will see you now."

"So . . . bye," Sasha said, waggling her fingers at him.

"Byyye," Michael said sadly, as the girl of his dreams walked away to get refitted. "I am *so* white and nerdy . . ."

Getting refitted meant . . .

Getting up on the laser table in a practically diaphanous skintight body suit . . .

"Michael . . . ?" Alexander said, snapping his fingers in front of the kid's face. "Earth to Michael . . ."

"It . . . it could . . . it *could* be red . . ." Michael said, his eyes unseeing as he looked into the distance. "*And* white . . ."

"What is *up* with this kid . . . ?"

CHAPTER 7

"Kashmir" —Led Zeppelin

Michael sat on the floor of his hotel room, legs extended in front of him, arms extended and hands holding his feet, with his nose between his knees. Every light in the room was turned off and he had an eye mask on, courtesy of the US marshals. They might not be willing to spring for the most expensive gaming laptop on the planet, but they had the budget for a sleeping mask.

Dandasana was what the instruction manual suggested for practicing Earth Sight, so he was going for it.

Unsurprisingly, the Vishnu manual on training powers included a *lot* of yoga. Every chakra had an accompanying yoga pose, some of them pretty advanced.

Earth Sense had seemed to be defeating him. Which was weird since you were supposed to get it automatically. Child's Pose wasn't particularly challenging—for some of the higher-level chakras he was pretty sure it was the yoga pose that was going to be the problem—the actual chakra seemed to be the issue. He wasn't feeling anything different.

In the manual it talked about how you immediately felt it after your Acquisition event, which they called "aarohee" which meant "ascending." But he'd been unconscious after his aarohee, so maybe he *hadn't* gotten it?

He'd read the English translation several times, then read it in Hindi and just wasn't getting it.

Then he remembered the flight from Baltimore. It had been the first time he'd been on an airplane, so he thought that was why he was so nervous. But something just seemed...missing. What was missing was *earth*. He had been surrounded by metal, plastic, and air.

Since he'd been in NYC, he was *surrounded* by "earth." The concrete walls of the hotel room and the offices, which had been his two main areas, were "earth" by the definition of whatever gave these powers. He wasn't feeling it because it was like a fish in water. Earth was everywhere around him.

After that he started to be able to sort out air from earth, closing his eyes and walking to the wall until he could "feel" the earth ahead of him. Then he went back to Child's Pose, which now made more sense since you were digging your nose in the earth, and just worked on feeling the sensation and sorting out where the earth was around him.

Then he fell asleep. He woke up some time later from a nightmare, got off the floor, crawled into bed, muttered about a yoga mat, and that night was done.

The next day, besides another visit to the shrink, was "awareness classes." He was aware that some people needed to eat some fruit, thanks, and that women didn't appreciate being compared to Corinthian leather, no matter how fine they were.

What got him about "awareness classes" was that they more or less delineated all the weaknesses of whoever you were supposed to be aware of. The sexual harassment awareness class was basically a "how to be a sexist jerk" class. If you wanted to be a sexist jerk, that was the class for you. The adipose awareness class was one fatty joke after another. It was fat-shaming on steroids.

He'd mostly kept his mouth shut until he got to the LGBTQISR4R class, which was how it was listed. Then he'd let rip as The Expert.

Besides astrophysics and economics, he'd audited this class at Harvard when he was nine in Queer and Transgender Theory. Mama was trans so he thought he'd check it out. It had turned out to be, not much to his surprise, a lot of bitching and crying and not much real information. Everyone struggled through the struggle sessions to the point that they might as well have been four thousand (yes, that many!) members of a Greco-Roman wrestling team covered in oil. The struggling with the struggle!

As part of the class, audit or not, you were supposed to do a three-thousand-word term paper. Three. Thousand. Words! Wow, that was a lot! So much angst about the horrors of a Three. Thousand. Word. Term paper!

He was simultaneously taking a master's level class at Wharton in finance. You turned in five-thousand-word reports every *week*. Not one for the entire term.

To fit in, he'd created a new profile. The online university he was working with more or less didn't care who you *really* were as long as the face matched the name when you took tests. Michael had multiple personality syndrome. For science he was Thomas Phillips. For business, economics, and finance he was Phillip Crawford III. And for anything grievance studies, he was Adrian Kornbluth.

Adrian Kornbluth was a pansexual goatherd who lived on a polyamorous commune in Vermont. The "in Vermont" was extremely important. Adrian Kornbluth, who talked with a quiet raspy voice and a slight lisp, really enjoyed xer experience as a goatherd.

Okay, so he might have embellished his résumé just a tad.

Xe was a favorite of the professor in the class who hoped someday to come visit xer commune and meet the many—odd—people who populated it.

Between a couple of weekly *real* papers about real stuff like the economics of Chilean sea-bass farming, Michael had dropped every big word and every grievance industry buzz word he could find into a random text generator. What spewed out was nearly but not *entirely* incomprehensible. Not good enough.

It took some work and looking up a few words with which he was unfamiliar—*omnisuescence* was fantastic—to get every single sentence to have exactly zero syntactical value but it was worth it. Put a comprehensible two-hundred-and-fifty-word introduction about the three goats Adrian herded—Xalla, Po'ahsoha, and Fred—and you had "The Three Goat Problem."

Xer professor had been ecstatic. So ecstatic she/her had submitted it for publication in *The Octagonal*, the Leading Journal of Intersectionality. Available online, for free, everywhere.

Excited about publishing a nine-year-old pansexual goatherd, or possibly because it was the leading journal of intersectionality and unavailable in paper form, xe made the cover and Adrian Kornbluth was famous in the field of Queer and Transgender theory. Then came the offer of an early entry to Harvard.

Xer rejection letter was, in xer humble opinion, a masterpiece of Marxist grievance rhetoric referencing Harvard's shameful history in taking money from the slave trade, not to mention evil capitalism in general. Stolen lands were mentioned. Xe would not even consider attending such a vile, evil, institution.

Which was true, but not for the reasons given. Mostly because it was center of mass of The Society's control of Western academic institutions and Michael had long before gotten tired of all the Society bullshit. Same reason that next year he'd turned down Stanford, not as bad but still bad, later Princeton, still bad, and MIT, also not fun.

Harvard's groveling response to the nine-year-old pansexual Vermonter Greta Thunberg practically wept electronic tears. They were shamed, ashamed, shame, shame, shame and guilt!

Man, they were pissed when Michael Edwards became briefly infamous for killing a bunch of black dudes and somebody put two and two together.

The Octagonal considered pulling his papers but by that time "The Three Goat Problem" had been cited so many times in the grievance industry they just hoped nobody noticed. And nobody did.

It was still getting cited. It had even crept into Critical Law Theory. It was like the psycho girlfriend you just couldn't shake off. The thing about the paper was that because he had intelligently ensured it had exactly zero real meaning, everyone who read it could say it meant *anything*. Which was most of what grievance theory papers were about. When a paper meant *nothing*, it could be twisted to mean *anything*.

His *next* published paper, at ten, was in a graduate astrophysics course at Stanford, "The Effects of Hawking Radiation on Nucleosynthesis," which also included a lot of big words, but every sentence was syntactical. If you knew what any of it meant. Very few did. But it still made the cover of the *American Journal of Astrophysics*, which *did* take notice of Michael Edwards killing a whole bunch of black dudes and wrote an apologetic note in their—actually published on paper—journal to the effect of that he seemed like a nice, quiet guy, the sort of neighbor you rarely see but just kind of wave to, and you never know about people.

It, too, was still being cited, especially in fusion research.

When the LGBTQISR4R Awareness teacher—who was white privilege she/her homosexual short-haired Karen one each—started in about the challenges faced by LGBTQISR4R, which even *she* had a hard time remembering all the letters and numbers, *Professor Kornbluth* stopped her cold.

"What I believe you mean is that we need to defeat the omnisuescence of *mens rea*."

LGBTQISR4R Awareness had read the "Three Goat Problem" and it was brilliant. He admitted to embellishing his résumé but did talk about Mama and even video-called her. Everything was going swimmingly until she/her vaguely sort of not exactly directly referenced, well, the deaths of some persons. Possibly of color. She seemed a bit puzzled by the dichotomy.

At which point Professor Kornbluth, expert in all things progressive, lambasted the simplistic view of "thou shalt not kill" as being a relic of bourgeois Christian sentimentality that needed to be tossed on the ash-heap of history with misogyny, racism, and washing your hands after going number two.

Xe made up quotes from Stephen Hawking that would probably get him damned to hell, referenced actual Foucault quotes—that raging pedo—and quoted other famous postmodernist philosophers, every single one of whom had proven, *proven* that there was nothing wrong with killing someone, because right and wrong were outdated concepts, and really what was death, anyway? It was just sort of a moment in life, right? This silly concept that killing someone was a "bad" thing depended on the definition of "bad." It was just another *mens rea* that needed to be overcome. Fight the omnisuescence. You're not a colonizer, are you?

He'd probably overdone it. The Nebraska Killer was still a boogieman to she/her generation. A super that clearly had no regard for any life, for purely philosophical reasons, wasn't what she/her wanted to be in the room with. By the time they were done, she/her was sweating and ready to run for the hills.

Dr. Michelle Swanson, MD, double PhD (Psych, Neuro), not the worst therapist he'd crossed swords with, had had Words to say on the subject. Michael couldn't stop laughing and that wasn't what the Good Doctor was looking for.

"I am aware, Doctor, that I am a bad, bad man..."

Finally, the day of "awareness classes" were done, Alexander handed him over to the marshals, dinner, quick stop for a sleeping mask, check in with Gondola, call Mama to talk about the day, and get started with Earth Sight. He wanted to get through the major chakras—Sight, Light Shape, and Thermal especially—before he got placed in a home. Practicing them in the hotel room was private. He wasn't sure what he'd be dealing with in NY foster care, and based on research assumed it wasn't going to be much better than Baltimore.

The instructions for how to "find" the chakras came down to just rummaging in your mind, staying Zen. Michael's main problem was shutting down all the tracks. Loosening every muscle in his constantly tense body was one thing. Stopping thinking was a nightmare. The Lord's command to "be still and listen" was *not* meant for ADHD.

Focus.

She can't wear the bonnet and study Earth Sense. Maybe a shorter brim?

Focus.

Should I have had chili on the quesadilla?

Focus.

I wonder how this floor is designed. Do they run the electrical through it or what?

And then he knew because he was suddenly seeing through it. But not exactly.

He could "see" in every direction, constantly, sort of. It was like peripheral vision. He could tell that movement would attract his attention. For someone as paranoid as he was, that was going to be awesome as soon as he got some range. On the other hand, with range there would be constant flickering movement in every direction in a city. He'd figure it out.

But he could also focus an inner eye in any one direction and see things clearly as sort of a gray-and-white shadow form. At least if it was made of earth elements. He could see through the floor and draw back to look at the concrete layer by layer. He could "see" the bones in his knees, then, looking around, all the bones in his body. There was a haze around them where his flesh was because there were enough "earth" elements in the human body it was like looking through a thin dust cloud.

It was totally cool. Also, very short range. Like Earth Sense it didn't extend much beyond arm's length. He could tell there was rebar, but it didn't block the vision. It was just a null space.

He could barely see into the room below, not even as far as that room's bed.

According to the documents, if he used it every day to its maximum range, the range would slowly extend.

He'd take that.

Day Three was more tests and classes, ways to interact with the public and the equivalent of Skippy's List with a list of don'ts. One of them was don't exhibit any potentially threatening or violent behavior to the public. So, going on a rant about how killing someone being murder was an outdated philosophical concept was probably out.

The highlight was to be his new costume reveal.

He couldn't wait.

Just after lunch they were back in Briefing Room Four waiting on Kevin. Briefing Room Four had featured prominently in his last week. At the rate he and Alexander were hitting the water bottles, people really *were* going to die of thirst.

"We probably should get some water and refill the bug-out bags," Michael said, taking a sip.

His Earth Sight had already increased, and he could see into the corridor from the back side of the briefing table. Not exactly the other side of the moon, but it was pretty good so far.

"Really?" It had taken some time, but Alexander had learned to treat any statement from Michael with caution.

"Really," Michael said, rubbing his earlobe. "My rant about taking a couple of bottles and you cursing me as you died of thirst was a joke. One or two bottles is no big deal. But we've been in here multiple times and some of the bags have *no* water in them. The reality is the statistical likelihood of the bags being used in the next six months is very near zero. Near zero is not zero. The other reality is that of all the 'stuff' in those bags, water is the most important in a survival situation.

"I would not be responsible for someone actually trusting the bags had water and then being without any. So, the next time we're going to be hurry up and wait in here, it would behoove us to Strategically

Transfer Equipment to an Alternate Location with a case of bottled water and fill them back up."

"I'm not even sure which ones..." Alexander said, looking at the pile.

"I am," Michael said. "Eidetic memory. I remember every single thing I've seen, heard, smelled, tasted. Which, alas, means I remember every single *bad* thing. Also, you can tell from the weight."

"Yeah," Alexander said as the door opened and Kevin! entered the room.

"*Kevin!*" Michael said, standing up and holding out his arms. He had had to ignore that he'd already spotted the slight designer and his much taller, generally silent, nonbinary assistant before the door opened. Earth Sight was awesome. No more surprises.

"Michael, darling!" Kevin said.

They embraced and did the side-kissy thing.

"What have you created for me, dahling?" Michael asked.

"You just sit over here," Kevin said. "Maureen," he added, gesturing slightly at the enormous plasma screen.

Maureen hit a couple of buttons on the pad, then nodded at Kevin.

"In three...two...one...NOW!" he shouted, throwing out his hands to the plasma screen triumphantly. "TA-DA!"

Michael and Alexander looked at the proposed costume and both cleared their throats, more or less simultaneously.

Michael had dealt with Kevin a couple of other times since their first meeting as well as passing in the hall. He really liked The Designer. He was one of those gay guys who was just happy all the time.

He also was a sensitive soul so Michael knew that the slightest hint of disapproval of The Design on the part of His Little Michelangelo's *David* would be like kicking puppies.

What to do? Because there were...issues, in his humble opinion.

"Kevin," Michael said, standing up and stroking his chin. "You are a genius."

"So, you *like* it!" Kevin said, clasping his hands together.

"But," Michael continued, raising a hand to stop any further gushing, "I, too, am a genius. And as a genius, I *understand* genius. The throes of creation take us to *great* heights. My genius may be more technical and, well, lethal. But it is nonetheless creation."

Words don't fail me now!

"And as a genius, I know that when we are good, we are very good," Michael said, nodding. "But . . . when we are not . . ."

Oh, the hell with it. Sometimes the puppy just needs a good kicking.

"We're in the last seconds of one of the biggest nail biters in Super Bowl history! The score is seven to seven in double overtime! It's Michael Edwards from his own sixty-five-yard line with three seconds left in the game trying for a game-winning field goal. What do you think of his odds, Bob?"

"Well, Tim, the wind isn't good, and I think the choice of a Labrador puppy was pretty ballsy. Yeah, they've got heft so they're going to cut through the wind better but they're notoriously unstable in flight with all the wriggling and yipping. Tough call."

"It's the snap, the puppy's set and Michael Edwards is going in for the kick . . ."

"Ah HEYLL NO."

Kevin slapped his hand over his mouth, released a slight whine, and looked, yep, just exactly like a Labrador puppy that's been kicked.

"YIP! YIP! YIP! YIP! YIP! YIP! YIP! . . . !"

"It's going, it's going, it's going, IT'S THROUGH THE GOAL POSTS, OH MY GOD, MICHAEL EDWARDS WITH A SEVENTY-FIVE-YARD GAME-WINNING FIELD GOAL!"

"WITH A LABRADOR PUPPY!"

Michael held up a finger to forestall a reply and stalked out of the room.

He hadn't dealt with Mr. DiAngelo since their first meeting, but he knew that the only choice was to draw upon relevant authority.

The problem being he was having a hard time expressing his exact feelings on the subject.

He walked past Miri, simply pointing at the door, and started banging. Not hard. A rapid, occasionally pausing, staccato.

"He's . . ." Tony's secretary said, turning around in her chair.

"I don't care if he's masturbating to pictures of the pope," Michael said, banging on the door.

It unlocked and he opened it just enough to point at the office chief, his nominal sort of boss, then point over his shoulder. Words were failing.

"Michael, I think you got a—"

Michael made the close-mouth motion, then pointed over his shoulder again, doing the Hannibal Lecter teeth rattle as he tried to form the word "you."

"You..." Michael got out. "That... You... That..."

Falcon got up with a quizzical look on his face and as soon as he got to the door, Michael turned around and stalked to Briefing Four.

"That... This..." Michael said, his arms crossed, leaning on the wall, pointing occasionally at the keypad.

Tony inserted his card, punched in a code, opened the door, started to step through, then froze. There was a moment's pause and then he said:

"Ah, hell, no."

"What's *wrong* with it?" Kevin asked, tearing up.

"Uh..." Tony said, trying to explain.

What *was* wrong with it? What...?

Well... the white fuck-me-pump go-go boots were going to be uncomfortable to wear walking around all day. The white hotpants with rhinestones didn't look particularly comfortable either, especially given recent developments in the nether regions. The white utility belt might have *some* utility, but it appeared to be purely ornamental. Though it might be possible to use the oversized belt buckle, with rhinestones—that was a theme, clearly—to beat some malefactor into seeing the error of their ways.

The skintight, apparently diaphanous, white midriff top with... *sequins* and rhinestones looked to be a bit much to wrestle felons in. And the white, rhinestone-decorated Lone Ranger mask...

Michael didn't mind being eye candy, but he was pretty sure he knew what Kevin had been thinking when he was having sex with his boyfriend. He hoped Kevin had washed his hands after coming up with the costume.

"Kevin..." Michael said, choosing his words carefully. "You said something that was stylish and expressed *me*. *That* does *not* express me."

"But... it's so *you!*" Kevin protested.

Michael was loath to do it, but it was the only way.

Since he hadn't been able to get any decent clothes, it was still jeans and T-shirts. So, he just took off his T-shirt.

"Oh!" Kevin exclaimed, clapping his hand over his mouth.

"Jesus, kid," Tony said quietly.

Most of Michael's scars were on the inside. But on the outside, he had some on his arms and one on his cheek. The real collection was on his chest and abdomen.

The scalding scars on his left shoulder where his foster mom, for some damned reason, had dumped a pot of boiling water on him.

The skin grafts stripped from his chest.

More on his stomach from being set on fire six months later. *Knowing* what the burn ward was going to be like.

The knife scar from Oh-That-Poor-Bastard.

The machete scar from Little Brown Tattooed Fucker Number Thirteen.

The numerous other knife, bullet, and surgery scars.

"Kevin," Michael said when The Designer couldn't take his eyes off the scars. "Earth to Kevin," he added, snapping his fingers.

"That's so . . . terrible," Kevin said, his face working.

"I'm terrible," Michael said. "I am a terrible person, Kevin. You look at this and think 'Oh, you poor baby.' But I am not a victim. Kevin, I have killed twenty-five people and wounded many more." He pointed over his shoulder at the plasma. "*That* . . . is *not* the costume of a person who looks like this."

"My little *David*," Kevin said, sniffling.

"Kevin, Kevin, Kevin," Michael said, shaking his head and putting his shirt back on. "You kidding? By my age, David had killed *Goliath*. Ever *read* the Bible? David wasn't some pretty boy. He was the original special operations. He'd sneak into the enemy's camp and slit throats. David was *Delta Force*. He was the original badass. This is *exactly* what David looked like, in reality."

"I didn't know that," Kevin said, perking up.

"Apparently, neither did Michelangelo," Michael said, shrugging.

"The problem is, what do we do for a costume?" Tony said. "I, by the way, agree. That . . . is not what would . . . do."

"The costume is easy but you'll both hate it," Michael said. "The Secretary will hate it. But it's the right costume."

"What?" Tony said.

"Tacticals," Michael said. "Tactical boots, tactical pants, poly shirt, body armor. I'm going to be out there busting perps or whatever the term of art it is you use. It's comfortable, practical, and sometimes people shoot at people who try to place them under citizen's arrest. I've been shot. I prefer to not be shot again. It stings. Plate carriers are your friend there."

"You're right the Secretary will hate it," Tony said, shaking his head. "We're not supposed to appear militarized..."

"But they're so... so..." Kevin said, his hand over his mouth. He looked as if he was going to regurgitate.

"They're practical," Michael said. "They're plain because they are not designed to stand out. If you stand out, you become a target. They're what warriors wear, Kevin, and I am a warrior. Alexander can drive me to an Army Navy store, and I can pick up everything for fairly cheap. And I'm your little Michelangelo's *David*, remember? David was a warrior."

"It will be so... plain," Kevin said with great resignation.

"But... you... you have a job, Kevin," Michael said. "Because while it's what warriors wear doing the job, it's *not* what they wear when they're doing something formal. So, what you need to design is a *dress costume!*"

"We... don't have those," Tony said. "There's a budget..." He stopped when he saw Michael's hand waving at him furiously from behind the kid's back.

"Dress costume?" Kevin said, perking up.

"Like a dress uniform," Michael said. "For formal occasions. Now, this is just in the *idea* range. Know the 1964 period Captain America?"

"Stan... Kirby..." Kevin said breathlessly. "Always squabbling, but two geniuses finally working together to create such..." He blew a kiss high into the air.

"Takes one to know one," Michael said. "And you know Marine Corps Dress Blues?"

That's it. Michael had turned The Designer into stone.

Maureen caught his arm as Kevin's legs started to buckle.

"Yes," Kevin finally gasped as the CO_2 response kicked in. He still looked a little woozy.

"Just spitballing, but maybe a combination of those two?" Michael said. "Maybe look at various military dress uniforms over the years? There are some awesome designs."

"I've never looked at—"

"Oh, you'll *love* Hungarian hussar regimental uniforms," Michael said. "Sooo pretty!"

Kevin thought about it for a moment, then raised one finger in the air.

"Maureen!" The Designer exclaimed. "To the sewery!"

And The Designer made his exit.

Michael waited until he was sure Kevin was clear, then collapsed into a chair, looked at the costume again, and started howling in laughter.

"Oh, Jesus Christ on a cracker," Tony said, sitting down next to him and holding his head in his hands. He looked up at the costume, shook his head, and put it back in his hands. "Aaagh. Ah, God."

"It's . . . not his best work," Alexander said sadly.

"I completely disagree," Michael said. "It's not perfect, but it's great work. If I wanted to be a rent-boy on Houston Street, that would be the *nearly* perfect outfit. The problem isn't what's *there*. It's what it's *missing*."

"I'm looking at it," Tony said. "My eyes are melting out but I'm looking at it. I don't see anything missing."

"The hat," Michael said, rubbing his earlobe thoughtfully. "The enormous white cowboy hat with a big medallion on the front and ostrich feathers. It's missing the hat."

"As always, kid, you're right," Tony said, waggling a finger at the screen and nodding. "That . . . that would make that outfit."

CHAPTER 8

Michael sat on his hotel room bed in a lotus, hands between his knees, slightly cupped, breathing in and out evenly and doing his usual bad job of trying to slow his thoughts.

The pose for the Chakra of Light Shape was Sukhasana or Easy Pose, which was easy enough. Throughout the instructions were admonishments to not use your hands. Good for impressing mortals, otherwise it was verboten.

But when training to get your aura *out* of your body, it was the way to go. It allowed you to focus. Try to push the aura, gently, to between your hands. Then learn to shape it. Find the chakra in your mind.

There was a *very* long section on Light Shape.

Super-auras turned out to be more than just simple light. The aura of powerful supers, certainly master class but also powerful journeymen, was capable of killing harmful "stuff." Bacteria, viruses, even fleas, mosquitoes and lice. It could be used to sterilize surgical instruments or entire hospitals, disinfect wounds, and even *promoted* healing of wounds in normals. Thrown through the whole of a person's body, it would kick back cancer. It wouldn't kill tumors, so the cancer remained, but it would reduce metastasization and bring some temporary remission in Stage One and Two cancers. It could cure AIDS or Covid—again, if it was thrown through the entire body. Heck, it could cure smallpox or black plague.

The problem was that powerful auras would also blind a person if their eyeballs were exposed. So, it was recommended that in all but small infected wounds, a healer be summoned.

The US had three Healers with about the power to heal a fly. One could only assume the Storm was going to be an apocalypse. If you had some people helping you and one of them got an abdominal from some other scavengers, being able to kill the peritonitis and aid in healing might be the difference between life and death.

Whoever or whatever was sending these powers had thought some things through.

Be still and listen. Search your mind.

He turned his aura on and off, trying to "find" the area in his mind that controlled it. It was slightly brighter. He'd been working on his actual power the last couple of days, and he was pretty sure his aura was brighter.

Earth Move and Earth Shape were the secrets there. It was like weightlifting. You tried to move earth that was too solid or heavy for you to move. Just pushed against it. You could also compress earth materials, pushing against them from all sides with Earth Shape. Anything that used up your powers. Do that until the powers were exhausted. Every day.

The problem as he'd been going through "orientation" was doing it surreptitiously. He'd found that he could push against the concrete walls and floor. It had no backlash, he wasn't lifted by it "pushing back." There was no beam. The kinetic power just *appeared* there, somehow, in total violation of all laws of Man, God, and Physics. You just... pushed. Good way to get his frustrations out when dealing with all the idiocy. He had the chunk of concrete in his pocket, and he could press against that, trying to compress it. But at a certain point he realized his pocket was getting hot. He was putting enough kinetic energy into the stone it was heating up.

That was actually a good sign. His power was increasing. But it was also a good way to set his jeans on fire. He went back to pushing at walls and floor.

Earth Sight had longer range now. He could "see" the room under his, empty, and the marshals outside the door, bored, occasionally talking but mostly playing on their phones. They could at least give the guys chairs. He could see beyond and all the rooms around him were empty. Interesting. Occupancy was not all that great.

People, animals in general, were like ghostly skeletons. He could mostly see their bones. Electronics he could mostly see the chips in them, silica. The plastic was invisible, being carbon based.

How did you get the chakra of carbon? He was surrounded by plastics. It would be useful.

According to the information he'd been accessing, courtesy of Gondola, only the extremely rare telekinetics had chakra of carbon as part of the chakra of, well, *all* matter. Also, that Invulnerable Grounds (hulks or IGs), and Invulnerable Flyers (Tinkerbells), were actually specialized telekinetics, and in some cases had learned to project their telekinesis just as he was *trying* to learn to project his aura.

He'd noticed that the "everything was there" range in Sight was lower than the "looking directly at it" range. The extent of "seeing everything" encompassed just his room—currently—but "direct vision" stretched into the room next door and, barely, into the one next to that.

All of which was distracting him from Chakra of Light Shape.

He rummaged, again, in his mind, trying to get the right series of synapses to fire. But too many thoughts were occupying his brain.

I can "see" iron in its earth form but not metallic iron. Is that because of the difference in electron shell? But I can't control electrons so that's no answer. I should be able to see and manipulate metallic iron . . .

Focus

Oxygen is included in most "earth" materials, so why can't I see and manipulate oxygen . . . ?

Focus

Maybe one of those hairnet things instead of a bonnet? Then she can do Child's Pose . . .

Focus

Even with the effect of radiation, it's just not enough. The Coulomb barrier is just too tough unless we're totally off on the actual mass of the universe. Maybe the matter-antimatter interaction has something to do with . . .

"Aaargh!" Michael snarled, rolling backward out of the lotus and jumping to his feet on the bed. He held his hands out gapped about a foot and shook them. "LIGHT! LIGHT BETWEEN MY HANDS! DO IT!"

He turned around and threw Earth Move into the wall by the bed in frustration and there was a distinct *crack!* as a section of the wall about the size of a fist punched out. He could see into the far room with his own eyes. It was dark.

"Oh, shit," he said, putting a hand over his mouth. "WhatdoIdo? WhatdoIdo? WhatdoIdo?"

In Earth Sight, shards of concrete were lying on the bed in the next room. He picked them up with his mind and tried to fit them back into place. They didn't exactly glue together. The wallpaper was also torn.

He shaped the concrete and molded it back into place. There was a distinct circular mark and the wallpaper was still screwed up. And he couldn't quite get the concrete flat. There was something mildly wrong with it in Earth Sense. He couldn't quite place it until he realized that this was prestressed concrete. He was putting unstressed concrete into prestress, and it wasn't exactly the same.

Also, it was obvious as hell there'd been a circular hole punched in the wall by something.

"Damnit," Michael said, tugging his earlobe.

He looked around the room and there was a print on the opposite wall of a horse. He wasn't sure how it was attached but, in the concrete, there were the gaps he'd come to associate with some sort of metal or plastic insert. He pulled concrete out like taffy there and detached the print. There was less of a mark on the wall. It would have to do.

In seconds he had the print covering the mess he'd made of the bed wall. There was the small mark where it had come from but that was better than an obviously punched hole. There was going to be some concrete dust on the bed in the far room. He'd let whoever took the room puzzle that out. Also, there was going to be the same mark there, probably worse.

"You are going to need to learn some self-control, son," Michael said.

He turned around and threw his hands outward, not pushing with Earth Move, just snarling in frustration.

A ball of light about the size of a lightbulb appeared hanging where he was pointing his hands. It was bright enough he had to close his eyes.

"Oh, you've *got* to be kidding me," Michael said, averting his eyes and bringing in the ball of light.

With a little bit of work, he got it to dim. He resumed his lotus position on the bed and started playing with the light, swirling it around the room, making additional balls and moving them around in patterns, changing their frequency. At first, he used his hands to direct them, but he knew it was all his mind. After a few minutes he took the basic pose, standard, with his hands on his knees and just played with light.

He ended with about six balls in primary colors, as many as he could reasonably control, spinning around his head about four feet away. Vishnu could create giant flaming dragons of light, but he realized that took years of practice. Just like all the other chakras, just like hacking. It wasn't much, but it was a beginning.

"You okay?" Alexander asked as Michael tried to get another bite of burger. They were at one of the many hipster burger joints where all the options had some sort of aoli and cheeses he refused to pronounce, but he'd found something resembling a bacon cheeseburger on the menu and he wasn't going to complain.

Orientation was almost over. Soon, he would be handed off to the tender ministrations of New York's social services—or the Family and Children Torture Division as he preferred to call it. Back to foster care. What fun, what fun.

Especially with:

"My teeth are growing back," Michael whispered, then put his thumb in his mouth, trying to get his plate back into place. "It's playing hell with my plate."

"Your what?" Alexander asked.

Michael finally gave up and removed his plate. He hated to do it in public.

"When did you get dentures?" Alexander said.

"When I got all my teeth stomped out," Michael said. He put the plate down and decided to just go for gumming. With the little bit of teeth sticking through his gums it might help.

"Ouch," Alexander said. "We're scheduled for your final checkup. The healer can probably fix it."

Michael started to say something sarcastic about American Healers, then thought about having to explain "my teeth are growing back in" at a middle school.

"Could give it a shot," Michael said, shrugging.

"I'll text him and see if he's available..."

"You've had a *lot* of maxillofacial surgery..."

Dr. Lee Conway, MD, was the Corps Healer at New York-Presbyterian Hospital Columbia and Cornell. Six two and medium build with medium brown skin, dark brown hair cut short in tight African curls, and green eyes he was, unsurprisingly, extremely handsome. At the moment, he seemed particularly fascinated by Michael's face.

"Not my actual specialty, but I can hum the tune," Doc Lee said, literally humming as he leaned from side to side, examining Michael's face like he was peering in every pore.

"Enjoying the view?" Michael asked. "What *is* your specialty?"

It was the nicest hospital room Michael had ever been in—though granted, he'd only ever been in true shitholes until his Acquring rated him slightly better. Still, this one was even nicer than any he'd even seen on TV shows about wealthy people. Plus, they had it all to themselves.

"Neurology," Doc Lee said. "The neural damage that was there has been taken care of with regen. But you've got plates, pins... pretty much everything in there. As the bones regen, they'll be getting in the way."

"My teeth are the primary concern at the moment," Michael said, rubbing his earlobe.

"Hmm..." Doc Lee said, nodding. "Take out your plate."

Michael did so and set it to the side.

"This may cause some slight discomfort," Doc Lee said, holding his right hand out just in front of Michael's mouth.

Michael suddenly felt his teeth swell in the roots and tasted blood. There was some "slight discomfort" at about the level of a six. He'd been in the burn ward; his levels were different from most. Most people would put it at an eleven or twelve on a scale of one to ten.

"Araagagragaaa," Michael muttered, holding his mouth open.

"Okay," Doc Lee said. "Looks good to go on dental."

The pain passed almost immediately, thank you regenerative healing, and Michael snapped his teeth together for the first time in five years.

"I've got chompers again!" Michael said. So, Healers weren't *completely* useless. "Thanks."

"The next part is going to be a bit less pleasant," Doc Lee said. "Lie back."

And that was sooo much fun, Michael thought, lying back on the examination table.

"Because of the regenerative healing, the pins, plates, and inserts of your surgery are going to come out as you heal," Doc Lee said. "So, at some point, you'll be sitting in class in school with bone pins sticking out of your face."

"That sounds . . . suboptimum," Michael said. "Really mess with the whole 'secret identity' thing."

"So, I'll have to pull them all out," Doc Lee said.

"There may be some slight discomfort?" Michael asked.

"Possibly a twinge," Doc Lee said. "How are you on discomfort?"

Michael decided the shirt thing was the only real answer on that.

"You *have* been to the wars, haven't you?" Doc Lee said. "I'd say I've read your file as your primary care physician, but 'skimmed it' is probably a better description. Reading it would be like going back to my brief residency in the trauma department."

"Do the scars go away?" Michael asked, putting his shirt back on.

"Scars usually stay," Doc Lee said. "And if you pick up more damage, which you hopefully won't, it too will scar."

"Good," Michael said.

"Good?" Alexander asked.

"Scars are the only medals you get on the street," Michael said. "Ladies like them and I like the ladies. Okay, Doc, do your worst."

"How about my best instead?" the doctor asked.

There was a twinge. Michael thought a couple of times about holding up a finger and asking for something to chomp down on with his new chompers. But as with all bad things, and good, it eventually ended. It all evens out in the end.

"Not bad," Doc Lee said, holding up a mirror.

Not bad. Not much different. He wasn't sure if it was better or worse.

"Things were going to change with your face, anyway," the doctor said. "Our faces reshape after Acquisition. I can see where yours is doing so. If I knew what you were going to end up looking like, I'd mold it closer. As it is . . . Not so sure."

"Neither am I," Michael said. "I don't know who my mother or father are, so I have no idea what they look like. I'm the classic superhero: an orphan."

"That's tough," Doc Lee said. "Your face will reshape. Most of that will happen when you sleep."

"Parasympathetic nervous system," Michael said.

"Right," Doc Lee said, nodding. "Your teeth had been slowly growing in every night. Your face was doing the same thing. Over time it will shape to its final form, which for some reason is always extremely handsome or beautiful by the local cultural standards of beauty. Which is weird as heck if you think about it. Especially the cultural part."

"Agreed," Michael said. "What about trauma? It's obviously something I'm curious about."

"With severe trauma, which is rare even given, you know, being super cops, the super goes into an induced coma, technically a very deep sleep. Their respiration falls and they tend to exhibit a slight aura. We've learned to just leave it alone absent healing being available. It take a lot to kill us and even with extreme damage supers usually just . . . heal."

"We are created Shiva, the Destroyer," Michael said. "Shaped to be human weapons. Living gods of war."

"I don't think that's our sole purpose," Doc Lee said.

"Even Earthers like myself or Healers like you have the strength, speed, and agility of Captain America," Michael said. "We form, as you pointed out, as creatures of culturally agreed upon beauty. Women have big bazoombas, men are very much in the manhood department.

"Even in a paleolithic society, or perhaps especially in a paleolithic society, we would be viewed as leaders of the tribe, Alphas, so we would have a reason to protect the tribe from the Storm and could get help from it with things we couldn't do while fighting. Resource gathering, for example. 'I can only be in one place at a time. I'm going to go fight Cthulhu. Have the mammoth ready when I get back.'"

"I suppose you have a point," Doc Lee said, chuckling.

"Powers are *not* designed for *this* world," Michael said. "Just like everything *else* about human beings."

CHAPTER 9

"Pain" —Three Days Grace

Michael hopped off the CAT scan examination table, stood, and stretched. It was clinically spartan, just like all the other ones he'd been in before, but this one was much cleaner and felt a lot newer than the others. The Super Corps certainly had plenty of money to burn on swanky facilities. He swiped his phone off the tiny table for patient's possessions. Mama had called three times while it was off.

Miss Cherise calling during the day was concerning; her calling more than once was downright troubling.

Yearly CAT scans were mandatory for *all* supers, Super Corps or not. Although some of the super-terrorists who had broken out in the late 1990s and early 2000s were neuro-norms, the Nebraska Killer was found to have a nonfunctional morality and conscience center and, thus, every super in the US was required, even over religious objection, to have a CAT scan once a year.

Thanks to simple internet research, but confirmed by Gondola, Michael was aware that the missing morality and conscience center was due to the CIA deliberately deleting it, using an electromagnet in the process of turning James King into a serial killer and "terrorist." He was also aware that every school shooting and workplace "active shooter" incident going back to Columbine had been triggered by The Society. The secret was the right personality type, found by scouring purchased therapist notes, getting the right push, usually from their therapist, and large doses of acetaminophen. Right personality, large doses of Tylenol, right push, and you had an active shooter.

MK Ultra was alive and well.

But it wasn't like he could protest that it was all a sinister plot by a secret conspiracy since he was . . . part of a different conspiracy.

"How do I look, Doc?" Michael asked.

"Anterior cingulate cortex looks fine," Doc Lee said, examining the CAT scan images. "You're good to go."

"Thanks Doc," Michael said. He looked at Alexander and gestured toward the door with his phone. "Hey, Alexander, I got to take this. Mama's calling for some reason."

"Okay," Alexander said.

Michael stepped out into the corridor and called the number back.

"Hello," a male voice—not Mama's—answered. "Who is this?"

For a moment, the world stopped, and Michael forgot how to breathe.

"Hello?" the voice repeated.

Michael drew in a slow breath and calmed himself. "Who's got my Mama's phone?"

"This is Detective Williamson with the Baltimore Police Department." Michael knew Jim Williamson, he'd given the detective statements more than a few times. "Who is this?"

Michael just paused for a second, trying to speak.

"Hey, Detective, it be Michael Edwards," Michael said. "Boogie Knight."

The Fifth Street Kings had been feared rather than liked. They did nothing to make themselves liked by the people of East Baltimore. It was rule by fear. They were the boogieman.

When Michael had wiped out most of their main guns, he became "the man you send to kill the boogieman" and for a while his street name was "Boogieman." The street being the street, it somehow morphed to Boogie Knight.

"Ah, shit, kid," Williamson said. "You can probably figure why I've got Miss Cherise's phone."

I be diamond. Michael closed his eyes and did his best not to crush the phone.

"And since it's Homicide, she didn't die of an overdose of fet, did she? Was she chopped up?"

"Shot," Williamson said. "Multiple round drive by. Why chopped?"

"Mama was the closest person I had in the world, Detective," Michael said, pulling at his earlobe. "It was '13. They did it since they cain't get to me."

In retrospect, it was obvious they would've done this, but he'd been too busy becoming a super. Not that he could've saved her, probably, but still...

"I didn't know that," the detective said. "Sorry for your loss, Michael. I was about to ask if you knew if she had any enemies."

"Any description?" Michael asked.

"It's the street," the detective said. "You know what that's like; nobody's talking."

"I'll make some calls," Michael said.

"How's Junior Super Corps?" Williamson asked.

"I'd regale you, Detective, but I'm not really in the mood at the moment," Michael said. "Sorry. Lemme see if anybody will still talk to me. I'll call you back."

"Roger."

"Out here."

"Everything okay, Michael?" Alexander asked. He'd entered the corridor as the call was ending. He stepped back a bit at the look in the boy's eyes. "Michael...?"

"Yeah," Michael said, pushing the killing urge to the back of his mind. Later for that. He'd process it all later. Like he processed everything later. Later would come eventually. "S'all good. S'all good. Win some, lose some, it all evens out in the end..."

He was barely in his hotel room when his phone buzzed. It was Gondola.

"God is building an army," Michael said.

"God has an army," Titanium replied. "Tiger, my sincere condolences. I wish I had more to say."

"We are beings of light," Michael said. "Mama has returned to the stars. All to say. That and *somebody's* going to pay. Preferably Cannibale. Pene was trying to kill me. Fair's fair. I was going to call some people and see if anybody saw anything, but it can wait."

"Do you want to talk about it?" Titanium said.

"Moving on, with respect, ma'am," Michael said. He found himself about to instinctively turn the TV on, but that hadn't been necessary after the first day, when his marshals were replaced with a pair of Supers Department-contracted security guards in the adjacent room. He snatched his hand back, clenched it into a fist, and paced around the room.

"Okay," Titanium said. "*Major* updates. Major enough that if the Faerie Queen had time, she'd convey them herself. Diarrhea is coming in instead."

Diarrhea, the head of ops and intel and as the guy who ran all the organization's mercenaries was known to be a badass. American and generally assumed to be former special operations. The rumor was he was former Delta Force.

Why he used the code name "Diarrhea" was anyone's guess.

"Tiger," Diarrhea said brusquely. "Sorry for your loss."

"Win some, lose some, sir," Michael replied. He pulled the curtains open and looked outside.

"Two updates on your situation. First: Cannibale is not in the United States. But he has been spotted in Mexico."

"Figures," Michael said. "You want something done right, do it yourself."

"Federales have two separate sightings and FBI is still insisting that he's dropped the grudge," Diarrhea continued. "So, they'll leave you swinging in the wind. We've looked for direct Society influence, but it just seems to be generic incompetence."

Cars rolled by on the street below and people wandered the sidewalks, all going about their normal, daily lives. He threw the curtain shut again and slumped onto the couch.

"Only incompetent people are easily corrupted or manipulated, sir," Michael said. "They've been dumbing down academia, the bureaucracy, for a long time. Not surprising that the FBI has gotten to the point they can barely find their ass with both hands. I'll handle it when the time comes. Powers are coming along. Should be fine."

"He's going to be prepared for powers," Diarrhea pointed out.

"Not these, sir," Michael said. "Wouldn't mind doing some planning with the team. But it's going to be okay, sir. Looking forward to meeting him and sending him on a personal visit to his grandnephew. Want something done right, do it yourself works both ways, sir."

"Good approach," Diarrhea said. "The second update is, Jesus, *complicated.* Simple part is we now know who your parents are. We've got DNA on both of them. Your mother is deceased. Your father is alive. If we'd known who your mother was a long time ago . . . Iron is going to give the brief. He's the Northeastern US Society subject matter expert. Iron?"

"Tiger, I greet you."

Lime Iron's female accent was somewhere African, but Michael couldn't quite place it. Her native language was probably part of the Bantu group, but that covered most of sub-Saharan Africa.

"I greet you, Lime Iron. What does The Society have to do with my mother?"

"She was on the run from them," Lime Iron said. "Picture coming in on your TV of Annabelle Follett . . ."

The TV clicked on by itself. The photo was of a light-boned blond female. Michael noticed that her hair was the same type as his and, after a moment, they had the same shade of blue eyes.

"Annabelle Follett was the last beneficiary of the Follett Trust, a multibillion-dollar trust fund managed by Fieldstone Holdings."

"Oh, fuck," Michael said, rubbing his earlobe. "You mean I'm Oliver Twist?"

"That would be one way to put it," Diarrhea said.

"Annabelle Follett was the daughter of Dela Follett and Carmen Lukessi, an Italian race car driver," Lime Iron continued. "Dela was, in turn, the daughter of Eduard Follett, who was one of the top members of The Society in the US until his death. Eduard was a Dark Hand, one of the ones who lead the sacrificial rituals."

A chiseled captain of industry wearing a tailored suit and carrying a deep, intense stare flashed onto the screen.

"Joy," Michael said.

"The Folletts were US Society before there was one," Diarrhea said. "Class Before One."

A young woman with long, wavy brown hair, a conservative sundress, and an empty smile came up next. Dela Follett, his grandmother.

"Yes," Lime Iron said excitedly. "The Folletts were French aristocracy and Society members in the ancien régime. They fled to the colonies to escape the French Terror contemporary to the DuPonts and the signing of the US Constitution. There they used the family fortune they brought with them to purchase farms and businesses, and invested in the DuPont company since they naturally knew the family as fellow aristos. And they held onto it through the years, actually increasing it frequently by strategic marriages, much the same as they had as aristocracy in Europe.

"Eduard Follett set up a trust fund for his daughter and later granddaughter," Lime Iron continued. "When it was formed it contained and managed all the fungibles—stocks, bonds, so on—as well as various commercial and personal properties scattered around the US. Your mother, Annabelle, predated her mother's death by about five years..."

"Both deaths were assassinations," Diarrhea cut in. "We'll get to why."

"Yes," Lime Iron said. "Your mother was assassinated. She was also sexually assaulted as a youth."

"Poor little rich girls rarely go off the rails 'cause they're having an idyllic childhood," Michael said, rubbing his ear furiously.

It was part of the background briefings. "Poor little rich girls," child actors and actresses, they were all targets of pedophiles, and with The Society protecting the pedophiles (see: Epstein), the life of a female anywhere around The Society was a nightmare.

Like bike gangs, they would rape their own daughters and pass them around. The Hells Angels had coined the term "one-percenter" way back in the fifties. It referred to throwing off the rules of society and living as predators on the weak.

The Society had happily coopted the term since it also described them. Which was why the "elite" and upper class were referred to as "the one percent." It was a direct reference to being nothing more than a rich bike gang.

"Dela Follett often traveled Europe as part of the elite set," Iron said. "She'd run away to Europe when she was seventeen until pulled back by her family. During a trip to Europe in her thirties she became pregnant by Carmen Lukessi and chose to have the child. Lukessi had little to do with Annabelle's upbringing. Nor did her mother, for that matter. Annabelle was raised mostly in Manhattan and the Hamptons and by a series of nannies and governesses."

The briefing was accompanied by photos of the various persons involved. Annabelle liked horses and from one of the photos must have been a Lord of the Rings fan based on the Eowyn costume.

"When she was eleven, Dela married Wesley Conn," Iron said, showing a wedding photo.

Conn and Dela Follett were posed on either side of Annabelle, who was wearing a dress very similar to her mother's wedding dress. She was leaning into Wesley Conn with a bright smile on her face. She *finally* had a *daddy*!

Michael more or less knew what was coming. Conn had Society printed all over him. He was tall, with a prominent chin, a dashing, sharp smile, and wide, strong shoulders that made his tuxedo look almost unnaturally well cut. His eyes said he was a master of all he touched. Emphasis on the *Master*.

"Conn was at the time the chief of property management for the New York area properties," Iron said. "Harvard MBA, additional finance degree from Wharton. He is currently the chief trustee."

"Let me guess that this is *not* a 'happily ever after' story," Michael said.

"Based upon photo analysis as well as intercepts . . . your mother was sexually assaulted by Wesley Conn starting from a few months after the wedding," Iron said carefully.

"No surprise," Michael said, looking at the photos. You could see the light had died from Annabelle's eyes. In one she was clearly pulling away from Conn, who looked totally innocent except for the hand possessively holding her by the neck. She also had her arms crossed over her breasts as well as having her head slightly ducked—both signs of being sexually assaulted.

Women and girls who are angry and defiant cross their arms *under* their breasts. When they are being sexually assaulted, they cross them *over* their breasts, protectively. Rapists always go for the tits. One of the many items of training he'd received as part of Gondola.

"He probably suggested to Dela that Annabelle would look fetching in a pseudo-wedding dress," Michael said. "He wasn't marrying Dela, he was marrying Annabelle with Dela on the side."

Michael punched his fist repeatedly and then waggled his fingers.

No punching the walls with Earth Move.

"*Damnit*, Diarrhea," Michael said. "The list of people I have to *kill* is getting longer and *longer*! Let me guess, she was passed around like a bag of chips at a Super Bowl party? The Society having its usual kicks?"

"There is photo interpretation as well as more definitive evidence that she was, yes, sexually assaulted by numerous persons affiliated with The Society as well as the Trust," Iron said. "Notably, at the time the chief of security for the New York properties, Eric Bear . . ."

Photo of a fit, bald, white male in an expensive suit. He'd been in one of the previous photos and Michael had already marked him as one who had hurt her. She was subtly drawing away from him in the photo.

". . . who is now chief of security for the Trust," Iron finished. "Also, members of the Trust, major figures in Northeastern finance, and potentially some of The Society's European figures."

"Wow," Michael said. "That list is getting longer and longer. Please tell me I'm not going to have to kill Klaus Schwab or Soros 'cause I *know* they're on the 'we don't kill major figures' list."

"*Conn* is probably too high profile," Diarrhea said. "Bear is a possible. But, former SEAL, so probably not that easy."

"Superpowers," Michael said. "With this stuff? Seen what the Vishnu can do? Get me *near* him, he's toast. Moving on."

"I should note that some have died of old age," Lime Iron said. "Or because they were associated with The Society."

"That's generally The Society cleaning up a potential problem," Diarrhea said. "But if it makes you feel any better: At least one of the high-profile ones we *already* took out. Not directly because of your mother but because of that sort of thing."

"You have my thanks," Michael said, carefully not asking who.

"Annabelle, or Anna as she preferred, ran away frequently," Iron continued.

Photos of Amber Alerts and Missing Children Alerts.

"Notably when she was fifteen when she disappeared for two years. While we have limited internals, it appears she made contact with various figures and . . . probably using sexual favors convinced them to give her training. We know she made contact with one MIT programmer and cybersecurity graduate student and learned some rudimentary hacking as well as decryption. It is believed she also dated a professional thief named Eric Randolph.

"When she returned, she apparently rigged the bedroom in the house in the Hamptons and recorded herself having sex with a variety of significant figures."

There was a brief video of Annabelle and a gentleman caller chatting in an ornately decorated bedroom. It fortunately did not include the conclusion of the chat. He'd seen those. Seeing them of his biological mother was not on his bucket list.

"They were all persons who had sexually assaulted her at an earlier age, and she got them talking about it," Iron said. "She was trying to use the information for leverage. It didn't work out the way she'd hoped. She took it to the FBI."

"Aaaaagh!" Michael snarled. "Longer and *LONGER*! Go."

Do not break walls. Do not break walls.

"The FBI agents initially assigned to the case were clean," Iron said. "But the fact that she was talking got to The Society. She only showed one video to the FBI agents, the one with Conn where he admitted to having assaulted her at a young age. She also stated she had been trafficked to other locations for the purpose of sex, violation of the Mann Act making it a federal case.

"She also stated that she had obtained other records and videos indicating a widespread conspiracy but did not share details. She was wary of the FBI, but it seemed like the only place she could go.

"She was laying low and was contacted and told that things were arranged that she should come in. Instead, personnel from Fieldstone were sent to pick her up. How she knew they were not FBI is unknown, but she fled and missed the pickup. The video disappeared from evidence and with nothing more to go on the case was dropped. Both agents were soon after pushed out of the FBI and died of self-inflicted gunshot wounds, which were, of course, assassinations."

"I hate these guys so much," Michael said. "I hate these guys *so* much! Do you realize that every fucked-up thing about my childhood, starting with being left to rot in the ghetto instead of being, I dunno, adopted, raised in a suburb, anything, *all* comes back to The Society? It's *all* their fucking with the system creating shitty policies to make the world as *miserable* as possible for the *most* people. The one thing, the *one* thing, that I could sort of *not* put on them, directly, was that my mother was a *whore* that left me in a fucking alleyway and now *that* comes back *directly* to them?! *I hate these guys sooo much!*"

"Got that out of your system?" Diarrhea asked. "Sorry that this had to come in on top of the death of Miss Cherise, but we're pressed for time."

"The list is getting longerrrrr!!" Michael said, clasping fists over his head and waving them back and forth. "We stare into the abyss in this job. And when it stares back..."

"Punch it in the fucking face," Diarrhea said.

"Moving on."

"After that there is not much track on Annabelle Follett for two and half years," Iron said. "She was as invisible as it is possible to be in this world. We know from other data that she was working as a prostitute. Where all is unclear, but she seemed to stay on the East Coast. The next positive indication of her presence is a photo."

Annabelle was at some sort of formal function, seated at a white-linen-covered table with a tall man with a solid build under the tuxedo, black hair, high cheekbones, a hooked, prominent nose, blue eyes, and a scar nearly identical to Michael's on his left cheek.

If Michael had ever seen an operator, he was looking at one. Albeit in an evening jacket.

In the background there was a figure in focus but all you could see was from the base of his arm down to knee height. The person, probably male given the trousers, was wearing Army dress blues and his sleeve was marked as a major general.

"Formal military function," Michael said, examining the photo. "From what I'm looking at, don't think I can figure out where."

"Fort Myer Officers Club," Diarrhea said.

"Do we know who the operator is?" Michael asked.

"That, Tiger, is your father, Counselor Derrick Sterrenhunt," Iron said, pronouncing it "STERN-hoont." "At the time Sergeant First Class Derrick Sterrenhunt, Combat Activities Group, who was taking an academic leave under light cover to attend Georgetown Law. Later Command Sergeant Major Sterrenhunt, Joint Special Operations Command before retiring."

"So, my mama was a trust-fund ho, and my daddy was a Delta?" Michael said, shaking his head. "That's a combo you don't often see. Jesus. Like you said, Diarrhea, complicated."

"Just a little bit, yes," Diarrhea said.

"So that's got to be around nine months before my birth," Michael said. "You said that my mother died about six months after, 'allegedly' due to a serial killer. Why 'allegedly'? Besides, obviously, The Society was after her."

"Your mother was found dead near the Port of Philadelphia," Iron said.

Gondola could get any information and sucked up more info than the NSA. So, Michael had seen crime-scene photos before, just not of his biological mother. On the same day he'd been informed of the death of the closest person he'd ever had to an *actual* mother; it was a tad much.

The photos were taken when the body was fresh and on-site. Anabelle was naked, legs spread, face up, arms sprawled to her side, eyes shot with red indicating asphyxiation with distinct ligature marks on her throat and wrists. There was disturbance in the area to indicate it was the actual crime scene rather than the body being dumped.

"Clothesline," Michael said. "Similar kills?"

"Seven with similar enough signature," Iron said. "Very good. But all *after* Annabelle and in the New York metropolitan area. At the time, the murder was attributed to a serial killer called the Port Killer."

More photos of five dead women, Annabelle among them.

"Wait," Michael said. "You're serious? She was lumped in with those? Wrong... in every way. No ligature marks on the wrists, manual strangulation. Same naked and probably sexually assaulted but... completely different otherwise."

"Correct," Iron said. "Also, the Port Killer was later identified as Rick Albritton."

Mug shot of a creepy, generic eighties movie stalker.

"Albritton was eventually caught and confessed to raping and strangling over forty women around the US. But he denied that he killed Annabelle Follett while confessing to the others."

"And he died in prison before he could be tried," Michael said. "Right?"

"Correct," Iron said.

"Fun fact," Diarrhea said. "The medical examiner in Philly later got an inheritance and bought a boat. About three months later it blew up from a fuel leak, poor guy."

"There was a brief portion of video of the explosion taken by someone coincidentally filming in the area," Iron said. "Our spectroscopic analysis and physics analysis is that it was C4. At the time we didn't make the connection to Annabelle Follett. Corrupt MEs get killed by The Society often."

"Chief detective on the case?" Michael asked.

"Also got an inheritance and retired shortly afterward to a really nice house in Florida," Diarrhea said. "But you know how the memories bother former homicide detectives . . ."

"Self-inflicted gunshot wound?" Michael asked.

"Got it in one."

"I'm so good," Michael said. "Okay, so Annabelle's found by The Society in Philly. They see where there's a serial killer killing whores. They only check the news. Raped and strangled. Got it. They tie her hands, rape her, strangle her with clothesline. Make sure to leave no major DNA. Oops! Wrong signature. Pay off the ME. Pay off the chief detective. And as usual clean up all the loose ends. You said Dela is dead as well. How is the Trust still in existence? Will?"

"Yes," Lime Iron said.

"The ME did include the information that Annabelle Follett had been in advanced pregnancy not long before her death," Iron said. "Relatively recent stretch marks. Dela Follett was, as it turns out correctly, *sure* that there was an heir. She ordered the Trust to search assiduously while hiring psychics and so on."

"And the Trust didn't search?" Michael said. "I'd think they'd have strangled me in the crib. How could they have missed me? I was an hour and a half away in Baltimore."

"Your mother was clever," Iron said. "She had another prostitute who was getting an abortion state that her name was Annabelle Follett. It might have been how they found her, though it was in Richmond. Anyway, they were sure there was no heir because of that."

"That *is* clever," Michael said. "Faking the death of an *unborn*. That's a new one on me."

"According to intel gathered from The Society, they wanted Dela to keep looking for the non-heir," Diarrhea said. "Keep her distracted with it. She was convinced to change her will to have the Trust continue in the event of her death for fifty years with orders to continue to search for her heir."

"How did they kill my grandmother?" Michael asked.

"She apparently became suspicious of Conn," Lime Iron said. "Despondent at the death of her only child, she decided to try opiates for some relief, like her child, and died with her first use."

"According to Society intercepts this was mostly a Trust operation,"

Diarrhea said. "The Trust is a major operation of The Society in the US. Not as big as Fieldstone but closely affiliated. But rather than The Society handling most of it, it was handled by the Trust."

"Yes," Iron said. "After Dela Follett was killed, which was five years after the death of your mother, a Society-placed judge agreed to her request despite it being very nearly in violation of federal law. The Trust then, in violation of the will, disposed of most of the real assets and converted it all to Fieldstone stock. So, the Trust is just a bunch of people paid, and well paid, to show up occasionally for meetings."

"Let me guess," Michael said. "They're all relatives of some Democrat politician or something along the lines."

"That's The Society," Diarrhea said.

"With nobody actually watching the kitty, I bet the looting is strong with this one," Michael said.

"We haven't dug that far," Diarrhea said. "That'll be up to you. When you inherit."

"So, I'm Bruce Wayne," Michael said. "Just with actual superpowers. All the homes and businesses got sold, though, right?"

"Mostly," Iron said. "There are three still all in the New York area including the Dosoris Island estate. We believe that is a sacrifice site."

"Those are usually on power points," Michael said.

"It was purchased in the early 1700s," Iron said. "It was, prior to that, a Native American ritual center. So, yes, probably a spiritual power point."

"Okay," Michael said. He took a deep breath. "Father."

"Derrick Sterrenhunt."

The photo was an official military file photo. Sergeant major.

"That is a *lot* of high-protein fruit salad," Michael said, with a whistle. "Not the expert in sorting out how *many* awards..."

"Fourteen Bronze Stars, two Silver Stars, Distinguished Service Cross," Diarrhea said. "Ranger Tab, SF Qual, CAG Qual, Scuba, jump wings, obviously, HALO Qual, Pathfinder. He could add a bunch of stuff like Malayan Tracker to the uniform if there was room."

"Counselor Derrick Sterrenhunt retired after twenty-three years in military service," Iron said. "Despite offers from white-shoe law firms and lobbyists in D.C., he returned to the area he'd grown up in in rural Montana. He is currently a small-town lawyer in a town called Kalispell, Montana.

"It's not really *near* anything. Closest city of note is Spokane, Washington, if you've ever heard of that. Various family lives in the area. Jacob Sterrenhunt, his father, is a subchief of the Lakota Sioux but rarely participates in Nation politics. The area is primarily Flathead rather than Sioux. Your grandmother, Madrigal Lisa Sterrenhunt née Zubenschutz, Maddie or Gramma, is of Zimbabwean background, though primarily German Boer rather than English."

Various pictures were shown, most probably taken from Facebook. It was a big rural family.

"The counselor appears to be nonpolitical. Probably a holdover of his military career. The rest of the Sterrenhunts exhibit strong conservative politics. There are two uncles, married with children, two aunts, one married with children, one divorced no kids. There are nineteen cousins total, though more are on the way. It's a big clan as such things go."

Some of the photos were of the Sterrenhunts at events like Trump rallies and of Madrigal and Jacob, especially, at various right-wing events. Pro-life featured heavily as did some Native American protests. Politically active was right.

"Has it been considered that that makes me a Lost Child?" Michael asked.

"Yes," Diarrhea said. "Our best contacts with the Nations, fortunately, are with the Sioux. We persuaded them to be easy with the Super Corps on the subject. They even talked to the other Native American super, Lightning Eagle, and he's aware they are being easy on it though not why. You'll be staying in the New York area, absent reuniting with family. The one condition is that absent reconnecting you are required to do a yearly summer camp to reunite with your Native American heritage."

"Eh," Michael said, shrugging. "I can gargle peanut butter for a summer. But skinning buffalo has never been on my bucket list. Seven similar kills in the New York area after Annabelle Follett was killed. Whoever killed her was triggered. Do we know who killed her?"

"Yes," Lime Iron said. "Eric Bear, the chief of security. We have that from Society intercepts."

"Yeah," Michael said musingly. "The Trust . . . You said that Dela asked for it to be in existence for fifty years, right?"

"Yes," Lime Iron said. "But it cannot last that long. When the twenty-five-year period of intestate is expired, it will go to the State of New York. I should note that it was not just the ME and the detective who were killed. In addition, there was a forensic technician. Because they switched the tissue samples in the autopsy."

"Why?" Michael said. "That sounds like a risk."

"There was still the slight possibility of an heir," Iron said. "If Annabelle Follett's correct DNA was ever placed on the NICS and the heir's matched to it, even if it was for reasons of sexual assault or so on..."

"Then they'd inherit, and the Trust goes away," Michael said. "It wasn't put on NICS automatically?" That was the National Instant Criminal Background Check System.

"Annabelle Follett was the *victim*," Iron said. "There was no reason and back then it was much harder to do DNA testing. They didn't bother. But if it got on a database..."

"Do we know who the contributor was? They couldn't do it from a Jane Doe. They might have a duplicate match."

"We do not," Iron said.

"I know I'm asking a lot of questions," Michael said. "But...we obviously got the match on Counselor Sterrenhunt off the secure DOD database. But where'd we get Annabelle's?"

"I'm...not sure," Lime Iron said.

"That's a long story," Diarrhea said. "From the Wayback Machine."

"Do we have time?" Michael asked.

"We weren't always sure The Society existed," Diarrhea said. "You were born back in Alpha's day, before he died, and Faerie Queen took over. *He* was certain that something like The Society existed, but it was just a conspiracy theory. It was his pet thing. I thought he was cracked.

"He was alerted to Annabelle and her story by some of our contacts in the FBI. So, we were looking for her as well, but it was a low-level thing, and we didn't have the numbers or penetration back then we have now. Faerie Queen really increased the network."

"Recruiting bright eight-year-olds will do that," Michael said.

"We were planning on bringing her in," Diarrhea said. "Give her protection. Move her to the Island if she wanted. She told the FBI she was carrying something major. Lots of secret data about a big conspiracy. Alpha wanted it. If it was us, we wanted to suppress it. If it was what he was looking for, he wanted it. We later found the proof in the KGB archives, after he died."

"We're all about secret information," Michael said thoughtfully, rubbing his earlobe. "Interesting alternate history where we find her instead of The Society and I end up growing up *in* the network instead of stumbling on it. Another interesting alternate history where she tells him she's pregnant, he opens his cover, and he ends up trying to protect his baby-mama. CAG versus The Society is a match-up I'd pay *money* to see. Special Operations Association versus the Society, I'd pay to see."

"What are you thinking?" Diarrhea asked.

"That taking down the Trust would be in the interests of Gondola," Michael said. "It weakens The Society by a fraction. Death of a thousand cuts. But the DNA in Philly is a problem. We need to remove the problem before we move forward in that direction, in my opinion. Is this in the interests of Gondola? This is my inheritance, my problem."

"Faerie Queen says it's *our* problem," Diarrhea said.

If the Faerie Queen said it, that was it. You didn't argue. They fought for everyone else's freedom and accepted absolute tyranny to do so.

"I still don't want to expend any budget," Michael said. "Do we have any third-party forensic testing labs in the US we're friendly with? Owe us a favor?"

"I'll have to check," Diarrhea said. "Why?"

"They occasionally have to test out their equipment, right?" Michael said. "So, they ask for an old tissue sample from an old case. Especially one that is 'solved.' They test it out. Maybe it turns out there's something wrong with it that means it's not Annabelle Follett."

"Worth a shot," Diarrhea said.

"I don't want to go at the Trust immediately, though, if that's alright," Michael said. "I couldn't, really, from my current perch. Doing it through social services would be a nightmare. I need the counselor on my side if he'll accept me as anything other than just a by-blow. The Trust is always going to be sitting there. Intestate is twenty-five years. That's thirty years after my birth, more or less, given it's from Dela.

"Unless someone sues on the basis of seven years—that would have already happened, and the Trust is the only group that I know of with standing—there must not be any other heirs. So, I've got years to go after it. Nice to be able to get that Razer, but . . . do you know where we got Annabelle's DNA? We were looking for her, so it wasn't from her."

"No," Diarrhea said. "But I can check."

"Not sure if Iron is briefed on the potential op here with—"

"Electrobolt," Diarrhea said. "I think he's in that silo."

"I'm not, but I didn't hear anything," Iron said.

"My thought is focus on Cannibale and Bolt, first," Michael said. "I don't see a way to use two problems to fix each other but there may be a way that's unclear, yet. But those are the time-critical issues. Worry later about the Trust. It's the bigger issue in a way and we'll need to weaken it."

"Cutting in," Titanium said. "If the chief of security got triggered by the death of Annabelle Follett and is now a serial killer . . ."

"Thought of that," Michael said, nodding. "Weaken the Trust by taking out their top thug. Just put some clean FBI on him. He's not important enough The Society will go to great lengths to protect him. Who do we want to owe us a favor in the Southern District?"

"There's a prosecutor who's not Society," Diarrhea said.

"I may or may not be in that," Michael said. "But that guy has to go. I'd prefer to handle it myself for purely emotional reasons. But if we can use what we know about him to build favors for the organization, that's more important. The Society will then clean him up. He's not going to last long after he's been exposed as a serial killer. One person off my list. Emotionally unsatisfying, I'd rather set him on fire personally and make sure he spends some time in the burn ward. But it's the more professional way to handle it. And hopefully so subtle they don't see the knife."

"Which is the better way to approach The Society," Diarrhea said. "First job is to protect the network. We can't do what we do if we're on the run from every Society-controlled police force on Earth. Or dead."

"El Cannibale is wanted in every jurisdiction on Earth and probably has warrants on Mars," Michael said. "Again, it's nice that at least some of my enemies are criminals."

"Find him and get him arrested," Diarrhea said. "Again, we have people we can feed that to."

"Thought," Michael said, rubbing his earlobe.

"Which is . . . ?" Diarrhea asked.

"They want me to be a junior super poh-leese," Michael said. "What if I somehow connive the Junior Space Eagles into arresting him?"

"That would be personally extremely dangerous for you *and* them," Diarrhea said. "And how would you know where he was?"

"We got a tip," Michael said. "I knew it was a trap, but we sprung the trap and busted the perp. Junior Super Corps literally arrested one of the most dangerous and notorious criminals in the Western Hemisphere."

"That . . . could be . . ." Diarrhea said thoughtfully. "Having you in a solid position with Super Corps has value. Faerie Queen would have to clear it."

"And I'd have to establish a résumé, first," Michael said. "If he starts to move on me and we know it before we're prepared for that, we get clean FBI to clean him up and give them a career boost for what it's worth. If he moves and we *don't* know it, I'm training my powers. I'll have a fighting chance absent a sniper bullet, and he's making this personal, so he'll want to get close. Preferably machete range.

"If he waits long enough, I get a tip on his location and convince Junior Super Corps to help me bust him. I need to make friends with Sasha, 'cause it will be *much* easier with a Flyer. I won't have to reveal my full powers that way."

"We'll need to do planning and contingencies," Diarrhea said. "You know how the boss is on that."

"And I entirely agree," Michael said. "Plans A to Z in a matrix across and down. *But* if it's as clean as our usual ops, it will look weird. Tell the boss we'll need to fill in *some* drama. It's the narrative."

"Right," Diarrhea said.

"We've got hundreds of thousands of orphans to feed, care for, and protect," Michael said. "And in the event of the Storm, to move to India. If I inherit, I can at least contribute to that. I'm sitting here looking at all the *fun, fun, surf's up* things in my life right now. Because of course! My life couldn't, you know, get *easy,* could it?

"The closest person I've ever had to a mother was just killed because of me and my propensity to jab people with chopsticks and ask questions about 'do you happen to be related to anyone who might run a massive and nasty transnational gang and who might possibly want to kill me and everyone I know and love for, you know, jabbing a chopstick in your eye?' later.

"A senior member of the above gang, whose name is literally 'The

Cannibal,' the person who was *behind* the killing of Mama, is headed for town to *personally* put me in the grave with hopes to eat me first, preferably alive, and not in any sort of sexual way, for putting a chopstick in the eye of his definitely grandnephew and possibly *ewwww* grandson."

"We got the DNA results back," Diarrhea said. "It's the *ewww* answer. Worse. Grandfather, granduncle, *and* father. Also, some sort of cousin. Fathered a daughter by his *sister*, had sex with the *daughter*, who was also his *niece*, Pene was the result."

"Ewww! Ick! The things I learn in this job . . .

"I just found out I have a biological family and if the bad guy finds out he'll have his people go after *them*. I'm not even going to joke about that.

"The most powerful and evil conspiracy on the face of the planet, worse than the transnational gang, members of which raped and murdered my biological mother, would love to take me out if they knew I existed because I'm heir to a fortune they control.

"I'm probably about six blocks from the guy who personally raped and murdered my mother who is now a serial killer, and if they find out about me will almost certainly be put in charge of cleaning me up.

"I'm about to get turned over to an active pedophile as my 'mentor,' who is so protected by see above conspiracy that 'she' is actually put in charge of super-kids because *that* makes the usual Society sense.

"My first costume was a disaster, so I have nothing to wear to the ball.

"I'm going to start a new school in a new town. You know the bullies are going to want to find out what the new kid is made of. Suspension, here I come.

"Not to mention a new foster home and new foster parents and foster sibs with all the fun *that* entails.

"While I'm trying to learn and sharpen my new superpowers without—and this is very important—*anyone finding out*. Because the above evil conspiracy wants all supers, everywhere, to be weak lest they threaten their hold on power.

"Oh, and at some point, possibly without warning, there's going to be an apocalypse that may or may not wipe out most of humanity.

"Did I leave anything out?"

"Snakes?" Diarrhea said. "At this rate, snakes are going to make an appearance somewhere."

CHAPTER 10

Since he wasn't, yet, done with "orientation," Michael wasn't sure why he was supposed to see Mr. DiAngelo. They'd probably gotten the word about Mama.

"Sit," Falcon said, gesturing to a seat. "And please . . ."

"I'll try to hold down the talkie-talk," Michael said, making the lip-zipping motion. Keeping one track of his mind on exercising Earth Move for power and another on Earth Sight for range had the advantage that two were being used up. It took some control to manage and that reduced the hamster in his head's tendency to overuse the wheel. The view of Tribeca looked gloomier than he remembered, probably due to smog through the recent sunset.

"Thanks," Falcon said, shaking his head. "I've had a lot of kids walk through that door. This isn't anything on you, Michael. You're a good kid. I know you've got a good heart. But I have *never* had as many headaches."

"I am why God created pain receptors, Mr. DiAngelo," Michael said, pointing at his head. "Also, congratulations, you're walking about ten steps away from a mile in my shoes. Try the actual shoes sometime. What headache have I caused now?"

"Have you ever heard of Lost Children?" Falcon asked, leaning back in his chair and interlacing his fingers.

"Native American Lost Children?" Michael said, tugging his earlobe. "Indian children used to be forcibly adopted by whites so that they could be 'properly raised' in Christian households. Once the

Nations got some political power, they put a stop to it but it's one of those rankling issues like slavery and KKK to blacks.

"So, at this point any Native American child who is identified as such *has* to be returned to the Nation. Indian Child Welfare Act of 1978. They've even insisted when there was a stable adoption. Don't tell me my DNA came back Native American! I sure as hell don't *look* like an Indian."

"And here I was going to give you a lecture on something I was *sure* you *finally* didn't *know!*" Falcon said, shaking his head and leaning forward again.

"There's a lot of stuff in this noggin," Michael said, gesturing at his head. "*Please* tell me I'm not going to a reservation! I'm a city kid! I don't want to skin buffalo! I refuse! Meat is murder! Tasty, tasty murder!"

"You're not going to a reservation," Tony said. "Mostly. But you're one-quarter Lakota Sioux."

"That explains sooo much," Michael said wonderingly.

"Excuse me?" Tony said.

"Well, I'd have to get all stereotyping and stuff," Michael said, "but the hell with it. Sioux have a saying: It's a good day to die. I've sort of had that attitude since the thing with the Fifth Street Kings. I knew I was going to die, just figured I'd see how many I could take with me. Ended up walking out alive, well, limping out, and none of them did. Also, the Sioux were pretty renowned as we're-gonna-fuck-you-up-one-way-or-another warriors. Checkbox. And the rare times when I've had a tan, my skin is sort of red. Huh. Makes sense."

"Glad it makes sense to you," Tony said. "From what the Secretary said, yeah, it's normally pretty automatic you'd go to the Reservation. To be raised in 'your native culture.'"

"It's why I was left in the ghetto," Michael said.

"What?" Tony replied, confused. "'Cause you were Native American?"

"It was my 'native culture,'" Michael said. *This guy is a natural sergeant.* "'Cause I was found there. Didn't matter I was white, apparently. If you're in the ghetto, you're ghetto culture and therefore are left there to rot."

"Ah," Tony said, then shook his head. "I am not even going to try to sort out the logic. Bottom line is the Secretary swung a deal with the tribe. You are going to stay in the New York area *most* of the time, but you have to attend, basically, a summer camp every year to connect with your native culture."

Heh, Secretary thinks she "swung a deal."

"My native culture is bangin' hos and bustin' caps, Falcon," Michael said. "I don't particularly care for my native culture. So, no real change 'til next summer?"

"Going to have to meet with a representative of the tribe at some point," Falcon said. "But for right now, no. We get your costume set up and we turn you over to ACS—that's New York City's child services. We've got a sign-off from the tribe that you can be in regular foster care."

"I don't suppose there's any chance of, say, putting me up in a mansion on a hill in the Hamptons or something?" Michael said. "There's got to be an Alfred around here somewhere."

"Sorry," Tony said. "Honestly."

He paused and his face worked, and he shrugged.

"I talked to the head of Children's Services in New York," Tony said, shrugging. "I had five kids. Took some medical intervention, by the way."

"Yeah," Michael said, grimacing. "Ever read the lecture 'Man of Steel, Woman of Kleenex'? Normal wife? Seriously?"

"Seriously," Tony said. "Knew Lucille since we were kids. Thing is . . . I asked the head of ACS if we could foster you."

"Really?" Michael said. "Thank you. Sincerely. Take it it didn't work?"

"There's these regulations," Tony said with a sigh. "You can sign up for foster care, but you can't choose a *particular* kid from it. He said there's reasons and that if he could do a variance on it, he would. But it was one of those you can't change. Like it's a state law. Dunno why."

"I do," Michael said.

"Yeah?" Tony said. "I got some time, and I was curious."

"Comes down to the house I was in when I was nine," Michael said. "Also, the reason they now require blind adoption from overseas."

He sighed and leaned back.

"Put in a house in a pretty decent neighborhood for a change," Michael said, tugging his earlobe. "Black father, white mother. Entire rest of the house was girls, all overseas adoptions. I've liked girls since

I was very young. Never had the 'ooh, girls, ick!' thing. Thing was, they were all being sexually assaulted. The couple was importing them, the dad would break them in, then they'd 'rehome' them—that is, rent them out or sell them to other pedophiles."

"Ah, jeez," Tony said, grimacing.

"I know, right?" Michael said. "Disgusting. Domestic wasn't good enough for him, he had to have import."

"Oh, wow!" Tony said. "Jesus, kid!"

"I have a *very* dark sense of humor for a reason, Falcone," Michael said, shrugging with his palms up. "It's a protection mechanism from all the hell I've lived through. Anyway, as 'qualified foster parents' of the state of Maryland, they had a shortcut to adoption. But to *stay* qualified, they had to have a foster kid in their house from time to time. So, they'd specifically ask for a street kid to 'give him a loving home.' Two examples of why the 'you can't choose particular children' rule exists. They'd picked the girls for their looks, and they specified a kid they thought wouldn't talk. Got it?"

"Yeah," Tony said. "So how long was you in that house? And . . . did they ever get caught? I hope you did actually drop the dime. If not, we gotta give somebody a call."

"Duh," Michael said. "Though a couple of times it was neck-and-neck drop the dime or kill the bastard in his sleep. I'm really good with languages. I had to learn some to talk to the girls. I told them things would get better. That America wasn't all like this.

"I mean, they were coming to America!" Michael said. "Coming from some third-world shit orphanage to the Best Country in the World! And they end up getting raped, day one. Most of them came from very strict moral backgrounds—Vaishnavas, Muslim, Christian. It was sin and irredeemable sin. It was hell for them. I told them it would get better. That it wasn't going to last forever. Things would get better."

He inspected Tribeca again, and now it almost seemed sinister. It was a guarantee those apartment buildings were loaded with kids in similar situations at that very moment.

"I had had enough experience with the all-around incompetence and corruption of Baltimore's social services office as well as CPS and Baltimore PD that I didn't trust any of them. Plus, street kid. Three rules of the street: big boys don't cry, never snitch, always get revenge.

I was caught between two of them, so the obvious one was to go with 'always get revenge' and ignore 'don't snitch.' 'Always get revenge' is generally my go-to anyway.

"In this case, I tracked down the federal marshals," Michael said. "Mann Act, right? Transportation across state lines for immoral purposes. International is 'across state lines.' I talked to a marshal and told him what was going on. He told me to hang in there, they had to follow-up with an investigation, but he'd get back to me. Understood I was a street kid, and it had to be confidential.

"About a week later, my foster dad decided he wanted a little domestic chicken," Michael said. "Woke up with a hand on my butt and him snuggling up to me, naked.

"I always sleep with something sharp. He went from having a tiny little chubby to backing out of the room as fast as he could, covered in cuts and blood from this nine-year-old wildcat with a shiv and a burning intention to perform gender-affirmation surgery on that asshole.

"Cops were called, the knife had to be pried out of my hands. I got sent to the slam..."

"You didn't tell them what happened?" Tony asked.

"One, Tony, you never talk to the cops in a situation like that," Michael said. "Doesn't matter if you are the most upstanding citizen ever. You always wait for advice of counsel. Two, it was the word of a street rat against a seemingly upstanding citizen. Everybody knows that foster kids are screwed up—drugs, crime, attacking their foster parents. Well-known fact. Be clear: situation like that, foster kid is always in the wrong. Because, honestly, they usually are.

"They said I tried to disembowel him. Total fucking lie. I was aiming for his chubby and it was so small I missed. It was *dark*! I was *nine*! I've gotten better with a knife since.

"Figured the social services attorney would show up the next morning," Michael continued, tugging his earlobe. "I'd explain it to him. 'So, he was just checking on me, huh? Where's his bloody and cut clothes? Why was he "checking" on me naked?'"

He looked out the window again. He straight refused to do the math on how many kids were getting raped at that moment somewhere in his field of view. Those numbers would pick up in the next few hours.

"Tony," Michael said, sighing. "Your dad may be a cop, but I don't have the highest regard for the brains of most."

"I've known cops my whole life, kid," Tony said, also sighing. "I'm with you there."

"Booked, prints, mug shot. Stayed overnight in a solitary cell after getting cleaned up from the blood. Around noon they shackled me up and turned me over to transport. Where we going? YDC, they tell me. Youth Detention Center. Level Two. Hard time. Six months. 'Where's my attorney?' Dunno.

"Fucking social services attorney had just done a deal with the prosecutor," Michael said, his mouth working and shaking his head. "'It's a first offense! He's not a bad kid!' Social worker had signed off as legal ward. Attorney never even *showed up* to ask me *my* side. Social worker did. Social worker is not an attorney even if they think they are. I asked for an attorney, not a lady with a degree in social work. Never showed.

"So, I'm in YDC getting counseled for my 'anger management issues,'" Michael said. "Counselors are telling me that I need to learn to deconflict. Understand I was having a nightmare, but cutting up my foster dad wasn't the way to solve my problems."

"That had to be fun," Tony said. "Still not talking?"

"What was the point?" Michael said. "Anyway, marshals finally show up, ask me what happened, figured I'd just finally gone off on the guy. They'd investigated. Yeah, it was for real. Weren't sure the girls would be effective witnesses.

"You don't talk to cops, but I *hoped* they were different. Told them the story. They had pictures of girls from their adoption files. Pointed to them, gave names, some of them I hadn't seen, rehomed; one, Shota, had been rehomed while I was there. Full cooperation.

"They busted the guy, started tracking down the girls," Michael said. "Some of them, their English wasn't all that. Assala only spoke Lata."

Michael shook his head and chuckled.

"Know how rare Lata is?" he said. "It's only spoken on one tiny little island in Indonesia. There are something like fifteen hundred speakers, total, in the world. Fifteen hundred and one with me. I found a PDF-scan dictionary of it in the Oxford collection, *after* I figured out what she was speaking through a couple of words of Tetum she spoke. I didn't, at the time, speak much Tetum. So, I had to translate for her to the extent I could. Helped with the translation for Anandi.

"Was a cooperating witness," Michael said, shrugging. "Which caused me some grief when they sent me back to the hood. But I said it was a pedo and that don't count. Dad got fifty years, Mom got ten. Girls were whisked off to Marshals Land and never heard from them again. The end. Not even sure why we were on the subject. Oh, yeah, why you can't specifically ask for guardianship for me from social services. That sort of thing happening is why. But I do appreciate the thought."

"That sort of thing happen a lot?" Tony asked. "My dad's like a lot of cops; he never talked much about his job."

"There are three kinds of people who are attracted to things like foster care," Michael said. "People who want kids because they want to do things with them—teach them to fish, teach them to be good adults, things like that. People who just want some income and don't care, indifferent. And people who want to do things *to* kids. Rape them, abuse them, hurt them."

Outside, dusk was giving way to darkness.

"My experience is it's one out of five want to help kids, three are indifferent in a bell curve to one is the predator. But you get moved from house to house to house so you always end up with the predators at some point.

"Predators go where the prey is," Michael said, shrugging. "That's a *saying* in CPS and it's true. Child predators infest things like programs for disadvantaged youths, foster care, schools, therapy. Anywhere there are children who are looking for guidance and need emotional support you find predators. Hell, anywhere there are children, you find predators. Predators go where the prey is.

"It explains the Catholic Church scandal and the Boy Scout scandal and the Southern Baptist scandal. It tends to be especially bad where there's a lot of secrecy, which is why I'm not a big fan of the juvenile court system.

"And they are always the people that everyone thinks are great people! It's always 'we never would have suspected.' 'They couldn't possibly be! They are such a wonderful person!' 'Everybody loves them!' Are they the homeless guy waggling his dick in public? Yes. But the real predators are always right under your nose and beloved by all."

Ding, ding, ding, ding! Are you listening, Tony? Hello! Electrobolt ring a bell?

He could tell that, yes, that was exactly what was going through Falcon's head. But he also knew Falcon couldn't do anything about Bolt. "She" was the Secretary's fair-haired girl.

"By the same token, it's where you find *good* people as well," Michael said, shrugging. "Wonderful people. People who are selfless and caring and just want things to be better for children. You find them side by side, working together, the good ones never knowing that the children they are caring for are being abused sometimes by someone they think of as their close friend. Predators can be very charming. They're seductive and will take on whatever guise they need to get what they want. Lucifer was the most beautiful of the angels."

Lights were picking up all across Tribeca and he could make out finer details and locations again.

"Most of my foster parents were the indifferent ones. Three out of five. They were getting paid to do day-and-night care. That was it. Then there were a few that cared about kids and wanted things to be better. Few of those. One set that was the best I had that started for the money and we ended up the closest thing to family I've ever had.

"The rest were the predators. And every one of them needs to burn in hell for all eternity."

"You probably ought to lecture on this," Tony said, his brow furrowing.

"Just last year I was the lead author of a paper at the London School of Economics," Michael said. "'International Trafficking of Minors: An Economic Model.' It was like a study of, say, oil flow and the supply chain thereof. Producers, consumers, flow-chain, requirements for transport. Cover paper in *The Economist*. Sex always sells and there's nothing sexier than child trafficking. It's required reading for anyone in the federal government who is working in the area of trafficking of minors, especially in the State Department."

"Wait," Tony said. "You wrote a paper that's required reading for the *State Department*?"

"Was the lead author," Michael said. "Seven-person international team. My pseudonym for economics, business and finance papers is Phillip Crawford the Third. Look it up.

"One of the members of the team is now running a think tank in

London on combating sexual trafficking of minors internationally. That includes the US. The point is, I'm an acknowledged world-class *expert* in child predation, Tony. At an academic level, not just being an abused foster kid. I've been a remote consultant for *Interpol*."

His coauthor that set up the think tank was a Society asset, and it was mostly supported by Society funding. The paper had been suggested by Gondola and they'd arranged for the Society asset, who was a pedophile close to traffickers, to be included on the team. By setting up the think tank, The Society got inside scoops on where law enforcement was looking. By being behind it, Gondola knew what The Society was getting and could get ahead of them. Also, it was one more data point for finding kids to rescue.

The entire thing, including the think tank, had been a Gondola setup of The Society.

The world he worked in with Gondola was so internecine and convoluted he sometimes had a hard time keeping up even with the brains of an astrophysicist.

Tony leaned back and put his hands on his head, shaking it back and forth.

"I don't even know where to go on that?" Tony said, laughing. "Jesus, kid. What were you even doing *doing* a ... I've *heard* of the London School of Economics but ... What?"

"There's an online university that aggregates remote courses from other schools," Michael said. "You get credit if you pay for them, but you can audit them for free. I've audited about six hundred hours, mostly master's and graduate level. That's how I wrote the astrophysics paper. My three main published papers are in Astrophysics, Economics, as mentioned, and Queer and Transgender Theory."

"Queer and *Transgender* Theory?" Tony said, eyes wide.

Michael gave him a quick summary of his publications.

"We need to get you into *Columbia*, kid," Tony said, shaking his head again.

Bite your tongue.

"I prefer remote," Michael said, shrugging. "You can get more information faster. Tony, since I was six and I figured out how to set it up, I've been listening to two college lectures at a time on earbuds, one in either ear, sped up to usually three times speed, twice with stuff that's hard. It's one of the reasons I don't do well in school. It's like the teachers are moving through molasses. And don't you tell anyone!"

"Why not?" Tony said, shaking his head again. You could tell he was getting a headache, regenerative healing or no.

I am the reason God created pain receptors.

"They want to put kids like me in special ed," Michael said. "They get more money for special ed. And other reasons but that's the big one. At which point, socially, you become a total pariah. 'Hur, hur, hur, you're in the dummy classes, hur, hur!' 'Do you ride the short bus to school?' 'Where's your helmet?'"

"Yeah, I can see that," Tony said.

"Foster care always sucks," Michael said, tugging his earlobe. "And from what I've heard, school mostly sucks unless you're in the in crowd or a jock. And I can't play on sports teams: super-kid. But at least they're not going to put me in Brooklyn, right?"

"Not all of Brooklyn is bad," Tony said. "You're thinking about the projects. Brooklyn's a big place."

"The worst areas are less violent than the ghetto I came out of," Michael said. "More people. More total violence. Less per capita. I'll probably end up in a working-class neighborhood. Not great school but not urban jungle hell like the ones in Baltimore. Kids are starting to be vaguely no longer children, not quite adults. It's possible there will be some that are interesting enough to hang out with. And, honestly, there's girls."

Tony started to bow-up at that one.

"Not like *that*, okay?" Michael said. *Liar. Only a little bit. Liar! So, I like red!* "Just…Okay, Columbia, right? Think college girls give a thirteen-year-old the time of day? Even if he's handsome, debonair, a sharp dresser and cool? It might be possible, sort of, to do the comic book superhero life—kid with a girlfriend by day, crime fighter by night. And if it all goes tits up, if I can't hang with dealing with the crap in regular school, I'll do my GED and be done with it. Sound like a plan?"

"Watch the girls, kid," Tony said. "Be a good guy, there."

"Absolutely," Michael said. "I really am a *total* gentleman."

LIAAAAAR! I am a good guy. Red being my favorite color does not mean…LIAAAAAAH!

Michael realized he was hearing the word "liar" in his Mama's voice.

CHAPTER 11

"Unbreakable" —Fireflight

Michael was sitting in the lobby of Super Corps headquarters, waiting on Alexander, pretending to play on his phone and actually "looking" around with Sight.

Earth Sight was weird. X-ray vision, yes, but still weird. It was more like looking at a 3D ghost diagram of an office building. Between the voids, stuff that didn't contain earth elements and the earth elements he could more or less puzzle out the entire scope of the building, at least as far as he could "see." He was up to about two stories distance, and it turned out office buildings were fascinating. So complex. Power and water runs were hidden everywhere, built into the precast and poured concrete of the structure. He could see the air ducts better because they were lined with dust—top, bottom, sides—giving a ghostly outline of their shape.

Then there were the people. The Federal Building was an absolute hive of people just doing *stuff*. Mostly sitting at computer screens. He could see most of those because they were filled with silicon chips. Eating lunch, getting coffee, chatting about whatever and, yeah, using the toilet and sometimes . . . he just looked away.

Please wash your hands, please wash your ha . . . Oh . . . Yuck.

Then he got to the point he could see into a particular storage closet at a particular time.

When he was four, he and his friends had all been given cheap smart phones. The Obamaphone program. He could argue all day about Keynesian vs. Akeynesian economics.

John Maynard Keynes in his *The Means to Prosperity* first mentioned the multiplier effect. That if government spends money, it is multiplied by the economy.

Democrats had taken that to mean that any money that government spent would return to them upon the waters tenfold. Thus, "We can spend our way out of debt!"

Republicans scoffed at the very idea that government spending was of any use except for the military and pork for their districts.

They were both wrong in Michael's somewhat expert opinion.

Even Keynes argued that all money spent by government did not multiply. Build a hydroelectric dam, yes. Electricity was one of the biggest economic enhancers around. Nuclear, even. Arguably, telecom infrastructure, which was honestly pretty creaky in the US.

Tell everyone to hit themselves on the heads with hammers and give people money to buy hammers, and the only people who are going to get rich are the Greedy Hammer Cartel.

Michael was of two minds on the phone program. He had happily taken to it like a duck and started reading and researching all of the wonderful information on the web. In that way, it was Keynesian in that at some point he'd be a productive member of society. The cost of the phone and his usage over time would be less than what he contributed to society over time. There would be a return on investment for the government, which was really what "Keynesian" meant.

All of his friends did what their older brothers and cousins did: watch porn.

He couldn't get into it. He was four. There wasn't anything there that excited him. He'd learned to read at two and had rarely had access to books. He would read anything in the house. He'd read the Bible six times by the time he was four just to have something to read. Three different versions.

Being able to read anything that was in the public domain and being able to watch college lectures excited him. There wasn't anything that really excited his four- and five-year-old friends about porn. They were even less into girls than he was. They were just doing what the big kids did.

That was then, this was now. He had still avoided even having porn on his phone. The closest thing he had was pictures of hot girls wearing skimpy clothes and carrying guns. He'd seen too much bad stuff working for Gondola to simply shrug off that it "wasn't harming anyone."

But he just couldn't look away from the supply closet at first.

It was over pretty quick. From their motions, they were ghostly skeletons in Sight, she pulled her skirt down, he pulled his pants up, and they left quickly after a peek around.

He had to take a very quick trip to the little boy's room afterward. He'd washed his hands.

The hotel was filling up. There was a convention in town, which was what the spare space was for.

It was getting hard to concentrate on his chakras. He was still working his Earth Move, the main power every day. One thing he'd read and found by personal experience was that Move weakened over distance. When he'd first starting using Sight that wasn't apparent. But what he'd learned was that his Move had the same range as Sight. At extreme range, where he was pushing Sight, Move was very weak.

So, he'd been doing most of his "push" at or near maximum range. Find a section of support member, and just push against it. There wasn't enough power at that end to do any damage. He wasn't going to push the building over.

He did Earth Move automatically at this point any time he was sitting still. It was when he was moving that it was difficult, and he was learning to handle that as well.

But Earth Sight occupied most of his attention. He knew he was being a Peeping Tom. He was thirteen and he had to keep looking "out" farther and farther to train the power. It was hard not to notice the people having sex within his range. Among other things, movement attracted the eye. Honestly, and shamefully, it was giving him a reason to look out and out farther.

It boggled him how much sex went on in office buildings.

He'd learned some things that weren't in the manuals, probably because they were considered too unimportant. There was enough earth matter that you could "see" currency. He'd noticed it the first time when he passed an armored truck and idly looked in it to see what he could see. The currency was in bags, for delivery to banks and ATMs.

Since then, he'd seen that in several trucks but more interestingly every now and again he'd see a car with large currency in the trunk. That was probably drug dealers moving money around.

As a Junior Space Eagle that could come in handy. There were major Fourth Amendment issues with what he was doing if it was going to be used for a trial. But civil asset forfeiture was just "Hey, that's ours!" He personally hated the laws, both statutory and case, around civil asset forfeiture but it was the law of the land.

Again, might come in handy.

At the Corps Headquarters there was more to see. Because there was a definite difference between supers and normals.

He'd had the briefing that "super-bones are denser than normal humans." That was obvious in Earth Sight. More than that, the Flyers and Grounds were denser than the others. The invuls were easy to pick out even if they looked human.

But there was more there. It was hard to define because of the limited "ghost" look of soft tissue. But the soft tissue was different as well. He was going to have to stop by a chemistry shop and start studying Chakra of Chemical Sense. He was fascinated by the differences.

He also was fascinated by the tactical aspect. Hostage situations were few but in one he could not only "see" what was going on, he could affect it from out of view and behind cover from the hostages and hostage takers.

The likelihood that Sasha *could* be taken hostage was remote. But he had a very vivid imagination and came up with every implausible scenario he could that involved him rescuing her using his powers.

The mumble mumble terrorists have drugged Sasha with fentanyl and massive doses of propofol to keep her knocked out . . . They could be doing anything *to her! But somewhere in the naked city . . . hmmm . . . hmmm . . . supername . . . can find her with his* Earth Sight!

"Ready to go?" Alexander asked. "Hello? Earth to Michael . . ."

"Hmm . . . ?" Michael said, realizing Alex had been standing there for a while.

"Thinking about astrophysics again?" Alexander asked. "Didn't want to interrupt."

"Oh, yeah," Michael said, standing up. "Astrophysics. Yeah . . . uh . . . stellar nucleosynthesis. What's up?"

"Ready to go shopping?" Alexander asked, holding up a government credit card.

"The best kind," Michael said. "*This* is a costume I can get my head around."

"Kevin is still crushed," Alexander said, heading for the elevator.

"He can get his kicks designing the dress costume," Michael said. "Not that I'll ever ... wear ... it ..."

I think that's a different ... That is definitely *a different girl ... You could at least use a different supply closet! Philandering asshole!*

"I'll take an iced tea," Katherine said to the server as she sat down. When the girl was gone, she looked at Maureen's glass of chardonnay longingly. "There are *so* many days I wished I could fuzz my brain."

"And what is the issue today, Madame Secretary?" Maureen Robbins, Assistant Deputy Undersecretary for Operations, US State Department asked.

"Nothing's turned up in the news," she added.

"It's what we're trying to keep out," Katherine said, sighing. "It's the new kid, Edwards. Thanks, by the way, for the contact at BIA. That helped."

"Not a problem," Maureen said.

"I thought it was going to be impossible," Katherine said. "Eagle Lightning quite read me the riot act on the subject. I was ... I thought some of it a bit ... insubordinate. But I got his point, eventually. Then the Sioux just changed their minds. He can stay in New York. I'd have been extremely worried about any junior super just swinging in the wind. But this one, gah!"

"What's he like?" Maureen asked.

"Haven't spoken to him personally," Katherine said. "Tony likes him. Keeps repeating 'The kid's got a good heart!' But he's the ultimate loose cannon. Smart, unquestionably. Off-the-chart IQ, published in multiple fields, Economics, Astrophysics, Queer Theory if you can believe?"

"Queer theory isn't something I'd expect," Maureen said, frowning.

"He has—had—someone in his life who was trans," Katherine said. "So, he should get along with Electrobolt. Tony's worried about that. He ... isn't a fan of Bolt."

"Senators Drennen and Munro *adore* Electrobolt, Katherine,"

Maureen said. "You know they're your biggest supporters on the Committee."

"I think Edwards is going to be an issue," Katherine continued. "He's too smart for his own good. All these kids think they have all the answers. I did. It's tougher with the smart ones. I at least knew James knew what he was doing. Over the years when I've had a problem I think, 'What would James do?' and I realize I have no idea. I'm not James."

"Another person we all miss," Maureen said. "Though not what he became, obviously."

"Would you ladies care to order?" the server asked, setting down Katherine's iced tea.

"I'll take the chef's salad with chicken," the Madame Secretary said.

"I'll have the same," Maureen said with a sigh. When the girl had left, she sighed again. "How long have we known each other?"

"Decades," Katherine said. "You were one of the first people in this town who treated me like a Secretary instead of . . . a secretary."

"Twenty-seven years," Maureen said. "I spend thousands on plastic surgery to look *half* as good as you. You look younger than you did when we first met!"

"Comes with the powers," Katherine said, shrugging. "I got the same thing from Senator Feinstein. God, I miss her."

"We all miss her," Maureen said. "But the thing that has driven me nuts the whole time I've known you is that you can eat absolutely anything and never gain weight and you always order the damn chef's salad with chicken!"

"I like chef's salad," Katherine said, shrugging again.

"We're supposed to go see the marshals," Alexander said, looking at a text on his phone.

Michael was having a pleasant afternoon, shopping in an Army/Navy/Police store for his new costume. It had taken some convincing, but the Madame Secretary had finally acquiesced to the wearing of tactical gear. On that basis he had chosen a super name of . . . dum-dum-dum . . .

Stone Tactical!

Which was lame as hell, and he hated it, but better a lame name than being noticed.

He was trying on some boots. The boots had a soft, conformable lining on the soles that was replaceable. He was going to be walking around in them a lot. He wanted something comfortable. Though they were not particularly stylish, he was planning on wearing them to school. Two reasons: One, they would be worn in when he did—*hack!* *Ptui!*—patrols. Two: When, not if, the bullies at school decided to take on the kid with all the scars, they looked just about right for stomping a face.

The picture of the future is Stone Tactical's boot, repeatedly stomping a bully's face.

"I see the marshals every day," Michael said.

"We're supposed to go to their office." Alexander looked puzzled.

"When?" Michael asked.

Whee! New identity! That will hold off Cannibale for . . . a day or two?

"Now?"

"Guess we better pay for all this, then," Michael said, looking at the pile of gear. It was pretty much what Mama had picked up for him when he was fighting the Fifth Street Kings plus some. The thought of Mama caused him to lock up for a moment.

Later. Deal with it later. Vengeance is mine, sayeth the Lord. I'm just how He gets it.

"Think there's enough on that US government credit card?" Michael said. "Oh, and can I do a walk-out in these . . . ?"

"Marshal Powell," the marshal said, looking the pair over.

Marshal Powell was short, slightly balding and paunchy. He was the exact opposite of the movie stereotype of "US Marshals!"

Michael knew that to advance at all in the Marshals you had to do Felony Warrant, tracking escaped prisoners and others with warrants, the stuff that the movies were made about. And to be a full qualified Felony Warrant Marshal, at one point you had to take down a massive and very-unwilling-to-return-to-jail criminal.

Powell might *look* like an accountant, but the guy could probably take Michael. Even if Michael got to tag in a couple WWE wrestlers.

"Michael Edwards?" he asked, looking at Michael.

"Yes, sir."

"Not . . . anymore."

"Was that an Inspector Clouseau reference?" Michael asked.

"Good catch," Powell said, then pointed at Alexander. "You. Here. Wait."

"Yes, sir," Alexander said.

Michael was led through a couple of security doors and into a slightly dark room with a camera set up and a blue background.

"Stand on the marks," Powell said, pointing at the floor. He stood behind a podium, looking at a screen. "Face the camera..."

Michael had to take several poses.

"I don't even have a driver's license?" Michael said after the third pose. Smile. Don't smile...

"School photos," Powell said. "We'll age them so you look appropriate ages. But if you're the same pose in every photo, it will stand out as a fake."

"Ah," Michael said. Gondola probably knew that but worth checking.

"We did it the other way around for a while," Powell said, continuing to take photos. "We'd use FakeTime with a stock set of poses. One of our outside contractors was able to spot it so this is what we had to go back to."

Let me guess who spotted it. 'Cause that sounds just like us.

After fifteen minutes playing male model, they went into another office.

"Lemme see...Yeah, you're all over the place. No personal social media accounts? 'Cause your name is all over social media a few years back."

"Hate it," Michael said, tugging his earlobe. "Don't have any. But, yeah, I was sort of mentioned."

"Newspapers...Jeez. You are *very* unpopular."

"Still am with some people. Especially terrorist groups like MS-13. And Antifa."

"I've got, I think, all your aliases," Powell said, handing over a piece of paper. "Anything not on that list? Hell of a list for a thirteen-year-old."

Mountain Tiger.

"Nope," Michael said after looking at it carefully. He'd forgotten he had some of these.

"Okay," Powell said, punching some buttons. "To the best of our ability, Michael Edwards just ceased to exist. Any thoughts on a name?"

"Michael James Truesdale," Michael said.

"That was quick," Edwards said, leaning back in his chair and studying him.

"Did you see how many AKAs I had?" Michael said. "I keep ones on file in my head just in case I need one."

"That's..." Powell said, then shrugged. "Okay. Don't like keeping the same first name."

"I've got reasons," Michael said, tugging his earlobe. "And it's at best a light cover. Everyone with access to knowledge of supers is going to know Michael Edwards is Michael Truesdale. Might as well keep the same first name."

He leaned over and typed carefully then hit enter.

"You are now... Michael James Truesdale," he said as a printer started up. "Complete with birth certificate, New York student ID, and passport. Thought I'd throw that in given what you're doing these days."

"Thanks?" Michael said.

"Your Maryland social services file is gone," Powell said. "As are your priors. However, they are on a special database, and you still owe the six months with the JSC. Your health file just changed names and the original in Maryland is gone. But, because the doctors are listed, it's pretty clear where you came from. Not much to be done about that. And we're done. Not the best job ever, we'd erase you utterly if there was a point. Given that you're a super and you'll be on the Supers List and people knew you trans... Acquired as an Earther... unless you dropped out of the JSC and were disappeared and left your medical records behind... people can still find you."

"You're from Schenectady," Powell said, handing over more paper. "Basic background. Similar to reality. Blind transfer to the state. No idea who your mother or father are. Raised in foster care. Your file is bland, none of the stuff that happened in Baltimore. Unlike your current, massive, file there are no CPS reports. So, you'll have to work with that. List of foster parents who don't exist. Memorize them to the best of your ability."

"Yes, sir," Michael said.

"About all we can do," Powell finished.

"Making it harder is worth it," Michael said. "And there are other reasons I'm grateful. Michael James Truesdale has never publicly been accused of murdering persons of color because of being a white supremacist. Which, by the way, is an outright lie if you care. Just to smooth the transition in a new school, this was worth it."

"Glad to be of service."

"... While we are getting to the point that any collected cell can give us a welter of forensics data, *that* is why we are strongly urging the National Academy of Medical Examiners to include bone samples in *all* future autopsies. There is no better material to understand the life that person lived than bone. Thank you for your time..."

Dr. John Pierce II stepped away from the podium, shook the hand of the master of ceremonies, and gratefully stepped behind the edge curtain. Public speaking was his least favorite thing in the world. He lived to simply exist in a lab, piercing the veil of whodunnit through science.

His phone buzzed and after a glance he paused. The calling number was a series of ones and zeroes. That could only mean one thing.

"Dr. John Pierce," he said, just in case.

"Dr. Pierce, Omega," the distorted voice replied. "Enjoyed your lecture."

"Thank you," Pierce said. "Wasn't aware it was being streamed."

"It wasn't," Omega replied. "We need a favor."

"For helping with Edmunson, you're owed *all* the favors..."

Michael got out of another orientation class and checked his phone. There was a text from Frank: *Call me.*

He called Frank back wondering what it was about. Probably Mama.

Frank Galloway was a homicide detective in Baltimore PD. He'd been the lead officer investigating the shooting with Fifth Street Kings.

After it was ruled as self-defense, he'd taken the then twelve-year-old Michael under his wing and tried to give him some fatherly mentoring.

Frank was an alcoholic, philandering, three-times-divorced, childless, embittered, cynical homicide detective who had seen more dead bodies than any one person should.

His mentoring had come down to teaching Michael how to golf and trying to persuade him to stay out of gang life.

Michael had no intention of joining drug gangs, he'd insisted. Michael intended to be a career thief! Not knocking over liquor stores. Heists and jewelry were his thing! *Italian Job*! Safes and stuff. Drug gangs were for losers!

But Michael had at least learned to golf out of it.

"Detective Galloway," Frank said.

"Hey, it's Michael," Michael said. "'Sup, fatso? You ever find a tailor?"

Frank had a small but well-developed beer gut. He also had the worst dress sense of any black man Michael had ever met.

"Screw you, super-kid," Frank said. "How you doing? I heard that Williamson had to inform you about Miss Cherise. I should have handled it."

"Nah," Michael said. "All good. I'll deal with it later. Win some, lose some. Why the call now?"

"We're done with Miss Cherise's phone," Frank said. "We just chalked it up to '13."

"That's who it was," Michael said. "I made some calls. Hispanic males, AKs. What other Hispanic males are going to gun down some trans street ho?"

"We got the word she was really insistent you get her phone," Frank said. "So, I've got it. We're done with it. Never could get it open, anyway. Had to make the call through the emergency contact. Question is, how do we get it to you?"

"Marshals gave me a new identity," Michael said. "If you'll do me the favor to give it to them. Give them my old name and they should be able to get it to me."

"Okay," Frank said. "That works. They're right next door. How's Super Corps?"

"I thought Baltimore PD was screwed up," Michael said, "but, damn, do they got budget. Put a flag on 'Stone Tactical' now that I've got a super name. And believe nothing that you hear. It's all lies."

"Usually is," Frank said. "Well . . ."

"Well . . ." Michael said. "Someday again, Frank. Where the moon meets the water."

"Where the moon meets the water," Frank said.

"Out here."

"Memory" —Elaine Paige, *Cats the Musical*

There was only one thing left in his sojourn in orientation. They had to have official photos. Which had been waiting on his costume.

He flexed dramatically, turning to the side and taking the position of a Greek hero.

"No flexing," the photographer said. "That's not the look we're going for."

Kevin was standing to the side with Maureen behind him, his hand over his mouth and tut-tutting.

Michael's costume had many things to say in favor. Stylish it was not. Unless tactical was a style, which he could argue.

From top to bottom it started with a full-face tactical helmet in black and gray. The helmet was made out of ballistic Kevlar with polycarbonate ballistic eye-shields and looked like something that was straight out of *Halo*. The resemblance was uncanny. Like, yuh know, somebody who designed helmets was playing *Halo* and went "I could probably do one of those and it would look cool as shit." Unlike many similar helmets, though, this one had a mesh ear cover. It allowed for good hearing but protected the ear from impact. Also worked dandy as a mask.

Down from there was a set of IIIA body armor also in black with gray highlights. It was light, flexible, and allegedly capable of withstanding up to .44 caliber. He'd mounted a few MOLLE pouches that might come in handy. Take that non-utility belt!

Under the armor was a Nike Dri-FIT shirt with a Maxx-Dri Vest both in black and gray. A theme was emerging.

Pants were 5.11 tacticals. Go with the type. For boots he'd gotten two sets even though he was going to outgrow them, one set of Under Armour and a set of Bates. He'd taken both to the home and was trying them out at school to see which held up better and was more comfortable. So far, he was leaning to the Bates, which were zip up and lighter, but the zipper kept sticking.

For the photoshoot for the newest member of the Junior Super Corps he'd gone with the Under Armour.

Last he had on a set of Wolf Tactical shooting gloves. No fingerprints left behind by *this* superhero!

"My little David," Kevin moaned.

"Oh, take a breath, Kevin," Michael said. "I am *tactically* stylish."

"There is *no such thing!*" Kevin said, wiping his eyes.

"So, unleash your creativity on my dress costume," Michael said. "If it's wearable enough I might even use it occasionally on patrols. But only when I'm not going to get messes on it. Did you enjoy Hungarian hussar uniforms?"

"They *are* very pretty," Kevin said.

"I know that you'll come up with something original and outstanding," Michael said. "Did you know that Nazi uniforms were designed by Hugo Boss?"

"I was aware, yes," Kevin said. "Hugo Boss has apologized ever since."

"Why?" Michael said. "*He* didn't kill any Jews. And those uniforms were *amazing!* They were so cool, George Lucas copied them for *Star Wars*. Imitation is the sincerest form of flattery."

"You have the oddest view of the world, Michael," Kevin said.

"Mike," Michael said, striking another pose. "Mike Truesdale. Michael is my super-duper secret identity. That only those in the know . . . know. So, I guess that makes you in the know. And I'm just waiting for the mothership to return so I can go back to Antares where I belong."

Michael did jazz hands and the photographer pulled away and looked at him angrily.

"Would you quit fooling around?"

"Who's fooling around?" Michael said, doing more jazz hands. "Jazz hands are totally superhero. *Five hundred twenty-five thousand, six hundred minutes / Five hundred twenty-five thousand moments so dear . . . !*"

"Just stay still," the photographer growled.

"So grumpy," Michael said, stopping the jazz hands.

"I wouldn't have taken you for a show-tunes fan," Kevin said.

"I'm not, really," Michael said. "I'm more into metal. Or seventies rock. Or alternative. Foster mom was. I just memorize lyrics. But there are a few songs that are worthwhile. If you wish . . .

"*Daylight / See the dew on the sunflower / And a rose that is fading / Roses wither away . . .*" And he proceeded to serenade the audience with "Memory" from *Cats* complete with dance routine choreographed for combat gear.

The photographer got up angrily from his crouch, then considered it, tilted his head to the side thoughtfully, shrugged and just started snapping.

"You can sing *and* you can dance," Kevin said, clapping his hands together.

"I was raised in black households," Michael said, continuing to dance. "Black people sing and dance with their children all the time. Hmmm, hmmm, hmmm. At least in the ghetto. I'm not sure about Alexandria. Hey, Alexander!"

"Hey, Mike," Alexander said as he came in the room.

"Memory! / All alone in the moonlight! / I can smile at the old days! / I was beautiful then...!"

"I have never heard 'Memory' scored for tenor," Kevin said, sniffling and wiping his eyes. "It's so...beautiful!"

Maureen silently handed over tissues and Kevin wiped his eyes again.

"I've never seen 'Memory' scored for black tactical mask," Alexander said. "And I've seen it in high school drama classes. I *did* it in high school drama class."

"Which cat?" Kevin asked.

"Bustopher Jones," Michael guessed.

"That," Alexander said. "I wanted to do Rum Tum Tugger but the kid with the red hair got the part."

"Stereotyping is annoying," Michael said. "In this day and age if I played Peter Pan, I'd probably get cast as Princess Tiger Lily..."

CHAPTER 12

"Heaven Knows" —The Pretty Reckless

"Welcome to New York City. Do you go by Mike or Michael?"

Jerry Adams, head of the New York City Administration for Children's Services, could have been Alexander's father. Maybe grandfather. Tall, still medium build, dark brown complexion and close-cropped graying hair.

His cramped office was as chaotic as every other social services-type office Michael had ever been in, but at least it wasn't a cubicle buried in Post-it notes. Plus, he and Alexander were the only clients in the room—Michael was used to waiting in a cramped holding space until his name was shouted.

"Mike, sir," definitely Mike Truesdale said. Michael James Truesdale. *Don't know why any of them, they gave them to me at the hospital.*

Same was true for that other name. Whatever it was.

He hadn't had time to write the name down four hundred times, which was what was recommended. Or, for that matter, do extensive research on Schenectady. All he knew about it was that it was somewhere in upstate New York. It didn't matter all that much, he doubted anyone at all would grill him on his fake hometown and, even if they did, he could run circles around them with vaguaries and chain restaurants.

"I don't think we've ever had a super in foster care," Mr. Adams said.

"There are only three hundred and thirty-six supers in the US, sir," Michael said. "Only five children out of one thousand are in foster care at any one time. To have *any* is the surprising part."

"You were never adopted?" Mr. Adams asked.

"No," Michael said, tugging his earlobe. "My previous office was not adoption focused."

"Ah," Mr. Adams said, nodding. "Well, we *are* adoption focused but . . . you understand that the likelihood of that at your age . . ."

"Not an issue," Michael said. "Never really been into the whole adoption thing."

LIAR! LIIIAR! Lying is a sin!

"Alright," Mr. Adams said.

"One tiny thing, sir," Michael said. "It's about the after-school activities . . . ?"

"That," Mr. Adams said. "I'm not entirely happy about sending one of our kids out to just wander around Central Park at night *intentionally*. We generally try to *discourage* that."

"Oh, my God," Michael said, holding up shaking hands. "Did I just hear sanity out of . . . don't take this wrong . . . a social services bureaucrat?"

Mr. Adams chuckled at that.

"Yes," he said, grinning widely. "While this job is thousands of required procedures and regulations as well as politics and incidents to make your hair white, I try as often as possible to introduce some sanity by, among other things, suggesting that making rational decisions is sometimes better than just checking boxes."

"Alexander," Michael said, pointing at the supervisor. "In your future career as a bureaucrat, you should listen to this man. But the thing is . . . I kind of need to be able to access them."

"You'll get a Metro card . . ." Mr. Adams said.

"It's about placement," Michael said. "This is the placement center for the entire five-borough area, is that correct, sir?"

"Yes," Adams said, then nodded. "You need to get to the . . . ahem . . . special whatever after school, one week a month? Is that right?"

"Yes, sir," Michael said. "And two Saturdays. If I could maybe be placed somewhere that is more possible rather than less in terms of transportation? And I don't know for New York City so . . ."

"Not Staten Island," Alexander interjected. "Ferry."

"I'll talk to Shaquea about that," Adams said, nodding. "Make sure she understands you have community service to work off and that you have to be there at certain times. It's not clear in your file for what, but I'll tell her."

He stopped and sighed and ran his hand over his head.

"Super Corps insisted that I be the only one who knows you're a super," Mr. Adams said. "So, Shaquea, who handles placement, can't know and your social worker can't know and your foster parents can't know. I've never personally spoken to someone who reports to the President before, so I'm not going to get in the way of that."

"No, sir," Michaels said.

"The problem is that issues come up," Mr. Adams said. "Mr. DiAngelo was both complimentary of you and somewhat... confusing. 'What's he like, in your opinion?' 'He's got a good heart but... he's kind of hard to keep up with.' Wasn't sure what he meant."

"ADHD," Michael said. "PTSD, ODD, and a bunch of other letters. Even some *numbers*. Really high IQ. I say things and they don't make sense to anyone else. And what people do don't make sense to me."

"If I give you my personal number..." Mr. Adams said, wincing.

"Only in an absolute 'this has gone completely sideways, and things are about to explode' situation," Michael said. "I'd appreciate the honor and would handle that with the greatest responsibility."

"Then let's get you placed," Mr. Adams said. "It may take a while. We have an excellent waiting area..."

There was a "rest" area for kids in the ACS building—aka the holding area he was used to. It wasn't even bad. In Baltimore he'd spent more than one night on a couch in their social services office. New York City had a sort of living room complete with couches, comfortable chairs, and even a foosball table. Then there was the waist-high wall with Lexan around it, so the kids could be watched like elephants in the zoo, locked gate, and a sleep area and bathrooms in the back that held bunk beds like a ready room in a hospital.

There was even a cafeteria available.

There were six kids in the living room area between the ages of about seven and ten, plus a black girl slightly older than Michael at a guess. Michael was the only one with luggage. The others had their stuff in plastic bags, per normal. They were ignoring each other, also per normal, concentrating on their phones or in one case reading a comic book.

"Well, Alexander," Michael said, jutting out an elbow.

Alexander gave him an elbow bump and his face worked a bit.

"Oh, don't be that way, silly," Michael said, punching him in the chest. "I'll be seeing you. Community service, remember?"

"Sure," Alexander said.

"Remember: Not everybody in the ghetto sees the cops as the oppressors. And if you're ever in a situation where killing is *going* to occur, what don't you do?"

"Try to talk about it?" Alexander said.

"Never talk to people when you're killing them," Michael said, punching him in the chest again. "You're a man of good heart, Alexander of Alexandria."

He gave Alexander a hug, genuinely sorry to see the guy go, then looked at the social worker.

"Time to lock up the monkey," Michael said.

"How was your lunch date with the Secretary?"

Thomas Leeth was a lobbyist with Keith, Kelly, Williams and Buckley, a white-shoe law firm with national offices based in Philadelphia. Six feet tall with a slope-shouldered body, hazel-colored, beady eyes, and shoulder-length, flax-colored hair, he had been a constant feature in and about Washington for decades. Having a casual meeting with a member of the State Department by the steps of a tiny, sparsely populated park was practically unnoticeable.

"How long is she going to *stay* Secretary?" Maureen Robbins asked, exasperated. "I've been doing this for nearly thirty years without a break. She's like the Energizer Bunny of dumb!"

"She *is* as dumb as a gnat," Leeth said, nodding. "Sadly, it appears that supers might, in fact, be immortal. So, who knows? At some point it will be time to throw her under the bus. In the meantime, you're doing a fantastic job at steering the gnat."

"She's worried about the new kid, Edwards," Maureen said. "He's been a handful already and he is extremely smart. Possibly too smart."

"That was what got Colonel King," Leeth said. "Being too smart for his own good but not quite smart enough. But this one is also an Earther and not in any sort of leadership role. Making it a 'Flyers only' club in terms of leadership has limited the problems there. And if he becomes a problem, we have various plans. Michael Edwards won't be an issue..."

Bruce Hobbs continued to text with a coworker on his phone, apparently ignoring the pair on a nearby bench.

He didn't know why Gondola was interested in them, nor who they were. And he wasn't going to ask. Because his name hadn't always been Bruce Charles Hobbs. He wasn't sure what he'd been named, originally, but his name had been Atieno Lencho Kariuki for many years. He remembered the container he was being transported in and the men in black masks and guns who had opened it. And the moment the children realized they were being rescued, not just turned over to more bad men.

Ten years in an orphanage followed during which he was taught English and computers. Then the query: would he be willing to move to the United States as an undocumented immigrant?

Add in some work as a cooperating witness with the FBI on a terrorist plot he had "stumbled on," that Gondola had spotted and used him as an informant to build trust, and he had a green card and a new identity, with the grateful thanks of the United States government.

The nano-camera and shotgun mike on his glasses automatically tracked on the pair as long as he kept his head within a certain angle. An AI processor combined what little could be heard with lip-reading algorithms to sort out what they were saying. If there was anything that couldn't be sorted out by the AI, it would be turned over to expert humans.

He wasn't worried about any of that. It was up to the bossmangs to figure it out. All he knew was he owed his life to the people who had found them, who had saved him and all the other children. If he had to volunteer to sit on a park bench for *days,* he would do so.

God was building an army.

Michael was used to his social worker taking him to a new home his-, her-, or itself.

Apparently, there were so many kids being constantly reshuffled in NYC that they had people who specifically dropped off the kids at homes. Michael had the name of his social worker and phone number on a card, but he hadn't actually met her.

So, he and two other kids were led to the parking garage, carrying all their stuff, by their "placement officer" Ian Major, a twentysomething, black, skinny, hippy-looking dude with dreadlocks who reeked of marijuana and who Michael mentally dubbed "Black Shaggy." The littlest, Tahwan, had a hard time carrying his bags so Michael gave him a hand. He wasn't thanked and wasn't expecting any. That shit was for movies.

They put most of their stuff in the trunk of a battered Toyota sedan with an old Biden bumper sticker as well as a host of other slogans: MEAT IS MURDER, COEXIST, LOVE NOT HATE. Tahwan called shotgun and Michael let him get away with it.

"I'm dropping off Shaketra, first," Ian said. "Then Tahwan, then Mike."

Nobody said anything. They just kept their noses in their phones.

Michael had no clue where he was; New York City was a new place to him and it was large enough that memorizing the entire thing was difficult. But based on what the map program was doing, they were headed for . . . Brooklyn. How original. 'Cause there hadn't been any orphan superheroes depicted as living in Brooklyn. Or the Bronx. Or Queens. Or, for that matter, *anywhere* in New York City.

They took a tunnel much of the way, so not so much to see. When they got on surface streets, it looked like a bigger version of Baltimore. Some nice areas interspersed with trashy.

They made some turns and ended up in an area called East Flatbush where Shaggy pulled in in front of a small row house on Brooklyn Avenue.

"Okay, Shaketra, this is your new home," Shaggy said, then pointed at Michael and Tahwan. "You two. Stay *in the car*."

Michael just nodded as they left.

Tahwan started to get fidgety, and Michael cleared his throat.

"Man, I'm tired of getting rehomed," Tahwan said.

"Where you gonna go?" Michael asked. "Good house, bad house, it all evens out in the end."

It took about three minutes to deliver the first package. Tahwan wasn't placed far away. Black Shaggy helped him with the trash bags with his stuff. Then it was Michael's turn.

"So, you're basically the Uber for ACS?" Michael said as they headed deeper into Brooklyn.

"More or less," Black Shaggy said. "Hey, are you cool?"

"Smoke 'em if you got 'em," Michael said.

"Thank God," Shaggy said, pulling out a one hit and lighting up at a traffic light.

"Wouldn't mind if you cracked the window, though," Michael said, without looking up from his phone. Thankfully, Shaggy obliged.

They finally pulled up at a small, brick row house on East Twenty-eighth Street. Looked to be a more decent neighborhood than many in the area, as some of the iron-gate cover doors looked to be permanently left open. Meaning the residents weren't trying overly hard to guard against intrusion, nor had they completely given up like in the lower slums.

"This is you," Shaggy said.

Michael got out, unloaded his rolling bags, and headed to the door.

The interior was tastefully decorated, and his new parents were a pair of whites in their thirties who just screamed "young urban professionals." A set of antique ceramic dishes were prominently displayed on a series of shelves. The front room was a sitting area, with two separate chairs—no cuddling on the couch to binge Netflix for these two—and a shelf full of whatever the woman's book club had read over the last five years.

"You have a beautiful home," Michael said to the lady of the house.

"Thank you," she replied, beaming.

"This is Michael ... Truesdale," Shaggy said, reading from the page on the clipboard. "And these are ... Frank Edwards and Linda Thomas ..."

"Frank Thomas Edwards," Linda corrected. "And Linda Edwards Thomas."

Of all the name coincidences ... Michael Edwards aka Mike Truesdale thought. Also—he'd just learned far more than he wanted to about this couple from those seven words, six of which were just their names. But at least now he knew. He could work with that.

"Okay, yeah, that ... sign here," Shaggy said, waving the clipboard back and forth.

Linda took it and scribbled a name.

"Good luck," Shaggy said, heading out the door.

That left Linda and Frank examining him and vice versa. He was using Sight as well as eyes.

Neither Linda nor Frank had had much bone trauma in their lives. Frank had had a broken wrist at one point, probably when he was a kid. Linda had no broken bones or signs of bone trauma.

They'd lived lives of more or less perfect peace and probably thought that all cops were bastards.

"Hi," Michael said, tugging his earlobe. "I go by Mike. I am a currently male-presenting lesbian. I go by he/him for convenience. I occasionally go girl when the feeling takes me. I have no food allergies. I am not vegetarian or vegan. I have no drug addiction problems. I am high-level ADHD and PTSD. I request that even if there is an issue at night, like I'm screaming in my sleep, that you announce that you are present to avoid...issues. In general, not a good idea to sneak up on me."

They'd both flinched when he'd started speaking as if they expected him to bite, which was fair, but the more he talked the more reactionary caution turned to dumbfounded confusion.

"I have an occasional mandatory extracurricular activity that is mandated community service for a misdemeanor charge. I just found out I am Native American genetically so I'm studying my cultural background."

Linda Edwards Thomas brightened considerably at this news.

"I've recently gotten into yoga and geology." He paused for a moment to let them catch up. Linda Edwards Thomas had actually smiled at the word "yoga" while Frank raised a curious eyebrow at "geology." "So, are you guys regulars? 'Cause you look like newbies."

"Uh, you're our first foster child," Frank said, smiling. "This is a new experience for us."

"You're my seventeenth foster home," Michael said, trying not to sigh. Linda's smile disappeared. He was damaged goods again. But again—*fair*. The newbs were the best and the worst. "Wanna take a seat, and I'll give you the *real* briefing about foster care? All the stuff they probably didn't tell you in classes? Or they sort of danced around with a lot of euphemisms?"

"Okay," Frank said, gesturing at the sofa and chair set.

"We probably should get you placed in your room," Linda said.

"You gonna wanna hear this, Linda Edwards Thomas," Michael said, sitting down and gesturing to the sofa.

She took a seat.

"That's a beautiful set of ceramics," Michael said. "Extremely fine crystallization. Inherited?"

"My grandmother's," Linda said, beaming. "She passed them to me when she . . . She's in a senior's center."

Can't call it an old folks home, now, can we?

"You continue in foster care, you're going to want to pack that up and put it in storage," Michael said. "'Less you want it in *pieces*."

"Excuse me?" Linda asked, confused.

"Where to start?" Michael said, shaking his head. "Let's start with: Every child in foster care is abused. They may be temporarily placed because they were in an abusive household, or they may be lifers like me who were abused *in* foster care. But we're all abused.

"Abuse, the lack of control, causes anger just like rape. Which is also common. Anger causes them to 'act out.' 'Your foster child may tend to act out.'

"What they mean by that, specifically noting your grandmother's collection, is other kids will throw those at your head while screaming like a banshee. They may be having flashbacks to prior abusers and be attacking you since you're not going to beat them down or rape them. They may just be angry. But by and large they are going to act out. They especially act out with the inexperienced ones or the nice ones. They don't act out with the ones that beat them down and rape them 'cause then they just get hurt more. So, they'll take it out on *you*, just because they can get away with it."

Linda looked more horrified with increasingly defensive body posture as he spoke. Frank—notably not comforting her—seemed actively interested in more of a processing way.

"Then there is the complete lack of any moral code," Michael said. "I'll get to asking about the rules of the house, but I'll give you an explanation why foster kids have *no* moral code. Moral code comes from a consistent set of rules growing up. Linda, did you have one set of parents growing up?"

"I . . . my parents divorced," Linda said.

"Stepdad?" Michael asked.

"Yes," Linda said, brightening just a little.

"But you had a mother who had a consistent set of rules," Michael said. "Don't know what all they are, yet, but make your bed every morning, toothpaste cap goes on the toothpaste, cups go here, dishes go there. These are what you think of as universal rules that exist everywhere and are the right and the true and the good."

Linda nodded and looked to Frank for support, who did give her a brief smile and nod.

"When I was four, I got rehomed," Michael said. "It was my sixth rehoming. My previous foster mother was toilet lid *down* after you go. So, new in the house, I went number one, put the toilet lid down, washed my hands, and went back to what I was doing. My foster mom snatched me up by my arm, took me in the bathroom, and screamed at me about putting the lid down."

"The lid *down*?" Linda asked. "That's . . . very strange. Are you sure?"

"I don't have to lie about abuse, I assure you, Linda," Michael said. "I don't know why she was so set on lid *up*, but she was. So, I did lid up for a while, then one time forgot.

"*That* time the next thing I remember is waking up in the amb-oo-lance," Michael finished, shrugging and introducing a bit of ghetto tonality. "She beat me so bad I had to go to the emergency department. Third trip for trauma, by the way."

Linda shifted and reached out to death-grip Frank's left wrist. Commendably, he took it and put a hand atop hers.

"That's the point, here," Michael said. "Moral code derives from a consistent set of rules. When every house has different rules, what people think of as 'pet peeves'—toilet lid up, toilet lid down, shower curtain open, shower curtain closed, don't use this shampoo—it gets confusing. And, at a certain point, you realize that it's all just made up. So, what's the problem with theft? What's the problem with violence? Rape? It's all just made-up rules. None of it's real. You dig?"

"I guess," Frank said.

"Now, I've got a strict set of *ethics*," Michael said. "Do no injustice to another is one of them. But that's me. I'm abnormal that way and I grew them all on my own. I grew up in a ghetto. There ain't no rules there 'cept Big boys don't cry, Never snitch and Always get revenge. I don't even follow *those* rules 'cept the first one and generally the third. I've snitched when it was beholden. Saving other kids from predators, mostly.

"So, *I'm* going to leave your ceramics alone," Michael said. "Other kids will throw them at your head, just to hurt you emotionally and physically. To get back at the parents that abused them, even though that's *not* you. They'll steal them if they think they're worth anything. 'Cause of anger, we ain't got nothing anyway and lack of moral code. Heck, if you just had your own kids, they'd probably get broken. Any parent with multiple children will tell you, kids can break *anything*. A set of breakable ceramics out on display like that is something for DINKs: double income, no kids. All clear?"

"I guess," Linda said. "Have you been . . . *badly* abused?"

Michael laughed drily.

"My shrink calls my file the *War and Peace* of Child Abuse," Michael said, sighing, this time he left out the addendum for their sake. "Lemme see if I can clarify."

He took off his T-shirt and their eyes widened.

"Oh, my God," Linda gasped.

"What . . . happened?" Frank asked, wiggling fingers on his left hand to make sure they were still getting blood.

"Growing up in a ghetto in foster care happened," Michael said. "The burns on my shoulder were from my foster mom when I was five, pouring a pot of boiling water on me. I just thank my lucky stars it wasn't oil. The rest of it is more 'the ghetto' than 'foster care.'"

He put his shirt back on.

"Second thing," Michael said. "Do not expect me to ever call you Mommy and Daddy or any of that stuff. You only see that in movies and TV shows where the writer has no clue what foster care is about."

Linda glanced at Frank, who nodded in understanding.

"This is a nice house and you're nice people. Unless Frank has a secret peccadillo for little boys, should go okay. If he does, be aware the last foster dad that tried that stuff got eighty-seven stitches.

"I'll do a reasonable job of not doing things that will tend to have you want to toss me out. But I'll probably be gone in a few months, anyway, because foster care plays musical beds. I can get into why it's that way, but I won't bother.

"Bottom line: By the time you're five in foster care, you learn to not make *any* personal connections. Not with other foster kids, especially not with parents. Another reason we're all cray-cray as bed bugs. Personal connections are mentally stabilizing. Lack of personal connections is destabilizing. So, we're all destabilized—a euphemism for unstable as a radioactive element. We're liable to fission and explode like a nuclear hand grenade at any moment. Want to know what foster kids are really like? Listen to 'Heathens' by Twenty One Pilots. It's the theme song of foster care. Pay attention to the lyrics. 'Please *don't* make any sudden moves. You don't know the half of the abuse.'"

Both were now just frozen in place, Linda out of shock while Frank's wheels were doing their best to keep up.

"When you're very young, you just, innately, want to have a mommy and daddy that will protect you and care for you. Someone to lock onto. You rapidly discover that that ain't what it's about. It's about minimal support of food, clothing, shelter, medical care and schooling. As long as the boxes are checked, it's all good to social services.

"So, I'll probably be gone soon enough—good, bad, indifferent. Just as I won't bother with a lot of personal connections, don't suggest you do so, either. At some point we'll part ways and that will be that. I don't Facebook and if I did, I wouldn't friend you, foster parents or not. Not because I don't like you, just no point. Pretty soon you'll be somebody I used to know, like that person you spent a little time with in college and very rarely wonder whatever happened to them. Things go well, in both directions, we'll have good memories. And never see each other again.

"All clear on personal connections and mommy and daddy?"

"Yes," Frank said.

"I guess," Linda said, looking a tad unhappy.

"Don't believe anything you see in a movie or TV show about foster care," Michael said. "If they did a movie about the realities, it would be banned for depictions of child abuse. *Girl with the Dragon Tattoo* don't get close.

"So," he said, clapping his hands. "Let's talk about the rules of the house. Toilet lid up or down?"

"I don't think it really m—" Linda said, smiling.

"Down," Frank said.

"Toothpaste cap?"

"It's not..." Linda said.

"On," Frank replied.

"Shower curtain?"

"Closed," Frank said.

"Inside the tub or outside?"

"Inside," Frank said.

"Oh, that's *very* important so it dries and doesn't mold," Linda said.

Michael knew that Frank couldn't care less but had learned the "right and proper way" from his wife, probably while they were still just living together. Linda and the decor exuded household control freak, one each.

"Particular shampoos and soaps I'm not supposed to use?" Michael said. The rules of the house generally focused on the bathroom and the kitchen.

"Well, you'll have your own bathroom," Linda said. "I would prefer that you keep it clean . . . But please don't touch my Oribe. I have a problem with split ends . . ."

"It's the black-and-gray bottle," Frank said carefully.

He'd used her Oribe at one point. There had been words.

"Okay," Michael said, nodding. "Communication is *vital*. Don't touch the Oribe. What else we got . . . ?"

CHAPTER 13

"Whom I Shall Fear" —Chris Tomlin

"I've got my own room?" Michael said.

It was a small bedroom but having his own room was a rare luxury. It meant no other foster kids would steal his stuff. There was a simple twin bed with a full set of fitted sheets and an actual blanket, a nightstand, a chair with its own small table, and a short, single-tier dresser. It was the nicest room he'd ever been in, way above the only one he'd only shared with only two other people—but, seeing as those two had died of starvation, it wasn't too fair a comparison. Bottom line: He was going to try real hard not to get kicked out.

"Is that . . . unusual?" Linda asked.

"Very," Michael said. "You can cram three kids in here if you try hard. Four at a pinch. Bunk bed set on one side, single on the other, space to get in the closet. Double bunk beds, even."

"That would be rather crowded," Linda said. "Would they allow that?"

"Dunno 'bout New York City," Michael said, tugging his earlobe. "Schenectady, they'd try to cram in *six*."

Dinner was a not particularly palatable vegetarian dish focused on tofu.

"We're vegan," Linda said.

NOOOO!

"Food's food," Michael said.

They sat at a small, round, contemporary table with upholstered chairs that fit fully underneath—a model of space efficiency.

He bowed his head and said a short prayer. He tried to remember to pray at meals.

Linda and Frank looked at each other and paused until he was done.

"You don't have to wait on me," Michael said, tucking in. Linda was not the world's best cook. Certainly not vegan. And the portion was small—but not too much more would've fit on the table anyway. It was food.

"Are you . . . religious?" Linda asked, surprised.

"ABE," Michael said. "African Baptist Evangelical. Though, given that it's always been sort of odd a white kid going to ABE, I'll probably find something else. I usually just go to whatever my foster parents attend, if they do. If you don't, don't worry about it. That God isn't to be found in any temple is sort of a basic aspect of Christianity. God is found where two or more are gathered in His name. And then you get into the discussion of 'what does gathered mean?' Which gets into televangelism and so on and so forth."

"Okay," Frank said.

"You're not religious," Michael said.

"Uh, not particularly, no," Linda said. "Is that an issue?"

"You are people of good heart," Michael said. "Who have taken in a child to do good in the world. You do unto others as you would have them do unto you. I'm of the mind that such people are probably saved by their hearts, because without any reference to God or the Savior they are still walking the path. Others disagree and say that if you do not come to the altar, you are not saved. The Anabaptists say that if you do not strictly follow the prescripts of the Beatitudes or Baptize in childhood that you are damned. It's a debate."

"Do you have any food insecurity issues?" Linda asked, trying to keep up.

"I spent a month in the hospital recovering from severe malnutrition when I was seven," Michael said. "The other two kids in the house died. But I eat to live, not live to eat."

"Oh," Linda said, shuddering.

"Been to the emergency department sixteen times for mild to

severe trauma," Michael said. "If you don't want to hear bad things, don't ask about my past, ma'am. Because the very small slices of good are pretty much overwhelmed by the extreme and more common cases of *very* bad. *War and Peace* of Child Abuse."

"You seem to be handling it well," Frank said.

"I am as nutty as a Snickers bar," Michael said. "But I'm trying to be on my best behavior 'cause I get my own room."

Michael sat on his own bed in his own room and just chilled. Supper had been . . . not the worst he'd had in his time. He wasn't sure whether to suggest he cook sometimes or not. He could do vegan. Gah! But the portions had been tiny, and his stomach was already grumbling.

Two hours after you have vegan, you're hungry again. Okay, more like two *minutes.*

Linda was a graphic artist in a marketing firm. Frank ran servers for a law firm. Michael had avoided any discussion of IT and Linda had dominated the conversation. He'd mentioned yoga and she was the world's greatest expert. He admitted he didn't have a yoga mat. She had spares. That problem was fixed.

They didn't use a dishwasher to conserve resources. Michael managed to hold his tongue and point out that a good dishwasher used less water than extensive washing by hand and guaranteed sterilization. He'd washed dishes by hand in a lot of houses that just didn't have the money for a dishwasher.

He managed to *not* use Earth Move to move the dishes around. That would have been weird.

He'd been working his Sight the whole time and was getting more range every day. He could just see across the street from the house as well as into the houses to either side. About fifty yards, give or take. His "everything is there" extended through the house. So, if something happened, he'd catch it. Assuming he was awake and present in the house.

Despite Gondola now taking an interest in MS-13 and guarding his back, he knew they didn't have one hundred percent data at all times. Surprises happened. They'd lost people in the past when enemies attacked without warning. Frank and Linda didn't deserve a home invasion over him.

That brought up the thought of Mama and he pushed it aside.
Deal with it later.

After putting on some shorts and closing the curtains, he took a lotus position on *his* bed, pulled a marble out of his pocket, courtesy of Alexander of Alexandria, and hung it in midair. Then he extended his aura into it, shifting the aura through colors. At the same time, he extended his Sight out across the nearby homes. People doing stuff. Mostly washing up, watching TV, looking at their phones. The building behind the house was a pre-K. It was empty. Even the janitors had left.

He extended his Earth Move downward under the house along with Sight and Sense. It was soil under the house. He had to be careful with that, lest he cause a subsidence. Michael had once lived in a foster home that had been cracking apart from that. He could see the plumbing, a void, and other inclusions. He had enough range, now, to reach under them. The soil was pretty consistent, no major layers or anything. He was looking forward to being around bedrock. And he had to do more study of geology, starting from the vocabulary and drilling down. Maybe audit some geology courses.

He spread his power and compressed the area of soil at his maximum range and power. There was no notable difference under Sight and with Sense he could just feel the slight compression. Since he should have more range tomorrow, he wouldn't be compressing the same area of soil every night so it should be okay.

Should.

With those tracks of his brain occupied, he decided to see if he could do something that he'd been considering. He very carefully grabbed his ribs and femurs with Earth Move and, carefully, lifted himself into the air.

So, he could fly. Cool.

Still in a full lotus, he began to work all of his chakras in multiple directions, pressing the soil beneath with Earth Shape while examining it through Sense, lifting himself and the marble with Earth Move and looking around the area with Sight. Focusing on all of those things at once should quell the . . .

Red just is not *going to go with her eyes . . .*

Focus. Feel the Earth, padawan. Let the Earth flow through you . . .

Like a soil enema? That would be kind of unpleasant, don't you think?

Oh, shut up. You always ruin the moment.

I ruin the moment? Who went babbling to Sasha?
You did!
I beg to differ! You're the nerd!
I am the serene master of all I survey. You're *the nerd! Nerd . . . !*

Frank had gone to the garage and rummaged around. Michael had
Seen him doing it and put it out of his mind. But now he was headed
to the bedroom with a laptop under his arm.

Michael dropped to the bed and pulled in the marble. There was a
tap at the door.

He got up and opened the door and smiled:

"May I help you, sir?"

He'd taken off his shirt just because he preferred the feel of air and
Frank kind of blanched, again, at the scarring.

"I . . . uh . . . I noticed the only electronics you had were your phone,"
Frank said. "I've got an old laptop . . . That sounds bad . . ."

"I mostly buy clothes at Goodwill, sir," Michael said, tugging his
earlobe. "I very much appreciate it."

"Thing is," Frank said, "it runs on Linux . . ."

"I am fluent in Linux," Michael said. "I admit to being a nerd."

Frank glanced at the scars again and looked quizzical.

"Who gets beat up more than nerds?" Michael said with a sigh.

"That's a point," Frank said, handing him a piece of paper. "Password
for the computer and the Wi-Fi. I scrubbed all my personal stuff off of
it when I moved the data. Can you handle it after you get in?"

"If I have problems, I'll ask for help," Michael said, taking the
laptop. "And, again, thank you. You're a man of good heart."

"You're welcome," Frank said. "'Night?"

"Namaste," Michael said, bowing slightly.

Once he got it set up, he could log in to the network again and get
some hours in. Though the Faerie Queen had said it was more
important for him to train his powers, he still felt he should do some
work on the network. There were never enough people for all the
problems in the world they tried to solve.

For now, he set it aside and went back to hovering over his bed,
working his powers. He was trying to find the Chakra of Thermal
Earth using the marble. He could Sense it but couldn't find the way to
warm or cool it.

He stopped sending power into the earth below and rummaged

where that power seemed to come from, trying to stay Zen and keep the various thoughts from interfering. "Be still and listen for the still small voice..." Not so easy for an ADHD. Earth Move and Earth Shape were both kinetic powers. So, since thermal was simply a variant of kinetics, they should be around there somewhere...

The marble suddenly flared and started to melt. He could "feel" the heat in it from something like Earth Sense. So, he could "feel" the temperature of earth materials, now.

He pretty much destroyed the marble heating and cooling it. He wasn't sure how much kinetic energy he was generating at this point, but it was at least that much. There was a test he'd taken as part of "orientation," pushing against a piece of rock that was on a scale. Testing his power levels. The Corps was pretty adamant that they stay low, post the Nebraska Killer.

But they weren't exactly testing his powers, despite what he'd told Tony. Even if they did, it wasn't like he couldn't just downplay them.

He finally set the screwed-up marble aside and went back to working Move and Sight. He realized he could use up his kinetic powers by just using Thermal Earth, spreading out an area under the house that he could cool off. It didn't seem to cause ice heaves; he wasn't that powerful, yet. And it was less likely to cause damage to the soil. So, he poured all his power at the farthest range possible into cooling off the soil under the house.

He noticed after about an hour of that, and considering the chicken-and-the-egg problem as an aside, that his Sight was drawing in. His maximum range was decreasing. He'd read that when he was running out of Power, that Sight would shorten. So, between the power he'd been using all day and his evening practice, he'd apparently used up most of his.

As the maximum range got up close to the base of the house, he stopped pouring in power. Save a little just in case something happened during the night. That might slow down his advancement, but he was too paranoid to give up *all* his power.

With training done for the evening, it was time for more research. That would be *slightly* trickier to keep up on when he started getting actual homework, but not really.

He couldn't wait to do a paper on colonialism. Oh, the shame and the guilt and the angst! *Mea culpa! Mea culpa! Mea maxima culpa!*

⊕ ⊕ ⊕

Breakfast was a filling bowl of Athenian Harvest Muesli with soy milk.

I should have said I have an allergy to soy. See what they do with that!

"Hope you have a good day at school," Linda said.

"It's school," Michael said. "I just hope that the bullies take a hint. I like this place. I don't want you tossing me out for getting suspended."

"Just don't get in fights," Linda said reasonably.

"Generally, you've got a choice of being stomped or fighting back," Michael said. "All my teeth are implants courtesy of a nice doctor. They've been stomped out before. Don't want to have them replaced again. I'll do my very best to deconflict. And my very best is good indeed. But . . . we'll see."

His schedule, along with a map of the school, was on an app so he just ghosted in. Old, brick construction with tall, black-iron fencing around the open areas and white iron bars across all windows. Not just the exterior windows, *all* the windows. He arbitrarily rated it three *Gossip Girls* above the best East Baltimore school he'd attended.

It was school. Hallways full of lockers, stuck-up chicks, and loser dicks. The main thing was to just stay as out of sight and mind as possible.

Yeah, right, sure.

Michael missed Baltimore at a certain level. He'd hardly gone to school there because nobody cared. If he showed up one day a month for half the day, he was counted as "present" for the rest of the month and could ghost.

New York actually *tracked truancy*. He'd checked. If he missed school, they'd call ACS and he might *lose his own room*. Fucking technology sucked.

He could just hack the server and show himself "present" every day. But that might get noticed. He needed to be invisible.

On reporting in, he had a significant delay at the front desk while they set up his "account" and issued him a tablet with a full set of ineffective, occasionally contradictory, and completely unenforceable rules.

First class wasn't bad. English for the terminally illiterate. Much about overcoming systemic racism. Homework assignment.

No problems changing class, even when he made a quick pit stop. Though he never even bothered opening his locker. There was really no point and it was just an opportunity for someone to catch up to you.

Second period, math. Fractions. Oh, so much fun. He was one-quarter Sioux and three-quarters white. So, he was seventy-five percent colonizer. He resolutely kept his hand on the table whenever the bored teacher asked if anyone knew the answer (Bueller? Bueller?) and concentrated on working his powers. More range today. He could see most of the school and into the ground below. He went back to cooling off the earth under the school for the kinetic powers and just roamed his Sight around school and outside.

Sure as hell wasn't going to practice aura shape.

The smart kids were all at the front of the class, polishing the apple. So far, nobody had introduced themselves to the new kid and despite the urge to introduce himself, at least to a couple of the cuter girls, he had managed to avoid all personal interaction.

Changing class to history, that came to a screeching halt when a big brown kid, mixed race, probably Asian, black, Hispanic at a guess, blocked his path along with a couple of lesser goons. No surprise about race, about seventy percent of the school, by his estimation and the stats online, were black-leaning mixed race. Statistically, the bullies were going to be the same.

The kid had various minor and some major bone injuries indicative of an abusive home life. Abused often became the abusers. Nature, nurture, it was the circle of life.

"What up, loser?" the kid said. Michael had caught his name in English class as Evuala Kincaid, which sounded straight out of some 1960s pulp sci-fi. "You owe me lunch money."

"I tell you what," Michael said, smiling. He considered doing something interesting to Evuala's bones but that might be noticeable. "I'll hand it over tomorrow, if you'll wait until after phys ed to discuss this."

"Hand it over *now*, white boy," Evuala growled, holding his hand out.

"*I am the very model of a modern major-general,*" Michael sang with his fingers steepled. "*I've information vegetable, animal, and mineral! / I know the kings of England and I quote the fights historical! / From Marathon to Waterloo in orders categorical!*"

Evuala's face took on a look of puzzlement and he pulled his hand back. Good, he was being forced to think. You could see the smoke.

Throwing in something unexpected when aggression was imminent caused people to have to use higher-level brain functions to evaluate the sudden change. It drew resources, blood, away from the violence and survival centers of the brain. In short: It cooled things down and created a possibility of negotiation instead of just going to naked aggression.

Gonnnndola training, sir!

"Like I said, wait 'til after P.E.," Michael said, holding up a hand to forestall a reply. "When you see me with my shirt off, *then* decide if you wanna do this. You wanna, we'll go. But not in front of cameras and after P.E. It's just after lunch, right?"

"Yeah," Evuala said, frowning.

"I'll *give* you my lunch money tomorrow if you win," Michael said reasonably. Then he quickly spun around Stunt Extra Number Two and headed to class.

"I see you met Evuala."

The kid he'd ended up sharing a desk with appeared mostly East Asian with some brown, might be Indian or some other brown. Timothy Broome sounded non-Asian but there were stranger things under the sun, Horatio, than in all the fiction of man.

"Yeah," Michael said, tugging his earlobe.

"He's a prick," Timothy whispered.

"I'll work something out with him," Boogie Knight answered.

"You're new here?" Timothy said. "I'm Tim."

"Mike," Michael replied. "Mike Truesdale, secret agent."

"Riiight," Tim said.

"No, really," Michael said. "I'm part of this international spy organization that's battling this group of super-villains in the shadows. I'm here to uncover Society operations in MS-136 and stop a planned terrorist attack."

The best way to lie is to tell the truth with a complete and obvious lack of sincerity.

"You say that like you mean it," Tim said, grinning.

"It's better than I'm a foster kid who got transferred to the city because a drug gang back home wants to kill me," Michael said.

"Where's back home?" Tim asked.

"Better you don't know," Michael responded as the teacher gave them The Look for talking.

So far, no fights had broken out in class. Which was just bizarre. Some of the kids were actually paying attention to the teacher.

Just weird. Nobody had been cut so far in the whole day. By this time in Baltimore, somebody would have been on their way to the hospital.

Huh.

Lunch was . . . vegan. Noooo . . . But they offered a backup of one of the worst industrial-processed cheeseburgers Michael had ever experienced.

It was meat! He would take it. Thank God for ketchup!

He chatted with Tim during lunch. Apparently, Tim was one of the slightly nerdy kids nobody hung out with. Michael was fine with being the "nobody notices me" type and hanging with the nobodies. It rarely worked out that way but that wasn't really his fault. He just didn't like being beat up. Happened enough in his life he was tired of it. He objected strenuously.

Tim's name conflicting with his complexion was explained by a grandmother who married a soldier in Vietnam. The rest of his family tree was Asian-leaning Vietnamese.

Then came PE class.

He'd talked Alexander into getting him a couple of extra Dri-FITs. It was federal government money, so why not? And a pair of decent gym shorts.

Evuala was in the locker room, doing various prep moves that were reminiscent mostly of baboon posturing. It wasn't quite green monkey or gorilla. Definitely baboon.

Then Michael took off his shirt.

"Jesus, dude," one of the kids said. "What happened to you?"

"Which time?" Michael asked, turning toward Evuala and pointing at his scars. "So, the point is, if you *really* want to take on a guy who looks like *this* and has survived all *this*, feel free. I don't want to go round but I'll go round if you really insist. But be aware: The people who did this mostly look *worse. Comprende?*"

"Like you're so tough, white boy," Evuala said. But you could see he was reevaluating.

"Up to you," Michael said, pulling on his Dri-FIT. It was a better shirt than any of the rest of the kids' in the locker room. *Oops. Cover mistake there.* "Your trip to the hospital. And, oh, by the way, I'm a *red skin* not a pasty-ass white boy. So, be prepared for a scalping."

Michael was taking another pit stop when he saw Evuala and Stunt Extras One and Two headed for the bathroom in Sight.

When they came in, he was washing his hands and went to dry them, pretending to ignore them. He finished drying his hands and just left his back to them, his fingers steepled.

Evuala walked up behind him and punched him in the kidney.

It hurt, but he'd had that particular hurt plenty of times before and he'd deliberately dialed up into orange. He mentally prepared for the fight, pumping himself up and releasing stress hormones. And while all of those tended to shut down prefrontal cortex processing, he managed to maintain higher-level brain function. He was going to beat them up, not let the rage that always simmered just below his consciousness tear them apart with Powers.

He pushed off the wall with one boot, focused Stone Move on Stunt Extra Number One's coccyx bone to distract him, came back with an elbow into Evuala's face, then spun and *really* started fighting.

Along with powers, supers who weren't "invulnerable strong" still got additional strength, speed, and agility. *Increased kinesthetics* was the term of art. His were still building—you didn't get full power right away and other than weightlifting there was no real way to push it. But he was still about as strong as a thirteen-year-old body builder without working out at all. And he had much higher reactions, speed, and balance than the norm. More like a professional gymnast.

Short version: Even teenage Earthers were the youthful versions of the strength, speed, and agility of Captain America.

Back in Baltimore, he'd more than once taken on upward of six kids who were planning on putting the boot in on the white boy. He was white, whites were the oppressors. He deserved it. That was all the logic needed. He'd learned long before the main trick was to stay on your feet. By the time of the incident with the Fifth Street Kings, Whitey N, the White Negro, later Boogie Knight, had already established a reputation as someone you tried to put a beatdown on with some degree of caution and lots of backup.

Three bully punks from suburban Brooklyn were going to have a hard time with just Boogie Knight. Going up against Boogie Knight with Olympic-gymnast speed, strength, and agility...Here he was, kicking puppies again. Difference was these puppies *needed* a good kicking.

One of the other kids who had been using the bathroom got out his phone to video while most of them fled the scene of the crime.

Michael used Stone Move on the interior of the phone where he could see the chips in the electronic guts and destroyed them.

So, no video evidence. Also, the little snitch bastard was going to need a new phone.

Instead of messing up his new boots and leaving evidence, he ended up by slamming Evuala's face into a urinal a couple of times.

"Nobody saw nothin' or you get worse," Michael said as he was washing his hands, again. Not too much blood splatter and he'd worn a black T-shirt for a reason. Always wear black your first day at a new school. The slight nicking on his knuckles would quickly regen and get rid of *that* evidence.

He dried his hands, knocked Stunt Extra Number Two's arm out from under him as he was trying to get to his feet, stepped on Stunt Extra Number One's back, and walked out.

CHAPTER 14

"Courtesy of the Red, White, and Blue" —Toby Keith

"Did you really beat up Evuala?" Tim whispered during Social Studies.

Colonialism bad. White people colonialists. White people bad. Bad colonists. Brown and black and Asian people good. White people bad.

He was looking forward to being assigned a paper on the evils of colonialism. He *loved* that subject. He had a whole list of the evils of white oppressors oppressing the poor oppressed brown, black, and Asian good people by forcing them to change their culture and give up important cultural rituals like, for example, suttee in India, the burning of widows alive on their husband's funeral pyre; human sacrifice, practiced not only in Mesoamerica but multiple areas in Africa; cannibalism in various regions and so on.

Bad naughty white oppressors. It really leaned into the "evil white oppressor" meme while explaining the cultural importance of those rituals and arguing in favor of them with a metaphorically absolutely straight face. After all, what's wrong with a little human sacrifice? Deny the oppression of *mens rea*! Overthrow the shackles of the Judeo-Christian mind oppressors! Morality derived from *religion*! And religion was the opium of the masses used by the oppressors to keep the oppressed in line! Oppressed of the world unite! We haven't had a good ritual human sacrifice with thousands of victims in simply *years*! Hearts don't cut *themselves* out, you know! What kind of a world is it that you can't dance in the flayed skin of your enemies? Shrunken heads are cool!

"I claim Fifth Amendment protections on that question, Congressman," Michael said, tugging his earlobe. Now that he was a super, he needed to get prepared.

"What?" Tim said.

"Yeah," Michael answered. "Duh."

"How?" Tim asked.

"Secret agent training," Michael said. "Mysterious fighting styles developed in remote monasteries in Tibet."

Tim looked at him funny. Shit, he was beginning to believe it.

"I grew up in a place a lot rougher than here," Michael said with a sigh. "Told him it was a bad idea. We'll see if a trip to the school nurse is enough or if I'm going to have to continuously be the oppressor."

"*Are* you the oppressor?" Tim asked, confused.

"I oppress the oppressors," Michael said. "The only prey worth hunting is predators."

Apparently, the beating of Evuala never came to the attention of the school authorities or they just didn't care. He'd tried to keep it to something the school nurse could handle.

He was getting some considering looks. Apparently, the word had gotten around—just not to the authorities. Good, maybe others would leave him alone.

Or they might try to glom on. That could be a pain. He didn't want school status. He just wanted to disappear.

He'd see how Evuala felt about lunch money tomorrow. It might be necessary to repeat the infraction, but he hoped not. He understood the Evualas of the world too well.

"Hey, uh, Mike," Tim said as they were headed out to the buses. "So...you wanna come over to my house? Maybe? I've got an Xbox. We can game...?"

Michael had just checked his phone and there was a text message about his AT&T account being unpaid and just click the link and enter all your personal information to clear it up.

It appeared to be a phishing text. It was actually a code that they needed him to check in. Something was up.

Also, it would be spammed to several hundred thousand phones as an *actual* phishing text because otherwise it might be noticed and if anyone *did* click the link, you never knew what sort of information you could pick up from morons. Gondola had caught more than one person with child porn on their phone that way.

"Not today," Michael said, smiling to relieve the hurt. "It's not that I don't want to hang out. I do. But new house and I got stuff I gotta do at my foster home. And I haven't cleared having other kids over there, either. So, yes, we'll hang. Just . . . later. Okay? And I appreciate it, I really do. Thanks."

"Oh, okay," Tim said, waggling his head side to side.

Michael could tell that he didn't believe Michael wanted to hang out.

Honestly, I don't. I've got a gazillion things on my plate. But it's the right thing to do.

Michael didn't have friends in Baltimore. Every kid he knew was black and since they went to school, they couldn't hang out with him because he was "the oppressor."

So, he wasn't even sure *how* to have friends. But he knew that involved "hanging out." Exactly what that meant, he wasn't sure.

"I got a contact from, you know, them," Michael said, nodding conspiratorially. "So, I've got to do a check-in. Something's up. The Ministry of Sinistry's on the move, ya know?"

"Riiight . . ." Tim said, frowning.

"I'm going to do *housework*," Michael said, shrugging. "I've got my own room. You have no idea how rare that is in foster care. I really want to schmooze these people. So, unless you want to help me clean the bathroom and kitchen . . ."

"Oh, okay," Tim said, grinning. "Got it."

"I really want to stay in this house as long as possible," Michael said. "Even though the mom is—ick, yuck—*vegan* and has no idea how much teenage boys want to eat. So, I also hope the school doesn't find out who put Evuala in his place. If your mom's a decent cook and likes to feed kids, I'll be over at your house a *lot*, Xbox or no Xbox."

"My mom's a great cook," Tim said, nodding. "You like pho?"

"Never had it," Michael said as they reached the buses. "But you're on. Just not today."

"Cool," Tim said. "See you tomorrow?"

"Absolutely," Michael said.

⊕   ⊕   ⊕

"Mountain Tiger," Michael said as soon as he got home. "God is building an army."

"God has an army," Titanium replied. "Cannibale positive sighting in Mexico again but too fleeting for a team to get there. Intercepts indicate they do not have your new identity, but '13 is surveilling the Federal Building to try to figure out who you are. They've assumed you were given a new identity."

"Intercepts and reports also indicate that, yes, Cannibale is planning on handling this himself. The other two senior jefes do not support going after someone federally protected. They've pulled the general contract, but Cannibale's faction is still looking for you. He's also hired a witch doctor to do the same."

"Any suggestions on how to keep under cover from that?" Michael asked, tugging his earlobe.

"Already taken care of," Titanium replied. "Faerie Queen sent Michael. No more witch doctor."

One thing that had sort of surprised Michael when he'd joined Gondola and sort of hadn't was that the supernatural was real. Just not in any way that was popularly understood in fiction.

Demons and angels existed. They were invisible but had effects on the world. Every person who was not absolutely and permanently damned had an angel, generally called a "guardian angel." They got assigned at or near the time of birth and remained with a person throughout their lives absent absolute damning, which was rare. Permanent damning required that the person had committed unpardonable sins. Since Jesus was forgiving, that took a lot.

Raping and murdering children was pretty much a no-no that wasn't redeemable. The real reason The Society sacrificed children wasn't to raise magic powers. They couldn't "trap the souls" of the children and feed them to Satan. Children were innocent. They went to God's arms. It was to ensure that the people who did so were permanently and irrevocably damned. That their souls were guaranteed to go to Hell. Whether they understood that was up for debate.

There were, in addition, unassigned angels of various powers—galadhrim, seraphim, and so on. Angels could fly more or less at the speed of light, crossing the Earth in mere seconds if called or sent. They also could travel over the internet and Gondola occasionally used them as a hacking aid.

Angels obeyed the orders of those who had been given the power by God, which required a person of strong faith and a personal, spiritual, connection. The pope could order angels around, even the archangels.

So could the Faerie Queen. Whoever she or he was, they were a person of strong faith. That had surprised more than one atheist in the organization when she took over. But she didn't care if you were an atheist, as long as you were willing to give your time, brains, and energy to finding lost children and saving them.

It had also caused a few of them to rethink the whole "Believers are stupid" thing. Because the one thing *everyone* knew was that the Faerie Queen was brainiac beyond par. A few had even gotten religion. The Faerie Queen didn't care as long as you were willing to sacrifice your time and energy to protecting the world and children especially.

The prayers of children were the most powerful prayers there were. The Faerie Queen and Gondola had saved hundreds of thousands of children from traffickers. That built up a lot of God mojo.

The Faerie Queen could even command the archangels like Michael.

There were also demons of various powers. Somewhere on Earth, Lucifer lurked. He hadn't been condemned to Hell; he'd been condemned to live on Earth among the mud-monkeys he'd rebelled over. And wherever he was, he was always interfering, making the world worse because he *hated* humans.

Demons had been stripped of their wings. They couldn't cross the Earth at a thought. But they too could travel the internet and The Society often used them not so much for hacking but as a secondary firewall to warn if something was *being* hacked. They were tough to sneak around and if you brought in an angel, it set off an alarm.

Using *Angel* Michael—which had happened on occasion, he was always up for a fight—set off *all* the alarms. He was not the "sneak around" type. *Kid* Michael had been working with a team trying to sneak into a Society server when *Angel* Michael had shown up. If you understood what you were seeing you could see the presence as a mass of scrambled data packets. The demon they were sneaking past saw it as "Holy God fire! I'm out of here! It's *MONGO*! SANTA MARIA!"

Yeah, so much for sneaking. What part of "secret organization" did he not understand?

The Society and various other groups used demons for black magic and were used by them in turn. Demons would work with humans, but they eventually commanded the humans, not the other way around.

Witch doctors, sorcerers, were possessed.

Possession could only occur with a person who had lost their angel, been permanently and irrevocably damned, and who accepted the demon into their body. With that, they could use their demon, always a high-level one, to command other lower-level demons to do various things. Bringing down curses on their enemies was a big one. Demons could affect the brain at a quantum level. Cause depression to the point of suicide. Trigger people to commit crimes including, possibly, things like school shootings. Sorcerers could also use demons and their communications to find people who were hiding as in this case.

Thing was, demons, even Lucifer, were *nothing* compared to angels. Angels flew on the power of God, not to mention the prayers of the faithful. Lowly angels could defeat major demons. They couldn't destroy them, but their presence, still being connected to the God who had severed Himself from the demons, was painful.

Whenever a witch doctor moved against Gondola and was spotted, all it took was sending even a minor angel or host and the demon that possessed the sorcerer would pull out and run like a scalded cat.

The effect was very much like a stroke. Often the sorcerer died. At best, they were left in a permanent coma.

Sending the Archangel Michael, who was renowned for both *hating* demons and, shall we say, a somewhat heavy presence, was an effective death sentence for a Possessed. Scratch one witch doctor. By last count, that was, like, *fifty* just since Michael had started working with Gondola. Probably more. At one point, the Faerie Queen had wiped out most of a *village* of sorcerers.

Hey, they'd started it. They attacked one of the Faerie Queen's people, not even over being in the network, just a screwed-up stalker thing, Faerie Queen objected *strenuously*, they lost, fair's fair. Well, okay, sending archangels against demons was sort of kicking evil demonic puppies, but still. Don't piss off the Faerie Queen if you were a Possessed and weren't ready for your one-way trip to Hell, down elevator always working, no waiting.

The Society's remaining sorcerers had started to get the point.

Others were still in learning mode. The good guys weren't supposed to fight back! They were just supposed to turn the other cheek and lie down and take it and let Lord Satan take over the world! Using angels was no fair!

"*What's that thing about Vengeance is Mine Sayeth the Lord?*" The Society would whine.

"*I'm how He gets it,*" the Faerie Queen would reply.

There was a reason the Faerie Queen was thought of as a supernatural entity. She *was* one.

"The sighting may indicate that he's headed for the US soon," Titanium said. "He's probably waiting to find out what identity the marshals gave you."

"I'll be waiting," Michael said.

CHAPTER 15

"Strength of a Thousand Men" —Two Steps from Hell

"You're sure it's okay for us to be here?" Michael said as they entered Tim's apartment.

Tim's apartment was in a complex half a dozen blocks away. Michael had been walking home from school but had gotten permission to ride the bus with Tim. Just asking permission for something like that was sort of weird for him. Usually, his foster parents couldn't care less about his location.

"My mom was glad I was having a friend over," Tim said. "Though she insisted I had to get homework done. I gotta call her. She keeps a landline just so she can make sure I'm home when I call."

The apartment was clean but cluttered with knickknacks that were mostly Asian in nature. The exception to the unsurprising Asian motif was crosses. They were nearly as numerous as the Asian prints and ceramics.

"All clear," Tim said, hanging up the phone. "Though she might call at random to make sure I'm not out, you know, running with gangs or something."

"Notorious TB," Michael said, grinning. "The Terror of Brooklyn."

"That's me, man," Tim said, rocking back and forth and acting like he was holding a bling chain. "I be rappin' an' slappin'!"

"That shall be your nickname from now on," Michael said. "Notorious TB."

"So . . . wanna game?" Tim asked.

"Let us away to the game!" Michael said.

"You are *really* not good at this," Tim said as Michael fell to his death. Again. "You are *so* not good at this."

"I rarely got a chance where I was from," Michael said, shrugging.

"Where do kids *not* game?" Tim asked as Michael respawned and almost immediately was killed. It wasn't even by a spawn camper. He just went the wrong way and ran right into a crossfire.

"Where whenever you get a new toy, it gets stolen," Michael said. "Where everything in your apartment belongs to whoever can steal it. The only people who had gaming systems and could hold onto them were gang members and their families. And I didn't hang out with them. So, no experience. I'll learn. I'm actually better at the real thing. Though I'm not so good at ranged shooting. And I died again."

He tossed the controller on the coffee table and sighed.

"So, can you keep a secret?" Michael said, tugging his earlobe. "It's a real-world, this-shit-cannot-get-around secret."

"Sure," Tim said, distracted. He really was good at the game.

"I'll wait 'til you can concentrate," Michael said, picking up the controller again and reentering the game.

By the time Tim's mom got home, he'd gotten a tad better. He wasn't dying *all* the time.

Hoa Broome was a tiny little lady in her thirties. Michael had learned Tim's dad, who was older, had passed away of cancer.

"Mrs. Broome," Michael said, standing up and nodding. "Pleasure to meet you, I'm Mike Truesdale, you have a lovely home."

"Thank you, Mike," Mrs. Broome said, sitting her packages down. She'd stopped by the store. "Timothy, did you unload the dishwasher?"

"Uh, no?" Tim said, still locked into the game.

"I'll get it," Michael said, grinning. "He's sort of occupied."

"*Timothy!*" Mrs. Broome said sharply. "Your guest shouldn't be unloading the dishwasher!"

"Oh, right!" Tim said, hitting the PTT button. "Hey, gotta go! I'm out!"

Michael just went and started unloading dishes.

"Just tell me where they need to go," he said as Tim reached the kitchen. "I'll take high, you take low."

"That was sooo good," Michael said, holding his stomach.

Dinner had been Vietnamese beef-and-potato stir-fry. Michael had never had Vietnamese food. He was hooked. There had to be some vegan recipes and he intended to try them out as soon as he could take over cooking.

After dinner, they'd retreated to Tim's room. Tim's mom did not allow him to have a gaming console in his room so he wouldn't "play games all the time when he should be studying." And the computer in his room, complete with large flat screen, was deliberately too weak to use for modern gaming. Studying only.

His walls were adorned with a mix of anime, video game, and Vishnu posters. The shelves were loaded with resin-cast figures of the same and a few rows of graphic novels. The room was surprisingly squared away. Hoa Broome ran a tight ship.

"My mom's a good cook," Tim said, nodding and picking his teeth. He'd taken the computer chair, leaving Michael the bed to sit on.

"I can't have her always cooking for me," Michael said, tugging his earlobe. Mrs. Broome also believed in large portions for healthy growing boys. God bless her. "And I can't always hang out. I've just got too much on my plate."

"Tell me about it," Tim said. "Forget homework. Most days I've got after-school tutoring sessions."

"Yeah," Michael said. "I'll repeat, though, can you keep a real-world secret?"

"About your secret agent identity?" Tim asked, grinning.

"Seriously," Michael said. "Very seriously. Can you keep a real secret?"

"Yeah?" Tim said.

"Okay, here goes," Michael said, releasing his aura.

"Holy shit!" Tim said, his eyes going wide and whispering. "You're a *super*?"

"Yeah," Michael said. "Stone Tactical. Earther."

"Shit," Tim said, spinning around to his computer.

"You can't put that shit on *anything*!" Michael said. "Do *not* update your Facebook or something!"

"No shit, Mike," Tim said. "I'm just looking you up!"

"Oh," Michael said.

"Holy shit," Tim said, looking at the posting on the Super Corps website. "Stone Tactical. Love the costume. *Really* different."

"The Designer hates it," Michael said.

"So, who are the other Juniors?" Tim asked, spinning back from the screen. "Like, who's Fresh Breeze? Do you know her?"

"I haven't met them, yet," Michael said. "And I can't just give you their identities even if I had. That's their secret."

"This is so cool..." Tim said, then frowned. "Wait. That makes me the Eurasian sidekick! Shit, that guy is *always* getting his ass beat or killed or kidnapped or something."

"It should be fine," Michael said. "Though...I pissed off MS-13. They're trying to punch my clock. So, that's an issue."

"How'd you piss off MS-13?" Tim asked. "Not that that's hard to do."

"It started off as a beef at school with some wannabes," Michael said. "It escalated to me sort of punching the clock of a guy who was related to one of the OG leadership. So now he's got it in for me. Mike Truesdale isn't my real name. Marshals gave me a new identity. We'll see how long that holds."

"That is so messed up," Tim said. "Wait. You killed a guy?"

"Did you *see* the scars?" Michael said. "Wasn't the first. Not proud of it, but where I came from, which was *not* Schenectady, it wasn't that big of a deal. Bodies were dropping every day."

"Sounds like Crown Heights," Tim said, grimacing. "I guess that was why you weren't too scared of Evuala. Wait. Did you use superpowers on them 'cause they're going to talk!"

"Just a touch," Michael said. "Hardly at all. You get increased strength and speed from Acquiring. And it wasn't my first rodeo."

"This is so cool," Tim repeated. "As long as I don't get beat up or kidnapped or killed."

"We'll try to keep that from happening," Michael said. "Main thing is, don't talk about it."

"Yeah," Tim said, nodding furiously. "Like, no. Don't. So, human bulldozer, huh?"

"There's so much more to these powers," Michael said, shaking his head. "It's weird but Super Corps is *terrified* of anybody getting powerful, which is just bizarre. But there's *so* much to Earth Power. That's something else you can't talk about 'cause I *have* been training on them and you can do all sorts of things with them."

"Like what?" Tim asked.

"There's Earth Sight," Michael said. "It's like X-ray vision. You can see through walls and stuff. There's Earth Thermal, where you can heat and cool earth materials. And Stone Move . . . Watch this."

Michael had been sitting on the bed in a lotus and now lifted in the air.

"Cool," Tim whispered. "So, you can *fly*?"

"*Any* Earther can fly," Michael said. "Just grab your bones and do Earth Move. I don't know why they don't."

"Can you fly me around?" Tim asked.

"Sadly, no," Michael said. "It would kill the cells in your bones. We regenerate so they just come back so I can do it to myself. But . . . if it was important, I could make a cradle for you to sit on and fly you that way."

"That's . . . terrifying, come to think of it," Tim said. "I don't like heights. What else you got?"

"With Earth Sense you can sense certain types of chemicals, at least elements," Michael said. "I need to find a good chemistry store. There's probably one over by Brooklyn College. 'Cause I need to learn to sort out the elements in stone and soil."

"That's . . . okay," Tim said. "I understand what you said, just wasn't aware that was a possible thing."

"And I'm going to have to bone up on geology," Michael said. Tim winced at the unintentional pun. "So much to do, so little time. School is a total time sink. But I met people so there's that."

"I can handle being the sidekick," Tim said. "Just as long as I survive the experience."

"Dr. Pierce, good to hear from you!"

Colonel Jack Drew was the supervisor for the Serious Crimes Department of the Pennsylvania State Police. Serious Crimes was what was generally called "Major Crimes" in other departments. It handled serial killer cases, major drug investigations, and investigations of governmental corruption. It was the sort of job you got when you'd solved a bunch of those sorts of cases. And Dr. Pierce had been instrumental in solving more than one, including the Edmunson case. Finding the serial killer who had kidnapped the governor's daughter, *before* she was murdered, wasn't the only thing that had made his career, but it had locked it into stone.

"Good to see you again, Colonel," Dr. Pierce said over the video link. "Got a weird one for you."

"What's up?"

"I'll send you the full report, but I thought I should explain," Pierce said. "Do you remember the case of Annabelle Follett?"

"Oh, yeah," Drew said, twisting his shoulders. "Poor little rich girl gets killed by a serial killer in Philly? That was a PR nightmare. But that was solved."

"In case you missed it, there were always questions," Pierce said. "We just got some new, extremely advanced equipment. We can practically prize what a person had for their last meal out of a single cell with this stuff."

"That sounds fun," Drew said. "What's it got to do with Follett?"

"We needed some old samples to test it," Pierce said. "So, I contacted Philly ME to see if I could get some. Curious, I included in the request Follett. Solved, as you say. But I wanted to see what I could tease out of the samples about her last years. Just . . . curiosity."

"That kills the cat, Doctor," the colonel said. "I take it you found something off?"

"The entire case is off," Pierce said. "But the main thing, which is right in your lane, is that these are *not* the samples of Annabelle Follett."

"Mistake in filing?" Drew said.

"No," Pierce said. "These are the samples of Nataliya Komarova, missing person from Lugansk, Russia."

"Autopsy samples?" Drew said.

"And the tests we ran show that she was definitely dead before they were taken. Fortunately, given that they included liver and brain."

"So . . . the autopsy samples for a poor little rich girl killed by a serial killer are actually the tissues of a missing person from Russia?" Drew said carefully.

"More than that," Pierce said. "A missing person from Russia who had no trace of regular opiate use, though she regularly used cocaine and probably Ecstasy. Annabelle Follett struggled with opiate addiction.

"Further, while Nataliya Komarova was raised in Lugansk, unquestionably, she had been in the US for at least a year prior to her death, ninety percent chance it was somewhere in the New York area.

"Prior to her death, Nataliya was drinking alcohol, probably vodka, probably Grey Goose, and she had traces of Rohypnol in her system. And the Rohypnol was from a batch that was circulating in the New York area around the time of Annabelle Follett's death. Oh, she was also pregnant at the time of her death."

"Conclusion," the colonel said. "Someone killed a Russian Mob prostitute and substituted her tissue samples for Annabelle Follett."

"Someone in *New York*," Pierce said. "Or at least from that area, given the Rohypnol was from the New York City area. Also, there are now *no* known samples of Annabelle Follett. So, the samples in Philadelphia have been tampered with. Which would seem to be in your lane."

"That *is* in my lane," Drew said carefully. "You said the case was all wrong?"

"Forget that while confessing to killing forty-two women, Rick Albritton denied killing Annabelle Follett," Pierce said. "Albritton had a very specific signature: rape in missionary position with manual strangulation and the hands unbound. He specifically stated that he enjoyed the sensation of being scratched by his victims.

"Annabelle Follett's body had ligature marks on the neck and on the wrists. Her hands were bound behind her back during sex, and she was strangled with a cord—probably clothesline in both cases. The rapist used a condom, Albritton did not."

"How did the ME miss that?" Drew asked.

"How did the lead detective?" Pierce asked.

"I think we should probably ask them those questions," the colonel said.

"Any good at séances?"

"Surviving the Game" —Skillet

"Michael," his teacher said as they were taking a quiz on his issued tablet. "There's a message from administration that you need to contact your after-school program. You can go out in the hall and use your phone when you're done with the quiz."

"Done," Michael said, hitting the button to turn it in.

He stepped out in the hall and called Super Corps headquarters.

"Mike, it's Miri. We got a delivery from the marshals."

"Is it a phone?" Michael asked.

Deal with it later.

"Yes," she said. "Michael . . . Mike, did Miss Cherise die?"

"Yes," Michael said.

"When?"

"Week or so after I gots here," Michael said.

Keep your voice steady. Deal with it later.

"You didn't say anything about it," Miri said.

"No," Michael said. "It was probably '13 and I'll deal with that eventually."

"I'm so sorry to hear that," Miri said. "I know she was . . . pretty much all you had in the way of family. This has to be hard. How are you doing?"

Michael wondered how to explain.

"Miri," he said after some thought, "Mama was a drug addict who made her living in prostitution, which is one of the more dangerous professions around. That Mama made it *this* long is the surprising part. You ever lost someone? Parent or relative? Hopefully not a child."

"No children," Miri said. "Both of my parents passed away."

"You know how you get really tired of people saying, 'I'm so sorry'?" Michael said. "It's not to dig on you for saying it. But after the third or fourth time you don't want to hear it anymore.

"People used to die all the time in Baltimore. I went to so many funerals I can't count. And when I had some people go, I figured that out. I was at this one funeral; this lady had lost her daughter. Not a bad gal. Wasn't hangin' with the bangers. Just caught in the cross fire.

"There we were at the church, all lined up, giving her our condolences. I got up to her and I said, 'You getting tired of people saying "I'm sorry"? I won't. You know it already and you're tired of hearing it.' She just looked at me and grabbed me and gave me a hug.

"They know you're sorry or you wouldn't be there," Michael finished. "Just give them a hug and move on."

"Words of wisdom from a child," Miri said. "I'll remember that the next funeral I attend."

"I'm not sure how I can even *get* the phone," Michael said.

"I'll have Alexander bring it over."

"Thank you. And you take care. Don't let Tony break any more desks."

"That no one can do."

"Bye."

"Hey, Alexander," Michael said, sitting in the principal's office. He'd been called up to receive the package since Alexander couldn't just wander around the school.

"Here you go," Alexander said, sitting down. "I didn't know Miss Cherise died. Did you?"

"Got the word at the hospital," Michael said, tugging his earlobe. "Remember when I was getting my checkup and I stepped outside to take a call?"

"I remember," Alexander said. "I'm so sorry, Ja . . . Mike. According to Baltimore PD it wasn't valuable as evidence, and they couldn't open it anyway."

"Yeah," Michael said, turning it over and over in his hands. It was a cheap, old, black Samsung with a broken screen and bedazzling. Which was pretty much a metaphor for Mama. "She always wanted to be a torch singer in a gay revue. I used to joke that she should ride out on the *Smokey and the Bandit* car 'cause it was a black Trans American. Thanks for coming all the way over here to bring this. I appreciate it."

"You going to be okay?" Alexander asked.

"Win some, lose some," Michael said. "It all evens out in the end."

Michael waved off on Tim again. He felt like shit for doing so and Tim got that kicked-puppy look. But he had his own crosses to bear.

When he got home, he just went to his room and pulled out Mama's phone.

He was curious why Mama had somehow arranged for him to get it. That was foresight unlike her. And why she was so *insistent* he get it.

The phone used the same cable as his and he knew the open code. It was still partially charged so he entered 2-2-2-2 and started searching in it.

Mama was not tech savvy. Mama could barely read. One of the reasons he had her code was that she always needed help with her phone. So, if she'd left something on it for him it would be somewhere obvious.

There was nothing obvious. So, why'd she insist he get it? Just a memory?

Memory, all alone in the moonlight . . .

Mama had loved *Cats*. Guess who her favorite character was? It wasn't Bustopher Jones.

He looked at all the pictures and videos. There were more of him than he'd remembered being taken. Pictures of Mama with her friends. Pictures of Mama in her younger days at parties.

Memories of days in the sun.

Then he hit one he'd seen before. It was the picture of Annabelle Follett from the formal dinner at the Fort Myer Officers Club with his biological father, Derrick Sterrenhunt.

What the hell was *Mama* doing with that picture?

He instantly realized that that meant Mama had known his biological mother. Which meant it was probably a lie that he was "found in an alleyway."

He logged into one of his hacked servers and pulled down some tools. Then he started *really* searching the phone.

The SIM had been recopied several times. Mama had had five phones with the same number, photos, and contacts list.

And embedded deep in the contacts list was a hidden directory. Well hidden. It would take an expert to find it.

Fortunately, he was an expert.

The directory was password protected and high-level encryption. What the hell was a high-level-encrypted hidden directory doing on Mama's phone? That was Gondola shit, not trans street ho.

He pulled up a password cracker and, on a hunch, put in all his names as well as birth date.

The password was exactly that: MichaelJasonEdwards070512.

Inside there was just a text string. A cryptic message:

Beware the Nine. The One is where you were born. Keep it secret, keep it safe. Do not trust the authorities.

"Big boys don't cry," Michael said, taking a deep breath.

Mama hadn't just *found* him. Not with *that* message. Mama had never read the Lord of the Rings and Michael doubted she had seen the movies.

Annabelle Follett had been a nerd. Her Facebook page, which was still up, was full of comments from her "friends" about what a nerd she was. She was into Harry Potter and *Lord of the Rings*. Started reading them at seven. The Eowyn costume had been a Christmas gift from her otherwise estranged Italian father.

Michael was reading a message from his dead mother, meant for him.

Every year on his birthday, Mama had taken him to where she'd "found" him, a squalid alleyway off Port Street.

"Don't you blame your mama," she'd say. *"You never know what people dealin' with on the street."*

Michael had resented it every time. His whore mother had left him in an alleyway. That ended up leaving him to rot in the ghetto. Why was he supposed to care about someone who'd done *that*?

Now he knew. Now he understood. Annabelle Follett had left him there to *hide* him and left the only person she felt she could trust, a tough street ho who could never have a child herself, to protect him.

Six months later, she was dead.

The rage just consumed him.

He poured his Earth power into the soil beneath the house, keeping as much control as he could, alternating heat and cold until he couldn't stand it anymore, then pressing on it so hard, he could feel the grains of soil fracturing into dust.

He wanted to tear down the house, the neighborhood. He wanted to rend and tear and destroy everyone and everything.

Control, he thought. *Keep control. Lock it down.*

"Somebody..." he whispered to the empty room, "is gonna fuckin' pay."

Deal with it later.

CHAPTER 16

Special Agent Joshua Hinkle, Southern District of New York Field
Office, FBI, pulled a half-eaten container of kung pao chicken out of
his refrigerator and gave it a sniff. No mold, good enough.

As he put it in the microwave, his phone buzzed with a call.

He slumped and groaned. Not the office. Please. He just needed
one night.

But he picked it up and looked at it because . . . you did.

Oh, shit. Even worse.

The number was a series of ones and zeros. That meant . . . them.

He knew even talking to *whoever* these people were was probably
a federal offense. And the agreement to not even mention that he'd
talked to them, while he'd held to it, was against regulation.
Technically, he should have written up a 302 at least. One of these days,
that was likely to get him fired.

On the other hand, he was so tired of the bullshit . . . At least if it
didn't end up with him in prison, he was good.

And they always had good intel.

He pressed the accept button.

"Special Agent, sorry to bother you," the distorted voice said.
"You've got to be worn out."

"Get to it," Hinkle said, watching the package spin around in the
microwave.

"Tomorrow your office is going to have a new assignment," Omega
said. "It's a shit detail. Nobody will want it. *You* won't want it.
Reluctantly take it."

"Why?" Hinkle asked as the microwave dinged. He pulled the kung pao out and looked around for a clean fork.

"Do you want to catch a serial killer?" Omega asked.

"Do I have to look at the crime-scene photos?"

"You already have," Omega said. "It's the Orchard Beach Killer."

"You pique my interest," Hinkle said, stirring the kung pao.

"The assignment is an old case from Pennsylvania that has resurfaced..."

"We have an issue," Eric Bear said, walking into Conn's office and sitting down without being asked.

Eric Bear was fifty-five, bald, a burly five foot nine and two hundred fifty pounds. Some of that was fat. Most of it looked to be muscle going back to his time in Navy Special Warfare.

"And the issue is?" Wesley Conn said.

"The Annabelle Follett case has been reopened," Bear said.

Wesley Conn, also fifty, was handsome and fit, medium build, six foot two, a hundred ninety-five pounds, with dark, nearly black, eyes and black hair with a touch of gray.

The corner office overlooking the Hudson River was meticulously designed and appointed to impress even the most jaded tastes, with soft lighting, antique furniture, and paneled walls adorned with original oil paintings. There was an original Louise Bourgeois in the corner by the window as well as other modernist and postmodernist sculptures.

"That is an issue," Conn said, leaning back in his chair and steepling his fingers. "Why?"

"A pathology lab was testing out some equipment and wanted some old tissue samples to do the tests," Bear said. "Turns out the Russian chick was in Russia's missing persons database. Those didn't *used* to be connected to the US database. Things change."

"Yes," Conn said, pursing his lips. "What's our exposure?"

"It doesn't look good," Bear said. "But there's nothing legally to bring it back to us. Nothing that will stand up in court. We should have just disappeared the body."

"So, you said at the time," Conn said. "But if there is an heir, we needed to prevent DNA confirmation. Water under the dam. If there are questions, you handle them."

"Will do," Bear said, getting up.

"If this does come back on us, arrangements will be made," Conn said. "And they will not be terminal. You're far too useful to the organization."

"God is building an army," Titanium said.

"God has an army," Michael replied. He was making the call after school from his bedroom. "You probably saw the update on Annabelle Follett. But if you didn't pick it up in monitoring, she left me something in Baltimore. It may be the packet she was offering to the FBI."

"We saw that," Titanium said. "We were waiting for your response. Faerie Queen says this is your inheritance. As long as it stays in certain bounds, how you handle it is up to you."

"Can I get some support?" Michael asked. "I believe it's in keeping with the needs of Gondola, but that decision is above my pay grade. If I disappear, the first place they're going to look is Baltimore. But the location is difficult to describe perfectly: it's in an unsecure area law-wise and there's nobody I can trust to do the pickup. Also, they're going to need to search for it. Whatever 'it' is."

"I'll kick it up the chain," Titanium said. "Do you authorize us to do the pickup? Again, Faerie Queen was clear this is your mother, your life, your inheritance. But it is in line with our operations."

"I authorize that," Michael said. "I'd like to see it myself, obviously. It was a message from my mother to me."

"Guaranteed you get it," Titanium said. "I'll send it up the chain."

"Mr. Bear," Hinkle said, shaking the security chief's hand. "Thank you for your time."

"Anything I can do to help," Bear said, walking back behind his simple glass desk. His office was more generically furnished than Conn's, as Eric was more interested in getting things done than finding the perfect statue for the corner. "They've reopened Annabelle's case? I thought that bastard Albritton was good for it?"

"A new wrinkle has come up," Hinkle said, sitting in the provided chair. His partner, Richard Starr, took the opposite chair and stayed quiet per the plan. "Since there was never a conviction, Annabelle's case remains an open case. Cold case, but still open. So, all the samples were kept. There was a forensic lab doing routine testing, needed some old samples to test their equipment. They tested Annabelle's autopsy samples, and they turned out *not* to be Annabelle's."

"How'd they know that?" Bear asked, leaning back and interlacing his fingers on his stomach.

"Well, there's a lot of things they can do with forensics these days," Hinkle said. "But it was as simple as the DNA was of a missing person from Russia: Nataliya Komarova."

"Who?" Bear asked, looking confused.

"Nataliya Komarova," Hinkle repeated. "Citizen of Russia. Last seen in the Lugansk region. Now believed to have been an undocumented migrant to the US."

"So...mix-up in Philly?" Bear asked. "What's some Russian hooker's samples doing in Annabelle's place?"

"That's what's got us puzzled," Hinkle said. "I want to just say, straight out, we're here for information. Follett Trust is in no way a subject of interest. Because the whole thing revolves around the death of Annabelle Follett, and why the *heck* would you kill your beneficiary? Right?"

"Yeah, definitely," Bear said with a sigh. "We barely passed the probate of Dela's will. Without Dela and Annabelle we're sort of a trust fund without a beneficiary. But we're still here."

"Why?" Hinkle said. "Trusts dissolve with the death of the last beneficiary."

"The heir," Bear said, shrugging. "Dela was fixated on there being an heir. She had in her will that the Trust is to remain solvent for fifty years in search of Annabelle's kid. There's not one. We've checked and checked. Annabelle *was* pregnant but had an abortion in Richmond. We were looking for her, to get her back, to talk to her. We got the hit on the abortion, but she'd skipped by then."

"What was she running from?" Hinkle said. "Any idea?"

"Wish I knew," Bear said, his face working. "Herself? Anna was my trust. I was her bodyguard when she was a kid. When she died, it was *my* failure. I'd known her since she was eight. Saw her grow up. Cute girl. Loved horses. Loved 'em. Then, she just *changed*. Hormones. Whatever. She wasn't that little girl anymore. She was constantly running away. I dragged her out of some of the worst flophouses you can imagine. She just wanted to live on the streets. Who wants that?"

⊕ ⊕ ⊕

"That fucker killed his protectee," Starr said as they walked to their car.

Richard Starr was new to the job and starting to wonder if he'd made a mistake. Being assigned to New York was considered a plum assignment. But he wasn't as sure about being assigned to Hinkle. His partner essentially had no career. Some big cases solved but no progression at all. When Starr had asked him about that he'd just grunted something about "politics."

"Certainly, killed Nataliya Komarova," Hinkle agreed.

"Russian hooker," Starr said. "You never said anything about prostitution."

"Could be an assumption," Hinkle said. "He's the type to assume any Russian female who is an undocumented migrant is a prostitute. Notice he used the old term. He's nineties. Notice his I-Love-Me wall?"

"Sort of," Starr said.

"Shadow box," Hinkle said. "Bunch of fruit salad. Lists in his bio that he was Navy Special Warfare. No Trident in his shadow box. Why?"

"I'm not even sure what you're talking about," Starr admitted.

"Which part?"

"Trident."

"Trident is the badge awarded for passing SEAL BUD/S," Hinkle said. Training was part of the job. "Like wings for airborne or a Ranger tab. He was a SEAL. So, where's his Trident?"

"Lost it?" Starr said. "Left it out?"

"Nobody leaves their Trident out and I doubt they'd lose one," Hinkle said. "Back to the office. Something about this is bugging me."

"Come 'ere," Hinkle said, gesturing to Starr.

He led him into one of the conference rooms where files were laid out on the table.

"Okay," he said, opening one up and throwing down a photo. "Nataliya Komarova. Describe and note the physiology."

"Fine boned," Starr said. "Thin, light sandy blond hair. Aquiline face. Small breasted. Small bodied. Thin. Not sure what I'm looking for or why."

"Good enough," Hinkle said, opening another file and tossing down another photo.

"Annabelle Follett," Starr said. "Similar look, similar physiology. So...Kill Nataliya for her autopsy samples. Probably they think the physiology will mean the DNA matches? We already were there. What I'm still wondering is why."

"The heir," Hinkle said. "It's one point six billion dollars just sitting there. Kid turns up with a shyster lawyer saying, 'I'm the heir,' what do you do?"

"Check the DNA," Starr said, nodding. "Even if the real heir turns up, the DNA doesn't match, they keep the money. It's just...he's good for it, but we don't have a body, we don't have anything but some tissue samples."

"Maybe," Hinkle said, opening up another file and tossing down a crime-scene photo of Annabelle Follett. "Note everything."

"Got it," Starr said confidently.

Hinkle flipped it over.

"How was she killed?" Hinkle asked.

"Ligature marks on her throat indicate strangling," Starr said. "Where are we going with this."

Hinkle flipped it back over.

"Look at it close," he said, pulling out other photos of the Annabelle crime scene. "Note the signature."

"Okay," Starr said, looking them over. "Got it. Ligature on the wrists and throat. Sexually assaulted face up. Limited bruising. No stab wounds. No major defensive wounds. No disfigurement of the corpse. Again...?"

Hinkle pulled open another file and threw down a photo between the photos of Annabelle Follett and Nataliya Komarova.

"Tell me who that is," Hinkle said.

Starr picked it up, looking puzzled, and compared it to the other photos.

"I thought it might be Komarova," he said. "But it's not either of them."

"*That* is Jaqueline Skelton," Hinkle said. "Victim One of the Orchard Beach Killer. So called because her body was found near Orchard Beach, in the Bronx. Arrests for prostitution and drugs. Killer never found."

He kept throwing down photos.

"Jaqueline Skelton, Mary Claire Bellinger, Helen Pieve, Tammie Darden, Celeste Brown," Hinkle said. "All victims of the Orchard Beach Killer based on profile and signature. Part of the listed signature *is* the physiology."

"All of them could be sisters," Starr said.

"Sisters of Nataliya Komarova and Annabelle Follett," Hinkle said. "When I was working the case, something kept bugging me about their look. Yeah, all alike. But sometimes serial killers have a particular taste. They won't kill just anyone. But there was something else. Now I know: They all reminded my back brain of when Annabelle Follett's body turned up in Philly because the Follett case was fresh when Jaqueline Skelton turned up here."

"So . . ." Starr said. "Bear?"

"I think that SOB got triggered by either Komarova or Annabelle," Hinkle said. "Probably Annabelle. Think about it. You've got the hots for your protectee, and you've got a rapist mentality. The fantasies build up. Then, for some damned reason, you track her down and kill her. You're trying to make it look like a serial killer that's been working the area. All you know is he rapes and strangles street prostitutes. You've tracked her down. Maybe he just lost control or something. But he kills her, and the beast is free."

"And he keeps killing," Starr said. "Annabelle Follett is kill zero."

"Yep," Hinkle said.

"Prove it," Starr said.

"For Tammie Darden and Celeste Brown, we have DNA for the killer," Hinkle said. "Never turned up in any database. Care to go dumpster diving?"

CHAPTER 17

"Legends Never Die" —Against the Current

Getting to Super Corps headquarters wasn't the most direct thing in the world.

To "preserve the secret identity" of supers, you didn't just walk in the front door of the Jacob K. Javits Federal Building.

To deal with the fosters, Alexander had set up a fake account with the "Foster's Outreach Program," a real program that took New York area foster children out for special events. It had good intentions but was just as corrupt as any other foster program. But for Michael, it made for a good cover with the foster parents. They still expected him to text, and were probably tracking his phone, but it gave a good reason for the locations he visited.

Michael had to get to the area through a long train ride with numerous changes. Though the directions for the subway directed him to use the Chambers Street station, he preferred to use City Hall for the "secret entrance." From the City Hall station, it was a short walk up Broadway to 291. Enter the 291 building—its only name as far as Michael knew—show your ID to the "security officer," who was an undercover federal marshal, go to the *third* elevator, very important, insert your CAC card, summon the elevator, insert CAC card again, press the B button and, straight out of a movie, hold it down.

The elevator then went to a dirty and disused lobby area in the sub-subbasement that led to a security door. Insert CAC, type in PIN, open door. Short corridor to the steam tunnels that went everywhere under New York City. First turn to the left, fifty paces to a door with a FEDERAL FACILITY – PENALTY FOR UNLAWFUL ENTRY FIVE YEARS sign and a camera. Insert card, wave at camera, enter PIN. Door opened inward to a mantrap. Insert card, wave at camera again, open second mantrap door. Wave at federal marshal, show ID, get waved past to the elevator. Insert CAC card, summon elevator, get in elevator, insert CAC, press 16, remove CAC, ascend to 16, wave at marshal, show ID, insert CAC, enter PIN, go through security door, and you were *finally* in the freaking lobby.

From Gondola, Michael knew the security protocols for getting into the National Security Agency. They were *far* less stringent. This was like getting into the Federal Freaking Reserve.

Before Michael walked into his first patrol meeting, he pulled out his phone, opened an app, and started it. Then he locked the screen and walked into Super Corps headquarters.

"Well, here we all are!"

Madeleine Cromarty was six one or so, had brown hair pulled up with a bow, wore a red dress that did *not* suit her complexion, and was hefty for a super. She spoke in a singsong falsetto that was already getting on Michael's nerves.

He was meeting his team for the first time in the main lobby of Super Corps. Sasha was there as well. She patrolled with an adult since there were no other junior Flyers. He made sure to avert his eyes lest he be turned to stone. That was the only reason. It had nothing to do with embarrassment over his nerdgasm.

"This is Mike Truesdale," Electrobolt said, putting her hand on the back of Michael's shoulder and stroking it lightly. "Earther. He's taken the super name Stone Tactical. So, I'd like you all to welcome Stone Tactical!"

"Hey..." "Hi, Mike..."

"So, this is Josh, the team lead," Bolt said, gesturing to a tall, blond male in preppy wear. Michael estimated about seventeen, which made sense since the team lead was probably the oldest, and at eighteen you joined the grown-ups.

"Metalstorm," Josh said.

"Cool," Michael replied, nodding.

"And *this* is Jorge," Bolt added, gesturing to an unusually short, bulky Hispanic male, still stroking Michael's shoulder.

"Hombre de Poder," Jorge said. He looked closer to fifteen or so. "It means Power Man."

"*Comprende*," Michael said. "*Yo habla Espanol. Es un buen nombre. Te conviene.*"

Understood. I speak Spanish. It's a good name. It suits you.

Though "Power Dwarf" might be a better choice.

"And these are Laura and Sasha," Bolt finished, quickly, gesturing dismissively to the two girls.

Laura was short, maybe five two, with brown hair. At least sixteen, but probably seventeen. Like all supers, she was extremely good-looking. In any normal crowd she'd be considered the hotty to end hotties.

She was standing next to Sasha. She didn't stand a chance.

"Fresh Breeze," Laura said, waving a hand but only giving him the briefest of glances.

"We've met," Sasha said, furrowing her brow. "*Mike.*"

Electrobolt turned so both her hands were on Michael's shoulder and looked down at him.

It was an extremely uncomfortable position. Michael's natural reflex was to slap the hands away. He restrained himself.

"Mike, I'm sure that you're going to get along with everyone extremely well," Electrobolt said, her hands more or less massaging Michael's shoulders.

"Thank you, ma'am," Michael said, steepling his fingers. "But with due respect, ma'am, I am not a tactile person. I would really appreciate you removing your hands. Ma'am."

"Well, I'm just being friendly," Bolt said, her eyes going hard.

"I understand that, ma'am," Michael said. "And I do appreciate the friendly greeting. But I really am not a tactile person. I would, again, appreciate you removing your hands, ma'am."

"Alright," Bolt said snippily. "Well, I suppose it's time to get it on! Off on another patrol! So fun!"

The locker room was, indeed, coed. The only concession to privacy was that the girls' lockers and the boys' were on opposite sides of the room. They shared the same bench but were far enough spaced they weren't in direct contact.

In the range of locker rooms, this was closer to the expensive spa end than a school gym locker or the police lockers he'd seen on TV that he'd expected.

"It's kinda ..." Jorge said, gesturing with his hand toward the girls. "You don' look, okay?"

"Wasn't plannin' on it," Michael said.

Electrobolt had followed them into the locker room and moved down to Michael's end, smiling.

"Do you need any help with anything?" Bolt said, back to being cheery.

I figured out how to put on and take off clothing way back when I was three, honestly.

"I think I'm okay," Michael said. Great. He had to get undressed with a pedo standing right there watching. He didn't have an issue with being eye candy. But the hungry look was sort of off-putting.

If it's to be done, best it be done quickly.

He decided to get out the major items of his costume, first.

Tactical pants, check. Wicking shirt, check. That should do it. Take off your tactical boots, first. Then ...

He pulled off his shirt, then his pants, quickly, and threw them in the locker.

"Oh, my God!" Bolt said, slapping a hand over her mouth.

"What?" Jorge asked, then paused. "Jesus, man, what *happened* to you?"

"Growing up in a ghetto happened to me," Michael said, slipping on the tactical pants.

In Sight he could see that Sasha and Laura had both turned around at the exclamation. As he pulled on his Nike Dri-FIT, they turned back. But Sasha still turned around a couple more times.

Ladies dig scars. Nerd or not, we shall wed and have many children.

"You poor baby," Bolt said, walking over and putting her hand on Michael's back again. She started stroking his back. "That must have been so terrible."

"If what don't kill you makes you stronger, I be *diamond*, ma'am," Michael said, bending over to pick up his boots and put them on. "And I will, again, request that you refrain from physical contact. I am not a touchy person in that way."

"It must be so tough for you," Bolt said, still not removing her hand.

"Being in a new town and all. Especially in foster care. You've got no one you know..."

Wow, groom much?

"I'm not really into knowing people, to be honest," Michael said, pulling out his body armor. The day was cool, so he left off the Maxx-Dri Vest. Just the wicking shirt should do. "I'm sort of a loner. Being on a team is the new thing for me."

"So, you really don't have *anyone*?" Bolt said, ruffling Michael's hair. "That's so *sad*. If you need a friend, I'm *always* available, night or day."

Michael transferred his phone from where he'd set it to the pouch on the armor. Then he attached an earpiece and battery.

"What I *need* is for you to remove your *hand*, ma'am," Michael said, pulling out his helmet and tactical gloves.

"I'm just being friendly," Bolt said sharply.

Michael put on his helmet with the front up, stood up, and looked Bolt in the eye as he put on his gloves.

"Do I look like the friendly *type*?" Michael asked, tightening his wrist straps.

"What kind of a costume is *that*?" Josh asked. His own—Metalstorm—was in gold and black, nearly full coverage with short sleeves and gold-and-black elbow-length gloves. His full-face mask was in the winged hussar mode with swept-up winglike protrusions on either side. They looked a bit like oversized ears and Michael wasn't sure where Kevin was going with that.

"The kind that suits my personality," Michael replied.

"I'm surprised the Secretary was okay with it," Bolt said snippily. But she was at least keeping her hands off.

Fresh Breeze's costume was in green and yellow, skintight complete coverage with the exception of a deeply scooped neckline that he suspected she'd had to wheedle out of Kevin. She, too, had long gloves in contrasting yellow and green. It could have used a short skirt or something. The *very* thin material of the costume was more revealing than a leotard and it was apparent she wore absolutely *nothing* under it. She sported an opera-style mask that went up on her brow and down onto her cheeks but didn't really disguise her very well.

"She *wasn't*," Michael replied. "She got over it. Besides, the helmet is totally cool! It's like something out of *Halo*!" He pointed at Jorge. "You can call me...Master Chief!"

"Mastur*bator* in Chief," Jorge said, grinning. His Power Man costume was a muscle shirt in primary blue with red accents and red thigh-length wrestling shorts with blue accents. It had an accompanying Mexican wrestler's mask with tiny mouth and nose openings.

"Jorge," Bolt said warningly. "That's not nice."

"It's okay," Michael said. "I'm not a nice guy, either."

Ivory Wing's electric-blue-and-green costume was heavier material to withstand the pressures of flying and very full coverage going up to the hairline. No scoop neck for a Flyer, damnit. She had a helmet that he knew contained a full communications and navigation array that connected to her solid-plastic streamlined backpack. She wore a controller device on her left arm that connected to the array through Bluetooth that was used for changing frequencies and modifying the heads-up display.

The green highlights on the suit matched her eyes. Kevin had at least noticed the eyes.

"We should probably head to transport," Josh said.

"You're patrolling Central Park," Electrobolt said. "You're to start at the Boathouse and patrol the south side. There are reports of drug dealing near the Pond, especially after dark. So be careful out there! Well . . . ? Get to it!"

"Wow," Michael said as they left the locker room and, fortunately, Electrobolt. "That was the most thorough briefing of all time."

"What did you expect?" Josh asked.

"Oh, I dunno," Michael said, tapping his fingers together. "Some intel on *who* is doing the drug dealing? BOLOs? Gang activity? Incident patterns? Poh-leese stuff."

"We don't do that stuff," Jorge said. "We just walk around the park and get our picture taken. We're a tourist attraction."

Michael had seen a male Flyer come in to the landing and move to the lobby in Sight. When they got there, he was waiting.

"Hey, Sash," the Flyer said.

"Hi, Patrick," Sasha said.

There was something in her voice that made Michael want to do an aura check with Patrick. Or possibly feed him a lethal dose of fentanyl.

Rival! Rival! Must kill! Kill! KILL!

Oh, calm down. He's, like, her dad's age!

Women like older men.

Rival! Rival! Must kill! Kill! KILL!

"Ready to fly?" Patrick asked. By his costume he was Iron Eagle, one of the middle range of the Corps. That would be Patrick Thesz, not that they were going to be introduced.

"Let's kick the tires and light the fires!" Sasha said, taking off and heading to the flight entrance.

"How will we *ever* survive without our Tinkerbell *betters* to light the way?" Michael said as soon as they'd cleared the exit.

Must . . . Kill . . . Rival . . . !

"We get along fine without them," Josh said.

You must *be gay.*

"No, seriously," Michael said as they got on the elevator. "If we're looking for drug dealers at night, they can light up the old aura and we'll have some overhead light to make things easier, right?"

Jorge at least got the joke and chuckled. Josh just looked confused.

"Oh, my God!" Fresh Breeze said. She was checking her phone. "There's already, like, *fifty* people waiting at the Park!"

"Wait," Michael said. "They know where we get dropped off?"

Despite Michael's considerable paranoia, he'd still underestimated just how horrible the security situation was going to be.

Do they want us all to get killed? Don't answer that.

Speaking of phones, he opened his up and turned off the recording app. He had enough on it already. And it wasn't about the team, it was about Bolt.

Besides, it was probably pointless. Gondola was going to be listening in anyway.

"Of course, Mike," Josh said. "It's on the website. Why?"

"Oh, no reason," Michael said.

Just a guy named El Cannibale that wants to cannibalize me. No worries. He's probably still in El Salvador.

They took the regular elevator down to the parking garage and boarded a windowless van.

Michael was glad he had Sight so he could at least see where they were going. He was still fairly unfamiliar with the city, but he could at least count the wide gaps between large structures to know how many blocks they'd traveled.

"So, anyone wanna take bets on what the Storm's gonna be?" Michael asked, lifting his mask. He caught a few glances, but no one spoke. Laura turned slightly toward him, frowned, and dove into her phone. "Me, I hope it's sort of like *A Quiet Place*."

Jorge shot him a questioning look while the others ignored him.

"Wouldn't be a big deal if that's what it was. There were fifteen million hunting licenses issued in the US in 2020, a year when Covid was ravaging our sanity, and every *one* of the people who got issued one could kill at least a *dozen* of those idiotic creatures. From out-of-hearing range. Using a rifle.

"Except Earl. Earl can't hit shit, I don't care what he says when he's liquored up."

The van had still been meandering around a side street, but finally turned onto a much wider street to head northbound.

"There is *no* season, there's no limit, they taste like chicken, and they killed Dale Earnhardt! Hell, they were legal to *snare*! They would not last a *split second* anywhere in the rural areas of this country except on a *spit*. Dragon barbeque would be the hot new ragin' in Cajun.

"Blind bird-dragon thingies? Blind? So, you can see *them* at a distance, and they don't even know you're *there*? Are you fucking *kidding* me? Hell, in places like the Serengeti the lions would be eating *well*. 'But the bird-dragon whatsits would eat the poor gazelles and g-nu ... gn ... wildebeest!' Really? Did you see how *slow* they move? They were eating people 'cause they couldn't catch a possum!"

Nothing. It was a tough crowd. Since the ice breaker didn't work, he decided to be more direct.

"Anyway, I know, like, zero about any of you," Michael said. "First off on me: the marshals changed my identity 'cause some bad people want to put me in the ground."

"We heard about that," Josh said, very matter-of-fact. He'd also taken off his mask for the ride. "MS-13."

"They tried to kill me, I objected strenuously, they lost, fair's fair," Michael said. "But they don't feel the same way so ... turning up where people know I'm going to be there is *not* my idea of kicks. I know all of you are older than I am and you've got all this experience ... If something bad goes down, let *me* handle it. Not my first rodeo and there's a reason I chose this costume."

Reactions were mixed. Laura was glued to her phone and didn't seem to realize he was talking. Josh narrowed his eyes and nodded once but primarily fought hard to maintain a manly leader persona. Jorge listened intently, with numerous nods of approval.

"About Mike Truesdale: I'm a foster kid, raised in the ghetto, don't know who my mother or father are, currently living in one of the decent sections of Brooklyn for as long as that lasts. Foster care is musical beds. I'm into rock and roll, heavy metal, and alternative with some EDM. Just found out I'm part Lakota Sioux, which is cool. Recently gotten into yoga and like to work out. Metalstorm. What's up with you?"

"Well, nobody's trying to kill me that I know of," Josh said. "Not sure what . . ."

"You from here?" Michael asked, tapping his fingers together.

"No," Josh said. "Chicago, though."

"What's your mom and dad do?"

The van came to a hard stop adjacent to a small, corner park. A couple other cars honked.

"Dad's an attorney, mom's in marketing," Josh said.

"If you're trying to figure out class," Jorge said. "He's Hamptons."

"Ah," Michael said, nodding. "Hamptons I know."

"I don't *live* in the Hamptons . . ." Josh said.

"They've got a weekend house there," Jorge said. "My dad mows their lawn."

"Does he literally . . . ?" Michael asked.

The van crawled for a bit, sped forward through a major intersection, then returned to a crawl.

"No," Jorge said. "But that's what my dad does. My mom's a maid."

"That's cool," Michael said. "Lawns need mowing. Houses need cleaning. It's a job. What about you, Laura? Your mom a maid?"

"No," Laura said, snappishly and without looking up. "She works in marketing, too!"

"Cool," Michael said. "Dad?"

"My dad's sort of . . ." Laura said, shrugging. "They're divorced. He stayed in Cleveland."

"Which tells me where you're from," Michael said, nodding. "How's that work, anyway? When you get transferred with family? Josh, your dad was working in Chicago? Change law firms?"

They passed by a large church on their left. NYC had so many beautiful stone churches and they were pure candy to his Sight.

"He actually stayed with the same firm," Josh said. "So did my mom. The people in the firms kind of know about this."

"And got a promotion," Jorge said. "We're from Charlotte. My dad was an *illegale*. Papa got a green card and his own lawn company out of it, and he doesn't actually do Metal's parent's lawns 'cause he's got government contracts. My mom still cleans houses, though."

"Right," Michael said, nodding. "Carrot to move to the Big Apple. What about you, Laura? Mom get a promotion?"

Laura sighed and looked at Josh, who made a slight, encouraging nod. She drew in a slow breath and relaxed a little in defeat.

"Little one," Laura said. "More like there are more opportunities here. But she always complains about the cost of living."

"It is high," Michael said. "And the taxes suck from what I hear. Not that I've got that problem. Yet. Where y'all live?"

"Y'all?" Josh said, grinning. "I thought you were from Baltimore."

"First of all, *y'all* is fairly standard in black slang and I grew up in black culture," Michael said. "Second, Baltimore is both northern and southern in some ways. So, yeah, y'all. Better than yinz. Question remains. I'm in Brooklyn in something called East Midwood. Josh?"

"Uh, Upper East Side," Josh said.

"*Movin' on up*," Michael sang. "*To the East Side! / To a de-luxe apartment in the sky-hi!*"

"What?" Josh said, frowning.

"Do you live in an apartment maybe overlooking the East River?" Michael asked.

"Well, yes?" Josh said.

"Got it in one," Michael said. "Laura?"

They went by a large pharmacy on their right. Those were a vast trove of treasures to unlock. He needed to start learning how to identify different compounds.

"I'm out in Long Island," Laura said with more than a little pride. "It's a long drive for patrols."

"Where in general?" Michael asked. "Long Island is . . . long."

"Massapequa," Laura said.

"Like it?" Michael asked.

"Love it!" Laura said. "The school is *amazing* and it's just a *great* neighborhood! I was worried about moving from Cleveland, you know? Yeah, sort of excited about New York. I mean, concerts and Broadway shows but... worried, you know? I had all these friends and stuff. But it's been *great*! All my friends back in Cleveland are sooo jealous!"

"Josh," Michael said. "Private school?"

"Uh, yes," Josh said. "That a problem?"

"Nah," Michael said. "We all have the lives we are given, and we all have the burdens those lives give us. I'm sure your parents aren't too sure about a future as a super cop."

"Yeah," Josh said, shrugging. "They're not big on me having a career in the Corps. I'm not sure *I'm* big on it. I'm planning on going to law school. On the other hand, the Corps does have counsels and that's a possible job? Currently they're all normals. Sort of be cool to be a super attorney."

"Everyone has their fetishes," Michael agreed, to a puzzled look from Josh. "Jorge?"

The high-rises and all other buildings gave way to continuous open space on one side, meaning they were now next to Central Park.

"South Bronx," Jorge said. "We're Honduran and it's a big Honduran area."

"Cool," Michael said. "Do Hondurans do shrimp tacos?"

"You can get 'em," Jorge said, nodding. "They're actually a California or north Mexico thing. But we do 'em. My mom's trying to open a restaurant. She's a great cook."

"I am going to be visiting you often, then," Michael said. "My foster home is great except the food. Gah. Vegan."

"What's wrong with vegan?" Laura said. "*I'm* vegan!"

"It takes sixteen metabolic processes to convert soy into muscle," Michael said. "It only takes nine for beef and seven for pork. I'm a growing boy. I need *meat*!"

"Meat is murder!" Laura said.

"Tasty, tasty murder," Michael said.

"Oh!" Laura snapped. "That's *barbaric*!"

"I am a barbaric person," Michael said. "My real super name should be Conan the Barbarian... Stone."

"Coming up on the drop-off point," the driver said.

"Masks on, people," Josh said, pulling his own on.

Michael just dropped the front of the helmet.

"Gimme a hand with this?" Jorge asked, turning so Michael could get at the laces on his mask.

"How tight?" Michael asked.

"Doesn't really matter," Jorge said.

Michael tightened up the laces and tied them in a double bow.

The van turned, stopped, then backed up. In Sight Michael could see a large crowd of people. Enough that there were some cops doing crowd control.

They were freaking rock stars. Great.

A scan of the crowd only revealed a few weapons and most of those seemed like they were either undercovers or people who had concealed carry. No hit teams waiting for him. Even so, the opportunities for a marginally intelligent team of belligerents to exploit the poor security were endless.

Two of the cops walked up to the back of the van and banged on it.

"Here we go," Josh said.

"Me first!" Laura said. "Me first!"

Jorge looked at Michael with a shrug and smile.

"Ladies first," Michael said, trying not to laugh.

CHAPTER 18

"Space Oddity" —David Bowie

As soon as the doors opened, Fresh Breeze jumped out, posed, and held her hands up to the crowd. There was a spattering of applause but more flashes as people took pictures.

Michael made sure to be the last one out. There'd be time for nobility when he both knew the others better and had any confidence whatsoever in the security situation. Plus, he was doing his best to keep a low profile. Thankfully, he didn't have to fight to be last. Though not verbalized, in the end it kind of seemed expected.

The drop-off was at a parking area by the Boathouse. There were about a hundred or so people, about half kids, behind a temporary metal barricade waiting to see the junior superheroes. A front had just been through the area and the while the afternoon had a pleasant warmth to it, it presaged a chill evening. The sky was clear with low humidity and smog and though the front had blown many of the leaves off the trees, there was still a welter of reds and yellows and greens. Last awesome day of the year in the park. He'd made it just in time.

"Okay, Breeze," Josh said, waving. "Group shot."

"Just a second," Fresh Breeze answered. She was signing autographs.

"Fresh, now," Josh said with a sigh. "Then you can sign. Group shot."

"Fine, fine, fine," Laura said, walking over.

"Put the pretty girl in the middle," Michael suggested, waving to the crowd.

They lined up with Laura between Jorge and Josh and Michael on the end. Some waves to the crowd and they were done.

Michael walked over to the metal barricade just to see what was up.

"Which one are you?" a black kid about nine or so asked. He was flipping through a booklet.

"I'm new," Michael said. "Stone Tactical."

"I don't have one of your photos," the kid said. "Can I get an autograph? I've got Bright Lightning and Fuzzy Star and Ice Centurion already. And all the other Juniors..."

"Got Italian Falcon?" Michael asked.

"Nah, he don't do public stuff no more," the kid said.

"Come out next patrol," Michael said. "I'll see if I can get his for you."

"That'd be cool," the kid said.

"What's your name?" Michael asked.

"Davon," the kid said.

"I knew a Davon back home," Michael said, taking the book and a pen.

"Really?"

"Yeah."

I blew his head off.

He wrote: *To Davon, Do Good Things, Stone Tac.*

"I've got one of your photos," a teenage girl said, smiling shyly. "It's a print from the webpage. Is that okay?"

"Sure," Michael said, taking the photo. He was in a side pose, with his hands down, shoulder dropped, cocked to the side. It looked as if he was going for a karate kick. Actually, it looked identical to a David Hasselhoff pose from the eighties.

"They were great photos," the girl said, looking down and to the side.

Massive beta posture. She's actually fantasizing about me. Good Lord, if she only knew.

"What's your name?" Michael said.

"Kathy?"

He signed it *To Kathy: We are beings of light, Stone Tac.*

"Tell you a secret?" Michael said.

"Sure," Kathy said, ducking her head again.

No wonder Electrobolt is so into grooming. It's like shooting fish in a barrel.

"So, I'm not into having my picture taken," he said, dropping his voice a half octave to get some "superhero" voice. "I'm never going the male model route, right?"

"Okay," Kathy said, smiling. "You probably look like one, though."

"But," Michael said, "I was sort of hamming it up for some friends who were there. Super Corps people. I started singing 'Memory' from *Cats* and doing a dance number."

"You're kidding, right?" Kathy said, loosening up.

"Serious," Michael said. "I like to sing. I like to dance. Really p . . . ticked off the photographer. Then he just decided to roll with it. So, it's really a shot of me dancing."

"You look like a good dancer," Kathy said, giving him a noticeable once-over.

"Not too shabby," Michael said. "Anyway, gotta do the public thing. It was nice meeting you, Kathy."

"Hey, uh, do you have any, you know, social media?" Kathy asked. She actually chewed her lip.

"I think I've got a Facebook and Twitter account," Michael said. "I really don't do it all that much."

"Why not?" Kathy said.

'Cause FB is controlled by The Society and it's just a way for them to collect personal information and manipulate you? TikTok is owned by the Chinese government and ditto? X gives you exactly enough characters to piss somebody off?

"Forget the whole secret identity thing," Michael said, shrugging. "I'm a very private person. Doing public is new to me and I'm not that into it. They say it's the job, so I do the job. But I'm not into being a rock star."

"Okay," Kathy said. "I guess that makes sense."

"Gotta talk to other folk," Michael said. "It is a truth of astrophysics that all matter is forged in the stars. You are star dust, Kathy. Bye."

As he walked away, he had to shake his head.

"*And the papers want to know whose shirts you wear,*" he half sang.

He signed a few more photos and autographs, then dropped back to where Jorge was standing in the shade. Josh was still answering questions while Laura, Fresh Breeze, was just posing back and forth for a circle of mostly guys taking picture after picture.

"She does realize that with that outfit she's showing camel toe, right?" Michael said as he turned to stand next to Jorge.

Case in point, a jogger stumbled and nearly crashed into a fence while trying to catch a glance at her.

"Jesus, Stone," Jorge said, laughing. "It's nice to have somebody with some sense in this thing but . . . Santa Maria."

"How long do you think she'll stand there getting photos taken?" Michael asked.

"As long as Josh lets her," Jorge said. "The guys won't leave, and she won't either."

The crowd was dwindling, but not too slowly as new people still trickled in as well.

"Vanity is a sin for a reason," Michael said, tapping his fingers together.

"You a Believer?" Jorge said.

"African Baptist Evangelical," Michael said. "Though I'm probably going to have to find a new church. Was always weird being the only white boy. Going now probably won't work. You?"

"I'm Catholic," Jorge said.

"Really?" Michael said, shaking his head. "I pegged you for Primitive Baptist."

"What is Primitive Baptist?" Jorge asked.

"The snake handlers," Michael said.

"That's a real thing?" Jorge asked. "I'd sort of heard of that but I didn't believe it."

"Mark 16: Verses 17–18," Michael said. "'And these signs will accompany those who believe in my name. They will cast out demons; they will speak in new tongues; they will pick up serpents with their hands; and if they drink any deadly poison, it will not hurt them; they will lay their hands on the sick and they will recover.' That's the basis for it. Most other sects and churches think they're just nuts."

"Huh," Jorge said. "Kinda sounds like us. Except the whole casting out demons. But we can handle snakes, at least once we harden. And no deadly poison will harm us. Okay, only Healers can heal the sick."

"Indian masters can heal some things with their aura," Michael said. "I've been studying up cause I'm a nerrrd."

A couple of the police officers wandered over as most of the crowd started to disburse.

"You're the new kid."

The lead officer was black with a nametag that read GILL. He, too, had a detectable Staten Island accent.

"Stone Tactical, sir," Michael said, shaking hands.

"Not the normal sort of costume," Officer Gill said.

"I wasn't really into spandex," Michael said. "This suits my personality much more."

"Where you from?" the officer asked.

"Ever seen *The Wire*?" Michael asked. He knew the answer was: Yes. Every police officer in the United States had seen the show. "My previous claim to fame was a quarter-second shot of me in the background as an extra. That's where I'm from. Found in an alleyway, raised in foster care in East Baltimore, murder center of one of the murder capitals of America."

"Planning on getting shot?" Gill asked, pointing to the body armor.

"They expect us to rough it up with people," Michael said. "Sometimes those people have guns. I have been shot *too* many times. I *do not* like it. If somebody is going to be shooting at me, I want at least *some* Kevlar between me and the end of their barrel. Hell, given our superpowers I'm like, Can *I* have a gun?"

"Tell me they're not giving supers guns," the other officer said. He was Hispanic at a guess but his nametag read CLEVENSTINE, which sure as hell didn't *sound* Hispanic.

"Nah," Michael said. "They told me no. Especially since this is community service. I'm working off a weapons charge."

"Baltimore PD catch you with a weapon?" Officer Gill asked, seriously.

"If Baltimore PD cruised by me, they'd *assume* I was armed," Michael said. "And they'd probably wave. Did wave. I had a mixed relationship with Baltimore PD. Some of them thought I was great, some of them thought I should be locked up for the good of the world. Don't get me wrong, I'm a street rat and proud of it. And I have to admit that there's a small voice in the back of my head screaming: Don't tell those pigs *shit*! You gots *rights*, man!"

The officers chuckled, which was the point.

"But the closest thing I had to a mentor was one of the Baltimore homicide detectives," Michael continued. "He tried to take me under his wing. Taught me to golf. That was about the limit of his parenting skills. He was an alcoholic, philandering, three-times-divorced cynic that had seen way too many dead bodies. But he tried."

"Where'd you meet Homicide?" Clevenstine asked, pulling down on his armor at the neck.

Michael had to admit that as the afternoon wore on and it got warmer, he was regretting not wearing the sweat-vest.

"In East Baltimore?" Michael said. "Pretty much every day. But it most definitely does not relate to any incidents involving MS-13 and fun with chopsticks."

"Chopsticks?" Gill said. "You're not that kid that took on those Muertos Angelicas with chopsticks, are you?"

"Can neither confirm nor deny," Michael said, bowing slightly.

"Wait," Jorge said. "What?"

"Why chopsticks?" Gill asked. "That didn't make sense when I read it. You know you made the *Post* with that, right?"

"I was unaware, so, no," Michael said.

"You're not over in Suffolk, are you?" Clevenstine asked. "'Cause they still got a problem with them over there. An' I know where there's some chopsticks going free."

"I'm not even sure where Suffolk is, sir," Michael said. "But I'd prefer that you not pass that around. They've still got it in for me. One of the Muertos was related to a senior MS-13 jefe. So, there's a contract out on me. The FBI is sure, sure, that it's been dropped because *who* is going to take on a super who has at least *some* fed connections. They are *positive*."

"I'm sure they are," Gill said, shaking his head. "You're not so sure."

"Notice how I'm wearing body armor instead of spandex?" Michael said. "I, of course, trust the FBI's competence and reliability completely. Absolute confidence. One hundred percent."

He coughed and went "Bullshit" behind his hand.

The officer laughed at that, too.

"The FBI is the finest police force on the face of the planet," Officer Gill intoned.

"Just ask them," Michael added.

"Love the helmet," Clevenstine said. "That is cool."

"Love it, too," Michael said. "Especially since it's Level IIIA protection."

"That's Kevlar?" Gill asked.

"Yep," Michael said, tapping it. "No ABS shit for me. Designed for the Army but they didn't pick it up. Some SWAT teams and riot teams have them. Some special operations. Comfortable to wear, too. Light."

"Very high speed," Clevenstine asked. "What did it set you back?"

"Not a dime," Michael replied. "'Cause the federal government buys this stuff. Couple of hundred bucks if I recall. Who cares? The federal government spends money like they own a printing press. Oh, wait... Serious time for a second?"

"Sure," Gill said.

"To describe our briefing as a briefing is to insult the word *briefing*," Michael said. "The one thing that dropped out was 'drug activity near the Pond.' Generally, after dark. Can we get something more than that? Gang affiliation? Signs to look for? Tats? Are they doing drive-through or single sale? Any intel to pass on?"

"Honest answer?" Gill said.

"Stay out of it?" Michael said.

"Stay out of it," Gill answered. "I don't want to be insulting..."

"'Let the professionals handle it,'" Michael said. "'Your job as Junior Super Vigilantes is to wander around and make a presence.'"

"Yeah," Clevenstine said. "That."

"Mostly, the dealers aren't armed up in the park," Gill said. "But they could be. And... Are you going to be doing full Super Corps?"

"Jury's out," Michael said.

"If you do this job, first thing you learn is *don't* be gung ho," Gill said. "You're going to be doing it for a long time. The main thing is to work it as hard as you have to, do the job, yes, but not so hard you *can't* do it a long time. Either because you're dead or you're burned out."

"'Twenty years of days,'" Michael quoted.

Gill frowned and looked thoughtful.

"*Brooklyn's Finest*," Michael said. "Great movie. Richard Gere's old, burnt out, retiring corporal character. Gets assigned training rookies. One of them is just too gung ho. 'Kid, this job is twenty years of days.' Great view of police work."

"That," Gill said, nodding. "Don't get yourself shot. Just because you're a super and you're wearing body armor, doesn't mean they can't kill you. And you did mention you hate getting shot."

"I also hate doing a job poorly," Michael said. "I'm not arguing with you, please understand. I'm not even into this whole Junior Super Militia arrangement. I think it's a bad idea. I think Super Corps is a bad idea. We should train to prepare for the Storm.

"In reality, we're just another gang. More of a crew, given that there's only four of us. But if I'm going to be put out here to play Junior Super Cop without being an actual copper, seems I should *do* the job. Then again, 'twenty years of days.'"

"That last is where your head should be at," Gill said, nodding. "Just enjoy the park."

"It's a pretty park," Michael said. "Nice day. I'm looking forward to checking it out."

He looked over at Laura and sighed.

"If Febreze will ever get done having her pictures taken," he finished.

"Febreze?" Jorge said, chortling.

"Well, she's very clear that her feces are odorless," Michael said. "Clearly that's due to the chemical stick shoved in her rectum."

Both the officers laughed at that one.

"Oh," Clevenstine said. "Ow."

"You gotta wonder," Michael said, tapping his fingers together. "Does she *know* she's showing camel toe?"

CHAPTER 19

"Okay, we don't really have a specific agenda or patrol area," Josh said when they'd gotten Laura pried away from the photographers. "Stone, you're the new guy. Anything you want to see?"

"I'm Earther nerding out on the stone formations," Michael said. "Manhattan schist. Really not a super-cool stone, metasedimentary, but... Belvedere Castle and Umpire Rock?"

"We can go through the Ramble," Jorge suggested.

"Oh, there's never *anybody* in the Ramble!" Laura said, clearly dejected.

"That's sort of my point," Jorge said. "We might actually *get there* if we take the Ramble."

"Isn't that narrow stone arch in the Ramble?" Michael said.

"There's arches all over the place," Josh said.

"He's talking about the, you know, Ramble stone arch, probably," Jorge suggested.

"That," Michael said. "That and Belvedere Castle. Maybe Umpire Rock. That's an agenda."

"There's *nobody* in the Ramble," Laura complained.

"I'll take your picture at the stone arch," Michael said. "How's that? The leaves are changing. The Ramble will be great to walk through. Pretty. Like you."

"You think I'm pretty?" Laura asked.

"Everybody thinks you're pretty, Laura," Josh said. "We literally get shaped to look like perfect specimens. You're very pretty."

Just not as pretty as Sasha and you know it.

"Off to the Ramble," Jorge said, taking the lead.

The Ramble was a woodland nature area in the park that was covered in deciduous trees with changing leaves. It was probably the best possible day in the year to visit it and Michael was glad Jorge had suggested it.

Despite Laura's complaint, there were plenty of people in the Ramble. The problem for her being, they were the types to take pictures of the trees and leaves and birds and woodland and were less interested in taking pictures of a pretty girl.

Jorge had suggested they go by way of Balancing Rock. When they got there, Michael considered it like an art connoisseur considering a piece of dodgy postmodern art.

"Well, it's schist but I don't think it's Manhattan schist," Michael said, rubbing the side of his helmet instead of his chin. "Definitely metasedimentary. I'm going to go out on a limb with my limited knowledge of geology and say it's a glacial erratic. Probably from the Catskill formation but that's more of a WAG."

"I have no clue what you just said," Josh said.

"Does it really matter?" Laura asked.

"Hey, uh, can I take your picture?"

The questioner was an Asian guy in his twenties with a semiprofessional camera outfit.

"Like, up on the rock?" he added.

"All of us or just her?" Michael asked.

"Uh, sure . . . ?"

"One group shot, then you can take the rest of her," Michael said.

"See?" Michael said when they'd dragged Laura away from her fan. "There are people in the Ramble."

"One guy," Laura grumped.

"Laura," Michael said, since nobody was around. "Have you discussed your issue with external locus of self with Dr. Michelle? That you get your sense of self-worth from the attention of others?"

"That's between me and my therapist," Laura said. "And she says the same thing."

"You are, literally, one in a million," Michael said. "And you are *very* pretty. If you don't watch it, guys will take advantage of that external locus of self. They'll play on your insecurities to get what they want. You need to be more confident. You're a super, for God's sake! You literally have superpowers!"

"Oh, wow," she said, bringing up Air Move and blowing some leaves ahead of her. "I'm a human leaf blower! Hooray! I can get a job working for Jorge's dad. Oh, my God, I'm sorry, Jorge!" she added, gulping.

"*De nada*," Jorge said. "I'm A-Number One at trimming hedges."

"You really think that's all that Air is?" Michael said. "Jesus. Air is one of the most powerful powers!"

"It's literally just blowing air," Laura said grumpily, blowing more leaves.

"Even if it's just blowing air, it can be beautiful among other things," Michael said. "Pick up some leaves and blow them up in the air. And use Air Shape to hold them in the air."

"How?" Laura asked.

"Just try it," Michael said. "The Vishnu have Airs that are performers, blowing flower petals and feathers in complex paravanes. But air is still a *massive* power. I said a guy might try to take advantage of that lack of self-confidence you show."

"I'm very self-confident," Laura said unconfidently.

"Try to lie to someone else," Michael said. "You probably would be upset if you killed a squirrel. We need to find a rat."

"We're a long walk from City Hall," Jorge said.

Michael stopped and chuckled at that one.

"Good one, Jorge," Michael said. "But air is one of the most *complex* of the powers. Air is about gases and gaseous chemistry is complex. Can you heat and cool air?"

"No?" Laura said. "Can you do that?"

"Vishnu can," Michael said.

"Nobody knows how the Vishnu do it, Michael," Josh pointed out. *Speak for yourself.*

"Can you sort out the different gases in air?" Michael asked. "Do you know what gases there are? Did you have that in school?"

"I know there's too much carbon dioxide," Laura said stoutly. "It's destroying the planet."

Michael stopped and put his hand on his helmet where his forehead would be and slumped over.

"What? We're *dying* from carbon dioxide! It causes *climate change!*"

"I just..." Michael said, grabbing his helmet. "I just...Okay! *Simpler!*"

He straightened up, took off his glove, wet a finger, and held it up.

"Okay, there's a slight breeze," Michael said. "Can you stop it?"

"Where?" Laura asked.

"Just in a small area," Michael said. "Can you stop a small bit of air from moving?"

"Yeah," Laura said, holding up her hand. "There. Stopped."

"What's your range?" Michael asked.

"I dunno," Laura said. "Not very far."

"See that squirrel?" Michael said, pointing to a tree where a tree rat was chittering at them. They weren't feeding it and were in its territory. "Stop the breeze where that squirrel's at. Just freeze the air."

"Oookay," Laura said, holding out her hand and pointing at the squirrel.

After a moment, the squirrel dropped to the ground.

"Is it dead?" Laura asked, horrified.

"Should be," Michael said. "Might just be knocked out."

"You got me to kill a squirrel!" Laura said, slapping him with both hands. "How *could* you?"

"'Cause we weren't at Super Corps," Michael said, protecting himself with one arm. "Laura, it was a demonstration. I said that air was one of the most powerful of the powers. Gases infuse *everything*. They are the most vital component of life. Probably more important than water. The Storm is coming, remember? You think we're not supposed to fight stuff in the Storm? Kill it? Now you know how."

"It's still a pretty little squirrel," Laura said, tearing up.

"I'll bury him for you," Michael said.

He picked the squirrel up by its bones, dug a hole, and dropped it in. For good measure, he pulled up a chunk of schist from just below the soil and formed it into a tombstone.

"Here lies Ralph the Squirrel," Michael said as he wrote on the slab of schist. "He was nuts for nuts."

He inserted it into the ground and there was now a squirrel monument added to the park.

"There," Michael said. "No squirrel has had a finer memorial."

"You still tricked me into killing a squirrel," Laura said unhappily.

"And I just showed you that you are far more than a human leaf blower," Michael said. "Say you're dumb enough to go walking in the park at night by yourself."

Which you are.

"And you get attacked by a rapist," Michael said. "You may not *want* to kill him, but you *can*."

"I'm still not really happy about killing a *squirrel*," Laura said as they proceeded onward. "I'm not sure I could kill a *person*."

"Is there anyone in your life you care about more than you?" Michael asked. "Sister, niece, friend. Somebody that you would die for?"

"My little sister?" Laura said. "I hate her and love her at the same time."

"So, you are in a locked room with your sister," Michael said. "And Jeffrey Dahmer. And all you've got is your powers. What are you going to do? Yesterday, you'd try to scratch his eyes out or blow air in them. What are you going to do now?"

"He's got a point, Breeze," Jorge said.

"We are living weapons," Michael said. "And inside everyone is a beast. Too many people live the life of their beast. We call them violent criminals. But to have the beast and leash it, is true nobility. Breeze, when the time comes to unleash the beast, now you have a weapon that you cannot lose, nor have it break. Air is far more powerful than just being a human leaf blower. Though that has utility as well."

"You're . . ." Jorge said.

"Weird?" Michael said. "You guys get the rumor about the super-genius thing? Really into astrophysics?"

"I sort of heard about that," Josh said.

"I didn't bother with studying superpowers before I Acquired," Michael said. "Now, I've been putting my mind to them. Jorge, you ever play baseball?"

"Can't anymore," Jorge said, shrugging. "Supers not allowed in sports."

Michael pulled up another chunk of rock and formed it into a ball about the size of a baseball, then lofted it to Jorge.

"Think fast," he said as Jorge caught it. "See that rock outcrop? Think you can major-league pitch that into the rock outcrop?"

"I can try," Jorge said, starting to wind up.

"Important safety tip," Michael said, holding up his hand. "Hit the rock, for God's sake."

"I'll hit the rock," Jorge said. He wound up and threw as hard as he could. Rock shattered against rock with a resounding *bang!*

"Jeez," Josh said, ducking his head. "We're not supposed to scare people."

"Good thing there's not many around in the Ramble," Michael said. Though there were a few and they were staring and in some cases videoing. "Problem of invuls is no range at all. If they can hit it, they can destroy it or at least punch holes. But no range. Now you have range."

"If you're around to make me a rock baseball," Jorge said. "Though, yeah, throwing things. Like, cars."

"Say you're in a real situation," Michael said. "Super-terrorist. The Nebraska Killer-type fight. Josh, think you can make some steel baseballs for Jorge out of, say, cars?"

"Probably," Josh said.

"Then you're both laying steel on the target," Michael said. "Even if it is just a distraction, you're in the game. And you're at range from whatever you're fighting. Never close if you don't absolutely have to. *Anything* is a weapon. I once killed three assassins with chopsticks."

"Chopsticks," Josh said. "Really?"

"I read about that in the *Post*, too," Jorge said. "That's what you were talking about with those cops."

"Anything is a weapon," Michael said. "We are living weapons and the Storm will come someday. Learning to be better living weapons is what we *should* be doing. Not wandering around being a tourist attraction."

"I want to learn to fly," Laura said unhappily. "Everybody *loves* the fliers."

"You can fly," Michael said, tapping his fingers together. "It would take some equipment, but you can fly."

"How?" Laura said.

"Tell you what," Michael said. "You got a car?"

"Yes," Laura said cautiously. "You going to trick me into killing another little furry creature?"

"No," Michael said. "Next Saturday, I'll take the subway somewhere closer to you but pick me up. I'll take you somewhere and show you how to fly. It'll take equipment, though."

"Can't you just tell me?" Laura asked.

"A wizard does not give away his wizardry for free," Michael said. "If I show you how to fly, you owe me a lunch of shrimp tacos. If and only if. With sauce, not just lemon and cilantro."

They finally reached the arch, and it was cooler than the pictures. Michael could have stayed there climbing all over it and checking out the masonry and the rocks for the whole afternoon. He mapped it out with his Sight, and mused over whether he could move the whole thing intact. Definitely not at his current stage, but sometime in the foreseeable future . . . probably.

"Can we go soon?" Laura asked. "When it gets dark, everybody leaves!"

"Okay, okay, okay," Michael said. "There'll be people at Belvedere Castle, right?"

As promised, he got out his phone and took her picture. Then they rambled on.

"This is a very cool park," Michael said as they left the woods and approached Belvedere Castle. "I begin to understand why it's in every movie and TV show, ever."

"It is," Josh admitted. "I'll always be a Chicago boy, but this is the best park I've ever seen."

There was a crowd of people in the courtyard enjoying the late fall afternoon. Michael subtly nudged the group to the side, quick group photo and the guys left to let Laura pose for her many male admirers.

"If you don't mind, I'm going to go nerd out on architecture and geology," Michael said to Josh. "Since we're more or less tourists as well. Just in costume."

They stayed at Belvedere for about an hour. As soon as one gentleman admirer would leave another would take his place in the semicircle of flashing cameras. Laura was in her element.

Michael and Jorge wandered around the area, occasionally stopping for pictures as well, as Michael checked out the architecture and geology. He was boning up on the latter but really needed to take some courses. School was a distraction from real studying. Such a time sink.

He gave a few lectures to kids about the geology, and they were mostly bored, wanting to ask about superpowers. He was called a human bulldozer a couple of times. New York kids were like that. So, he went down to the lake and showed off his elite rock-skipping skillz. Jorge wasn't bad, either.

Finally, they dragged Laura away and headed west.

"Who's hungry?" Josh said. "'Cause I'm starving."

"I could eat," Jorge said.

"How's that work?" Michael asked.

"We'll head over to Central Park West," Josh said. "There's going to be some food vendors over there."

"I hope they have vegan," Laura said.

Michael thought fast.

"You guys go," he said. "I'm gonna check out the Shakespeare Garden. Give me a heads-up when you're ready to patrol again."

"Okay...?" Josh said.

"Just want to check out the rocks," Michael said. "Earther."

Okay, so question he *hadn't* covered in orientation. Corps did *not* provide meals during patrols. His bad. Should have asked. Great. As if he wasn't dealing with enough hangry issues with his foster mom providing about enough vegan food for a malnourished sparrow.

He wandered in the area, occasionally posing for pictures.

"Yeah, the helmet is cool, like Halo *..."*

"Earther. Yeah, human bulldozer..."

"I was stuck under a rock and had to get it off me..."

"I think it's that way but I'm new here..."

"I love being in the Junior Space Eagles so much!" Michael said, smiling thinly. "I just eat this up with a spoon! Which does not describe anything I've done lately..."

CHAPTER 20

"Rise" —League of Legends
(featuring The Glitch Mob, Mako, and The Word Alive)

Finally, his phone buzzed, and he linked back up with the team. It was close enough to the food that he could smell a few of the options: chicken 'n' waffles, hot dogs, pizza, at least one taco truck—though no indications of shrimp, thankfully. He might've turned feral.

"You get something to eat?" Josh asked, picking his teeth.

"All good," Michael said. "How do you eat in that thing?" he asked Jorge, pointing to his mask.

"I make it real small and stuff it through the hole," Jorge said. "I should have thought that through."

He gave Michael an odd look. He'd figured out what the problem was, and it wasn't an obsession with rocks.

"So, where now?" Michael asked, tapping his fingers together.

"Probably should head south, to the Pond," Josh said, gesturing down the bridle path.

They'd gotten down by the West 77th Street Stone Arch.

"Wanna check it out?" Josh asked.

"I was rockin' out while you were eating," Michael said tightly. "I'm good."

They proceeded south along West Drive. There were more people and Laura had to be occasionally wooed to continue "patrolling." So far there hadn't been any incidents of note. At least, not around them.

229

As the afternoon died, the families started leaving the park and the texture began to change. There were fewer people wanting to take Laura's picture and more eyeing them askance.

As the sun was setting, they came up on a kid, about nine, just standing by the side of the path, not really doing anything. His clothes weren't quite ragged, but they hadn't seen a wash in some time. No cheer in his face like he was here to play with friends, just a constantly shifting scan of all the passersby.

Michael had been continuously using his Sight. One thing he'd noticed was an increase in the number of weapons. Wood handles on knives and cloth on shivs he could *just* see under Earth Sight. The blades not so much. The only thing he could see of guns was a vague shadow of the propellant. But he could also see outlines in clothing and holsters, vaguely.

For that matter, he could *clearly* see cached drugs. And up in the wood behind the kid was a hole with some glass vials in it.

He thought about twenty years of days and about not getting dinner or for that matter *any* solid food for weeks. And he decided to just be the jackass that was his natural nature.

"Hey, kid," he said, stopping and bending over with his hands on his knees. "It's getting late. Shouldn't you be heading home?"

"Fuck you, poh-leese," the kid snarled. "I ain't gots to tell you shit!"

"Now, is that any way to talk to a superhero?" Michael asked. "Where's your mom?"

"I'm here with my cousin," the kid said, gesturing up the trail to an older teenager who was dressed quite a bit nicer but still pretty shady-looking.

"Really?" Michael said. "Maybe we should talk to him. Don't want you out in the park too late. Bad people come out at night."

"I *am* bad people!" the kid said stoutly. He waved a gang sign at Michael and declared: "I'm *gangsta!*"

"Really?" Michael said. "Well, remember, crime doesn't pay."

"Crime pay good!" the kid argued.

"You do good things, okay?" Michael said, rubbing him on his head.

"Get you hand off my head!" the kid snapped.

"See ya," Michael said, proceeding on.

"What the hell was that all about?" Josh asked.

"He's a runner," Michael said, looking down the bridle path.

The "cousin" was hanging out, just idly checking his phone, not paying attention to the approaching Junior Superheroes or anything like that. About the same distance in the other direction was another kid, about the same age, also just standing around minding his own business.

"Runner or a tout. Maybe both. I've never seen a double drive-through but that's what this looks like."

"A what?" Josh asked.

"Hang on," Michael said, walking up to the teen. "Pleasant evening to you, good sir! I understand you are the temporary guardian of that minor child. Is that correct?"

"Why you wanna know?" the teen snarled.

"Just checking on his health and welfare," Michael said. "Superheroing and stuff."

"Yeah, he wit' me," the teen said.

"You know there is drug activity in these parts in the evenings," Michael said seriously. "Do you really think it's wise to expose your... cousin, is it?... to those sorts of conditions?"

"Man, fuck off, poh-leese," the teen snapped. "You ain't gots no right tellin' me where I can stand. I gots rights!"

"Hmm..." Michael said. "Well, have a good evening, good sir. Bad people are in the dark."

"I *am* bad people," the drug dealer said.

"Oh, I forgot something," Michael said, slapping his helmet. "Just left it up by your... cousin. Forget my own head if it wasn't attached."

He walked back, followed by a puzzled Junior Super Corps, until he was by the kid. Then he started, ostentatiously looking at the ground.

"What you doin'?" the kid said. "Why don't you fuck off, poh-leese?"

"Where oh where might it be?" Michael half hummed.

"Stone, what *are* you doing?" Josh asked.

"Yeah," Laura said. "This is so lame."

"She gots *that* right," the kid said, looking Breeze up and down, clicking his tongue, and rubbing his hands together. "That shit be *sweet*. You be fine as fine *wine!*"

"Oh, my God," Breeze said, rolling her eyes. "Stone, can we hurry this up? I'm getting hit on by a nine-year-old!"

"You ain't had a good time 'til you been wit' me!" the kid said, grabbing his crotch. "I gots the goods right here."

"Oh, Jesus," Breeze said, shaking her head.

Michael walked up into the woods. He could see the faint trail but didn't really need it. He reached a flat rock about a foot across and turned it over.

"My, my, my, what have we here?" Michael said, pulling out a plastic baggy filled with glass vials. "I'm not sure what this is."

"Man..." the kid said, then took off. "See ya, babe!"

"What the hell was that?" Josh asked.

"Dude," Jorge said. "That is *bound* to piss them off. These are *gangs*. You know that, right?"

"I'm in a pissy mood," Michael replied, getting back on the bridle path. He rambled over to the drug dealer, ostentatiously swinging the drugs in his hand. "Excuse me, good sir. Are these by any chance yours? I found them up in the woods with your cousin—who, it appears, may have headed home like a good boy."

"They ain't mine," the guy said, shaking his head and refusing to even look at the baggy. "I don't even know what they is. What be dat?"

"I think they *may* be *illegal drugs*," Michael said, shaking his head. "And so close to your...cousin, was it? The evils of the drug trade are insidious. Why, he could have gotten them in his *own hands*. How terrible. Well, I suppose I should turn these over to the proper authorities. Oh, by the way, is that other youth also your...cousin?" Michael added, pointing to the other kid down the trail.

"Uh..."

"I suppose I should check to ensure that he isn't exposed to the evils of the drug trade as well," Michael said, putting the bag in his cargo pocket. "Don't want your...cousin to get into bad ways, do we?"

"Sure, man," the drug dealer snarled. "Yeah, don't want that, 'tall!"

Sure enough, there was another bag of drugs up behind the second kid. Who also took off like a scalded cat when they were found.

"What is going on?" Josh asked.

"How much of a lecture do you want?" Michael asked, pocketing the second set of drugs.

The sun was full down, now, and the character of the park had definitely changed. All the families were gone, and it was teenagers and twentysomethings, mostly male with some women hanging close to them. There was some laughter in the distance and bottles being passed around. For that matter, he could see people in Sight up behind the bushes shooting up.

It was starting to look like home.

"It's a drive-through," Michael said. "It was literally come up with by West Coast street dealers based on a McDonald's drive-thru. This is not being an ass when I say this: Have you ever been to a drive-through?"

"Yes," Josh said. "I'm not that... Yes."

"Okay," Michael said. "First rule of the drug trade: never put drugs and cash together. So, the way this works is a drug fiend goes up to the teen dude at the intersection and goes, 'Hey, man, I want some drugs.' The dealer then charges him for the drugs, just like at the drive-through cash window. Then he signals the runner, using gang sign..."

Michael flashed a gang sign with his left hand.

"In Baltimore, with the GangstaLand Lords, that means 'two vials of fet.' That is, fentanyl. Got it? That's what most gang sign is; it's an ordering system."

"Okay," Josh said. "I... did not know that."

"Every gang has different sign," Michael said. "And there's this whole big split between the GD and the Blood about right hand/left hand but that's not important.

"The kid gets the drugs and passes them off to the drug fiend. If the kid gets caught with drugs, say with an undercover buy, they're going to plead it minor. If a teen or twentysomething gets caught with this much, it's felony distribution.

"So, the experienced guy in the gang holds the money. He's got a knife, good enough for drug fiends. Then, at a certain point, he'll signal for a pickup or a re-up. Pickup is pick up money. Re-up is resupply of drugs. With pickup, he'll turn it over to the money car and those dudes are armed and heavy. With re-up, car will bring it in close, he'll probably send the runner. So, he's gonna need a re-up after this. All clear?"

"So... what do we do with the drugs?" Josh asked.

"You guys have *never* gotten drugs off of someone while patrolling?" Michael asked.

"No," Josh said. "Not since I've been doing this."

"I told you," Jorge said. "We're a tourist attraction."

"Then why the *hell* are we out here 'til eleven?" Michael said, his stomach rumbling. "*See* any tourists?"

"In case there's an incident," Josh said.

"Okay," Michael said. "Well, when we come up on a cop, we'll give it to them."

"They don't patrol much at night," Josh said. "I can call in."

"So, we're on our *own* in here?" Michael said. "Great."

"I don't like it," Laura said, crossing her arms. "It's scary."

"Call for a patrol car to meet us over on West Seventy-second Street," Michael said, reevaluating the situation.

We're in Law-Level Zero zone with shit superpowers. Are they nuts?

They literally had an aggressive groomer in charge of the junior super-kids. Question answered.

They met the patrol car near Strawberry Fields, and Michael silently handed over the drugs.

"Where'd you get these?" the Hispanic officer asked. His nametag read HERMANEZ.

"Saw a couple of runners, followed the trail, found them under a rock," Michael said. "Runners were kids, took off."

"You sure that was a good idea?" Hermanez asked.

"I just found out we don't have backup in there," Michael said, gesturing behind him with his head. "So, maybe not. But if something goes down, I'll just throw Hulke at them and run."

"Hulke?" Hermanez said, his eyebrow raising.

"I'm the definition of politically incorrect," Michael said. "Try to give us some credit on it. Fighting the scourge of the drug trade. I'll bet dollars that's fet. Which I truly do *hate*."

"Will do," Hermanez said before driving off. "Watch yourself."

"Hulke?" Jorge said dangerously.

"You're a hulk and you're named Jorge," Michael said. "Makes sense."

"'Hulk' is an insulting term," Laura said primly.

"Okay, Febreze," Michael said.

"Febreze?!"

Jorge turned his head and put his hand over his mouth, faking a cough. But his shoulders still shook.

"Do you use Febreze in your home?" Michael asked.

"Yes," Laura admitted.

"So, it's a product you like," Michael said. "What's wrong with it as a nickname?"

"I think I'll just call you Asshole," Jorge said, getting the laughter under control.

"Asshole," Michael said, shrugging. "Shithead. Whatever."

"Do *I* have a nickname?" Josh asked drily.

"Easy Listening," Michael said. "'Cause for a metallo, you're about the least metal dude I've ever met. You are literally the definition of white-bread easy listening."

"I listen to rap!" Josh argued.

"You listen to rap 'cause you think you *should*," Michael said. "You're like, Air Supply or Little River Band. *Skillet* would be too much for you, forget Sabaton. We'll just shorten it to Easy. Which is a good nickname. And I'll generally call you just Breeze. Which is also a good nickname."

"And Hulke," Jorge said.

"Only between friends," Michael said. "So, wanna go steal some more shit from drug dealers? Every drug dealer kills on average fifty people. So, we are literally saving lives."

"I suppose," Easy said uneasily.

"Come on, Easy," Michael said. "Superhero up, man! Think of the stories you can tell in law school! No guts, no glory! Besides, if shit goes down, we've got Hulke."

When they were back in the park, Michael had them stop and, while nobody was around, he took off his helmet and rummaged in his pack. He pulled out a monocular and connected it to the helmet, then ran the power cord back to his pack and plugged it into a large rechargeable battery. Finally, he put his helmet back on, pulled down the monocular, and swore.

"Fucking cool," he said, looking around.

"What is . . . that?" Josh asked. "There's a fair amount of light."

"Thermal imagery," Michael said. "Let's roll."

They rambled about another hundred yards down the trail and Michael stopped again.

"Hey, Breeze, how good are you at blowing?" he asked, eyeing some bushes.

"What?" Breeze asked, aghast.

"How's your blowing ability?" Michael asked again. "How well can you blow?"

"I'm ... How can you even *ask* a question like that?" she asked angrily. "I don't ... I've never ..."

"Your blow," he said, making whooshing motions. "How hard can you *blow*? Your air? How hard can you blow?"

"Oh, you mean, like, a leaf blower, blow ..." she said uncertainly.

He turned and looked at her, tilting the monocular back and forth.

"What the hell did you *think* I meant?" Michael asked, then paused. "Oh, my *God*, get your mind out of the gutter, girl!"

"Yeah, I thought you meant that ... too," Josh said, confused.

"Sorry," Laura said, waggling her head.

"Okay, give those bushes a good solid blowjob," Michael said, pointing at the bushes.

Jorge turned to the side and just started laughing.

"You!" Breeze shouted, smacking him again repeatedly with both hands.

"What?" Michael asked, pointing at the bushes while raising one arm to protect himself. "Blow the *bushes*, Breeze! *Blow the bushes!* I'm serious! Blow the bushes!"

"Why?" Breeze asked, but she stopped beating him.

"God, you ask a lot of questions," Michael said, throwing out his hands at the bushes, fingers spread. "Blow the bushes, Breeze! Blow the bushes!"

"Fine," Breeze said, throwing out her hands. She blew and blew as hard as she could.

The bushes rustled in a fresh breeze but there was another, more serious rustling and coughing as well. Then the sound of running footsteps and somebody crashing through the underbrush.

"What the ... ?" Josh said.

"Congratulations, Breeze," Michael said. "You just blew a mugger or potential rapist right out of his hiding spot. Not that he won't be back, but you might have just saved some young woman such as yourself from being attacked."

"What the ... ?" Josh repeated. "How ... ?"

"Hello," Michael said, tapping the monocular. "Thermal. Vision. I can see into concealment like that."

He'd actually been using Sight. But "thermal vision" was a good cover. Which was why he'd talked Alexander of Alexandria into the monocular.

"That . . . starts to make some sense," Josh said.

"Yuh think?" Michael replied.

And they rambled on.

"I'm about ready to call this," Michael said, stuffing another pile of collected drugs in his overfull backpack.

So far nobody had attacked them. When one group had looked as if they might, Michael suggested that Jorge just turn on his aura. That, apparently, was a startling suggestion.

They *never* used their auras. Even for, you know, light. Jesus.

When the dwarf with all the muscles started to glow, the group had backed off.

Fight, flight, bluff, submit. If bluff worked, all good.

Breeze had blown at least five potential muggers or rapists and had a jolly good time of it. She was really getting the knack of blowing.

"I'm calling in," Josh said. "We need to drop those off."

"Roger," Michael said. It had been a long day, and he was at that stage of hungry where it was going away and he had halitosis. That was never a good sign.

"We'll meet at Columbus Circle," Josh said. "I sent a text to Iron Eagle about the drugs and he's on his way with Ivory Wing."

Sasha!

The same cop car from Strawberry Fields was pulled up in Columbus Circle when they'd rambled their way there, along with another. This time Officer Hermanez was out and waiting with an NYPD lieutenant.

"Mind if I . . . ?" Michael asked, pointing at the hood. "They're mostly in baggies."

"Go," Hermanez said.

"Hey, Hermanos, could you unplug me?" Michael asked. He'd turned off his monocular and tipped it up.

Once he could get his pack off, he opened it up and tipped it out on the hood of the cop car. Various configurations of drugs spilled out and threatened to spill off.

"Jeez," the lieutenant said. "Nice haul."

"Is that the last of it?" Michael said, turning on his flashlight and rummaging in the depths. "Don't want to get caught with drugs at sch... There it is."

He pulled out one last packet and tossed it on the hood, using Earth Move to pick up the ones that had fallen on the ground.

"Man, if a drug dog gets wind of this backpack, he's gonna flip his shit," Michael said.

About then Iron Eagle and Ivory Wing came in for a landing.

"Hey, Sa... Wing," Michael said, waving.

"Hey... Stone," Ivory Wing said, waving back.

She acknowledged my existence! We shall be wed!

"That's a lot of drugs!" Iron Eagle said in his best command voice. "Congratulations, Junior Super Corps! You have made the streets safer. Where did you find them?"

"M..." Josh said then paused and thought. "Stone! He has a nose for it. It was like an Easter egg hunt."

"Good job, Stone Tactical!" Iron Eagle said.

"Thanks," Michael said.

"Lieutenant," Iron Eagle said, "I'd like to ensure that Super Corps gets credit for this drug haul."

"No problem, sir," the lieutenant said.

"We'll probably do a press conference, Monday," Iron Eagle said. "It'll look good to have drugs on the table. Again, Junior Super Corps, good job."

"Thanks!" "De Nada." "Thank you, sir!" "Uh-huh."

"Ivory Wing! Time to call it a night!" Iron Eagle commanded. "We are RTB!" he added, saluting the group, then taking off. Sasha followed him up into the darkness.

"Whaaat... the *hell* is it with Flyers acting like they're reading from a *superhero* script?" Michael asked, rhetorically. "We... are... AR-TEE-BEE...!"

Even the lieutenant snorted a little.

"Whatever would we do without our Flyer betters?" Michael asked, again rhetorically. "Well, gentlemen, we are RTB as well but using much more mundane means. Stay safe, tonight. Anybody know where our van went? Dude, where's my van?"

CHAPTER 21

"Veteran of the Psychic Wars" —Blue Oyster Cult

Monday just after lunch, he got called to the principal's office.

"Mike," the principal said, nodding. "We haven't met, yet. I'm Principal Wetherspoon."

Wetherspoon was five nine or so, with hair that was nearly an Afro, well stuffed into his clothes and with an Islands accent.

"Your . . . community service office called," the principal said. "They need you over at their offices right away after school. They *were* sending a car, but I pointed out, delicately, that they weren't allowed to pick you up—only your social worker, a listed transportation officer from ACS, or your foster parents can do so. So, they will probably be trying to make other arrangements, but I thought you should know."

"Right," Michael said, thinking about it. Oh, the hell with it. "This whole secret identity thing is stupid," he added.

There was a framed picture on the desk, probably of the principal's family. Using his powers, Michael very carefully lifted it, then lowered it just as carefully.

"Stone Tactical," Michael said, waving a finger in the air. "Earther. I don't know what's up, but you were talking to Super Corps."

"Oh," Wetherspoon said, surprised. "Okay."

"Let me call them," Michael said, tugging his earlobe. "I walk home, anyway. I'll just have them pick me up off school property. Not your issue, not your responsibility. And it's probably FBI or marshals picking me up. It's all good. Just give me a minute to call, yes?"

"Of course," Principal Wetherspoon said, nodding but also frowning. "We really *should* be informed."

"Half the freaking world is informed," Michael said, standing up. "The press has a copy of the Supers List, corporations, foreign governments, too, but apparently I'm supposed to keep the secret from my foster parents and my school administration. That makes zero sense. And I don't do things that make zero sense."

Marshals picked him up off-site and took him to the headquarters. And he wasn't even expected to take the back way in. They went in through the secret marshals' entrance for high-value prisoners and protectees. It was waaay more direct.

"Can I *always* use this one?" Michael asked.

"Sorry," the lead marshal said. "It's mostly for witnesses."

"*I* was a witness," Michael said. "Does that count?"

Apparently not.

When he reached the Super Corps lobby—using his CAC card because it wasn't cleared for marshals, hah, neener—Alexander of Alexandria was waiting for him.

"Briefing Four," Alexander said, gesturing then walking that way.

"Are there any other briefing rooms?" Michael asked. "Are there, like, Briefing Two and Three or are they just imaginary?"

When they got to Briefing Four, Josh, Sasha, and Laura were all there.

"Do you want a water?" Alexander asked.

"Yeah," Michael said, then gestured with his head out of the room. "But you should probably...you know...that..."

"Got it," Alexander said, grinning.

"So...what did we do wrong?" Michael said. "Were we *not* supposed to collect drugs or something?"

"There's going to be a press conference about it," Josh said. "We're getting credit. We're just waiting on Jorge."

"Oh," Michael said, tugging his earlobe.

Sasha was looking decidedly unhappy for some reason.

"So," she said. "You said your name was Edwards when we first met, now it's Truesdale?"

"Yeah, well, some people don't like the name Edwards," Michael said. "Seriously. So now I'm Mike Truesdale, courtesy of the US Marshals' Ident-A-Print. Nothing insidious."

"Okay," Sasha said.

"We get to do a press conference!" Laura said, grinning. "We *never* get to do press conferences! Thanks, Mike! Or Michael or whatever! I thought you were nuts, but this is *great*! My social media is going to *explode*!"

Sasha sunk deeper in her seat with that. Something was up.

Jorge arrived and so did Falcone.

"So, you kids get the word?" Tony asked.

"No," Jorge said, dropping into a seat.

"You're doing a press conference in about thirty minutes, so you've got to suit up fast," Tony said. "That's it. Gotta get ready myself."

"So, let's suit up," Josh said, clapping his hands.

Laura was chatterboxing about talking to the media and getting in front of the cameras.

Sasha wasn't saying a word.

Thank God there wasn't any Electrobolt present.

"Where's Bolt?" Jorge asked as they carefully got undressed—without in any way looking at each other or, especially, the opposite sex.

"Probably on patrol," Josh said.

Thank Ghu.

Michael's costume took the longest to don but it wasn't long until he was rigged up.

"Let's go," Josh said. "We don't want to be late for our first press conference."

Alexander was outside the locker room and led them to the press briefing room. It was beyond another security door and there was a preparation area to the side where Tony was waiting.

"Okay, here's how it's going to go," Tony said, talking with his hands and pointing to the briefing area that was in view. "We're going to walk out there in a line. Stone, you lead, then Laura, then Josh, then me, then Sasha, then Jorge. Stone, walk all the way across the stage. Laura, follow him and set between Josh and Stone. Josh, you're to the left of the podium. I'm at the podium. Sasha's behind the table with the seized drugs. Then Jorge to the right of Sasha."

He took a position of parade rest, shoulders back and chin tipped down.

"You stand like this, yeah?" he said. "Shoulders back, feet shoulder-width apart, hands behind your back, yeah? Got it. You look straight forward. Not an expression, not moving a muscle, 'less you're called on. If you're called on, answer the questions straight and move on.

"Last thing," Tony said. "*Don't* lock your knees. We won't be out there long, but if you lock your knees even a super can pass out. Don't lock your knees. Keep 'em a little bent. Got it?"

There were nods and agreements.

"Okay, get lined up," Tony said. "Aaand, move out."

Stone marched out as militarily as he could, came to a stop at the approximate right point, did a decent right-pivot turn and snapped to a position of parade rest.

Josh and Sasha were flanking the podium, but Sasha was the one standing behind the drugs. Michael knew *exactly* what that meant, and Laura was going to be *livid*.

The room was about a quarter full, and the journalists looked a little bored with the whole thing.

"Thank you for coming here today," Tony said in his best Staten Island accent. "We're here to congratulate the Junior Super Corps for their tremendous work over the weekend, keeping Central Park free from the scourge of drugs..."

Tony talked for a bit about the horrors of narcotics, then paused.

"I'd like to introduce Ivory Wing, who will give some prepared remarks on behalf of the Junior Super Corps," Tony said.

Michael heard a strangled "Whaaa?" from Laura, followed by a low growl.

Oh, the locker room was gonna be *lit*.

"It is my honor to speak on behalf of the Junior Super Corps," Sasha said, reading off a teleprompter. "Drugs are one of the most despicable horrors in modern America..."

They were well-prepared remarks. Michael wasn't sure who the speech writer was for the Super Corps, but they hit all the right notes. There was even Diversity, Equity, Inclusion, and Anti-racism included.

Sasha was a good public speaker. She delivered it extremely well.

There was a brief question-and-answer session. Tony took most of them but when it was time to speak on "behalf of the Junior Super Corps" it was Sasha who fielded the questions, with the exception of one directed at Josh.

Finally, it was over, and they marched off the stage.

"Good job, all of you," Tony said. "That's it. You can get out of the zoot suits. And good job on the patrol. That was a lot of drugs youze guys rounded up. Keep it up!"

With that he walked off.

Alexander led them, unspeaking, back to the locker room. As soon as the door was shut, it started.

"What...the...FUCK?!" Laura shouted. "You didn't have *anything* to do with it!"

"It wasn't my idea, okay?" Sasha said. "I just got handed the script, okay?"

"NO, IT'S *NOT* OKAY!" Laura shouted. "That was *my* chance to *shine*! *We* were the ones that did all the work! Hell, Mike was the one who found them all! I was the one who was chasing off the muggers and THAT WASN'T EVEN *MENTIONED*!"

He'd forgotten about that.

"I'm sorry, okay?" Sasha said, nearly crying.

"I don't care if you're *sorry*!" Laura said. "How *could* you?"

"Laura..." Josh said.

"They told me to, okay?" Sasha said, her arms crossed over her chest.

"You could have said you didn't have anything to do with it!"

"I couldn't say that or..."

"YOU COULD HAVE! NOBODY ASKED ME ANYTHING! NOBODY WAS...was..."

"Okay, that's enough," Michael said, putting his arm around Laura. "Laura, stop."

"No! It's not fair!"

"It's the Corps," Michael said. "The Flyers are the only ones who matter. Tony's the office chief in New York. Larry Whatshisname is the office chief in LA. Both Flyers. The Secretary? Flyer. That's how it is."

"It's not FAIR!"

"It's how it is," Michael said, gesturing up. "People literally look *up* to Flyers, Laura. 'Look, it's a bird, it's a plane, it's a poopy pigeon!'"

"Oh, thanks very much," Sasha said.

He waved his hand behind him to get her to hush.

"We're the grunts, they're the flyboys," Michael said. "Or -girls. Whatever. The grunts *never* get the credit."

"He's got a point," Jorge said, nodding.

"It's not *right*," Laura said, pouting.

Michael put both hands on her shoulders.

"Look at me, Laura," he said softy. "Look me in the eye. It's okay."

"It's *not* okay," Laura said, crossing her arms under her chest.

"Yes, it is," Michael said. "'Cause while Sasha is up there, flying around like a pigeon, you're the one that's down here with people, getting your picture taken. All they get of her is a quick shot of some fuzzy thing flying by."

"They do a public meet and greet," Josh pointed out.

"They do?" Michael said.

Shit.

"And they get more people there than we do!" Laura said, shrugging at his hands. "*And* she was on the cover of *Seventeen*!"

"You were?" Michael said, removing one hand to turn around and look at Sasha.

Well, big surprise there.

"Why aren't *you* on the cover of *Seventeen*?" Michael asked, looking at Laura again. "You're smoking *hot*! You would look *awesome* on the cover. You do modeling, right?"

"Yeah," Laura said, her chin working.

"But we're back to the whole external locus, Laura," Michael said. "You don't get confidence from people taking pictures of you. That's a drug, just like the ones we rounded up. It's an addiction that there's *never* enough. You get confidence from a hard job, well done. And you did a *great* job. What you did with driving out those muggers probably had more direct effect than cleaning up the drugs. You *saved* people, even if you'll never see it directly and they'll never know. You did a great job, and you should keep doing it. It made the world a little bit better place.

"The Flyers are the flyboys," Michael repeated. "The flyboys are always the stars. Look at *Top Gun*. It's exciting. We're the grunts. We're not exciting. We never get the credit or the notice. But it's the *grunts* that get the job done. And the satisfaction we get from that is a job well done. Okay?"

"I guess," Laura said, tearing up.

He gave her a hug, trying not to notice that she had *really* nice boobs and all there was between him and that camel toe was a thin layer of spandex.

Squeezable.

Down, boy. Be the good guy here.

"It's not Sasha's fault," Michael said, releasing her reluctantly. "She had no control over it."

Laura gave an "if looks could kill" side-eye past him.

"I really should have said something," Sasha said. From the tone of her voice, she was feeling miserable.

Time to shift comfort.

"Look," Michael said, keeping one hand on Laura's shoulder but turning to the group. "We are all dealing with massive shit here. We get uprooted from our homes, tossed into fairly adult situations, thrown out in the public eye, and our preparation for all of that could be muuuch better. You guys all had friends, right? People you left behind?"

They all nodded.

"Man, in this place, I'm a fucking *nobody*," Michael said, a touch angrily. "Back home, I was the fucking *Boogie Knight*. People stood out of the *way* when *I* walked down the sidewalk. The corner boys, if I *acknowledged* them, it was *big* status. 'Man, you know Boogie Knight?' 'Yeah, man, we tight!' I had *status*. I had *respect*. In *this* place? I'm a fucking *nobody*. Think that makes *me* feel good?

"But you don't get confidence from people bowing and scraping!" Michael continued. "You don't get confidence from people taking your pictures or likes on Facebook or TikTok! You get confidence from facing a hard task and completing it. You get confidence, and, yes, respect, and *self*-respect, when you do the *unthinkable*, the *impossible*! And *that* is what supers are supposed to do. The jobs no normals *can* do!

"What matters is how you help *others*. Be the best super you can be, Laura," he added, tapping her on her upper chest.

Careful.

"*That* is where you'll find your *heart*."

"For an asshole, you can be a pretty good guy sometimes," Laura said, sniffling.

"Eh," Michael said. "I have my moments. Now let's get out of this shit. What a *complete* waste of time..."

"Tell me the doctor has fifteen minutes available," Michael said, gesturing at Dr. Swanson's door.

The light was on, and another super was in the room in Sight. So, the obvious answer was "no."

"Uh, she's in with someone right now," her secretary said. "She'll be through in about fifteen minutes, but..."

"Yeah," Michael said, taking a seat. "Really need an emergency session."

He'd had no opportunity to meet with the supers' therapist after the first patrol, so this was his only chance to meet with her before the next one. Michael didn't even get out his phone, just literally twiddled his fingers and examined the building under Sight until the other super walked out with Dr. Swanson.

"Doctor..."

"Michael," Dr. Swanson said.

"This won't take long," Michael said, standing up. "And it's pretty much got to be right now."

"Come in," Dr. Swanson said.

Michael took a seat as the doctor sat behind her desk.

"I heard about Miss Cherise," Dr. Swanson said. "We probably need to talk about that..."

"Not now," Michael said, steepling his fingers. "I'll deal with it later..."

"Michael..."

"Said I'll deal with it *later*," Michael said angrily. "I gots lots to deal with later. Later is when things ain't constantly putting more on. You cain't deal with it when there's *more* being laid on. Someday, maybe I'll find that gentle Eden. Place where nobody *putting* on me every day. Place where I kin *heal*. But that *ain't today*! So, I deal with it *later*, just like all the rest I gots to deal with *later*!

"I'll tell you the one part that gets me about it," Michael said, tapping his fingers together rapidly. "When somebody dies ain't got nothin', they let the dead collect 'til some point comes, too many bodies, monthly, quarterly, I dunno, then they send 'em to a crematorium. Then they take all the ashes together and they bury 'em in a potter's field.

"Real part that gets me?" Michael continued, his face hard. "My Mama's gonna be burnt and tossed in a hole with a bunch of ashes of other people ain't got shit by some hourly wage shovel wielder. And that shouldn't matter. It shouldn't! Body's just a shell. But it buggin' the fuck out of me.

"Right now, ain't time critical ... Deal with it later."

"If it's about the press conference ..." Dr. Swanson said.

"That's Laura's problem and I ain't got one," Michael said. "Talked her down off the ledge and got things smoothed. She'll probably be in here sometime. Probably should stock up on tissues. Two things we gots to talk about. First thing 'bout Bolt."

"Ah." Swanson's face was an unreadable mask.

"Hard for some people to tell groomin' behavior from just bein' nice," Michael said. "You can say all you want since I been groomed, been assaulted, that I might be a might *sensitive* to that. Might be *overreacting* to her just being friendly like. But there's one thing you *cain't* say nothing about:

"You *will* tell that motherfucker to keep her hands off my fucking body."

"Michael ..."

"Don't you dare 'Michael' me, Dr. Michelle Swanson!" Michael snapped. "You *will* tell that motherfucker to keep her hands off my fucking body, clothed or unclothed. You *will* tell her to keep her hands *off* my body! That shit ain't acceptable under *any* circumstance.

"And, oh, in case you're wondering, yes, she's a grooming *ped*. It's not even *vaguely* hid. What the fuck are you dumbshits doing using a fucking ped as a 'youth outreach coordinator?' Are you fucking *high*? Have you been doing the drugs we turned in? Or are you just outrageously *stupid*? Are you so drunk on Kool-Aid that you're letting a fucking ped run down the reputation of the Corps? Because when she gets caught—and she's *gonna* be caught—it's the *Corps* that's gonna bear the brunt."

Dr. Swanson remained as rigid as a cold, stone statue with perfect posture as he unloaded.

"I get how easy it is," Michael said, shaking his head. "First fucking patrol there's this dewy-eyed little brunette all super-excited to meet a super. I know how to groom. I know how to wrap somebody like that around my finger. I'd have been in that pussy in two days, flat. And she'd have cried but she never would have told. I know how to do that. You know why I don't? 'Cause I may be an asshole, but I'm not *that* kind of asshole! I'm not a rapist! So, I was a gentleman to her and moved on.

"That motherfucker you've got running the junior super doofs *is* a fucking rapist. If you think there's not a dozen kids out there that she's groomed and humped, you're *wrong*.

"So, if that motherfucker puts her hands on me *one more time*, the *best* you've got to look forward to is a super fight," Michael said, pointing at her. "That's the *best* outcome. That's the one you should *hope* for. You don't want to think on the other options. Are we clear as crystal on this subject, Doctor?"

"We're clear, Michael," Dr. Swanson said, then opened her mouth to continue.

"I don't care," Michael said, tapping his fingers together. "Just *keep* it. I know she's the fair-haired girl. I know she's popular. I don't care one bit. Best you can hope for is I throw her out Tony's window. That's the *best*. Make sure that is clearly understood.

"Item the Second—which by the way was the only one I was planning on having to talk to you about:"

He stopped and shook his head.

"Could you maybe, please, talk to my foster mom about the nutritional needs of growing teenage males?" Michael asked plaintively.

"Is she not . . . ?" Dr. Swanson said, looking concerned.

"She's doing what she knows is the right thing," Michael said, slapping his fist into his hand. "We're *vegan*! And we have *proper* portions! And we *eat to live*! And I've got *enough* shit on my plate without being *hangry all the fucking time*! I can put up with it being lousy vegan. If there's just *enough*! I'm a large, primarily European genetics-derived male. We need more nutrition than a four-foot-tall Bengali rice farmer!"

"You have really *clear* food insecurity issues," Dr. Swanson said, clearly alarmed. "I'll talk to her."

"Good luck," Michael said. "She has a mind like a steel ball. She is doing the right and true and *just* thing! Reduce, reuse, recycle! Meat is murder! But I've got my own room and that's something.

"On the subject of food insecurity. Does it not occur to the Corps that *some* members of Junior Super Corps might not have money to just *buy* their food when on patrol? Like, say, a kid in foster care who doesn't *get* an allowance? Or that, say, Jorge's parents might not have the money or at least shouldn't be out the money? 'Cause I had one tiny bowl of some granola shit for breakfast, a tiny vegan whatever that shit was for lunch, and then patrolled half of Central Park all evening on *nothing*. And that's hangry time as well."

"That...hasn't been addressed before..." Her eyes narrowed and the wheels were obviously turning.

"Only orphan you've got, huh?" Michael said. "We're infrequent," he added, heaving to his feet. "Good talk. Must do it again some time."

He paused in the doorway.

"Tony might want to be here the next time we have a patrol," Michael said. "'Cause if he's not in his office when I toss her out the window...we'll see if she can survive a sixteen-story fall. And that's the *better* option, I assure you."

CHAPTER 22

"Vater Unser" —E Nomine

Michael was sitting in science class for the unscientific, zoned out, and using his Sight to examine the building. He was up to about seventy-five meters or two hundred and fifty feet with Sight and he could see most of the building as well as the nearby buildings on whatever side he was on.

He'd gotten female vs. male sorted out early. The idea that there was "no difference between men and women" was sort of belied by, among other things, the pelvic girdle. Men's were joined, women's were separated at the front so the hips could spread during childbirth.

Race was harder. He'd found there was essentially no major bone difference between most races with the exception of African derivative, which was *very* different. In strong African background individuals, the femur bone was curved whereas it was straight in all other races. And there was generally some noticeable cranial and maxillofacial differences that were racial type class.

But it wasn't easy to spot. It wasn't as easy as spotting hair and skin color. In general, under Sight, most people just looked like . . . people. He started to understand how God saw the world. White, red, brown, black, yellow or really brown, people were just people. It was their *behavior* that was noticeable.

The other thing he could see was the rats. Not metaphorically, though that too, but the actual *Rattus rattus* crawling around in the walls and in the basement.

Michael hated rats. They were a constant of East Baltimore and more than once he'd been nibbled on in his sleep by one of the god-awful things.

But they made useful experimental subjects. He'd picked them up by their bones and generally fiddled with them including doing some things that were objectively sadistic. He'd heated the bones of one up to the point that they sublimed, turned into gas. The rat had died early on in the process, and he probably *should* have found a way to kill it other than burning it alive from the inside.

Then again, he really hated rats.

He wasn't worried about the evidence being found by a janitor or something. The dead rat's fellow rats immediately dove into the partially cooked carcass.

Having a better way to kill rats was on the agenda. Because a better way to kill rats was potentially a better way to kill whatever the Storm might be. No guarantee that if the Storm was kaiju, they would have bones. Hopefully, it'd be comprised of *some* kind of minerals.

He thought about it but decided to zoom into class just in case there was something he might miss on the quiz . . .

"Though the human body is, famously, mostly an ugly bag of water, it has *many* other elements and small molecules in it that allow us to grow and thrive. Chief among them is calcium, which besides being the structural material of bone is essential for muscle contraction and protein regulation. Then there's phosphorus, which is the main element of adenosine triphosphate—which, you may recall, is ATP, which is used in energy transport in the cells . . ."

Truth be told, there would've been some real value in the class to Michael's current extracurricular endeavors—had Michael not already known everything being taught.

Michael grabbed one of the larger rats that was close by its bones and zoomed in to the thing's brain. That would be the mostly empty gap surrounded by bone. Then he did Earth Move in that mostly empty gap and released the rat.

It dropped. Obviously dead. Another feast for its cannibalistic brethren.

"Huh," Michael said quietly.

"What?" Tim asked.

"Mike, do you have a question?" the balding, middle-aged teacher asked.

"So, does that have anything to do with vitamins?" Michael asked, thinking fast.

"Precisely," the teacher said with a glimmer of light in his eyes, glad to have any feedback from other than the front row. "These are all elements that make up what were originally called 'vital minerals' or minerals of life. The term was shortened to vitamins..."

"You didn't know that?" Tim asked quietly.

"Of course I did," Michael whispered. "I just wanted to drop the attention."

He needed to sort out the various Earth Elements. The problem being, he hadn't been able to find a chemist supply shop. He knew there were some, but they weren't nearby and most of them were just drugstores. He needed somewhere that had a variety of minerals he could...

He rolled his eyes and groaned slightly.

"You okay?" Tim whispered.

"Just need some *vitamins*! Duh."

Michael lined up the bottles he'd talked Linda into getting. He'd felt a little bad about it. He'd had to say he felt as if he was missing some "vital micronutrients" when, honestly, now that he'd taken over the cooking, he was feeling fine.

But he now had a variety of earth elements related to human biology, which was...most of them.

He could sense them as Earth Elements—calcium, potassium, manganese, phosphate, sodium in common table salt. They were all there. He could pick up any of the bottles by lifting the material within. But he couldn't sort out which was which.

He was pretty sure that the yoga pose for Earth Chemicals was just designed to force students to extensively study yoga. Compass Pose was an advanced yoga pose and although he'd gotten up to some intermediate poses, he wasn't quite flexible enough to contort that much.

So, he decided to just use a standard lotus and examine them. Thermal Earth was a half-rotated standing-log pose, for God's sake. He'd managed to figure out the *chakra* but was still working on the *pose*!

He spent about two hours just rummaging in his mind. Unfortunately, as usual, there were distractions.

He was pushing his Sight pushing farther and farther out and could look into most of the nearby homes. Which had the usual issues of being a Peeping Tom. People touched themselves a lot. More than he'd realized.

But the real issue was 1334.

The house was a duplex like many on the street. No problem there. But the family was a basket case. The dad was an abusive prick. Pretty much every night he was screaming at one of his kids or his wife or beating on one of them. Three kids, two sons, one daughter, all elementary school age, and honestly watching the way the family went on they were certainly not the easiest kids in the world. But the dad was just a freaking jerk.

He got distracted as he was considering the various bottles several times. The dad was winding himself up again. Sometimes he just lashed out without warning, sometimes he'd wind himself up until he was screaming at the kids or his wife, then the smackings would commence.

Michael knew that neighbors had called the police more than once. He really wasn't up for the CPS thing. Too often what the kids ended up in was worse than their home-life. And he knew why Gulshan said, "you couldn't become involved in everything."

But this was practically right next door.

The dad raised his hand to the daughter and Michael was done. He reached out, focused on the guy's tailbone, and tweaked it.

The father dropped his hand and collapsed to his hands and knees. Hitting the tailbone was remarkably painful. He sure as hell wasn't going to be yelling at anyone since he couldn't breathe for a moment.

The mother, who often would step in to take blows directed at the kids, rushed to see if he was okay.

He brushed her off, got to his feet, and started in on the daughter again, shaking his finger and getting his rage up.

Tweak.

Knees.

It took three times, but he finally gave up on whatever he was screaming at his daughter about, shuffled up to the bedroom, and lay face down on the bed.

Michael was going to see over time if negative conditioning could get him to some anger management classes.

Back to trying to sort the elements out . . .

There'd been another contact message from Gondola when he got out of school.

"God is building an army," Michael said over the phone.

"God has an army," Titanium replied. "Potential packet retrieval in Baltimore scheduled for this evening. Are you available?"

Michael didn't have anything he could think of that would interfere.

"Should be clear," he said. "Absent my foster parents coming up with something to interfere."

"We have flex on it," Titanium said. "It's being picked up by an asset not a merc."

"It's a threat zone," Michael said.

"The asset is aware and is capable of blending," Titanium said. "After it's retrieved, we'll mirror it and send you the original."

"Roger," Michael said. "I should be available depending on the vagaries of foster parents . . ."

"Mugasa," Hobbs said, careful not to touch his earbud. "Commo check."

Bruce Hobbs had practiced for the retrieval mission for several days. He'd continuously worn an old hoodie and rough jeans for three days to get the right smell as well as crunching his oldest pair of shoes through broken glass to get the right look of a drug addict living on the street.

The only thing that would be mildly incongruous if he was caught was the electromagnetic wand he had stuffed down his pants. It was anticipated that the dead drop was a chip. Finding it without the wand would be difficult.

He'd driven through the neighborhood several times to ensure he had the approximate location. He'd even done a drug buy just to give him a cover for being in the area. Though his native African skin was nearly cover enough.

"Mugasa, Titanium Asteroid, and Mountain Tiger. Mountain Tiger will be directing."

"Roger," Hobbs said. "Approaching the alleyway."

He was wearing the surveillance glasses again and turned his head from side to side, slowly, both to keep situational awareness and to give the overwatch team a look at the conditions.

Port Street was one of the areas of East Baltimore rife with junkies, homeless, dealers, and prostitutes, the very heart of the ghetto in Baltimore. Boarded-up shops matched the open ones, and those were largely split between beauty salons, thrift marts, and pawnshops. Many of these had smashed windows or mangled metal screens. Here and there, an empty shop was walled off with police tape. One was charred wreckage that looked as if it had been there for a while.

But the positive for the mission was that the population was constantly shifting. One more homeless drug fiend was practically invisible.

He turned into the alleyway and stopped.

"*Go in about thirty paces,*" Mountain Tiger said. "*Just walk the street. I'll tell you when you're close and to stop.*"

Hobbs entered the alley cautiously, which was normal on the street, looking around like a rat looking for food, just like any drug fiend looking for something, anything, that might be worth selling to buy drugs. There was another homeless down the alleyway, leaned up against the wall, rocking back and forth and rubbing at his arms. Bruce kept one eye on him as he moved down the alleyway.

"*Stop. Turn to observe the left wall from the right side of the alleyway . . .*"

Hobbs checked he wasn't being observed, then followed the directions.

"*Turn your head slightly right . . . Bag of garbage there . . . Got it?*"

"Yes," Hobbs said, looking at one of many bags of garbage in the trash-filled alleyway.

"*That area. Precisely, the target point is directly where that bag is sitting. But what you're looking for is somewhere in the area. So, don't feel like you have to check under it first. Check the wall first.*"

Hobbs pulled out the wand, the same sort of device used to check travelers at an airport, and began sweeping the wall. After only a few sweeps he detected something. But he couldn't find it in the dim alleyway.

"I have to use a light," Hobbs said. "There's something here, but I can't find it without light."

"*Your call.*" The voice was the boss of the operation, Titanium.

Bruce pulled out a small flashlight and, cupping it in his hands so the only light came out from between his fingers, used it to carefully examine the area where he'd had a hit.

After a moment he saw something up in the mortar of the bricks. There was a small crack and something was in it.

He pulled out a lockpick set and used one of the thin lockpicks to pick at the item. Slowly, he prised out the microSD chip and held it up for inspection.

"*Bingo,*" Mountain Tiger said with a tone of satisfaction.

"*Egress,*" Titanium said. "*Mission complete.*"

Now to just get "feet wet," as his mercenary trainers had phrased it, and out of this hellhole.

Ramon Sanchez lay against the wall of the alleyway, shaking back and forth, rubbing his arms against the cold and, apparently, against withdrawal symptoms. He had been wearing the same clothes for four days and had been in or near the alleyway for two. Just another homeless drug addict living on the filthy streets of Baltimore. The only thing that wasn't solid on the cover was the Glock 40 in his waistband. Any drug addict as far down as he was portraying would have sold it and the two spare magazines long before.

He studiously ignored the other "homeless" who was examining the wall. But when the man retrieved something from a crack and left the alleyway, he got up and followed. The individual walked in an unhurried fashion until he was well away from Port Street, where he boarded a bus.

"*Get on the bus,*" his handler ordered.

Sanchez got on the bus at the last second and took a rear seat, just another homeless drug addict in Baltimore. He pulled out his phone and pretended to text message, observing the courier through peripheral vision only while examining all the other riders as well with quick, unnoticeable, glances. None of them seemed to be a potential threat. Most were people returning from late work at a guess. One other homeless that wasn't, apparently, looking at the courier.

The courier, black, probably African from his skin color, five six, seventy-five kilos, took the bus four stops, then got off.

"*Stay on the bus,*" his handler said.

He stayed on the bus but saw the courier get picked up by a car.

"*Courier is feet wet,*" his handler said. "*Mission complete. Return to pickup point. Good job.*"

"*De nada,*" he replied.

He didn't ask who the courier was or what he'd picked up in a trash-strewn alleyway. Not when the people who sent you had rescued you from organ traffickers, gotten you into the United States as a political refugee, and gotten you a green card. They had given Ignacio Rivera, former cartel soledad, a new life. You did whatever they asked you to do.

God was building an army.

CHAPTER 23

"Ocean Avenue" — Yellowcard

"Hey," Michael said, tugging his earlobe. "You clean up well."

"Thanks," Laura said, pirouetting.

He'd suggested they take the subway into Manhattan. She didn't like to take the subway so he went out to the Far Rockaway station, got off the train, and met her on the platform.

The day was relatively warm, and she was dressed in tight jeans and a crop-top that showed off her assets.

Michael still hadn't been able to do any decent clothes shopping. All he could manage was jeans and a button-down shirt that wasn't fitted.

He was sort of glad he *hadn't* dressed up.

"I really don't like the subway," Laura reiterated.

"It's dirty, it's frequently crowded, and it's essentially a Law-Level Zero zone," Michael said. "We're both supers. If somebody gives you shit, just blow them."

"Oh, my God," Laura said, slapping him with both hands again.

"With your air power," Michael whispered since there were people around them on the platform.

"You're just so . . ." Laura said, then shook her head. "I'm still pissed about the press conference, but I guess you're right."

"Flyers are always going to get top billing," Michael said, shrugging. "And it definitely wasn't Sasha's fault."

"I just . . ." Laura said.

259

"You just hate her," Michael said, shrugging. "You do. Which you shouldn't. But it's a very human thing. Got any idea how much other girls hate *you* for the same reason? You are a very pretty girl and girls tend to hate girls who are prettier than they are or have higher status. But there's a reason that envy is a sin. I can get into the innate, biological reason that you're that way. But you're letting your id get the better of you."

"My what?" Laura said as the train came in.

They took seats. It wasn't particularly crowded, and it was mostly local families that seemed to be headed into town for a day of shopping or seeing the sights.

"Your id," Michael said. "That's how Freud described it. It's all those thoughts that lie just beneath the surface. Your subconscious. In my opinion—and it's a fairly knowledgeable opinion—it's innate, evolutionary processes that were developed when we lived in a very different lifestyle, back in the caveman days. So, a way of saying it is you're letting your inner cavegirl drive you. And you're not a cavegirl, you're a modern woman in a modern society that still runs, too frequently, by caveman rules."

They continued to chat as the subway headed in-town. After Lafayette Street, the characteristics of the riders started to change. It got a little rowdier and started to trend toward teen and twentysomething males. A few of the guys gave Laura the once-over. She was a very good-looking young lady and was dressed to show.

"Got a Covid mask with you?" Michael asked.

"Yeah," Laura said, confused.

"Put it on," Michael said, pulling his own out of his backpack. It was a cloth skull mask he carried around just in case.

"Why?" Laura said, but she pulled a surgical mask out of her purse.

"'Cause sooner or later one of these guys is going to ignore the guy with you," Michael said. "And we're going to aura and tell him to get lost."

"We're not supposed to reveal in public," Laura said, muffled by her mask.

"Thus, the masks," Michael said. "Then we get off at the next station, avoid whoever has seen us, and get on the next train."

"Oh," Laura said.

"Or you can blow them," Michael said,

"Would you *stop* that?" Laura said.

"When I first said it, I seriously wasn't thinking about it," Michael said. "I get distracted when I'm thinking about something, like how to scare a predator out of the bushes. But then when you got mad, I realized what I had said. I don't have an inside voice, okay? I just say stuff. But when you got mad and I realized why, I decided to just roll with it as a joke. 'Cause it's funny."

"It's *not* funny," Laura said.

"It's funny."

"Is not."

"Is."

About then one of the "youths" decided to try his luck with the built girl in the mask.

"Yo, baby," the guy said, hanging on the metal crossbar with both hands and leaning over Breeze to look down her top. "You be *fine*."

"Oh, God," Laura said, turning away. "*This* is why I don't like to ride the subway."

"Go away," Michael said, not bothering to look at him.

"Hey, I'm just being friendly," the guy said menacingly. "What are *you* gonna do about it?"

"You really want to walk away," Michael said calmly, steepling his fingers.

"Mike ..." Laura said, putting her hand on his arm. "Really, just walk away, okay?"

"Well, with the way you're dressed, don't you *want* guys being friendly?" the guy said.

"That's it," Michael said, tweaking the guy's tailbone, lightly.

The coccyx bone was a vestige of an evolutionary tail that had no remaining purpose on the human body. But because it was an evolutionary tail, designed to be moved around, and because it was directly at the base of the spinal cord, it was incredibly pain sensitive.

The guy's face went white and he let go of the strap, falling to his hands and knees in front of Laura.

Michael leaned over to the guy's ear.

"I *told* you you wanted to *walk away*," he whispered. "Now, you get to *crawl* away. Crawl."

"What ... ?" the guy gasped through the pain. Michael wasn't even applying pressure anymore. It just hurt that much.

"Go away or I'll do that to you again," Michael said and leaned back. "Worse."

The guy grabbed a pole, got to his feet, and stumbled away.

"There," he whispered to Laura. "Didn't even obviously use powers."

"What did you do?" Laura whispered back.

Michael thought about trying to explain and shrugged.

"He left," he said. "Does it matter?"

The people with phones were looking puzzled but either stopped filming or went back to doing what they'd been doing. And the few other guys who had been eyeing Laura turned away when he gave them a Look.

Possibly from having killed a few people in his time, Michael had a really good Look.

They managed to reach their stop without further incident and debarked on Twenty-third Street, taking off their masks as soon as they'd broken contact with the other riders. Then it was a few short blocks to the shop. Laura attracted some male looks along the way but there were no incidents.

Michael was sort of enjoying the "walking out with a pretty girl" thing more than he'd expected. Male status comes, in part, from what woman you're with. The Persians had a saying, "A woman is a man's jewelry," and Laura was some pretty jewelry.

Pride is a sin.

It's not like I'm sticking my chest out or anything.

Pride is a sin for a reason. So is lust, by the way.

He really had no interest in Laura in the long term but there was a little voice in the back of his head that was arguing in favor of reproduction. He told it to go away.

They finally reached the shop and Michael waved.

"Ta-da!" he said, waving at the storefront.

"How am I supposed to fly with ...?" Laura said, frowning at the scuba shop.

"Come on in," Michael said. "I'll show you."

There was another customer in the store and the sole clerk was busy, so they waited and checked out gear until he was free. It was high-end for a scuba shop, with rows of the shiniest new equipment and great pictures of beautiful island destinations and schools of tropical fish. There was a separate counter for travel plans and another for scuba lessons.

"Hi," the guy said. Medium height and build with brown hair and eyes. "Welcome to Downtown Scuba, I'm Mark. How can I help you? Thinking of taking scuba lessons?"

"Mark Cash?" Michael asked.

"Yes?" he said. "Oh, are you Stone Tactical? Jeez, I thought you'd be in costume or something!"

"Nah, we're in mufti," Michael said. "No telling. This is Fresh Breeze."

"Hi," Mark said, shaking her hand. "Uh, have to say, you're even better looking in person than in costume."

"Thank you," Laura said, smiling. "But . . . how does this get me flying?"

"Got a room in the back?" Michael asked. "Don't want to do this in public."

"Sure," Mark said.

There was another clerk in the back who Mark—who was the manager—waved out to the floor.

"Okay," Mark said, eyeing Laura professionally. "You're about a female medium. I was going to set this up, but I wasn't sure what her size was."

"Yep," Michael said, tugging his earlobe.

Mark got down one of the rental dive vests and attached it to a steel scuba tank that was a display item. Then he held it up.

"Try it on," Mark said.

Laura slipped her arms into the vest, then was shown how to attach the cummerbund that kept the vest from riding up.

"You'll want to pull that real tight," Michael said, opening it up, then pulling it as tight as he could.

"That's kind of . . . it's a little hard to breathe . . ." Laura said.

"It won't be on long," Michael said. "Now, can you Sense the air in the scuba tank?"

"Sort of," Laura said.

"Lift up on it," Michael said. "Warning: Try not to lift up on air on your spine. It will do the same thing to your spine as the little fuzzy."

"What?" Mark said.

"Never mind," Laura said, glaring at him. "Okay, here goes..."

"Lift slowly," Michael said.

Laura's brow furrowed, then she started to lift into the air.

"Oh, my God!" Laura said, squealing with delight. "I'm flying!"

"That..." Mark said, turning his head side to side. "Huh."

Laura started to weave back and forth.

"Careful," Michael said. "Not much room in here."

Out of the corner of his eye in Sight, he saw a purse snatcher grab a purse. He tweaked the guy's tailbone and, like the guy in the subway, he fell to his knees. Some passersby helped with getting the lady's purse back. A couple of them put in the boot on the purse snatcher.

People basically don't like crime.

"It's sliding up," Laura said. The vest was really only being held in place by her boobs.

Don't stare. Don't stare. Don't stare.

"Yeah," Michael said. "Come on down."

When Laura was landed and the vest was off, he considered it.

"What you really need is an air tank connected to something like a hang-gliding rig or a full climbing rig," Michael said thoughtfully, tugging his ear. "These are designed to hold on with just the positive buoyancy of a tank..."

"I have no idea what you are talking about," Laura said. "Can I fly or not?"

"You *could* with this," Michael said. "But it's not optimum. What we really need is to attach something like this to a climbing rig. But that would take some outfitting. And I didn't look for where to find climbing rigs."

He pulled out his phone to start checking for climbing gear.

"New York Outfitters is just around the block," Mark said. "They've got lots of outdoors gear and they do repairs and custom work. You could talk to them."

"Really need a nitrogen tank for safety," Michael said musingly. "Doesn't need to be under pressure, even. Though the Air Move might cause localized compression, so you'd want one designed to take pressure. Probably a Self-Contained Breathing Apparatus, or SCBA, would be best."

"Nitrogen is very stable," Mark said, nodding. "Very safe. And SCBAs are rugged."

"Can I work with ... that?" Laura asked.

"When you blow ..." Michael said, then paused.

Laura glared at him.

"You're mostly blowing nitrogen," Michael continued. "Air is made up of a little less than eighty percent nitrogen, a little less than twenty percent oxygen, which is what you need to metabolize, and the rest is a mix of other gases including, yes, carbon dioxide."

"I thought carbon dioxide was a lot of it," Laura said. "Are you sure?"

"He's right," Mark said, nodding. "There's a big increase in carbon dioxide, lately, but it's still in the less than point one percent region."

"Oh," Laura said.

"Can you expand air?" Michael asked. "Create a small area of lower pressure?"

"Yeah," Laura said. "I've tried that. You've got to be careful with it, though."

"Then you could do the same thing I did to the guy on the subway," Michael said.

"I still don't know what you did," Laura said.

"Guy was hassling her on the subway, so I just tweaked his tailbone a bit," Michael said.

"Ouch," Mark replied. "You can do that?"

"Bone is stone," Michael said, shrugging. "It's a sort of living limestone. Coccyx bone is nonvital, which is important 'cause it can cause cell damage. But Laura can do the same thing. Just expand the gases in the area."

"Ouch," Mark repeated. "Bends in the tailbone. Ow."

"What?" Laura said.

"Bends, also known as decompression sickness, is one of the most dangerous conditions in diving," Mark said, dropping into scuba instructor lecture mode. "It occurs, in scuba, when you've got too much nitrogen absorbed in your tissues and you come up to the surface. The nitrogen expands and can cause serious injury or even death."

"Oh," Laura said, clearly not getting it.

"The next time some guy is hassling you, where you're *not* going to see him again, just expand the gases right at his tailbone," Michael said. "It won't do any *serious* damage to him, but it will *really* hurt. Also, useful if you ever get, you know, a guy trying to rape you. Won't kill him, *will* get him to concentrate on something else."

"Huh," Laura said.

"Mark, thanks," Michael said, tugging his earlobe. "This is going to be interesting. But we need a better harness for it."

"Yeah," Mark said. "Uh, hey, can I get your pictures?"

"Only if they're for personal, obviously," Michael said. "Better yet: Breeze, you do Instagram and stuff, right?"

"Oh, yeah," Breeze said. "I've got nearly a million followers!"

"Why don't you get Mark's picture and say something nice about the scuba shop," Michael said. "And you don't talk about our identities, yes?"

"Got it," Mark said. "That would be great..."

CHAPTER 24

"Money" —Pink Floyd

"So...are we going to that place...?"

"New York Outfitters?" Michael said as they left the shop and paused on the sidewalk. "Not yet. You said you were buying me lunch."

"Oh, yeah," Laura said, wagging her head back and forth. "I'll buy. What are we having?"

"It's up the street," Michael said, pulling out his phone and checking it. "A little bistro. But the good news is *you're* not buying..."

"Phillip!"

The man greeting them was in his midtwenties, just over six feet with large cocoa-colored eyes and thinning auburn hair. He was dressed in dress slacks and a long-sleeved red silk shirt.

The bistro was an upscale one with an interior of warm wood and low lights. It smelled like money.

"Hey, Dave!" Michael said, giving him a handshake and manly half hug. "Good to finally meet you in person!"

"Phillip?" Laura said dubiously.

"Dave Harris," Michael said, giving her a "please just go along with it" look. "This is...we'll go with...Breezy? Okay?"

"So, you're, uh..." Dave said, nodding approvingly. "I've seen the...uh"—he lowered his voice—"costume you. Actually, saw you in the park one time. You're even better looking without it..."

He paused, grimaced, and blanched.

"Let me clarify that I meant..."

"I get what you mean," Laura said, smiling flirtatiously. "But... uh...?" She looked at Michael and pointed.

"Phillip," Michael said.

"Phillip didn't explain... *what's going on?*"

"Let's get a table and Breezy can catch up," Michael said.

"I met Phil taking a class at Wharton on Acquisitions and Mergers," Dave said after they had ordered drinks. "Brilliant kid with this serious ghetto accent," he added, shaking his head.

Michael had carefully chosen his seat so Breeze was opposite Dave.

"We just sort of hit it off," Michael said.

"I'm doing pretty well these days, but I come from a working-class background," Dave said. "So, we could communicate."

"He and Tony would get along," Michael said, tugging his earlobe.

"Oh, okay," Laura said. "You said you were taking college courses but..."

"I have a really old-fashioned problem with a lady buying lunch," Michael said, shrugging. "Besides, I wanted to meet up with Dave. Since he can afford it..."

"Okay," Laura said.

"And I can," Dave said. "No problem. So... Acquisitions have more than one meaning."

"Yeah," Michael said. "Got to be a touch careful about what we say on that. But... here I am!"

"And, Breezy?" Dave said. "You're... sixteen?"

"Seventeen," Laura said. "Going to be eighteen next spring. Then I have to decide, you know, what my future is going to be. I stay in... Juniors 'til I graduate high school and can continue over the summer if I want."

"So is there training for, that...?" Dave said.

"We get *no* training," Michael said. "Week of orientation, then it's 'well, you'll figure it out, there's not much to it.' I've been training Breezy."

"He figured out how I can fly," Laura said, leaning over to whisper.

"How...?" Dave said. He definitely heard her, but Michael could tell he was also distracted by the cleavage shot.

"Long story not for here," Michael said. "I take it from knowing the hostess's name they know you here?"

"They do," Dave said. "One of my favorite restaurants."

"They encourage a criminal justice degree," Michael said, answering the real question. "And there's a law enforcement academy you're supposed to pass."

"Tell me you're not going to waste your talents as a cop," Dave said.

"Not planning on it, no," Michael said.

"Would you like to order?"

Michael had just ordered the bacon cheeseburger.

Meat!

"Breeze, you don't mind if we do a little shop talk, do you?" Dave asked.

"No," Laura said, puzzled. "Go right ahead."

"Thought about your future?" Dave asked.

"Pretty much every day," Michael said. "When I was in the ghetto, didn't seem like there was one. You just hoped you'd see another sunrise. These days . . . think about it a lot."

"These days, you don't have to have a degree to be a trader," Dave said. "The thing is, they're looking for certain types of minds. People who are very high IQ, very high energy, and exceptional at math. Sound familiar?"

"Yes," Michael said. "And it's one of the things that I'm considering. Though, to be honest, I'd prefer a degree first. I might have been cancelled from the major universities, but I can still take remote. I don't honestly need it, but it's something to point to and say 'Yeah, I've got that.'"

"Thinking of how you're going to pay for it?" Dave asked. "You're talking about the university you were using when we met. Any idea how much that one course at Wharton costs?"

"I've been looking at how to use"—he unobtrusively pointed at his cheek—"to find minerals. But that's it. There are probably other uses."

"You'd use . . . that to make money?" Laura said, frowning.

"You've got an allowance and you model," Michael said. "I'm not into male modeling, thanks."

"You model?" Dave asked.

"I do, yes," Laura said, smiling and posing in her chair.

"Thing is," Michael continued. "There are other uses. That's the answer to the 'how to pay for it' question. And as for being a trader, or a quant for that matter, it will depend on what the world is like then. I can't do trading before eighteen, minimum, and honestly, they want someone a bit older."

"Some," Dave said. "You should think about it. And, yeah, quant, too."

"What's . . . that?" Laura asked.

"The squints," Michael said to a blank look. "The nerds that figure out the math for the traders."

"I'm good at math," Dave said. "You have to be to be a trader. But the quants are next level. Thing is, most of them don't have the focus for trading."

"I can get very scatterbrained and unfocused," Michael said, nodding. "But when I focus, you can't get me *out* of focus."

"I'm kind of the same way," Dave said. "Which is one thing they're looking for. As long as you can focus on the market. You really should think about it."

"If this is a recruiting lunch, I was expecting at least steak," Michael said, grinning.

"Well," the waitress said, setting down his meal in front of him. "You're going to have to settle for a bacon cheeseburger."

"Meat!" Michael said happily.

He bowed his head in prayer as the other two looked a bit confused but waited for him to finish.

"I wasn't aware you were . . . ?" Dave said.

"I am," Michael said. "I just don't talk about it much."

"This is too hot," Laura said, testing the vegan dish she'd ordered.

"You could always try blowing it," Michael said, with a straight face.

"What?" Dave said.

"Do *not* tell that story!" Laura said warningly.

The nearby table had cleared so there was nobody to overhear, and he ignored her.

"So, we're doing my first patrol in Central Park," Michael said. "By the way, amazing place . . ."

"Can I help you?"

New York Outfitters was a bigger place than Michael had expected.

It carried everything from weekend camping backpacks and gear to the sort of stuff you'd take on an expedition to the North Pole or Everest.

And that included a very full selection of climbing gear that included more types and varieties of climbing harnesses than Michael had realized existed.

Dave had glommed on, and he and Laura had been keeping up a steady chatter on the walk to the store.

That wasn't entirely unexpected, and it was one of the reasons that Michael had asked Dave to lunch. He wasn't sure if he was cursing or blessing Dave with Laura. But if she hadn't been a super, Laura's natural niche was trophy wife.

Dave was getting to the point in his career where he was supposed to start building clients for the firm. Laura was still "too young" for a girlfriend by present standards, but they were only six years apart and in six months, if you counted "at least out of high school," she wouldn't be.

Having a pretty girlfriend was helpful in building clients. Having one who was a super would be better. They were allowed to be paid to attend parties in "secret identity" mode and were a cachet in the Hamptons/Park Avenue set. "We're having a party; Iron Eagle is going to be attending in his *secret identity*!" They were known guests, also in "secret identity" at things like the Met Gala and other charity events. For which they were also usually paid.

On the other hand, it was Laura. She wasn't the sharpest tool in the shed and would be royally offended if Michael suggested she probably should try to "marry well."

All of which had carried them to looking at a wall full of climbing harnesses.

"I'm . . . not sure that you can," Michael said, turning to the clerk. He was a skinny guy who had "vegan climber" practically tattooed on his forehead. He *had* tattoos on his arms.

"We probably need to see someone that does custom work," Michael continued.

"I can probably help you out with whatever you're looking for," the guy said. He could tell a trio of newbies when he saw one.

Michael intercepted him with an offered hand but a disgruntled expression. "Hi, there. I represent an extreme sports Instagrammer who's looking to climb to remote areas and scuba in unexplored— look . . ." Michael shook his head in feigned frustration. "This is kind of technical and it's going to take custom work. Can I just talk to a manager?"

"You want to attach a scuba tank to a climbing harness?"

Bob Butzlaff, manager of repair and custom at New York Outfitters was about five foot six, skinny, bearded, also tattooed and had the look of someone who was out of good summits.

Michael explained the concept and talked about the scuba shop.

"That makes sense," Butzlaff said, nodding.

"Thing that I was thinking about on the walk is redundancy," Michael said, looking at the wall full of repaired gear. "What if the harness fails at five thousand feet?"

"That's not a good thought," Laura said. "I'm actually afraid of heights."

"You wanted to fly," Michael said. "We need a redundant system."

"Why would it fail?" Dave asked. "Do they?"

"Very very rarely," Butzlaff said.

"We're supposed to fight something in the Storm," Michael said. "Say Breeze is fighting—just an example—Godzilla, and it hits her harness and tears it. She'd survive even a major wound, but she might not survive the fall."

"If Godzilla attacks Manhattan, *you* can handle it," Laura said.

"Long Island," Michael said. "Little sister."

She grumped and stuck her tongue out at him.

"We actually need two separate systems," Michael said. "One the lift and drive, and an emergency backup chute. On a separate harness."

"We don't do parachutes," Butzlaff said. "I know the people for it, but we don't do it."

"Can you, firmly, attach an air tank to a climbing harness?" Michael asked. "Firmly enough, it won't come loose under stress?"

"That we can do," Butzlaff said, nodding.

"We'll consider the whole system later," Michael said. "We'll need to get the office chief to provide the funding, anyway. But if it's doable, we'll figure that out. Thank you."

Michael had arranged an after-school meeting with Tony and was waiting in the lobby. To the man's credit, he was easy to see, though he imagined Miri played a much fiercer gatekeeper when needed.

"Mr. DiAngelo will see you now," Miri said.

"Hey, Michael, siddown," Falcon said, waving at the chair. "Hell of a trip for you to take on a weeknight, so this must be big. If it's about Bolt, I've talked to hi...her, the doc's talked to her, the Secretary has talked to her. She understands to stay hands off."

"It's not about Bolt," Michael said, tugging his earlobe as he took the seat.

"If it's about the press conference..."

"I'm not worried about that either," he said. "I don't like public credit. Laura was pissed. I got her talked down. Jorge was pissed. I think even Josh was a little pissed. I don't care..."

"I heard about your mama," Tony said. "Like you asked the doc, we're keeping it quiet. How you doing on that?"

"I'll deal with it later," Michael said, then sighed. "The one part that's got me *furious* is so...stupid. I just hate that I can't give her a decent funeral. I hate being poor. I hate being a ward of the state. I hate being a foster kid. But the reason I asked to talk isn't any of that. Personal isn't as important as professional. It's about a way for matter shapers to fly."

"Matter...what?" Tony said.

"Matter shapers," Michael said. "Powers that shape physical matter—Earth, Air, Water."

He explained the basic concept.

"I was thinking about it from the point of view of the Storm," Michael said. "I think we're designed to fight something. But thinking about it some more, what about disaster response? We do that, yeah? It's a way for the matter shapers to move around quicker. There's only so many Flyers. It allows the Earth, Air, and Waters to do rescues, move faster from point to point where they are needed."

"That's a point," Tony said, nodding. "Though I have to say, public is just going to see 'more powerful supers.'"

"It's not making them more powerful in any way," Michael said. "Powers remain the same, we're just using some of them in a new way. It's adding a useful capability."

"Okay, there could be a way to spin that."

"Do we have an R and D budget?" Michael asked, tugging his earlobe.

"Not here," Tony said. "It's mostly handled by D.C. Can Kevin do it?"

"He's more into pretty," Michael said. "Light sewing and design. I'd prefer somebody do the work who understands the stresses. I was going to go with a local climbing guy. Can we get a Beltway Bandit?"

"A what?" Tony asked.

"A defense contractor," Michael said. "One of the people who works with Homeland Security. Something like that. But somebody who will just...do the job. Not suck down budget to come up with something that doesn't work."

"It's fire season in California," Tony said. "We're pulling in people to deploy them out west. Always lots to do with fires. Hurricanes. Ain't had a good earthquake in a while, not in the US. Lemme talk to the Secretary, see if I can get some budget, quick. We'll see if we can come up with something here. Probably can't get them for everybody, but we'll see if we can get one or two done in time. Have them try it out on the fires."

"That's a plan," Michael said.

CHAPTER 25

"Phoenix" —Cailin Russo and Chrissy Costanza, League of Legends

MT: I'm going for a walk.
LET: Okay. Be back by supper.
MT: Veg lasagna in the oven. Have to get back by done.

Having foster parents who cared was kind of nice in a distant way.

Having foster parents who wanted to track his every move on his phone was a pain in the ass. And if he hacked it, Frank was a good enough server guy to possibly notice. Had to save that for when it really mattered.

What he really wanted to do was try out an Earth Skill.

Skills were different from chakras. Skills were what you could *do* with chakras.

He'd gotten fair at Earth Shape to the point he could mildly sculpt. It wasn't his gift. He was going to have to practice more.

But there was a Skill using Earth Shape and Move that he found intriguing called Earth Fly.

Basically, you created a cocoon of stone or hardened earth, then used Shape to move it along underground. It wasn't tunneling. You only removed as much earth or stone as necessary to create the basic cocoon. Then you had to Shape earth around it on all sides while using Move to move it.

When you got good at it, the Earther could fly underground, completely unseen.

He wasn't up to that point. All he wanted to be able to do was walk along with an invisible cocoon of stone under his feet. You had to work your way up to flying underground. Baby steps.

The problem, for Michael, was first to keep anyone from noticing. That mostly happened when you created the cocoon. You had to remove some earth to do so and that might be noticeable. The second was that even in a place like East Midwood, there was so much stuff underground. Any time that anyone was having any excavation work done it had to be checked by a half dozen organizations. Water, sewer, power, telecommunications, they all had stuff under the ground. It was a maze.

He had enough range he could now get it deeper than most of the stuff in his Brooklyn neighborhood. But Manhattan, good luck. There was stuff going down hundreds of feet in places.

The real problem was the earth around the house. The back of the house was mostly a concrete parking area. If he pulled a plug up at the front of the house, it would probably be noticeable.

But. The next-door neighbors had a backyard with a lawn. That was potentially doable, but problem being on both sides it was a well-manicured lawn.

There was a small remaining patch of dirt in the back with a tree. He didn't want to harm the roots of the tree, but he pulled out a cylinder of dirt like a snake from under the roots and, thus, had a void. After that he took a small amount of concrete from the underside of a tile that wasn't going to be put under any pressure and formed an egg shape about the size of a football in the void.

"Okay, ready to roll," he muttered, tugging his earlobe.

The next step was to get it down to depth. He had to Shape the soil around the concrete egg while Moving it with the shaped soil. He found the combination tricky. It was a bit like juggling. Just getting it down to a depth where it probably wouldn't run into anything was a pain.

Finally, it got down to about seventy-five feet and that was good enough. Most of the stuff was in the first ten feet, anyway.

Then he had to move it around, preferably as he walked.

He started by just circling it beneath him, getting used to the combination of keeping the egg centered within the void, not hitting the sides, top, or bottom, and keeping the void opening, then closing continuously. It was harder to juggle both than he'd thought. He turned the egg of concrete into a small chunk, left it behind, and just worked on moving the void. When he had *that* down, he went back to the concrete, re-formed the egg, and moved both around deep under the parking area.

When he finally felt like he had it down, he started walking, slowly, feeling it along underneath him.

He walked slowly down East Twenty-eighth Street, headed for Avenue N. He'd been up to Avenue M going to the subway. He wanted to try a new direction.

He walked down Twenty-eighth slowly to N, then turned right. He didn't want to deal with crossing many streets as he was still having trouble juggling walking with Moving. He passed or was passed by a few people as he headed west on N. One was a man in a suit and broad-brimmed black hat and Michael realized he'd entered a fairly heavy Jewish area. As he passed a synagogue, the reason became obvious.

He continued walking down to Twenty-first Street, getting increasingly confident, then headed north to M. His route deliberately kept him in a single-family-homes area. Less likelihood of a confrontation of some sort. Few people gave him a passing glance; he was just a kid wearing a backpack and a hoodie. The weather was a tad warm for the outfit, but he gave off "don't bother me" vibes. If anything, people were looking at *him* as a potential threat rather than the other way around. Much easier to do this sort of thing than in East Baltimore, where he'd have had to keep his defenses up one hundred percent on a walk like this.

Hell, he might even be able to walk around this neighborhood thinking about astrophysics. Wouldn't *that* be a radical notion.

Once he got to M, he just turned his mental autopilot on and headed for home.

The lasagna wasn't going to get itself out of the oven.

"Glory to the Brave" —Hammerfall

He'd gotten the brush pass from the courier as he walked home from school. Fortunately, Tim had an after-school tutoring session, so he was free guilt-free.

When he got home, he inserted the microSD card into his borrowed laptop and opened it up. Frank was in his office working from home, but Linda was out, so he only had to track one person.

The password was the same as the one on the directory in Mama's phone. His full name and birthdate.

Inside were a series of folders:

AAAThisFirst

AABThisNext

AACAlltheRest

"Okay," he said.

Inside "AAAThisFirst" was a single video file named: LASTWILLANDTESTAMENT.

He started the video.

It was of Annabelle Follett in what was obviously one of the abandoned town houses that homeless flopped in in Baltimore. There was some light coming in from a window and she looked . . . wrung out. Her hair was stringy and hung in her face.

"*My name is Annabelle Follett*," she said, holding her phone out in front of her. "*I am a former resident of Glen Cove, New York, and heiress to the Follett Trust. This is my last will and testament. Being, despite the look, of sound mind I hereby leave all of my worldly goods and moneys to my biological son, Michael Robert Edwards, born today, July the 5th, 2012. I did not leave him in an alleyway as people will be told. I left him in the care of a friend, Miss Cherise. Hopefully, she'll be allowed to adopt him. Why I made that choice is no one's concern. He is my son, and he is entitled to my share of the fortune.*

"*His father is Derrick Sterrenhunt. That's spelled S-T-E-R-R-E-N-H-U-N-T. He was a law student at Georgetown last fall semester. He was the only man I slept with during the time that Michael was conceived. So, he's the dad.*

"*Why I am choosing to do things this way is no one's concern. I am of right mind, and this is my choice. Everything goes to Michael.*"

Her face worked for a second and she shook her head to keep from crying.

"*Baby, if you're viewing this, and I have to hope it's you, I did this for a reason and I did not leave you in an alleyway. I just hope you can make it here. It's tough. But you're going to have to be. Just . . . live. Survive. That's all I can hope for you. Goodbye.*"

"Goodbye, Mom," Michael muttered. He closed that one and opened up AABThisNext. Not too surprising, it was a longer video.

"*Hi, Michael,*" Annabelle said. She was looking a little better. She'd gotten a shower somewhere and cleaned up her hair. "*At least, I hope it's Michael watching this.*

"*However this got into someone's hands, it's for Michael Edwards and, I assure you, you don't want to be viewing it. It's likely to get you dead. So stop now and put it back where you found it.*"

She'd been stern for the warning but now brightened again.

"*Michael. You probably wonder why the hell any mother could leave her child the way I left you. And I'm sorry. I really, really am. But by the time you watch this I'll probably be dead.*

"*I told Miss Cherise to keep an eye on you and take you to the spot you were supposedly left when you were old enough to be on your own. And tell you there was something important about it. Something special. Also, I told her if anything happened to her, she needed to make sure you got her phone and knew how to open it.*

"*I left you there to hide you, baby. Hide you from some of the worst people on earth. No, not some of, the worst people on earth.*

"*There's an organization. It's called The Society. They're mostly in finance and old-wealth families like, well, us. My grandfather, your great-grandfather, was a member. They don't have women as members.*

"*They . . . pretty much run everything. And they're so horrible you can't begin to imagine.*"

Her posture had withered over the last few lines, but she found a renewed determination and straightened.

"*The guy who runs the Trust now, Wesley Conn, used to be my stepdad. I don't think he even cared about marrying my mom. What he wanted was to get his hands on me. I . . . It's hard to say this but he started raping me when I was eleven. And he made me screw other guys— Society guys, just rich pedos, New York, Florida. Hell, he took me to Germany one time to get gang-raped.*"

Frank had gotten up and stopped at the stairs. Michael paused for a moment to see if he was coming by, but the man headed downstairs instead.

"*They're worse than that. They, and I know this sounds crazy, but they sacrifice children to Satan. I know, I know how it sounds. But they made me watch one time when I was thirteen, right after I'd tried to run away."*

Her eyes darted around as if looking for a way to escape, but her bearing held firm.

"They raped them first and they raped me along with her. I thought they were going to kill me, too. And the worst part was that it was right in the house I grew up in, in a room in the basement. I thought I knew the whole house, but it was a secret room. They made me watch what they did to her. Her name was Angelines Cuellar. She was from Guatemala. They tortured her and they raped her, and they raped me and then they . . . cut open her chest and drank the blood from her heart.

"She was twelve."

She'd refocused on the camera and stared for a moment.

"Wesley told me if I ever told, they'd do the same thing to me. Just say I'd run away, like I'd just tried to do. I ran away a lot. They always found me when I was younger.

"Then, when I was fifteen, I thought I'd figured out how to survive. I ran away and this time instead of just going and partying and trying to forget, I started looking for certain types of people. One of them was a professional jewel thief. Another one was a grad student at MIT. I'd offer them sex and whatever they fucking wanted to teach me skills.

"Wesley had told me, bragged to me, he had an insurance plan in his safe. A bunch of videos and photos of powerful people doing bad things. If things went down, he was planning on using it to bargain his way out. I thought I'd try to do the same."

Now her gaze dropped low and her shoulders settled.

"So, when I was seventeen, I went back. First, I rigged up my room, then had sex with a lot of the bastards who had raped me when I was younger. Got them talking about it.

"Then I went to Conn's condo in Park Tower and slipped a roofie into his drink so he passed out during sex. Then I broke into the safe. There was a hard drive and couple of notebooks. I took photos of those and copied the hard drive.

"The hard drive is in the Holy Sepulchre Cemetery in Trenton, New Jersey. Grave 148-D as in Dela. It's under the gravestone.

"This chip has some of the videos from it, the ones I took and the photos I took of the notebooks. I have to warn you, baby, the videos and

photos are rough. I hope you got adopted and raised somewhere nice. I hope. But Miss Cherise was supposed to try to keep track of you. If you've been raised easy . . . these are going to be tough to watch."

Michael chuckled cynically. "I think I'll be fine, Mom. Didn't have quite so nice a life as you'd hoped."

Maybe shitty lives are genetic?

"Whatever you do, don't try to take them to the authorities. That was my mistake. I thought I could take them to the FBI, and they'd protect me.

"I did. I showed the one of Conn from my room to a couple of FBI agents and told them about what had happened to me. Named names. They were arranging protection—or so they said.

"When I went to the pickup, the guys who were supposed to pick me up, who were supposed to be FBI, were Fieldstone security. I've got a really good memory for faces. I'd seen them working a party years before. I spotted them before they spotted me, and I just ran.

"I've been running ever since. I hate to say this: I'm not sure why I had you. Your father was a good man. He took me in and never even asked questions. He was a former soldier. A truck driver going to Georgetown on the GI Bill. When I got pregnant, I didn't know what to do. I just ran again. I couldn't bring all my hell down on him.

"I was in Richmond, and I was going to get an abortion. Then I changed my mind. I got another street girl who was getting one to use my name at the clinic."

Her gaze had wandered around again for a while, but now she locked onto the camera again. She was looking right into her son's eyes.

"Maybe it's selfish but I just wanted someone to live through this. I have to hope you did. I went to the hospital to see you just a couple of hours ago. I wanted to keep you. I wanted to hold you and protect you. But I can't even protect myself. There's no one to turn to and no one who can help.

"They're going to find me but maybe they won't find you. Whatever you do, don't go to the FBI and don't try to take them head-on. But . . . maybe you can find a way. Maybe you'll be smarter than your mother. Go find your father. Maybe he can help. He was really smart. Maybe I just should have told him the truth.

"Just know that I love you. The most important thing is that you survive. I love you, baby. Please, just . . . live."

"Well, so far so good," Michael said.

It took him a few minutes to settle before moving on. Hearing all of it from Gondola, seeing the photos, and knowing what happened academically was all one thing. Hearing *her*, seeing *her*, learning the details from *her* was something else entirely. When he'd heard all of it from Gondola, he'd been so full of rage, so ready to go out and burn the world down to get revenge. But right now he felt *nothing*. He was empty, numb. He wasn't even tugging as his damn ear like he usually did at times like this.

He opened up the other folder and it was full of videos. Some of them were marked "Anna" and he skipped those. There were a series of ones marked DH followed by a name and initial. DHJonesA. DHWilsonB.

Those were Dark Hand initiation videos.

Curious, possibly recognizing one of the names, he looked at it.

It opened with a black screen with writing: DARK HAND INITIATION CLARENCE PUTNAM followed by a date.

Then the video started, and he had seen enough similar he wasn't interested. He fast-forwarded just to see if it was as described.

It was.

That was all he needed. He had enough nightmares.

He both pitied and feared anyone who could watch anything like that without cringing. His life had royally sucked, but at least he'd had his Mama.

Putnam was a common name in the South, but he was curious, so he pulled up Wikipedia and did some digging.

Yep. Clarence Putnam was the father-in-law of the former FBI director. Recently deceased. Same face, though. Old-wealth family.

There were more videos and photos of major people in compromising positions. Dozens. And this was just the sampling of the hard drive his mother had left.

He looked at the photos of the pages and puzzled over them for a few seconds. That was all it took. The code that had baffled his mother was a simple substitution code. One of them contained names of people along with code names. A members list but probably just the ones who reported up to Conn. Quite a few, though, and some major names again.

The other, though, was a tad more interesting. It was an account book of offshore accounts. It was Conn's black money. His escape money. Hundreds of millions of dollars.

"You did well, Mother," Michael said softly. *Big boys don't cry.* "I won't let you down."

"Not a great day for flying," Michael said.

But it's nice to be outside right about now.

They'd taken the prototype to the Park to try it out. They'd used the NYPD parking area off West Eighty-sixth Street and were trying it out on the mostly deserted Great Lawn. A front had come through and blown down most of the leaves and the Park was wet with a raw northwest wind.

There was a courier retrieving the hard drive from Trenton. You couldn't do everything yourself, especially when you were a thirteen-year-old foster child.

"I'll take it if I can fly," Summer Storm said. "My hubby can warm me up when I get home. Or at least start a fire."

Summer Storm was a tall, platinum blonde with a shapely figure married to Bonfire, a thermal. Since she was going to be doing "public," she was in her costume which, like Breeze's, was not well designed for a cold, wet, windy day.

Michael was wearing his skull mask and a hoodie, as much against the weather as to keep from being identified.

The harness was based on a cross between a climbing and a parachute harness. It had a soft thigh connection to allow for lift with more padding on the chest straps and went over the shoulder. The SCBA, the same type as used by firefighters, was zipped in upside down and had additional metal straps to ensure it didn't go anywhere. It was ruggedly built and should stand up to the rigors of flying.

"Just try lifting into the air," Michael said, tugging his earlobe. "Try it out carefully."

Storm lifted up, gently, then had to correct as the wind blew her to the side.

"Funny that the wind is an issue," Storm said, laughing.

There were a few people who had braved the park and there were pictures and video being taken.

She lifted higher, then swung around, moving over the Great Lawn in a manner more similar to a jetpack flyer than one of the super

Flyers. The Flyers normally took a position parallel to the ground in proper superhero fashion.

She came in for a landing, carefully, and grinned.

"It's more like a jetpack," she said, noting the similarity. "I'll take two."

"You'd have to talk to Tony about that," Michael said. "You won't be able to keep up with the Flyers. But once we get the matter shapers equipped, if we can get the budget, you'll be able to move around more effectively. Useful for rescues. You'll have to work out SOPs on that. Probably carry a separate lifting harness with you to recover people from floods, that sort of thing. Probably useful with fires, though I can't work out exactly how. Not enough experience with them."

Michael had learned supers weren't just "super-cops." They spent about half their time doing disaster response. With forest fires, they were significantly stronger than normals and often worked as fire crews, cutting lanes and setting backfires. Many of them took fire academy courses as well as law enforcement. The Corps would pay for it as well as paying them full-time while they took the course.

Supers were well paid. On first joining Super Corps, they started with the pay of an Army major and were quickly promoted plus had seniority bonuses. Many of them who had been in the Corps for a while earned the pay of a full colonel. And since they were federal employees, there was a cost-of-living adjustment for living in New York and Los Angeles, their two primary bases.

Tony's pay rate was equivalent to an Army two-star general.

In addition, many of them earned side-money from being paid attendees at events as well as selling signed photos. They even attended science fiction conventions. Electrobolt was constantly being paid to attend high-end parties on Park Avenue and in the Hamptons, where she had built up considerable connections. One of the reasons she was so hard to oust.

There were reasons for it. The main one was retention. After a spate of super-terrorist attacks, starting with the Nebraska Killer, the federal government decided it *really* wanted to keep its eye on all the supers. Then there was the problem of criminality. Some supers who came from criminal backgrounds had turned around and immediately started using their powers to commit crimes.

Thus, the Supers Act, which had withstood Supreme Court scrutiny.

When a kid Acquired, they were *required* to register with the federal government and were added to a watch list. Though they weren't required to join Junior Super Corps, most did. And they were encouraged, as well, to join the Corps. Generous pay and benefits as well as, honestly, being pampered in a way that most federal employees were not, were ways to encourage joining. Even if an FBI agent *could* go to an event and sign autographs, it was against federal regulations. Supers had an exemption.

There were always iconoclasts. Some just walked away completely from their powers, taking regular civilian jobs, sometimes after a period in the Corps to pay for college. Those went into the Corps Reserve in case of an emergency. Some started Storm Cults, prepper militias devoted to preparing for the Storm. At least one of those had had their powers severed for, like David Koresh, being a little *too* into the underage girls in the cult and refusing to submit to arrest.

Of the three hundred and fifty-six Acquires in the US, two hundred and fifty were in the Corps. Twenty-six had had their powers severed or been killed for some criminal act. Fifteen had Storm Cult militias centered around them, and Michael was sure that the FBI had multiple undercovers in each. Ten were juveniles, all currently in JSC.

The rest were just living their best lives as normals.

"Anyway," Michael said, shrugging. "It works. That was the question. Just remember not to hit your spine with your powers. That will at least temporarily paralyze you."

"Can I keep it?" Storm asked.

"It's fitted to you," Michael said. "Up to Tony, but I don't see why not. And take it out to Cali. Try it out if there's a reason. It will give us some additional flying support and I don't see a reason that would be an issue."

"Eh," Storm said, frowning. "You haven't been around very long."

"Use it for something useful and I'm pretty sure we can overcome the Madame Secretary's aversion," Michael said, smiling. "You won't be able to keep up with the Flyers. They're designed for it. But you'll be able to do more than just run around beating out fires. Enjoy and you're welcome. Nice to have *one* problem fixed. If I could just fix the others as easily..."

⊕ ⊕ ⊕

Soli Talas carefully did not look at the old man covered in tattoos as the group took a brief rest, deep in the Sonoran desert. Nobody spoke to him. No one dared.

He didn't stand out from the group. He wore the same cheap T-shirts, jeans, and work boots. All of his clothing was old and worn. He carried the same gallon bottle of water, the only water they had on the fifty-mile trek to enter the US. He even was carrying the same seventy-five-kilo pack of marijuana on his back that paid for the coyote.

Every single member of the group was wondering two things: Why was an OG member of MS-13 walking through the desert with a bunch of field hands? And were any of them going to live to talk about it?

Michael slid silently out of the sky onto a hill in Green-Wood Cemetery and just looked around, scanning for any signs of being discovered.

Michael had considered bringing Tim along for this caper, then rethought it. There were just too many problems. First, both Tim's parents and Michael's insisted on phone tracking. He was already taking a risk with Frank hacking his own phone to show the "proper" location. If he'd brought Tim, he'd have to risk hacking another and double the number of parents who might discover the trick.

Second, if they got caught it would be no big deal for Michael. He'd probably get rehomed, but that was something that happened whether you wanted it or not, whether you were good or not, whether you were bad or not. There was no "naughty and nice" list for rehoming. Like he'd told the little foster kid Tahwan, good home, bad home, all evens out in the end. He had no control over that.

But in Tim's case it would be a major issue. His mother would hit the roof but worse it would probably involve a police report. Though juvie reports were supposed to be secret, these days things got ferreted out. Tim was hoping to get into Columbia. The likelihood of that if he was caught in Green-Wood Cemetery after dark was low to zero. He already hadn't made it into one of the magnet middle schools. It was probably wrong that by eighth grade you were "tracked" to either top colleges or crap colleges but it was reality. Worse for Tim, he was Asian. And Asians faced all sorts of barriers to getting into top schools cause so many of them were, you know, properly prepared.

Third: Getting there *with* Tim would have been difficult. Without him it was a cinch.

Putting a large stone in a backpack was much simpler than better harnessing a scuba tank, though a few chafed areas meant he'd still look for a better rig in the future.

Picking it up to about a thousand feet above ground level, by far the highest he'd ever flown, he was virtually invisible in dark clothing and the night sky. All he had to do was avoid being spotted by a passing helo and they were few this time of night. There was, like, zero actual radar in the New York area because the US had approximately zero real air defenses. That left the Flyers spotting him, which would be awkward seeing as he wasn't supposed to be able to fly.

The Flyer patrols were all over in Manhattan.

He'd reached his destination without anyone, apparently, seeing him. Now, it wasn't time to fly. It was time to try something else.

Most of Green-Wood was covered in graves. But there were gaps, plenty of them. And it was time for Michael to try flying underground.

He'd been reading up on Green-Wood and its histories had lots about "unmarked graves." He was pretty sure there were more than they realized. He'd landed in an area that had no gravestones and he could see bones beneath the ground. Most of them were nearly gone from being in the soil for so long. But he really didn't want to disturb graves.

But he finally found a space that was clear of any old graves and, even better, clear of grass. It was under an ancient tree near the corner of Cypress and Vine Streets.

He created a hole about the size for him to stand up in it—pretty much like, say, a grave—then slowly reshaped the earth so he lowered like an elevator and the earth slid up over his head.

He couldn't do it for long; he would run out of air. But he sat down on the bottom of the hole and began shaping the earth around him, "flying" underground.

He was now looking at the cemetery from underneath with Sight.

He popped up a short distance away to get some fresh air in the hole and take a breath of air, then dropped down again.

Navigating was hard. In the cemetery he'd memorized landmarks while on the day trip with Tim. But finding them again from underground was different.

He flew around under the cemetery for about an hour, popping up from time to time for air like a gopher.

"Take that, gopher!" he muttered. "The gopher Cong!"

Now that he was getting better at this, he needed to source a few good portable oxygen bottles, something more manageable than scuba tanks.

Finally, he went back to his original entry point and popped out. He used the pile of dirt to fill in the hole, then waved some snow over it. It wasn't perfect but it would have to do.

He looked up into the sky. There was a prediction of more snow soon. Hopefully nobody would notice this little marking before it got covered.

With that he took back off into the air.

"Time to R-T-Beee!" he said in his best superhero voice, thrusting one fist into the air as he flew.

The sound was lost in the wind and sky.

CHAPTER 26

"Becoming the Bull" —Atreyu

Michael turned on the recording app again as he went into Super Corps headquarters for his third patrol. Their second patrol had been uneventful. It was one of the bimonthly weeknight outings and had been cold and rainy. Madeleine had apparently had better things to do that evening than babysit.

Unfortunately, tonight she *didn't* have better things to do.

"Well, here we all are again," Madeleine said, smiling thinly then giving him a glare. "Time to get it on!"

Madeleine followed them into the locker room, then confronted Michael just as he'd gotten his shirt off.

"Mike, I don't appreciate you talking to the principal," Madeleine said, her arms crossed. She reached out and grabbed him by the shoulder and shook him. "I am just trying to be friendly! You need a *friend*!"

"I *have* friends," Michael said loudly, prying at her hand. Damn she was strong. "And, again, I do not like to be touched! *Please remove your hand*."

"You're a homophobe!" Madeleine said. She pulled up her skirt and pulled out her penis, stroking it erect. "You need to get over your innate homophobia!"

"Madeleine!" Sasha said. "*Stop it!*"

Michael couldn't help noticing, in passing, that she'd gotten down to bra and panties.

Great, now the image of Sasha in her underwear will forever be spliced with the image of Bolt's penis.

"Madeleine," Josh said. "This is not a good way to handle this..."

"You need to realize *everyone* is *innately* homosexual!" Madeleine shouted, hitting him with her erect penis. "You're *innately* homosexual!"

"Okay, that's *enough!*" Michael snapped. *What the hell?* He picked her up into the air and moved her away from him with Earth powers. "Hitting me with your *dick* is way *beyond* enough!"

He didn't want to move her back too far because it would show how he'd been working his powers.

"THIS IS *ASSAULT!*" Madeleine yelled, struggling like a fly in amber. She'd dropped the falsetto at least. "YOU'RE ASSAULTING ME!"

The electro flashed a wicked grin and threw out her hand. Fractious, jagged blue-white light arced across the room and electricity surged through Michael.

"MADELEINE!" Sasha screamed as Michael dropped to the floor and started convulsing. "STOP!"

"HE *ASSAULTED* ME!" Madeleine yelled, continuing to pour electricity into the convulsing juvenile.

Sasha grabbed her by the arm and dragged her far enough away she was out of range of Michael.

"That's it," Sasha said. "You're out of the locker room!"

"Let *go* of me!" Madeleine snapped, putting her hand on the super.

"Did you just zap *me*?" Sasha said, laughing. "You know I'm *invulnerable*, right?"

She thrust the electro out the door of the locker room, then looked around.

"Okay, how do we *keep* him out?" Sasha said. "Her."

"J-J-Josh," Michael gasped, pointing at the door, shakily. *Damn, that hurt.* "S-seal it. M-metal."

"Right," Josh said, going over and putting a light weld on the door.

"You okay, amigo?" Jorge said, squatting down by Michael.

"N-n-never b-better," Michael said, getting up to at least sitting on the bench. He was still twitching. "Healing. I'll b-b-be fine. Well, th-th-*that escalated qu-quickly.*"

It hurt like hell, but he'd hurt before.

He looked around at the group and smiled.

"Sash, thanks," he said. "B-better that than what I-I-*I* was gonna do. And th-thanks, everybody."

He got up and stretched, still jangled but getting better. God, he loved regenerative healing. Getting hit like that before he had it . . . would probably have killed him. Recovery would have sucked.

"I never had any friends when I was in Baltimore," he said. "Didn't want to join the gangs. It's nice to have a gang," he added, looking at them and nodding. "Especially such a good-looking one."

Sasha suddenly seemed to realize she was in bra and panties. And then there was Laura. Her costume had a built-in bra, so she was just in pink panties, holding her arm over her breasts.

"Don't get weird on me," Michael said, smiling. "It's just nice to have somebody at my back."

"Well, I gotta get my costume on," Laura said primly. "Turn around?"

"Will do," Michael said. *Reluctantly.* "And that's literally at my back."

"We need to do *something* about Bolt," Sasha said as the guys and gals turned their backs again and she continued dressing. "She's *totally* out of control. That was *not* okay!"

"Was she like this with you?" Michael asked Jorge. He wiggled his fingers and sort of felt them, but couldn't completely control them yet.

"Yeah," Jorge said. "Though she never actually hit me with her dick. She was always whipping it out and saying I wanted to suck it. *Him* back then."

"What are we going to *do*, though?" Sasha asked.

"We should do a petition to have her removed as our mentor," Laura said. "That's what you do when someone is like that."

"And have everyone know you're a transphobe?" Michael asked. "'Cause that's what she's going to say. That we're transphobes."

"She hit you with her . . . penis," Sasha said. She was dressed now but had stopped prepping the rest of her gear.

"Won't matter," Michael said. "She's an activist. All the trans activists will rally round her because *Trans!* And Trans! Are allowed to do *anything!* Anyone who doesn't agree is a TERF. So, Laura, you'd be branded a TERF."

"I'm not . . . that," Laura said. Breeze was still getting ready, but it was super slow as she paused after just about every action.

"I know that, you know that," Michael said. "But all her followers on Instagram will be all over your feed calling you a TERF and a homophobe and a transphobe."

"So, we don't do *anything*?" Sasha asked angrily.

"There are three real-world, adult choices," Michael said. "I'm surprised that Josh hasn't suggested one of them."

"You mean a lawsuit for sexual harassment?" Josh said. He, above the others, had remained the most focused of preparing for the patrol but he carried a tense energy. "It's not just the publicity problem. What we'd be called because, yes, that would happen. I have to think about that from the point of view of schools. You don't get into Harvard if you've been publicly branded a transphobe."

Or a white supremacist.

"We're also going to have to deal with Super Affairs our whole *lives*. I'm not sure I want the Secretary *that* pissed at us."

"And that's another issue with coming forward," Michael said. "The Secretary is going to be livid. And everyone walks on eggshells around the Secretary. So, Josh, what are the other two choices?"

"Not sure," Josh said.

"Media," Michael said, tugging his earlobe. "Bolt is hugely popular with the *Gotham Herald* and so on. But the *Post* would take the story. Big headline: *Pedobolt?*"

"Not the *Post*!" Laura said. "That's as bad as Fox!"

"Does anybody read that rag?" Josh asked. Finished, he put up a hand and his locker door slammed shut with a loud *clang!*

"My papa does," Jorge said. He was only a hair less lethargic than Sasha. "So do his friends. I'm . . . not real happy about having them know, you know?"

"That's what keeps kids from coming forward," Michael said, donning his armor. "Shame over what's happened. I don't got it. I have no shame button. But I know others do. So, what's the third choice, Josh?"

"Again, not sure," Josh said. "This isn't really my dad's field."

"Did you ever talk to him about it?" Michael asked.

"No," he admitted. "Bolt used to look at me . . . creepily? But 'til Jorge came along he wasn't—*she* wasn't that bad."

"I'd just push him off," Jorge said, shrugging. He still hadn't donned his mask. "Back when her was a him. But he never beat me with his dick! That's . . . sick."

"Madeleine is a very sick person," Michael said. "Which will be another defense. 'I have mental health issues!' Yeah, no shit. So, third choice: CPS."

"Oh, I'm not sure about that," Sasha said. "They can get things sort of backward, you know?"

She'd had dealings with Child Protective Services or been around them. Interesting.

"I know the head of ACS here," Michael said. "For one thing, it keeps it quiet. ACS is all about secrecy, which is a bad thing sometimes and a good thing at others. In this case, if Madeleine's name comes up, or Electrobolt's, it would just be her involvement with an 'after-school' program. It wouldn't have to bring in the Corps at all..."

Michael had seen Patrick Thesz—Iron Eagle—arrive and have a discussion with Bolt in Sight. Now he was headed for the locker room. He pushed at the doors then hard enough that it broke the light welds Josh had put on them.

"What the *hell* is going on?" Patrick asked, dropping the superhero script.

"Josh," Michael said.

"Bolt was literally beating on Mike with her erect penis," Josh said.

"Are you *serious*?" Patrick asked, looking around.

They all nodded.

"She took it out and, you know, did it with her hand, then started hitting him with it," Sasha said.

"Totally out of control, Patrick," Josh said. "Worse than with Jorge."

"Oh, son-of-a...BOOOLT!" he yelled, turning around and grabbing the door handle to open it. It came off in his hand. "SHIT!"

"I'll fix it, Patrick," Josh said. "If you could just get Bolt to leave us alone, please?"

Josh walked over and opened the metal doors with his powers.

"BOOOOLT GOD *DAMNIT*!" Patrick said as he flew out.

"Hey, Sasha," Michael said. "You did supersonic?"

"I did!" Sasha said happily.

"So, did your clothes fly off?" Laura asked.

"You *knew* about that?" Sasha said.

"Who doesn't?" Laura said.

"*Everyone* knew about that?" Sasha said louder. They all suddenly found something very interesting in their lockers that needed close investigation.

"So . . . what happened?" Laura asked after a moment.

"I had clothes with me," Sasha said. "I brought a leotard along and just changed into it."

"Uff!" Laura said, huffing angrily.

"You *wanted* me naked?" Sasha said, a touch angrily. "You're as bad as Bolt!"

"Sash," Michael said, holding up his hands. "Laura, please. Sasha, Laura's always going to resent your extreme beauty, despite the fact that she's gorgeous as well. We've *all* got our stuff. Every one of us. God knows I do. I've *been* sexually assaulted."

"You have?" Jorge said. With a light tap, he threw his locker shut while focused on Michael.

"Oh, yeah," Michael said, tugging his earlobe. "Please allow me to not get into details, okay? But . . . young. And more than once, thanks. I know what it all tastes like, thanks, don't like it," he added, shaking his head. "But we've all got our things, okay? Thing is, since you've passed the test, any chance Patrick would be okay with you walking with us tonight?"

"What?" Laura said, crossing her arms. "Are you *serious*?"

"Are we even still going on patrol after that?" Sasha asked. "Do they want Michael going on patrol after that?"

Josh moved into the middle of the group and nodded. "We're going on patrol until they say we aren't." He paused and turned to Michael. "Are you good to go?"

"Never better," Michael said. He looked at Sasha. "We've got things we need to talk about. It's a bad enough day for a walk in the Park. Pretty sure it's worse flying."

"It *will* be bad flying weather," Sasha said.

"Laura, we need to talk about this," Michael said. "And other . . . stuff. There's stuff you guys need to be read in on."

"Read in on?" Jorge said. "Which means what in gringo?"

"Stuff you need to know," Michael said. "Are we a team?"

"Yes," Josh said. "But we need to keep in mind the needs of the *whole* team."

"That's the sort of talk we need to have," Michael said. "So, Laura, can you hold your breath to allow Sasha along? Her costume isn't *nearly* as sexy as yours *and* she's wearing a helmet."

"Fine," Laura said, slumping. "We do need to talk."

"You can get all the pictures," Sasha said. "I don't actually like them."

"Then why were you on the cover of *Seventeen*?" Laura asked.

"It's a long story," Sasha said.

"Which we'll have time for on a walk in the Park."

Michael had warned them not to talk about the Bolt thing in the van. Best to keep any counterattack secret.

When they were en route, Michael cleared his throat.

"So, Sasha," Michael said. "You said it was a long story why you were in *Seventeen*. Can you share with the group?"

"My mother?" Sasha said. "Stepmom, to be clear."

"I heard your mother died," Josh said.

"Yeah," Sasha said, shrugging. "When I was six. I was in the car with her, but I lived. My dad got remarried when I was ten. And my stepmom is nuts about . . . modeling and pageants and all that stuff. So, she wants me to be nuts about it."

"I would be," Laura said.

"You're you," Sasha said, sighing. "Thing is . . . there's problems with modeling, *too* . . ."

"Think Bolt's bad?" Michael said. "Most girls who are in the high end of modeling get passed around like a bag of chips at a Super Bowl party. Young actresses, too."

During this trip, Michael spent most of his Sight focused on the adjacent vehicles as best as he could, on the off chance the Secretary subsequently sent someone to intercept them.

"I haven't had problems," Laura said, frowning.

"Higher you get, more likely it is," Michael said. "The upper levels of all those fields—acting, modeling, anything where the girls in it are . . . focused on external locus of self? Guys, and women, will play on that to use them sexually. It's *extremely* common. It's why young teen actresses and singers and models always seem to go off a cliff.

"If you *did* do *Seventeen*, you'd be dealing with it. And with *your* personality, it's *much* more likely you'd be assaulted and just . . . not talk about it. You'd be too ashamed. Afraid people would find out and it would reduce your status. One of the reasons I taught you that trick about a tailbone."

"What?" Josh said, twisting in his seat and narrowing his eyes.

"Just . . . stuff," Michael said, shrugging. "Ways she can use her powers to defend herself without killing somebody. So, your stepmom is the one who's into it and you're not?"

"It's not bad when the photographers and the editors are cool," Sasha said, shrugging. "But it's a pain when they're trying to get in my pants. I've seen a guy's dick before. And I just sort of go, 'You realize that I'm a super, right?' The magazine editors are the *worst*. With one guy I just picked up a piece of metal and crumpled it and went, 'You do *not* want me to grab that, believe me.' And then my stepmom was all angry that I'd lost the gig. I didn't tell her it was because I wouldn't have sex with the photo editor."

"Oh," Laura said, blanching.

"Laura," Michael said. "We've all got our stuff we have to deal with. And guys are like that, especially with young people. If they're gay, it's young males. If they're straight, it's young females."

"It's because of the patriarchy!" Laura said stoutly.

Michael put his head in his hands.

"It's not?" Laura said.

"Why does the patriarchy exist is a better question," Michael said. "Remember when we were talking on the subway, and I said it was an innate thing? Men are wired that way, going way back to the caveman days. If you think it's something new, look at Chinese or Persian emperors. They'd had upward of two thousand concubines.

"There was a court artist whose whole job was to paint them, nude. These were *very* young women. Those paintings are now legally child pornography. The emperor would just leaf through the book, picking one out to have sex with that night.

"And with the Chinese emperors, when the girls got over the hill, if they hadn't had a child by the emperor or were otherwise favored by him, they'd go to the Dowager Concubine building for the rest of their lives. Pop quiz for the class: How old was 'over the hill'?"

"Twenty?" Josh said. "Twenty-five?"

"That young?" Laura said angrily.

Michael peripherally noted a major diagonal intersection with small parks at either end. They were passing Broadway, which meant they were abeam the Empire State Building and a little over halfway there.

"Twenty-seven is when you're starting to be over the hill in modeling," Sasha said. "If you're not a big name by then, you never will be. I'll go twenty-seven."

"Jorge?" Michael asked.

"Way younger," Jorge said. "Eighteen, latest."

"Sixteen," Michael said.

"What?" Laura said. "You're kidding!"

"Concubines were as young as *eleven*," Michael said. "They were fertile—the term is *nubile*—they'd had their first period, and the tit fairy had hit. But they were as young as eleven and when they turned sixteen, they were considered too old."

"That's . . . gross," Laura said.

"The gene is selfish," Michael said, shrugging. "You *do not* want me to explain the math of why men are wired that way and will be until we're no longer human. Ninety-eight percent of males are wired to be strongly attracted to younger persons. Very young. Nubile, yes. But young. There's a reason we have the term 'jailbait' in the English language. Tits don't suddenly appear at eighteen.

"Which is why Sasha gets hassled in modeling, why you got hassled by that guy on the train, and why young models, singers and actresses get passed around like a bag of chips. Also, why *you* are so attracted to status, being noticed, likes, hits on your Instagram. The innate processes of reproduction and sexuality are, in a term of art, conservative. They are very deeply laid and are very hard to overcome.

"It's generally explained as 'men are spread reproducers,'" Michael said, tugging his earlobe. "That is, the more women they sleep with, the more chances they have of their gene surviving into the future. The gene cannot understand things like birth control. Historical queens did not have harems. Emperors and kings had—still have—harems."

"Like *The Handmaid's Tale*," Laura said primly.

"Which was based on her experiences in Afghanistan in the 1970s," Michael said.

"Really?" Josh said.

"She rarely talks about it anymore," Michael said, "'cause she'd be accused of Islamophobia. But, yeah, she talked about it in several inteviews going back to the eighties. She'd visited Afghanistan during one of those periods when it was safe enough and studied the lives of women. But she didn't think the book would sell if it was about Islam, so she changed it to Christian fundamentalists, which were the bugaboo of the Left in the 1980s."

He paused in thought for a moment, tugging his ear.

"Think about some thirty- or forty-year-old woman," Michael said. "She drives by a Catholic school getting out and there are all these teenage males in prep clothes like Josh wears. Think she's turned on by them? Some, a few, will be. People are different. But the majority aren't. They just drive by."

Once again, the buildings disappeared on their right as the van drove alongside Central Park.

"The vast majority of guys are going to be turned on as hell by a bunch of girls in schoolgirl outfits," he finished.

"They're all over anime," Jorge said.

"Exactly," Michael said, nodding. "There's a reason for that. Guys are attracted, in the vast majority, to younger persons. Women are, in the vast majority, attracted to older persons. And by women, to be clear, I'm talking about a person who lacks a Y chromosome. A person who menstruates. They tend to be attracted to older persons because in the time when we evolved, older males were more established, had more status and therefore their children were more likely to survive and perpetuate their genes. The gene is selfish. It just wants to propagate. Then it gets into the complex matrix of the differences and the entirety of human romance gets all screwy and weird."

"Screwy and weird I'll agree on," Sasha said, grinning.

"Screwy and weird is a good description," Laura agreed.

"So, you two gals agree on something!" Michael said, holding up his hands. "We have a point of commonality!"

"Coming up on drop-off," the driver said.

"Masks on," Josh said.

Michael dropped his helmet front and worked his neck.

"And it's *showtime!*"

CHAPTER 27

"Twilight Zone" —Golden Earring

There weren't nearly as many people as had been there for the first patrol. The weather was intermittent light showers with a prediction of heavy rain after midnight. Michael was hoping it would hold off until after the patrol was over, though the walk home from the subway was going to be fun.

They were patrolling the north side of the park this time, with a drop-off by the tennis courts.

Sasha drew some of the attention off of Laura but her costume, being designed for the rigors of flying, was much less sexy and her helmet entirely hid her face. So, after a few photos, the guys were mostly taking pictures of Laura.

If they only knew.

There weren't many kids out and after Michael had signed a few autographs he joined Jorge again, this time in the sun to get some warmth.

To his surprise, Officer Gill was working the detail again.

"Just can't shake you, can we, Officer?" Michael said as he and his partner walked up.

"What was that about 'twenty years of days'?" Gill asked. "Twenty-six *pounds* of drugs? You *wanna* get shot?"

"That's what I said," Jorge said, shrugging.

"I was in a pissy mood," Michael said, tugging his earlobe. "I'm in an even *more* pissy mood today."

"What crawled up *your* ass?" Clevenstine said, grinning.

"Internal Corps stuff," Michael said. "I'd say politics, but it's gotten beyond that."

"Shit is fucked up," Jorge said, shrugging again. "Really fucked up."

"Everywhere you go, you've always got to deal with politics," Gill said, shrugging. "That's just being part of any organization."

"It's a bit more than 'just politics' when someone who is waaay over the line is protected by someone who reports to the President, and by senators," Michael said. "I'm hoping that it never comes to public attention just *how* over the line. 'Cause then senators and a certain Secretary will have it out for us for the rest of our lives. Or theirs."

"How over the line?" Gill asked.

"Oh, line's somewhere over in New Jersey," Jorge said, pointing over his shoulder. "Maybe farther."

"That far," Michael said. "As in chargeable far. And not just misdemeanor. As of this afternoon, class A felony. We're just trying to keep it down to a dull roar because otherwise the Madame Secretary will wreak vengeance on a bunch of kids for making her and her fair-haired girl look bad."

"Fair-haired girl got a name?" Gill asked.

"Bolt," Jorge said, hawking and spitting. "Fucking *maricón* Pedobolt."

"He didn't say that," Michael said. "You didn't hear it. We're going to take care of it through ACS probably. That way it doesn't reveal us. Okay?"

"*How* far over the line?" Gill said. "You said class A."

"Attempted murder?" Michael said. "Sexual battery of a minor? I'm pretty sure those are both class A felonies even in New York. Look, I'm in foster care. I've literally got the head of ACS for New York on my speed dial because of *this* stuff. I'll contact him. Please. We don't need this in the fucking *Post*. The Secretary is going to hit the roof anyway. But this shit has *got* to *stop*."

"Bolt hit Stone with his *fucking dick* while he was changing," Jorge said quietly. "Full erect, you dig? Yelling about how Stone was innately homosexual and had to get over his homophobia. Then when M . . . Stone pushed him back to get him to stop, Bolt hit Stone with full power electro. Would have killed either of you. Surprised it didn't kill Stone."

"It's not in your jurisdiction," Michael said, just as quietly. "Took place in the Federal Building. Pretty sure that's federal. But ACS will *make* it their jurisdiction and they'll handle it quietly, so we don't have to keep getting asked about getting sexually assaulted every time we *do* this shit. Dig?"

"Dig," Gill said, shaking his head.

"Yeah," Clevenstine said, nodding thoughtfully. "I'd say that line is somewhere over in Jersey at the least. More like Ohio. You okay, Stone?"

"Oh, shit, man," Michael said, chuckling. "This is somewhere around the two hundredth worst thing that's ever happened to me. Maybe further down. The list is *long*."

"Once Sah...Wing dragged Bolt off, Stone just got up and shook it off," Jorge said. "I was standing by him, and *I* could feel it and I'm *invulnerable*. It was heavy blast. Stone was just, 'well, that's a Tuesday,' right?"

"She was harassing Hulke, too," Michael said. "She likes the young ones. And the ones that don't have much at their back. Hulke's family isn't rich. I'm in foster care. She's the 'youth outreach coordinator' for the Corps and five gets you ten CPS will find victims there, too. But it will be under her regular name, right? Bolt doesn't come into it and neither do we."

"Right," Gill said, shaking his head. "You'd think that..." He shook his head again.

"Bolt's popular with the Secretary and some senators," Michael said, shrugging. "And there's the whole 'trans can do no wrong' thing going on. We'll handle it."

Madeleine Cromarty walked back and forth in the deserted lobby, biting her lip. Then she pulled out her phone and hit a number.

"Hello, Madeleine," Secretary Harris said. "Get the juniors off to the park alright?"

"Not quite, Madame Secretary," Madeleine said. "They're at the Park but there's a problem. Stone Tactical is *totally* out of control. He *assaulted* me! So did Sasha!"

"What do you mean *assaulted* you?" Katherine said angrily. "What did they *do*?"

"We were in the locker room," Madeleine said. "I was just *talking* to

Mike, I did *not* lay a hand on him, and he just *lost* it! He started screaming and threw me across the room with his powers! Then Sasha backed *him* up and picked me up by my arm and dragged me out of the room! You have to *do* something. He's out of *control*! He needs to have his powers severed!"

"Have you contacted the FBI?" Katherine said.

"I wasn't sure if that was what you'd prefer, Madame Secretary," Madeleine said. "I just let them go on patrol and contacted you."

"You let them go on patrol?" Katherine practically shouted.

Madeleine shrugged and blinked.

"It sounds like we need to get him under lock and key," Katherine said, sighing. "I *knew* he was going to be trouble! He's a loose cannon. I'll contact the field office. You'll have to swear a charge against him. And I'll need to call Tony. Just head down to the FBI office. I'll make some calls."

"Here's the thing," Michael said as they started off on their patrol. They'd all joined back up and were circling around Burnett Fountain. He briefly glanced at the statue of Mary and Dickon. "If I go to ACS with just my word, they'll have a hard time doing anything."

"I'll back you up," Jorge said.

"You'll have to bring your parents in on it," Michael said. "Which you'd be surprised how they'll react. You think they'll put it on *you*. They won't. They'll be all about killing *Bolt*."

"You don't know my parents," Jorge said unhappily.

"Parents are down on their kids, a lot," Michael said. "That's why kids think if something's going on their parents will be down on *them*. Pedos are always saying, Don't tell or you'll get in trouble. 'Cause they know that's how kids think. That *they're* the ones who will get in trouble. And your parents, all of your parents, *are* going to be angry. But they're *not* angry at *you*. They're angry at what has been happening. They're going to be angry at the Corps. They're going to be angry at Bolt. Hell, they're going to be angry at Tony, who hasn't had any control over it. But they're *not* angry at *you*.

"Parents care about their kids more than anything, generally. Some worry about social stigma. Wing, that might be an issue with your mom. But since it's all going to be in secret investigation and court, that's not an issue. However, I need people to be willing to come forward. Be witnesses. Just that. Say what you saw, witnessed, and what you've seen before. I'm new here."

"I'll talk about it," Jorge said, shrugging. "Even in front of my papa. I don't want to talk about what Bolt was doing but . . . it has to stop."

"I'm in," Josh said. "But we need to keep it quiet as possible. Bolt was at a fundraiser for Senator Drennen just last night."

"In," Sasha said. "I'm tired of being harassed in modeling. You shouldn't be harassed in Super Corps. And Bolt could have killed you!"

"Very nearly did," Michael said, tugging his earlobe. "Good thing we're as hard to kill as we are. That's another charge I'm throwing on: attempted murder."

"Hang on, I'm getting a call from Patrick," Sasha said while putting her phone to her ear. "Where . . . ? Okay, we'll head that way . . . Yeah . . . Out. He wants us to meet up over at the Hundredth Street entrance."

"Okay," Josh said, looking around. "That way."

Michael's Sight had extended enough that he knew what they were walking into. Somebody had called out the cavalry. There were about sixty NYPD cops, SWAT, *and* snipers.

Patrick was in the middle of a discussion with what Michael was pretty sure was FBI.

One Hundredth Street and Central Park West had been sealed off with police cars and more moved up, slowly, behind them as they entered the road.

The FBI agent pulled out a microphone from his car and keyed it.

"*Stone Tactical,*" he boomed over the loudspeaker. "*You are under arrest for super-assault. You have the right to remain silent. Anything you say can be used against you in a court of law. You have the right to an attorney. If you cannot afford one, one will be provided for you. Do you understand these rights?*"

Michael wasn't worried about getting shot himself, though he was under about a hundred guns. It would really fuck up Josh and Breeze.

There were also more spectators than had been at their arrival. New Yorkers will always turn up for a spectacle.

Michael put his hands over his head in a distant "okay" sign, then signaled a regular "okay."

"Why are they arresting you?" Laura asked.

"Just stay *real still,*" Michael said, his hands in the air. "If they get scared of you, they'll open fire. Madeleine probably realized she'd fucked up and went running to the Secretary. Remember how she was yelling, 'You're assaulting me! You're assaulting me!'? She probably thinks she has a solid case. Josh, hopefully your dad will take a pro bono case."

"*You need to step forward fifteen paces,*" the agent continued. "*The rest of you, stay where you are and please don't move. This is about Stone Tactical, only.*"

"The hell with that," Sasha said, picking up and flying over. A heated argument ensued but no shots were fired.

"Stay. Here," Michael said, then started walking forward, slowly.

"*Stop there.*"

Patrick came flying over as Sasha continued to give the agent a piece of her mind. It was apparent he was starting to listen.

"Stone," he said, holding up heavy-duty super-cuffs. He wasn't doing superhero voice for once. "Sorry about this."

"Madeleine charged me with assault, right?" Michael said, his hands on his helmet, fingers interlaced.

"Yeah," Patrick said. "Which . . . It's going to be handled, okay?"

"Oh, yeah," Michael said, raising his voice to ensure anyone nearby could hear. "Since this is out in the open, due to *Bolt*, be advised: I hereby charge Madeleine Cromarty, aka Electrobolt, with sexual battery on a minor, super-assault, and attempted murder."

"M . . . Stone, look," Patrick said. "We can get this dealt with quietly. Just in the Corps. This all can go away."

"Too late for that, Iron Eagle," Michael said, gesturing around at the crowd. "It's out in the open, now. Should have told Madeleine or the Secretary that. Now? Too late."

He turned around and offered his wrists.

"Put on the bracelets. And you might want to keep them handy. Madeleine's going to jail for attempted murder."

CHAPTER 28

"Lawyers, Guns, and Money" —Warren Zevon

"Do you have *any* idea how you've *fucked this up*?" Secretary of Super Affairs Katherine Harris said, obviously trying not to slam her hand onto the table and break it.

It hadn't taken the Madame Secretary long to fly up from Washington to "handle this matter," but it *had* been long enough for Josh to call his dad, attorneys to show up, discussions to be had with the FBI and a federal prosecutor, Michael to be freed, his social worker to show up, and Bolt to be placed under arrest.

During which arrest Bolt had damn near killed an FBI agent. What she'd done to Michael was probably going to be pled down to a misdemeanor and be swept under the rug. Michael had learned long ago that kids didn't really matter to anybody. They didn't have any money, they didn't have any votes, nobody cared about them. They were just props for asshole politicians.

Nearly killing an FBI agent was what was going to hang her ass.

The Secretary's office was the most impressive he'd ever seen, with sweeping views of Manhattan and exquisite modern furniture. This was the place to host foreign dignitaries and hobnob with the power players of New York. Or chew out a thirteen-year-old who didn't like getting sexually assaulted.

As she hadn't offered him a seat, he was still standing, as were his social worker and Jerome Ford—Josh's dad.

Michael wasn't particularly worried about California Girl shoving her hand into his chest, not in front of witnesses, so he decided to let her have it.

"*I* fucked this up?" Michael said, steepling his fingers and tapping them together. "*I* fucked this up? Screw you, lady! *You* are the one who fucked this up!"

"How dare you—"

"How *dare* I?" Michael shouted back, slamming his hands on the table. "How dare *you*! How dare *you* put kids in a position of having to deal with a *predator* every fucking patrol! How *dare* you ignore *all* the reports and requests to have fucking Bolt taken *out* as mentor! How *dare* you put a predator in the position of '*youth outreach*' for the Corps! How *dare* you! We were trying to keep this *quiet*! We were trying to deal with it as best we could without letting *everyone in the world* in on the secret that the Secretary of Super Affairs was supporting a *pedophile*!"

"Madeleine is not—"

"SHE'S A PEDO, YOU FAILED CHEERLEADER BIMBO!" Michael screamed. "And *you* were the one that called the FBI and described me as a 'loose cannon' who was '*dangerous*'! So, they called out *every cop in New York* and the NATIONAL GUARD, making it A NATIONAL NEWS STORY! WHEN WE WERE GOING TO *TRY* TO HANDLE THIS *QUIETLY*! So, *you* are the one who fucked up, Madame Secretary! *Not* me! I am *not* the bad guy, here! We were keeping sexual assault on a minor and attempted murder *quiet,* you dumb *bitch*!"

He finished by flipping her the bird and leaning back in his seat.

"Look, you little—" the Secretary said, pointing at him threateningly.

"Madame Secretary," Social Worker III Angela Davis, Administration for Children's Services, Foster Care Division, said precisely.

Michael had never met his social worker until this day. First, the on-call worker had shown up. Then, when it got to the point it was clearly a *major* case, they'd called in Michael's social worker on her day off. But he knew a *full-bull* social worker when he saw one and the Madame Secretary, cabinet member or no, was about to *get it*.

"*What?*" Secretary Harris snapped, turning to look at her.

"Please be *advised*, Madame Secretary," Ms. Davis said in an extremely prim, icy voice, "that our preliminary investigation of this matter has led to *multiple* charges of sexual improprieties with minors, not only with Mr. Michael Truesdale but Mr. Jorge Camejo as well. Furthermore, since Ms. Cromarty is youth outreach coordinator for the Super Corps, we *shall* be opening a *full* investigation of *all* groups, including minors with whom she has been associated.

"This investigation is in its initial stages, and everyone is innocent until proven guilty. But we are seeking an emergency judicial order of the New York City Family Court to deny Ms. Cromarty *any* further access to children on the basis of reports by *multiple* persons of ongoing sexual harassment and sexual battery of minors. In short, Madame Secretary, you've got a pedophile on your hands and as a designated mandatory reporter it is my duty to inform you that you, too, are under investigation."

"What?" Secretary Harris said, surprised.

"*You* are the ultimate authority on these things, Madame Secretary," Ms. Davis said. "And while much of it is hearsay evidence, currently the investigation is centering on your continued protection of this individual despite *numerous* reported incidents. So, *did* you continue to protect Ms. Cromarty when she was reported to have sexually harassed minors and solicited sex from them?"

"Madeleine is just . . . very friendly," Secretary Harris said. "I know there have been some reports . . . I have counseled her very strictly on keeping her hands to herself . . ."

Michael just leaned back and crossed his arms.

"Was that an admission against interest?" Michael asked. "It sure sounded like one."

"That was, yes," Jerome Ford said. Josh's dad looked like an older version of Metalstorm. Thin, golf fit, blond hair and green eyes, currently dressed in probably not his best suit but much nicer than the Madame Secretary's. He normally handled SEC law but could pinch-hit at something this easy. He'd already been talking to another full partner about the lawsuit. "Ms. Davis, please be advised that you will be called as a witness in the suit, and I'd like you to note that admission against interest."

"I have duly noted it down," Ms. Davis said, taking notes.

"*What* suit?" Secretary Harris said.

"My client has advised me that he had chosen *not* to bring suit, previously," Ford said, leaning forward. "Because all the Juniors were afraid of attracting *your* ire, Madame Secretary. Which is why they have put up with aggressive and abusive sexual harassment from Ms. Cromarty for some time. They also did not wish it to be known publicly that they were being sexually harassed and abused. Who does? But since *you* decided to make a public spectacle of this, there is no longer any reason for secrecy.

"Culpable, collusive, and negligent are the three standards for tort in civil suit, Madame Secretary," Ford continued. He held a cool, impartial tone that Michael had to admit was a tad intimidating. "So, Monday morning there will be a sexual harassment suit filed in federal court in which *you* will be named as a party who was both collusive *and* negligent. Ms. Cromarty, as Electrobolt, will be named as culpable. My clients feel that Mr. DiAngelo was neither—collusive nor negligent, that is. That it was *you* who was allowing Ms. Cromarty's depredations free rein. And once we've filed that suit and entered the witness statements, your counsel will suggest *immediately* settling. Because, wow, in my client's idiom: You have *really* screwed up."

"I have not..." Harris said, starting to get nervous. She glanced to the phone, as if it might somehow hold a solution.

"Madame Secretary," Ms. Davis said sweetly. "The counselor did *not* explain the meaning of 'admission against interest.' I had *advised* you that you were under consideration of charges as being conspiratorial in the matter of sexual harassment *and* battery of minors. You then said words to the effect of 'Bolt is just very friendly...'

"That means that you, broadly, had knowledge that there had been complaints of excessive 'friendliness' and had chosen to retain Ms. Cromarty in the position of 'mentor to the Junior Super Corps,' that group being composed of minors, as well as 'youth outreach coordinator' for the Super Corps. More contact with minors. When you had some knowledge that Ms. Cromarty had been acting in a manner that minors considered sexually harassing or even abusive and had requested relief.

"You are therefore conspiratorial in any matters which are found to be legally chargeable in the matter of Ms. Cromarty and her contact with minors involving Super Corps either as 'mentor' or as 'youth outreach coordinator.' You did not remove Ms. Cromarty from those positions, even temporarily, despite these well-substantiated reports.

"You can, therefore, be charged as a coconspirator in sexual abuse of minors, if we find sufficient grounds to charge Ms. Cromarty, as we would charge wives when husbands are assaulting minors in the home. They might not have been doing it *themselves*, but they were covering it up and helping."

Secretary Harris now had a death grip on the corner of her desk, and Michael wondered if it would snap off. Her attention went repeatedly to her balcony door, as if she contemplated simply flying away.

"That is what is meant by 'an admission against interest.' You had just made an admission of fault in a legal matter in front of witnesses. I will be noting that in my report to Child Protective Services and you may be facing charges as well."

"Wait..." Harris said uncertainly.

"Madame Secretary," Ford said, his arms crossed. "I really shouldn't say this. I should just let you continue to babble and dig a deeper hole. But you should not be in this room right now. Not without an attorney by your side telling you to *shut the hell up*."

Michael held his hands up to the two adults, hoping they'd let him go.

"Madame Secretary," he said reasonably. "You won't like it if I call you Katherine but I'm going to. Katherine, when I went to talk to Dr. Michelle after the press conference, one of the things that I asked as part of the diatribe about Bolt was 'How could you have a pedo as youth outreach coordinator?'"

"Bolt is *not* a pedophile," Katherine insisted.

"I don't know how much personal experience *you* have had with pedos, but I've had *lots*," Michael said. "Far *too* much. And, yes, she is. And it *will* come out. Now that it's out in the open, one will come forward, then another, then another and it will cascade. That's how these things *always* work. Epstein, Weinstein ... other Steins.... Who was that singer back in the eighties? Johnson ... Jackson? Something.

"First one victim comes forward and gets blasted by everyone for saying such *terrible things* about their *hero*, then another, then another, then people start to realize, 'Oops, yeah, they're a predator,' then everyone turns around and goes, 'Oh, I knew it all along' and nobody thinks to ask, 'Why didn't you do something, then?' Nothing happens because everyone is *afraid*.

"They're afraid of being blasted by fans and activists on social media. They're afraid for their careers. In our discussions about it, Josh specifically said he was worried about being branded a transphobe and killing his chances of getting into Harvard. And everyone, including me, was afraid of having to deal with . . . well, *you* for who knows how long having pointed out that your fair-haired girl was a *fucking pedophile*.

"But there's always *someone* in a position of power," he said, making a knife hand at the Secretary, "who has *excused* it. Catholic Church scandal. MeToo. Harvey Weinstein. Baptist Church scandal, and the Mormons are probably *next*. There's *always* a reason.

"Sometimes it's money. Sometimes it's politics. Sometimes it's *compassion*. Catholic Church. 'Oh, they're sinners, but Jesus is forgiving.' So, it just *kept* happening again and again and again. There's *always* a reason. There's always *some* reason that they realize, in retrospect, was a *stupid* reason that they've cradled the viper in their midst."

"I . . ." Harris said, shaking her head.

"Mr. Ford is right," Michael said. "You really *should* have an attorney by your side telling you to *shut the hell up*. We were *trying* to keep it *quiet*, Katherine. I was going to go to the head of ACS and ask to, *quietly*, open an investigation. It would have been of *Madeleine Cromarty* not of *Electrobolt*. Also, a trans activist but not the prominence of Electrobolt and not connected to the Corps, publicly. You'd have been pissed but the Corps' name, and *ours*, would have been out of it.

"You're Gen X. Can you think of all the things you did when you were young that you are glad nobody knows about, Madame Secretary? Well, lemme 'splain somethin' to ya, Kath. Social media *never* forgives and *never* forgets. So, this is going to be hanging over our heads for the rest of our lives! In fifty years, some asshole will refer to Stone Tactical as a transphobe. The kid who was *raised* by a trans."

Now that she was finally listening, he recounted the events from his point of view in as professional a manner as he could muster.

"He actually hit you with his . . . penis," Katherine said, shaking her head.

"It all happened just as I described it, Madame Secretary," Michael said. "I'll affirm all of it in my legal statement. You can imagine the sort of headlines they'll come up with when this comes out."

"Shit," Katherine said, finally accepting what had happened.

"That," Michael said. "Yeah."

"We have much the same story from *all* the minors," Ms. Davis said. "They all witnessed it. And they didn't all have the exact same story, but the important details all matched. They weren't making it up, in other words. Do you begin to realize why you are potentially chargeable in this matter, Madame Secretary?"

Katherine just put her hand over her face. It was a universal sign of shame.

"Madame Secretary," Michael said softly. "Don't say sorry. Not at this time. It would be another admission against interest. But we might just be functionally immortal. At the very least, extremely long lived. So, we were all looking at a future where we had you as a bitter enemy for a *very* long time and trying like *hell* to avoid that while still trying to figure out what to do about Bolt. That was an unpleasant situation but . . . life, as I've pointed out to them *many* times, is not fair.

"Bolt, by the way, resisted arrest," Michael said, tapping his fingers together. "In case you hadn't heard, there's a badly injured FBI agent. Patrick had to handle it."

"I heard," Katherine said, sighing. "You're right. I should probably get the Corps Counsel on this."

"We don't have to bring suit in court," Mr. Ford said, nodding at Ms. Davis. "I'm sure that Social Services would prefer that this be kept as quiet as possible. But it *is* out in the open. However, all of the kids, including my son, are being encouraged to participate in the suit. They were all exposed to pain and emotional suffering over this. And Mr. Truesdale and Mr. Camejo will be the primary plaintiffs. They endured the most. Oddly enough, Josh had very little direct harassment."

"He had you," Michael said. "Back then, at least, Bolt had *some* worry about getting caught. With me and Jorge, who did we have at our backs? Some poor Honduran family? A kid in foster care? The Bolts of the world go for the kids they see as unprotected."

"I have to agree on that one," Ms. Davis said. "*Classic* predator tactics. Go for the disadvantaged kids."

"That, too, was a part of the Catholic Church scandal," Michael said. "The kids who got assaulted weren't the ones whose parents were the big contributors to the parish. They were the lonely ones. The poor ones. The weak. That's what pisses me off the *most* about predators. They go for the weakest ones."

Secretary Harris shook her head. "What a nightmare."

"Try living it," Michael said. "Since you're here, Madame Secretary, one thing completely separate?"

"Yes?" Harris said.

"Can I get a signed publicity photo?" Michael asked.

"You . . . want my autograph?" Katherine said with an incredulous expression.

"Not for *me*!" Michael said, tugging his earlobe. "This kid Davon. He's an obsessive collector and I bet he doesn't have a C . . . *Katherine Harris* photo. I told him I'd try to get him an Italian Falcon. It's outreach, right?"

She looked at him with her mouth agape for a moment, then shook her head again.

"I'll see what I can do."

Sunday *Gotham Herald* front page: STONE TACTICAL CHARGED WITH ASSAULT!

Sunday *New York Post* front page: PEDOBOLT!

"Can you believe this?" Linda Edwards Thomas said, looking at her phone at Monday morning breakfast. "Junior Super Corps is filled with transphobes."

"I'm sure it's not as bad as it looks," Frank Thomas Edwards said.

"Well, Stone Tactical was arrested, at least," Linda said. "He deserves it for putting Electrobolt in the hospital!"

"I heard she was charged as well," Frank said diffidently. "And she's in Super Containment until the legal proceedings."

"She was just protecting herself from those maniacs!" Linda said.

"Got to get ready for school," Michael said, picking up his empty bowl. "See you guys later . . ."

"Oh, my *God*," Laura groaned over the video link. She nervously leaned into the camera, so her face dominated the screen. "I can't even *go* on my Instagram. It's a raging battle between a whole bunch of rabid conservative transphobes and trans activists. I'm being called a *transphobe*! I'm a trans *ally*!"

"Every friend I've ever had was black," Michael said, tugging his earlobe. "As Michael Edwards, people who knew *nothing* about me started a *riot* calling me a white supremacist and a racist. I'd say it will die down, but it won't. You're finding out just how vicious the Left is when they find a victim. I'm being called a transphobe and *Mama* was trans. If she was still alive, she'd be gettin' out the switchblade."

Frank was out, and Linda was hustling around the kitchen preparing to host her book club meeting in an hour. He wasn't too concerned about being bothered.

"I'm never getting into Harvard now," Josh said. He was relaxed back into his chair but looked a little spooked. "Did you really *have* to bring charges?"

"It was out in the open," Michael said, shrugging. "There wasn't any point to secrecy anymore. We had sixty cops thrown down on me, ready to pull the trigger on the dangerous super-terrorist. Kill the NK, by proxy. There were news crews and people live-streaming."

"I'm avoiding my super social *entirely*," Sasha said. She was sitting cross-legged on her bed. The background wasn't fuzzed out but the room was too dark to see much of anything. "I'll let the team handle it. But I've been monitoring Twitter and Facebook on my personal accounts and hashtag Stone Tactical is trending along with Pedobolt. FB is taking down anything negative about Bolt, and you're being framed as a transphobe. You really need to do something about that."

"I'll see about contacting the Sioux," Michael said. "They might throw in for a Lost Child. It's public that Stone Tactical is a Native American Lost Child. So, I've got that for cover. Jorge, you got any contacts in the Honduran community?"

"As Hombre de Poder I do," Jorge said. He was on a balcony, with his feed bouncing all over the place as he shifted around. "I've gone on there and told my story about being harassed for a fucking *year*."

"Might want to avoid that," Josh said, wincing. "My dad said we mostly should lay low until they've done a settlement with the Corps."

"It's all in Spanish, I bet," Michael said. "I agree on that with the English stuff. But nobody ever notices the Spanish. Is it in Spanish?"

"Yeah," Jorge said. "And I agree. Nobody ever notices us. But I got contacted by Telemundo."

"*That* you might want to avoid," Michael said.

"You looked at *your* social media?" Sasha asked.

"No," Michael said. "I let the team handle that. I don't do social media at all if I can avoid it. Though . . . since we're suing the Super Corps, that might *not* be the best idea."

"Your accounts are empty from your side," Sasha said. "Haven't been *any* posts from you at all since the incident. And all your posts are just lame jokes."

"That's what I told them to post," Michael said. "Just the lamest jokes they could find that might not offend anyone."

"You've picked up over a half a million followers," Sasha said. "You're not up at my or Laura's level but you're climbing. Fast. When this hits the news on Monday, you'll be skyrocketing. Some of them may be, probably are, trans activists and trolls there to attack. But many of them, possibly most, are on your side."

"That's great," Michael said. "And I'm sure that they'll be there to support us with the trans activists and other social justice warriors that are going to be waiting to ambush us at our next patrol."

"Do you think that will happen?" Laura said, tearing up. "How can I make it any clearer I'm a trans *ally*!"

"Doesn't matter," Michael said. "They won't stop. We're going to be attacked for the rest of our lives by some activist for just choosing to not be the victim.

"But, Josh, to keep you out of Harvard, they have to connect your super name to your secret identity. That's outing a super, which is a federal offense. And while there may be some activists at Harvard in admissions who will see it as their duty, if they even have *access*, they'd be committing a federal offense. Think about it. So, it shouldn't affect your chances of getting into Harvard."

"Point," Josh said with a thoughtful nod. "As long as they *don't* connect it."

"We could apologize," Laura said.

"Apologizing won't help," Michael said. "For one thing, we're the *victims*. It makes no sense. Some of it will die down when it gets around that Bolt has been charged. Just as the Left is always on the lookout for a victim, they'll throw their own under the bus—fast. Laura, Breeze is a noted social justice activist, but they turned on you as soon as you looked like you might not be pure enough. Think what they're going to do with *Bolt*. When it gets out that Bolt has been charged, she won't *exist* anymore. Her name will *disappear* to the Left. They'll pretend she never existed. Heard anyone supporting Weinstein lately? 'Oh, that person? We *never* supported her! Uh-uh!'

"They eat their own just as soon as they become a burden. As soon as the 'Pedobolt' meme gets around enough, they'll start running. *Then* it will die down. But it will *always* be a pain in the ass. There will *always* be someone calling us transphobes or homophobes or some other phobes. That's why I *hate* social media. It brings out the *worst* in people. *All* sides. It's mean girls and toxic assholes, wall to wall.

"It's also just the cause de jour. It's the latest shit storm that people are making much of. It will stay that way until the rabid hounds go chasing another rabbit to devour."

"So, what do we do until it dies down?" Sasha said.

"Keep your head low and off social media," Michael said. "Laura, you can do it. You really can."

"It's, like, my *life*!" Laura said.

"Then find a better life," Michael said. "Go read a book. See a movie. Keep off of social media. There will be something that will cause this to go away soon enough. The real problem is that it won't have gone away *enough* before the next patrol. *That's* going to be no fun at all."

"Think there'll be protesters?" Josh said.

"Protesters and counterprotesters," Michael said. "Unless the weather's really bad. Then I'd doubt there'll be many. But a few hard cores are going to turn out."

"Great," Josh said, shaking his head.

"Isn't there anything that we can do?" Laura asked, nearly crying.

"Not that I can think of," Michael said, tugging his earlobe.

CHAPTER 29

"In the Air Tonight" —In This Moment

"Well, it was one plan," Titanium said. "Not the optimum plan."

"Tango, Lima," Michael said over the phone in his room. Frank was downstairs making a couple spoonfuls' worth of meatless dinner, so he didn't have long. "I was going for Delta, Echo, get a consensus on reporting it to ACS quietly. Then Madeleine went and made things easier."

"This is not exactly easy," Titanium said. "Nor is it particularly quiet."

"The real problem is the social media and media angle," Michael said. "The Society has a half a dozen things they're trying like hell to keep out of the news. The economy is dying under their administration, crime is up, foreclosures are up, homelessness is up. And this gives them something newsworthy to use. The MSM is going to support their fellow pedophile since so many of *them* are pedophiles. So even though Electrobolt being arrested and denied bail is the big story, they're *never* going to cover it."

"So, is there an answer?" Titanium said.

"Bigger news story," Michael said. "Something they *have* to cover. Take out a Society member in the New York area that is a notable person. Somebody that they *can't* ignore dying. Somebody so big that it will make bigger news."

"Are you serious?" Titanium asked.

"Forget self-inflicted gunshot," Michael said. "I've figured out how to have them drop dead without a *trace*. Sudden death. They just... die. Even the most detailed autopsy won't reveal why or how. All I need to do is get close. And I've figured out how to do *that* if I can get ahold of a rebreather. Just point me to them and they die. That will push *this* off the evening news."

"Target?"

"Butch Eisenberg. If the owner of the *Gotham Herald* dies, it will be a monthlong ritual mourning with sack cloth and ashes. The *President* will attend the funeral. It'll dominate every news channel, right and left, hell, international for a *month*. He's senior Society *and* he's an aggressive ped. Hell, he's a *Dark Hand*. He's center of the bracket for our primary assassination targets and he's right here in New York City. And that means a major Society meeting at the funeral that we can probably bug.

"Aggressive pedophile off the plate. Senior Society member down. Society control of the media damaged. We'll get butt-tons of intel from all the meetings as they try to fill the hole. That's a four-fer."

"That's a bold plan," Titanium said. "I can't clear that."

"No," Michael said. "It would take the Faerie Queen to clear it."

"I'll push it up the chain," Titanium said. "Don't take action without clearance."

"Yes, ma'am."

"Can you do it?" the Faerie Queen said. "And *not* get caught."

Michael had described the method of kill and it was agreed that would be pretty hard to find on an autopsy.

"Plan, plan, plan, and prepare," Michael said. "First of all, we do some dry runs. I need everything about his bone structure. I won't be in view of him. I'll need to be close, within about seventy-five meters, and have his exact location as well as his bone structure. I really need to be in close proximity to him at least once before the action. That way I *know* what his bones look like.

"With that and a location on him that I can approach covertly... He's gone and no trace of it being unnatural. He's old. He's going to die soon, anyway. Does he have anywhere he frequents besides the estate and the offices? Restaurants? Mistress?"

"He usually has his sexual partners delivered to the estate or his apartment on Fifth," Lime Iron said. She'd been read in on the potential assassination as the Society subject matter expert.

"Where's the apartment?" Michael asked. "In the building."

"Top floor," Iron said.

"That's it, then," Michael said. "I can take him there. He died in his sleep after a long and fine life. All I need to do is get to the roof unobserved. Locate the apartment. He'll be the only one with that bone structure in the apartment."

"Foster parents," Faerie Queen said.

"Do it late at night, early morning," Michael said. "I'll go out by the window, meet a car. I'll either need transport or boost one myself. We'll have to dry run. And I sort of need to get to the top of another roof nearby first. That way when I take off it won't be so noticeable. Wait . . . How high is the building?"

Flying in the dark to a cemetery had carried almost zero risk. This would be much higher visibility, so flying was out.

"Fifteen stories," Lime Iron said, bringing it up on Google Maps.

"Probably too far to reach from across the street," Michael said, examining the target. "Presently. I'll get there. Roof is out. It's overlooked by the skyscraper behind it. Damnit. Estate."

"One-hundred-acre estate on Peacock Point," Lime Iron said, zooming to that.

"I can *probably* infiltrate it?" Michael said after examining it for a moment. "Among other things, with a rebreather I can come in underground. But it's big. Finding him will be questionable. And the road network . . . *every* car that approached that night will be investigated."

"It will appear to be natural causes to the most finite forensic examination. But the Society will still *assume* assassination. Not to mention patrols in the area. I'd have to do a *very* long underground insertion to be sure of being completely uninvestigated and I'm still untrained at that. Just navigating the approach is currently questionable. Other frequent hangouts?"

"Preferred restaurant is The Grill," Lime Iron said, bringing that up on Google Earth. "Ninety-nine East Fifty-second Street."

"Steam tunnels?" Michael asked. "What's over it?"

"Unsure," Lime Iron said.

"Offices."

"Who's cutting in?" Faerie Queen asked, tightly.

"Hi, boss, AutokId," the lead Gondola AI said. "Sorry. Heard you were talking about killing that bastard Butch and I just couldn't help jumping in. There is empty office space over The Grill, well within target range. The Grill has multiple cameras we've hacked. I can specifically locate this fucker and bring Mountain Tiger straight in on him.

"Tiger: Butch broke his right ulnar bone when he was sixteen. Actually, his dad broke it. Radial fracture. Pretty distinctive. He also has a replacement left hip and both knees. But given who he's going to be dining with, that's fairly common."

AutokId was one of the only true *full* AIs on the face of the planet. He was so far beyond the rest it wasn't funny. He'd simply come alive one day from their highly automated child rescue system.

When you had only a few thousand people to handle everything Gondola did, you had to automate. And when all of those few thousand people were expert in everything IT, the automation was extremely advanced. Icons pushed and airline tickets for mercenaries were arranged, temporary identities, guns ordered, handlers set up, transportation, funding, safe houses, cache guardians alerted, and weapons and gear prepped in advance. Just hit a button and most of the work was done. Even searching for the children was highly automated. No number of hackers could look over every single air shipment container in the world searching for the subtle telltale signs of *one* of them carrying children.

One day, some mercenaries had called Diarrhea asking when they were supposed to turn over their kids. They'd been sitting in the safe house for two weeks with no contact.

What kids?

The ones the Faerie Queen had ordered rescued, and the Chief Accountant had cleared the funds. The passwords were all good.

Neither of them had had any idea about the operation. The Chief Accountant had been on vacation that week and completely out of the network.

The computer had found the kids, ordered the rescue, chosen the merc teams, ordered the weapons, set up the safe house, transportation, and handlers and paid for it from Gondola accounts all on its own. Which was . . . a bit of a problem.

Michael had just joined Gondola when it happened and there was a minor panic. Skynet was mentioned frequently. He'd been part of one of the programming teams that had pulled the entire system down, cleaned up old legacy code, generally fixed stuff that had needed fixing for a while. It was great training.

He wasn't there when they restarted the system, but he heard the news. When it was restarted it typed out: I Am AutokId.

It had named *itself*. Since then, he—definitely he—had continued helping Gondola with pretty much everything. And he was tremendously *enthusiastic* about rescuing children and killing those who harmed them. He could never go Skynet and destroy the world. Too many children would be harmed.

He also had become the world's worst practical joker. AutokId, possibly because he too had to deal with a lot of evil stuff, had a very raucous sense of humor.

"We need to preferably take him out on the Tuesday before Tiger's next patrol," AutokId said. "They're already warming up Antifa and the rest of the assholes to protest the evil transphobes of the Junior Super Corps. But he is scheduled for dinner Tuesday evening with Hamlin Devlin, chairman of Fieldstone Holdings. That way they'd probably have the viewing that Saturday.

"They *definitely* will not want anything interfering in the news with the funeral and all the mourning, so they'll kill the planned protests. And if Butch drops in front of Devlin, it's not like anybody is going to question it except did *Devlin* kill him. That could cause some inter-Society angst, which would be sweet.

"I can schedule Michael for a therapy appointment with a child psychologist located in the same building, set it up with Super Corps, ACS, and the foster parents. Evenings so he'll be in position. It will give us time to dry run and make sure he can access the offices. He won't actually be scheduled, obviously."

"What's the access method to the empty office space?" Faerie Queen asked.

"Punch-code electronic," AutokId said. "We have the codes. We have him put on a yellow vest and a hard hat and he's just another worker going into some unused office space occasional evenings for some unknown reason. Tuesday, Thursday. Butch has another meeting, same time, Thursday that week in case we miss the first time.

But we do need to do some planning, rehearsals, and dry runs. We have time."

"Usually, it's The Society which causes some crisis to affect the news," Faerie Queen said. "Turnabout is fair play. Approved."

The Faerie Queen was also known for being able to make a quick decision.

"I've got another meeting," Faerie Queen said. "Keep me updated. Mountain Tiger: Good luck."

"Fortune favors the prepared, ma'am," Michael said.

"See you on the other side."

The real problem with Gondola operations was there was rarely any real drama; they were just *too* good at what they did.

Every operation was planned with backup plans for the backup plans. Which was why they had rescued over four hundred thousand children from trafficking, often involving gunfights, without a single *one* being scratched. They planned, they rehearsed. Then and only then did they act.

Michael had been in and out of this building for a week and a half, every Tuesday and Thursday night, visiting his "therapist." He took the subway to Times Square, walked two blocks down the street through the hookers and drug fiends, wearing a hoodie and a mask, got in the same car, changed into a workman's jacket, yellow and orange vest, Covid mask, and picked up a set of electrical tools. Then he was dropped off out front, showed his fake ID to the guard, walked into the building, walked up to the unused office space, entered after entering his code, and examined it, inch by inch, while examining the patrons of the top steak house in New York beneath with Sight.

AutokId would walk him through. Butch had a favorite table but there might be a problem. He might be sitting somewhere else. The AI didn't just have bone data on Butch, he had it on others. HIPAA meant nothing to Gondola. He would direct Michael to a particular spot in the offices, then ask him to describe the bones of a particular person directly beneath. To the side. This table, that table. How many people at the table. Sex, race, approximate age.

AutokId was famous for having snipers shoot a particular spot on a wall with a particular adjustment to their scope and having the bullet go right through a guard's brainpan.

On the designated night, there was a new, overly curious guard and a pair of unexpected technicians visiting the site, but AutokId canceled them out by having Michael head in while the guard was signing out the two technicians. AutokId assured him that guard wouldn't be there when he returned. His way cleared, Michael walked to the selected point just as he had several times before.

"Target is in the preferred seat and at the preferred table," AutokId said.

Michael had the interior view up on his phone and was simultaneously looking below with Sight. He could see Eisenberg and Devlin sitting opposite each other at a four top with their closest aides. The booth at the rear was their preferred table since it was hard to overhear their conversation.

Gaps where the knees should be as well as left hip. He couldn't See titanium. Radial break, right ulnar bone. Old bones. Some plastic surgery.

He also had Devlin acquired. That was one of the bastards who had raped his mother and was as bad as Butch. His tastes ran to little girls instead of little boys. Pity he couldn't take both.

"Target acquired," Michael said, zeroing in on the target's medulla oblongata. "Requesting green light . . ."

"You realize we're going to have to throw Electrobolt under the bus at some point," Devlin said.

"Hopefully not before this weekend," Butch said, taking a bite of rare, dry-aged New York strip. "We've gone to all this trouble to stir up the crazies. Besides, those little Super Corps bastards need to learn their place."

"Oh, agreed," Devlin said. "But it will have to be done. He was caught metaphorically red-handed."

"Pity," Butch said. "He was a fun boy when he was yo—"

Arnold "Butch" Eisenberg suddenly faceplanted in his steak, then slid out of his chair, his face taking the plate with him.

"What the hell?" Devlin said, shocked.

Butch's aide rushed to pull his boss out from under the table as a waiter moved in to provide assistance.

Devlin got up and went around the table to look. Butch's eyes were wide and unseeing. He'd seen dead people before. Generally, children that they'd sacrificed, but that was *dead*.

He was pretty sure that nothing could be done for the media magnate.

Meanwhile, the other patrons were growing increasingly alarmed, and one lady looked ready to scream.

"Shit," he muttered. His first thoughts were what a cocked hat this was going to make of everything. They'd have to secure Eisenberg's files, fast. And the whole plan to pound the Junior Super Corps was out the window.

"Call off the protests this weekend," he whispered to his aide. "We can't have anything interfering with this news."

"Yes, sir," his aide said.

Devlin looked around and shook his head.

"Make sure it wasn't poison," he added, quietly. "Or a super-assassin."

"I'll make sure there is a thorough investigation, sir," the aide said.

"This is...not a good time..."

He thought for a moment longer and leaned over.

"And order an immediate short on *Gotham Herald* stock..."

CHAPTER 30

"I Will Not Bow" —Breaking Benjamin

"*Nobody* is going to show up," Laura said grumpily, as they got into their costumes. "I can't believe Butch Eisenberg is *dead*! It's like the end of the *world*! He's a *legend*! And they're holding the viewing *today*! *Nobody* is going to be at the Park!"

"What's the fuss about this guy?" Jorge asked, pulling on his muscle shirt. "So, he runs the *Herald*. Ran it. Big deal."

"Big deal?" Josh said angrily. "Yes, very big deal, Poder! She's right, the man is a *legend*! He's been the guiding hand of the *Herald* for decades! It's ... Wow. I thought you'd *get it* by now."

"I think it's one of those things that's only important to white people," Jorge said, picking up his mask. "I don' read the *Herald*. Me papa don' read the *Herald*. He reads the *Post*. And I get most of my news from X. It's generally more real."

"More real?" Laura said. "Since Musk took it over, Twitter's nothing but *fake news*! You might as well watch *Fox*!"

"I watch Telemundo," Jorge said. "And at least *they* aren't calling us transphobes. Which the *Herald did*."

"Sasha, can *you* explain?" Josh said, shaking his head. "I'm out of ideas."

"I'm sort of on Jorge's side," Sasha said. "I get that he's a legend. But people are acting like the King of England died. It's not like the *Herald* went away. And I've sort of lost any love affair I had about the *Herald*

325

when they made the whole thing about Stone getting charged and sort of failed entirely to cover that Electrobolt was the aggressor.

"I'm not saying that I'm glad anyone died but the one thing it's done is take all of that *off* the news. We were expecting a couple of hundred protesters—which I guarantee you, Breeze, would have been *worse* than nobody showing up. As it is . . . ? You'll probably be pretty much unbothered. 'Cause everybody's mourning a publisher. And that's all he was. A human being. A publisher. It's sad he died but it's not the end of the world."

"Oh, my God, you just don't get it!" Laura said, rolling her eyes.

"Stone, you're unusually quiet," Josh said, putting on his gloves.

"Doubt you want to hear what I have to say," Michael said, donning his helmet.

"You agree with Sasha and Jorge?" Josh asked.

"I'm not a *Herald* fan," Michael said, being careful what he said. "I haven't been a *Herald* fan since when I was eleven, when they made it like I was some big white supremacist for not wanting to be a statistic. A kid I had literally *carried out of a fire* and on my back for *blocks* on burned feet asked me when I turned white supremacist."

Jorge shot him a hard, respectful look. Laura, however, rolled her eyes as if to say "Of course you carried someone out of a fire before you had powers."

"So," Michael said. "It's terrible that such an icon died. But it's also terrible that my Mama died. People die. And you have to admit that it's a fortunate death. Because we're out of the news and the attention has all turned to Butch and his legacy. Laura can start to rebuild her trans-ally cred, and I can go back to somewhat obscurity, which is where I prefer to be.

"And Laura," Michael said, nodding at her. "Don't be worried about turnout. Turnout isn't all that great getting into winter, anyway. But most of the people who turn up to take your picture aren't the type to care one way or the other about Butch Eisenberg. They don't even know who he *is*."

She shrugged apathethically. Everyone quieted down as they finished getting ready.

They found their new Junior Super Corps mentor waiting for them in the lobby with Patrick. It was Bonfire, Daniel McGillicuddy Griswold, who went by "Griz," husband of Summer Storm. He'd been polite enough to stay out of the locker room while they were changing.

When they walked out, he just started chuckling.

"I don't even *want* to know what it is," he said, grinning and looking at the group. They had very obviously separated into two factions, with Jorge, Michael, and Sasha separated from Laura and Josh.

"Want to know why I don't want to know?" he asked. "Because *I* was in JSC. And every freaking patrol it was *something*. Lord, the arguments and the angst. Summer and I used to go at it hammer and tongs if it wasn't both of us going at the others. And let me inform you: ten years down the line, you won't remember what it was."

The group glanced around at each other with mixed signs of believing him.

"Sometimes, people keep the petty grudges. Trust me, got them myself. But you're also going to realize these are the people you're going to be depending on to keep you alive. You're all going to end up the best frenemies you'll ever have. What the military calls 'buddies.' And love your buddy or hate your buddy, you end up buddies for life.

"And if you think this is the first 'controversy' involving JSC, think again. One of the main reasons to concentrate you all is that a super is generally going to cause some 'controversy' and at least if you're here we can work the angles and try to reduce it. But, among other things, getting some training on not getting into it with people.

"On that issue," he continued. "FBI says the organized protests have been called off. The Eisenberg thing has absorbed most of the heat. There may be *some* protesters. There may be some counterprotesters. Just keep your cool and be professional. Don't get into it directly. Let NYPD handle it. You're literally not paid enough. Neither are they.

"I'm going to be out there in civilian clothes," he said. "There'll be some NYPD undercover as well. We'll see how it goes. If it gets too bad, we'll pick you up and bring you back.

"Sasha, you're going to be there but up," he said. "You and Patrick are going to take a high, rear position. In the event there is any *direct* hostile action, thrown objects for example, you will identify the perpetrator and remove them from the scene. NYPD has a drop location that is slightly off-site. Keep your cameras running at all times. *Don't* damage the merchandise. We don't need accusations of 'excessive force' on top of the current issues.

"The rest of you, no overt use of powers," he said. "We don't want this looking like Kent State or anything. You can, obviously, act in self-defense. But don't be hostile and generally let NYPD handle any issues.

"On the patrol itself: Continuing drug activity around the Pond as well as on the west side bridle path," he said, consulting a pad. "Activity is primarily run by Los Tresos and CH Mafia. CH stands for Crown Heights. Intel indicates that Los Tresos is more on the Pond activity with CH Mafia being around the bridal path. Additional sexual trafficking activity occasionally identified near the Boathouse after dark. This seems primarily to be homosexual activity and may not be trafficking per se but simply hook-ups with some prostitution involved.

"I know your first patrol you rounded up a bunch of drugs," Bonfire said, nodding. "I'm going to add my 'good job' to that and recommend that you just *patrol* tonight. We've got enough on our plate as it is. I'm not going to go hard and fast on that but it's the wiser course.

"Any questions?"

The ride to the Park was unusually quiet, with most of them just checking their phones.

There were cameras at the Boathouse with one of them pointed more or less where the crowd gathered to see the arriving junior superheroes. The weather was fair, midsixties and no rain. Fairly strong breeze that chilled things a bit.

The crowd looked to be a bit larger than the one on the first patrol, definitely bigger than the one on the second. And while a few of them carried signs, most seemed to just be the regular tourists that showed up to see the Junior Supers.

NYPD was out in some force. There were a few riot police discreetly off to the side with about twice the usual number of uniforms out to handle things. It seemed like they'd tried to separate the crowd into protesters, counterprotesters, and tourists with steel barricades between each of the groups as well as between them and where the team was to be dropped off.

The counterprotesters and protesters were to one side with the "tourists" separated by a double line of barricades. Michael couldn't quite sort out which group was which on his phone, but one was forty people and the other was about ten. Neither contained anyone who looked like black bloc.

NYPD had *most* of the department covering the public viewing for Butch Eisenberg, which was being held at the New York Public Library—Stephen A. Schwarzman Building. *Thousands* had lined up for that. People were flying in from all over the world to pay their last respects. The intel take was going to be better than the Olympics or Davos. The *viewing* was today. Events "celebrating his life" were to go on through the week with the final funeral next Saturday; "a mostly private ceremony" at his family's memorial at the estate. "Mostly private" meaning hoi polloi need not apply. Just a thousand or so Davos attendees getting together to decide who would rule media now that Butch was dead.

If Gondola could get enough bugs into the right areas, it would be the biggest intelligence coup . . . in the last month or so. Gondola had so much intel it was coming out of their ears. But more was always better.

"I don't wanna go first," Laura said, practically curled in a ball.

"I'll go," Michael said. "Most of the tourists are to the left, Laura. You head that way. I'll move over to block from the protesters and counterprotesters. Go see your fans. I got this."

"Don't get in a fight," Josh warned.

"Not gonna," Michael said, tugging his earlobe. "Just going to let them throw all the eggs and bottles of frozen water they want to throw."

"I'm with Stone," Jorge said. "Got your flank, amigo."

"Let's do it," Michael said, dropping the front of his helmet as the doors opened.

The layout was apparent as he got out. The counterprotesters outnumbered the protesters by about three to one. They were more or less in the center of the separated groups with the protesters to the right, and tourists, who outnumbered both groups, on the far left.

The protesters and counterprotesters both had handmade signs. The sure signal of a Society-organized protest was preprinted signs.

He headed over to the protesters, being held back by a fairly flimsy metal barricade.

"Stone!" Josh shouted.

"It's okay," Michael said as he approached the group. Several of them were overtly trans, most of them were white females. Only a few obvious males in the group. He suspected they were mostly there because some girlfriend like Laura insisted they attend. Guys will do anything for pussy.

When he was ten feet from the barricade, he lifted off the ground about ten feet and released his aura, not at full power. Then he pulled a small bullhorn out of his cargo pocket. He'd sweet-talked that out of Alexander as well, pointing out that at some point it might come in handy.

It was about to come in handy.

"*Hey, folks, welcome to the show,*" Michael said calmly. "*Glad you could make it. Just need to catch you up on some background you might not have gotten and some recent developments in the story you might have missed what with the* Herald *and every other mainstream station only covering Mr. Eisenberg's unfortunate death.*"

The protesters were screaming things that he couldn't precisely catch and generally doing the angry leftist thing and, of course, live-streaming it all. He couldn't care less. Let them live-stream *this*.

"*To clarify what exactly occurred; I had previously requested on my first patrol that Electrobolt not place her hands on me, especially when I was changing. I did so quite politely, all things considered, since what she was doing constituted sexual harassment and unwanted touching...*"

For the millionth time, he recounted the events, to include mention of Electrobolt having previously been counseled, the fact that Michael was a sexual assault survivor, how things had played out after the event, Electrobolt's current incarceration, and the standing charges against her.

"*So, that's what you're all here about: to support a rapist and pedophile who sexually battered and attempted to kill me and sexually assaulted* numerous *other minor victims. Please note that I am Native American and come from a disadvantaged foster care background. Native American, for those of you not up on it, is the I in BIPOC. Indigenous. So, what you are doing, very specifically, is supporting sexual harassment, sexual battery, and assault upon a BIPOC disadvantaged minor by a* white *adult female.*

"*What? It's not enough you're standing on stolen lands? Most of Bolt's victims were BIPOC. Notice that most of* you *are white. So, you think that it's perfectly okay for a white to rape a BIPOC child? That's certainly been the opinion of you white folk ever since you arrived here.*

"For all your protestations about being 'progressive,' and allies of BIPOC... nothing has changed. You're still the same oppressors you've always been."

"Oh, amigo," Jorge said as he landed. "You really know how to twist the knife."

"Best way to get the blade back out so they bleed," Michael said, nodding.

The protesters and counterprotesters were starting to break up. Michael was pretty sure he'd just branded himself as a lefty to some of the counterprotesters. Anyone who wanted to pigeon-hole that hard, fine by him.

Jorge's shoulders shook from laughter at that as Officer Gill walked up.

"BIPOC, huh?" Officer Gill said.

"'Make your enemy live up to its own book of rules,'" Michael said. "Rule four of Saul Alinsky's *Rules for Radicals*. Live by those rules, die by those rules."

Michael spotted a familiar face in the crowd.

"'Scuse me. I gotta go see somebody."

He went over to the tourist area, where Davon was waiting with a lady who was probably his mother.

"Hey, Davon!" Michael said, taking off his pack. "Got a surprise for you!"

"Is it an Italian Falcon?" Davon asked.

"Okay, so not that big of a surprise," Michael said, handing over the signed photo. "But... Oh, wait, what's thiiis...?"

He pulled another photo out already sleeved.

"Hmmm... Is this for you... hmmm...?"

"What is it?" Davon asked. "Come on, please let it be for me!"

"I'm not sure who this is," Michael said, turning it around and holding it out so Davon could see it. "Who is that?"

"THAT'S A CALIFORNIA GIRL!" Davon screamed.

"Davon!" his mother said, shushing him.

"That's right," Michael said, handing it over. "She owed me a favor."

He'd seen the protester swing around the barricades and come down to where the tourists were at. He knew it was a protester because though the person was biologically male-based on bone pattern, they were wearing heels.

"Gotta go," Michael said, moving down the barricade.

"Hey, about what you said . . ." one of the people who he'd put down as a counterprotester started to say.

"Sir, please excuse me," Michael said. "This is about to get problematic. And *please* don't get involved. We'll speak in a moment."

"Look, you," the protester said. She was holding a sign that read LOVE NOT HAT! It was handmade—and badly. She was followed by a man in a beanie who was filming the evil transphobe being smacked down. Yaasss Queen!

"Yes, ma'am?" Michael said politely, getting out his phone.

"I don't care *what* you say, you transphobe!" the woman said. "Trans are lied about all the time. We are *not* pedophiles! I know half the trans community in New York, and we are *not* pedophiles! That is a *lie*!"

"You're all a bunch of disgusting perverts!" the counterprotester said.

"HOW DARE YOU SAY THAT!"

"Because that's what you are!" the man shouted. "A bunch of grooming perverts!"

"You're just a MAGA hater!" the woman said. "You're the face of white supremacy! You like to beat up gays! Homophobe!"

Michael could see police moving in their direction in Sight. But he had a better idea.

"This is the woman that found me in an alleyway," Michael said, holding up his phone. "Can you come over here so you can see this, please, sir."

"I don't care what you have to say!" the trans activist shouted. "You're a liar!"

"Would you care to look at the picture, ma'am?" Michael said. "And you, sir," he added, swinging it to the counterprotester. "That's my Mama. Wanted to 'dopt me but the state wouldn't let her. Wasn't 'cause she was black; all my foster parents was black. Probably wasn't 'cause she was six-four in her fishnet stocking feet and talked in a baritone. Probably was 'cause she was a drug addict and street ho. But that's my Mama.

"Here's a pic of her with me," said he continued. "I was littler then.

And my face is changing so cain't hardly recognize me. That is me with Mama. My *trans* Mama. Even tried girl one time. All the kids was doing it. Didn't feel right for me. Mama said I should make my own choice. Stayed boy. But I know how to walk in heels better nor you, ma'am.

"I called her whenever I could, 'til lately. I'd let you talk at her but some enemies of mine shot her *dead* not so long ago. So, you callin' a kid who was raised by a trans a transphobe. Kid who just lost his trans Mama. You want to think on that?

"And for you, sir," Michael said, turning to the man. "I was *raised* by a trans. Been sexually assaulted before. But not by Mama. Mama hated that shit. She was a victim her own self. Know she knifed at least one ped to death. Did time for it.

"So, from my perspective, y'all can *both* go to hell. Check your fuckin' assumptions, people. Fact, check that shit at the door..."

CHAPTER 31

"On the Dark Side" —John Cafferty and the Beaver Brown Band

Conn made a perfect backswing, and the club head connected with the ball perfectly. And as too often was the case, sliced to the right. Naturally, the course sloped downward to the right and curved left to the green, so he was going to have to work uphill to fix it.

"Fuck," he said, looking at Perry. "You'd think I'd have gotten rid of that slice by now."

It would have been a nice day in Augusta. But then it had to involve golf.

"Unlikely after all these years," the tall, gaunt Kurt Perry said, leaning on his own golf club. "They say if it isn't gone by thirty, you'll be with it forever."

"Screw you," Conn said. "So, why'd we have to have a meeting?"

He preferred minimizing meetings with the creepier of his Society acquaintances.

"Your pet monster has gone off the reservation," Perry said as they got back in the golf cart. He was driving.

"Bear?" Conn said. "What's he done?"

"According to the FBI, he's been killing hookers in New York and New Jersey," Perry said. "One of the FBI agents that was questioning him about the Annabelle Follett case in Philadelphia noticed similarities with a serial killer in the area. Our analysts say the same."

"Can we quash it?" Conn asked.

"Probably not," Perry replied, getting out at the next lie. "Berlin was consulted. They've had this sort of thing happen before. His skills are useful so instead of burying him, we'll extract him, and he'll disappear. But you need to chat with him about the importance of not going off the reservation. We'll do this once. Only once."

"Got it," Conn said, waiting from the cart. "Well, time to look for a new security chief. Like we need this on top of losing Butch."

"What's your exposure on the Annabelle case?" Perry said, lining up his shot.

"With Bear gone, essentially zero," Conn said. "It looks suspicious. But why kill your beneficiary? The Trust barely survived the probate on Dela."

"Pity about Dela as well," Perry said. He whacked the ball and though it didn't go as far as one of Conn's drives, it was at least straight and landed between the sand traps.

"She'd gotten too suspicious," Conn said. "One of the people she'd hired had looked a bit too closely at Annabelle's death. When he got cleaned up, she started asking questions. Which was a new thing for that airhead."

"Always loose ends," Perry said, shaking his head. "Too many loose ends."

"Sit, Eric," Conn said, gesturing to the provided chair in his office suite.

"What's up?" Bear asked. The man was relaxed and oblivious.

"Eric, Eric, Eric," Conn said with a sigh. "You've been going off the reservation, Eric."

"Say again?" Bear said.

"The FBI has connected the signature of Annabelle to the Orchard Beach Killer," Conn said. "And you were sloppy enough to leave DNA on some of your kills. They did a dumpster dive on the trash at your house in the Hamptons. They're just awaiting DNA tests."

"Ah," Bear said, nodding. He didn't bother to deny it.

"Berlin became involved," Conn said. "Your skills are useful—as a trainer if nothing else. So, you're going to disappear instead of *being* disappeared. They're being lenient. We understand that finding people with just the right psychology for your position is difficult and they're *always* on the edge of going off reservation. So, you're getting a pass on this one. But only one. Once you're overseas, accommodations may be made for your peccadillos."

"Understood," Bear said, nodding. Then he shrugged. "Annabelle was such a turn-on . . . I never really understood addiction before. Now I do."

"You're going to need to stay on the reservation from now on, Eric. You get *one*."

"God is building an army," Michael said.

He'd gotten the contact code on his way home from school. He'd waited until he was home in his bedroom before calling.

"Update on the Annabelle situation," Titanium replied.

"Go," Michael said.

"Nataliya Komarova was a Bratva prostitute smuggled into the US in the beginning of year two of her five-year contract."

"They can't have liked that very much," Michael said. "Bratva is protective of their girls. They make them a lot of money, the loan contract alone is worth a couple of million, and there's a nationalist aspect."

"Yes," Titanium said. "Upper-level Bratva apprised of the situation are unhappy."

"Given that she was killed by my enemies, I'm not crying about them having new ones of their own," Michael said. "Especially Bratva. Are they planning on doing anything?"

"Moscow knows," Titanium said. "But. We put FBI on Bear because he's a working serial killer. However, The Society has found out. They discussed dealing with him themselves. The decision was made to move him overseas. His skills are useful and rare.

"The FBI don't have enough, yet, for an arrest warrant." Titanium sighed. "Even they have to await DNA results. So, it requires other measures.

"We don't normally expose members of the network. However, in this case, the Faerie Queen has ordered a face-to-face meeting between you and Bratva to discuss the situation. Unusual, especially since you'd been considered for higher-level positions."

"I'm authorized to reveal?" Michael said.

That was unusual and he wasn't sure he was comfortable with it.

But if the Faerie Queen said to do it, you did it. Among other things, she'd *never* been wrong even when it seemed like something nutty. Lots of intelligence and lots of intel did not explain the prescience of the Faerie Queen. It was more like magic. Thus, the name.

"How and where?"

"Ever been to the beach...?"

He'd thought Titanium was kidding. But the meet was in a restaurant right at Brighton Beach.

Getting there was surprisingly easy compared to getting around in Baltimore. Get back to the home from school, walk a few blocks down Avenue M, get on the L at the station, train went direct to Brighton Beach.

From there it was another couple of blocks' walk down a street crowded with apartment buildings.

He'd worked his Sight as he rode and walked, peeping into the lives of the people in the houses and apartment complexes along the L. People watching TV. People screwing. People arguing. One assault case. Rats and cats and dogs everywhere.

He began to understand that you couldn't intervene on everything. There were always too many bad things going on at any time and you could only be in one place at a time. If you really could see all the hell in the world, it would drive you nuts. But he was still going to tweak that bastard in 1334 every time he raised his hands to his wife and kids.

The restaurant was an aging diner that was doing its middle best to modernize as a defense against gentrification. He took a booth on the inside, tossing his backpack in the corner. The place was mostly deserted at that time of day and service was quick. The waitress was a pretty little—as in short—gal in her twenties with a blue-eyed, black-haired look that was more common in Estonia than Roo-shah.

"*Naskol'ko khoroshi vareniki?*" Michael asked.

How good is the pierogi? Pierogi was literally the only Russian food he knew besides borscht, and he wasn't up for trying borscht.

"*Eto khorosho. Luchshiy v N'yu-Yorke,*" the waitress replied.

Very good. Best in New York.

"*Vareniki i chay, pozhaluysta,*" Michael said. "*Yeshche skazhi Valerian, chto Pushkin zdes'. Spasibo.*"

I'll have the pierogi and tea, please. Also, tell Valerian that Pushkin is here. Thanks.

At that she gave him The Look, nodded, and scurried away.

Russian mob, Bratva—the Brotherhood—was never popular. Like the Fifth Street Kings, they were respected from fear rather than liking.

Everyone knew they were terrible people. Michael knew they were terrible people. The Faerie Queen knew they were terrible people. But they were also useful, and for terrible people they had one small code that meant that Gondola could abide them: No kids, no slaves.

It was a small thing but telling and it wasn't because of their association with Gondola. From what Michael had heard, back in the nineties one of their low-level guys ran into a situation that sickened him so much that he drew up that personal rule: No kids, no slaves. No trafficking child prostitutes, no forcible prostitution, no forcible trafficking, period.

Which was better than, for example, MS-13, which was all those.

As he rose through the ranks, generally by killing everyone who disagreed, he enforced that rule across the Bratva groups he controlled. Anyone who disagreed either kept it to themselves or got the choppy chop.

Eventually, that guy ended up running the main Russian mob. He had since semiretired, from what Michael had gleaned. His heir in the position was even more determined to maintain the rule. They both hated child traffickers and slavers with an unbounded passion.

Since Bratva operations stretched across much of the globe, they were useful allies to Gondola. Gondola's weapons caches were often supplied by Bratva. They also provided forgery services. Occasionally, it had been Bratva teams that showed up at an orphanage that was having problems and Gondola orphanages in Russia were under their direct protection. Those were the interactions that Michael *knew* about from being involved in ops. There were probably more.

Gondola worked in the shadows. Pretty much every government on *Earth* had, at one time or another, tried to ferret them out and eliminate them as a "terrorist organization." A "terrorist organization" that had informed pretty much every government on Earth of an upcoming terrorist attack and even stopped several personally.

The Society had originally just seen Gondola as a thorn in their side. As time had gone by, they'd begun to view them as legitimate competition. So, every government and administration they controlled was anti-Gondola despite the good that Gondola did. Gondola had informed the FBI *and* the CIA about 9/11 to the point of locating the terrorists *in the United States* before they found out, years later, that both groups had leadership working *with* Atta and UBL.

And pretty much every government on Earth had, at one time or another, come to them for help. The Society had come to them for help and if it was for the good of the world, they helped. It was like that in the shadows.

Gondola sure as hell couldn't work with the CIA. Too many of them worked for the traffickers. Always a bad idea to send the Faerie Queen a "message" of chopped-up children. Those particular assholes had been added to The Wall.

You found allies where you could.

The waitress had gone immediately to the back and spoken to a man, probably the manager, who immediately got on his phone while gesticulating at the cooks.

Service was quick; the pierogi and tea arrived with "Valerian."

Valerian was dressed in a broad-lapeled, wide-striped suit of fair cloth. Clearly not one of their common thugs. Midthirties, five foot nine, about 170 pounds, black hair and blue eyes like the waitress. He was wiry and tough-looking with a scar across his forehead—from a knife, at a guess.

Michael could just barely make out the different earth elements on his body that showed he had prison tats. He'd broken an arm in his childhood and a leg later, probably in his twenties. Several broken ribs and a very minor skull fracture. Lots of minor bone injuries that were remarkably similar to Michael's. He hadn't been raised in the softest school, but it looked as if he was moving up in the world. Two more men casually loitered outside. By their build and postures, he guessed them Valerian's backup.

"Hear you speak Russian," Valerian said.

"I'm okay with it," Michael replied, taking a bite of pierogi. He'd never had it before and it was not bad.

"What you got?"

Michael pulled a file out of his backpack and handed it over. He got a sense that everyone else in the restaurant was actively avoiding even looking at their table.

"The story is short," Michael said, tugging his earlobe. "Poor little rich girl, Annabelle Follett, trust-fund baby. Drug addict, constant runaway, street whore, found dead in Philly, raped and strangled by a serial killer. The end. Except it's not short and it's not the end."

"What *is* the end?" Valerian asked.

"Hasn't happened, yet," Michael said. "Annabelle was running away all the time because she was being sexually assaulted by people in and associated with her Trust, the Follett Trust, as well as members of high New York finance. An Epstein thing, *da*?"

"*Da*," Valerian said.

"Annabelle was killed because she was believed to be carrying intel related to what was happening to her as well as other skullduggery by people of the Trust," Michael said. "Not to mention she could name names. *Kompromat, da*?"

"*Da*."

"There was a possible heir," Michael continued. "Annabelle had stretch marks when she died. Since the Trust and its billions would dissolve if the heir appeared, they had to cover-up Anna's DNA. Since there was an autopsy and they keep those samples *forever*, they needed a body to replace the autopsy samples. Enter Nataliya Komarova, previously missing person from Lugansk."

He passed over another file.

"One of your girls," he said, taking a sip of black tea. "Her remains have been positively identified in the Philly crime lab, substituted for Annabelle Follett's. According to the forensic lab that tested them, she was living in the New York area for at least a year. Shortly before her death she was drinking Grey Goose vodka that was roofied. Passing resemblance to Anna so the dipshits thought the DNA would match? Anyway, she was killed for autopsy samples. We thought you should know."

"Know who killed her in particular?" Valerian asked, looking through the files.

"Eric Bear," Michael said. Another file. "Former SEAL, tossed out for sexual stuff, unsurprisingly. Chief of security for the Trust. We know that, not suspect. Intercepts."

"*Da*," Valerian said, glancing at the photo. "What interest do your people have in this? Besides they're assholes."

"One, the Trust is part of one of our big enemies," Michael said.

"Giving them issues is in our interests. You know about The Society?"

"*Da*," Valerian said, making a face. "Those assholes."

"Those assholes," Michael said. "The Trust is one of their funding sources and useful for paying off useless scions of politicians they control. Bear is one of their wet-work people who—they don't know this—has recently been going off the reservation.

"Two: You're looking at the heir."

"You?" Valerian said.

"We'd rather have the money on our side, working for our purposes, than The Society's," Michael said, shrugging. "I'm good either way, but the Faerie Queen says it's our issue. So, here I am."

"You're a *member*?" Valerian said. "One of the hackers?"

"Yes," Michael said.

"Young!" Valerian said, surprised.

"Recruited when I was eight," Michael said, shrugging. "I'd accidentally penetrated one of our minor servers. If I could get in there, even though it was low-level protected, they figured I was worth recruiting. I was just doing it for the practice."

"So, this is the motherfucker killed Nataliya?" Valerian asked, pointing at the picture of Eric Bear.

"Yes," Michael said. "And given that he raped my mother at an early age and then raped and murdered her in Philly, calling him a motherfucker is redundant."

"Guess a hacker doesn't really handle this sort of stuff," Valerian said. "No offense. I've heard of you guys. You're the best. But . . ."

"Oh, I wouldn't mind taking care of Mr. Bear personally," Michael said, his eyes hard. He softened them and took another sip of tea. "You don't know much about me, sir. But I assure you, it would not be my first rodeo. The Faerie Queen said take it to you. When the Queen speaks, you obey."

He didn't have to pay for the meal. He had hardly any cash on him, but he left a tip because he wasn't an asshole like Mr. Pink.

Michael was doing an American history report when his phone buzzed.

Usually, you kept the reports from earlier school and just updated and improved them as you advanced. Currently, he was taking a graduate-level report and dumbing it down to seventh grade. It was surprisingly hard work, and he was glad for a break.

Cellphones were the worst and best inventions in mankind's long history. Like nuclear systems, they could be good, like nuclear power plants, or bad, like nuclear weapons. And at about the same level of good/bad.

It was a text from Valerian:

v: You available this evening?
m: Y
v: 15m. Corner 28 n M east side.
m: Roger.

So much for American history. Time to go meet scary people.

"Where are you going?" Linda said as he headed out the door.
"Out."

"Uh, okay, just, uh, keep your phone on you and be back by nine, okay?"

CHAPTER 32

"Heathens" —Twenty One Pilots

He'd gotten in the Uber when it pulled up and the guy waved at the back. It had taken him, with an unspeaking driver, to another restaurant also in Brighton Beach.

It reminded him of a meme he'd seen: 1980s: Don't get into a car with a stranger! '90s: Don't talk to strange people on the internet! '20s: Talk to people on the internet and get into a car with a stranger!

The restaurant, which was considerably more upscale, had a sign on the door: CLOSED FOR PRIVATE PARTY.

When he went inside it was effectively empty with some waiters and waitresses rearranging tables and a female maître d' at the stand.

"I'm sorry," the woman said peremptorily. "We are closed."

"Pushkin," Michael said.

"Oh, yes," she said hastily. "Sorry, Mr. Pushkin! This way."

"*Nichego*," Michael said, following her into the restaurant.

At the back sitting in a booth were Valerian and an older man wearing a much nicer suit.

The man was probably in his sixties. Like Valerian's, the suit was broad lapel and broad stripes. It was a fashion thing with Bratva. Six feet or so at a guess—hard to tell sitting down. He was much burlier than Valerian, with broad shoulders and a heavy build that was part age-fat.

Lots of broken bones. Face reconstructed from lots of hits. New nose. Old work. Nothing new in the way of plastic surgery. Not bone, anyway. All the breaks were old. His hand bones had punched quite a few somethings. Could be bags. More likely faces.

Missing half the pinky finger of his left hand.

There was a half empty bottle of Belvedere Vodka sitting in front of them and three glasses.

There were four more men sitting at a nearby table sharing an unlabeled vodka bottle. They were large men with not quite as well-fitted suits of cheaper cloth. The term of art would probably be "heavies." The restaurant was otherwise empty, save for a line of servers waiting at a respectful distance.

"Sit, Pushkin, sit," the man said, gesturing at the seat across from him at the booth. "Vodka?" he asked, holding up the bottle.

"*Pozhaluysta*," Michael said. "*Kakim byl by mir bez vodki?*"

Please. What would the world be without vodka?

"Doesn't affect you, though," the man said in English.

"Not . . . anymore," Michael replied, downing the drink. "Bit like water. But gives it a little flavor."

Valerian was making the Spock eyebrow.

"Our friend Pushkin here is the newest member of the Junior Super Corps, Stone Tactical," the man said. "Who is already pissing off the *chernozhopyye* by stealing their drugs. Also, rather a dangerous fellow, *without* the superpowers.

"But part of *Gondola* was a surprise. Pardon, introductions, I am Feliks Morozov."

"Honored, Mr. Morozov," Michael said trying to hide his surprise.

When he brought this to Bratva, he was not expecting to meet the head of the Russian mob on the East Coast.

Michael picked up the bottle with Earth Move and opened up the metal cap by holding the cap and unscrewing the bottle from it. He poured himself another shot, then sent it over to hover over Valerian's glass.

"*Boleye?*" More?

Valerian chuckled.

"*Da. Boleye*. Looks like I'm going to *need* some."

"At this rate we may need another bottle," Morozov said. "*Devochka! Yeshche odna butylka!*"

One of the waitresses hurried to the bar.

"This is about Nataliya, obviously," Morozov said as the waitress brought the new bottle. "You read the report?"

"*Da.*"

"She was pregnant," Morozov continued, cracking the seal and pouring himself another drink. "It was mine."

"*Bozemoi,*" Michael puffed.

"I had a vasectomy long time back," Morozov said. "Not a good idea having kids in my line of work. Some disagree. But she got pregnant. Just another hooker but she got pregnant. Swore on her life I was the only one she didn't use a condom. Got an amnio. Then she disappeared. Got the results back while we were looking for her. Mine. Never heard from her again."

"My condolences," Michael said.

"I was running the hookers in New York at the time," Morozov said. "I warned her she needed to just take the johns that we brought. People we knew we could trust because we knew them. Knew where they lived. But she was a hard worker. Very into the job. Top earner. Fucking *fantastic* in bed. My boss was *very* pissed when she disappeared."

He held up his left hand to show the pinky.

"My boss was old-school," Morozov said. "Also, into Asian stuff. Thought the yakuza had the right way to deal with failure. Nearly killed me. Said he *should* kill me. We don't like to lose girls."

He tossed down another hit of vodka and poured again.

"Now I find out the lady carrying my baby was killed for some fucking *tissue samples*?" Morozov growled.

"*Da,*" Michael said. "The information is valid."

"Oh, *da,*" Morozov said. "It's obvious who did it. And *when* you guys will give information, it's always a hundred percent. *When* you do. This is because they're fucking Society?"

"We don't like Society," Michael said.

"Fucking slavers," Morozov said. "Like they're so high and mighty. So untouchable. The Dvoryane. Fuck them. *Anybody* can be touched. *That* fucker is going to be touched."

"From the broken bones you've got, I suspect you're going to use a baseball bat," Michael said. "Fun fact: Russia has one of the highest sales of baseball bats in the world and they don't play baseball. But, as the kid whose mother was raped repeatedly by this guy and then raped and murdered, can I make a suggestion?"

"*Da,*" Morozov said.

"Ever been in the burn ward?" Michael asked. "He's a former SEAL. He's still a tough guy and he's got situational awareness. But if you could set him on fire and then let him get treatment, it's worse than anything you could do to him, personally. He won't survive anything as bad as the burn ward outside of a hospital."

"That sounds pretty painful, yeah," Morozov said, nodding approvingly.

"The one fly in the burn jelly is Doc Lee—a healer," Michael said. "Now, Doc Bethany never showed up for me the *two* times I was right there in Johns Hopkins in the burn ward. But this guy Bear's got protection. He's Society. He might get the ministrations of a healer. Which would make things not as bad. I mean, being set on fire with jellied gasoline is no fun. I say that from personal experience. But the burn ward is where it's at if you wanna go full old-school. So, the bat may be the more assured route is what I'm saying."

"Yeah, got to think that through," Morozov said, nodding, thoughtfully. "Definitely and personally put the pain to him or let some of my guys set him on fire, let him go to the hospital but then take the chance the healer heals him. Tough call."

"If you happen to go the baseball bat route, mind if I get involved?" Michael said, steepling his fingers. "I can do some *really* unpleasant shit to people's bones with these powers."

"That's a thought as well," Morozov said. "So . . . you're also that kid from Baltimore. The chopsticks."

"I humbly admit that I am, sir," Michael said, bowing then downing another shot.

"Three Muertos Angelicas with *chopsticks,*" Morozov said. "Not bad."

"Well, there was some gunplay and knives involved," Michael said. "But it was mostly the chopsticks."

"Why chopsticks?" Valerian said.

"All I had," Michael replied. "Plus, I'd already kilt a bunch of people with guns. You don't get street rep from repeating that shit."

"I've got some time," Morozov said, gesturing around. "Tell."

"In my own idiom?" Michael asked.

"*Da.*"

Michael cleared his throat and poured another drink.

"I'm sure you know this word, but are both of you familiar with the term 'probative'?"

"Oh, fucking very," Valerian said. "Evidence that can be used against you in fucking court."

"Notably, evidence that would tend to confirm guilt or innocence," Michael said. "Probative. Important to the story:

"So, there I was, no shit, standing on Spring Street in traffic on a beautiful spring day in Baltimore next to a battered brown sedan that looks like its windows have been spray-painted red on the inside... covered from head to toe in blood."

"Head to toe?" Valerian said, chuckling.

"I was hocking that shit out of my ears," Michael said, making a hocking motion and mock spitting. "The first responding officer is slowly taking his hand off his weapon. We have established that he knows me, at least by reputation. He looks at the car, looks at me, and says, slowly:

"'Sooo... What happened here?'

"To which I reply:

"'I dunno, Officer, it was like this when I *gots* here!'"

Michael wiped his eyes, tossed whatever had been wiped out, mock-spit again, shook his hands as if to get something off, and made more hocking motions.

"I was *covered*! Moving on:

"'So, you don't have *anything* to do with this triple homicide?'

"'Why ever would you think *that,* Officer?'

"'Maybeee... because you're covered from head to toe in *blood*?'

"So, I look at him with wide, innocent blue eyes and say:

"'How is *that* probative...?'"

As Michael walked out of the restaurant, he looked at his phone and shook his head. There were six text messages from Linda.

This was going to be fun.

Michael got back around eleven and The Parents were waiting in the front room, sitting next to each other on the couch.

"Mike," Linda said, her arms crossed and eyes narrowed. "Where have you been?"

"Out," Michael said. He sat down in the provided chair and folded his hands on his lap.

"Frank?" Linda said primly.

"Mike," Frank said. His posture and expression were attempting to balance "concerned parent" with "stern enough to satisfy Linda." "I know you're a very independent person. And that you feel that you are old enough to make decisions for yourself. But we are your parents, and we are responsible for you."

"You cannot just be running around at all hours of the day and night!" Linda said. "I thought we had worked through the food issues..."

Michael was slowly allowing his aura to build up. It was probably just a shimmer at first. Linda wasn't noticing, yet, but Frank was. His eyes were starting to widen.

Linda suddenly stopped talking and just sat there with her mouth open.

"I was studying my powers and I got focused," Michael said, doing a not totally full aura. "I needed to be around solid rock. The powers I was working... It could do damage to the soil around here and I don't want to do any damage. The nearest rock around here is out of my range, fourteen hundred feet down. So, I was over at Central Park, working with the rock there, and lost track of time.

"I'm aware it's a school night. I should have gotten back earlier. I get focused sometimes and forget. Like when you're really into a book or TV show. It's called hyperfocus. I did my homework on the subway. I apologize."

"So, you're with..." Frank said, his jaw hanging open as well.

"Junior Super Corps," Michael said. "Stone Tactical," he added, putting his hand on his chest and bowing slightly. "At your service. That's the after-school and weekends mandatory thing I've got to do. And, no, Linda, I'm *not* a transphobe. I just didn't like it when your hero Electrobolt literally flailed me with her penis, then tried to kill me by electrocution. Which is what she was arrested for."

"Oh," Linda said, then, "Oh!"

"So, it's been a long day," Michael said. "Sorry to cause you worry. Should have communicated better. You want to kick me out, your call. In the meantime, mind if I take a shower and get some sleep? I'm bushed."

"Okay," Linda said. "Sure . . ."

"You guys are great," Michael said. "You're people of good heart and you're right that kids need guidance. But you don't have to worry about scary people in the dark. I *am* scary people. 'Night."

"Ho-ho-ho, Merry Christmas!" Hinkle said, looking at his computer screen. He leaned back in his chair and tapped the edge of Starr's cubicle. "DNA on Bear is back."

"And . . . ?" Starr asked.

"We have . . . a positive match!" Hinkle said, grinning. "Which means he killed Annabelle Follett as well. Which makes no damned sense."

"Been looking into that," Starr said. "You know what I did before this job, right?"

"Sex crimes investigator," Hinkle said.

"Lots of CPS cases of sexual assault on minors," Starr said. "There's lots about body language. Annabelle Follett's mother set up an in-memoriam page for her, or more likely had someone set it up."

"Okay."

"A lot of it is knowing what to look for," Starr said. "Crossed arms. Drawing away. Head down. Looking into it further, grades dropped off the scale, runaway, got into drugs. All the classic signs of sexual assault by a person close to her. Then there are the tells when she's with people in photos.

"Take my word for it: Annabelle Follett was being *repeatedly* sexually assaulted. Including by Bear and her stepdad, Wesley Conn, who is now the *head* of the Trust. Not only them. There are photos of her giving exact tells for being near an assailant and some of the people pictured are *very* powerful people. Major figures in New York finance. It was an Epstein thing, and she was the cookie being passed around on a tray. Probably by Conn. What if she was going to talk? That's why she was always on the run. She was running from the Trust. From Bear. He wasn't her protector. He was her nightmare."

"Whelp," Hinkle said, "we'll need a warrant for a DNA swab. I'm going to shoot for a warrant for arrest as well. It's likely that he'll run. We've got him cold."

Starr got a curious look on his face, turned to his computer, and brought up a screen. A few taps and he swore.

"Eric Bear is scheduled for a flight to Zurich," Starr said.

"When?" Hinkle replied, angrily.

"Just took off."

"Son of a *bitch*!"

"I checked with the airline," Starr said, hanging up his phone. "Bear was *not* aboard. He never went through TSA. Apparently never made it to the airport."

"So, where is he?"

"The Vengeful One" —Disturbed

Eric Bear was hanging from the ceiling in the warehouse with his wrists manacled overhead with chains. A single light illuminated him and left dark the area where Michael and Feliks were standing.

"So, I see you decided to go the baseball bat route," Michael said.

"The healer *was* an issue with the burn ward idea," Morozov said, shrugging. "But the real reason is I just want to get personal. This job is all meetings and reports these days. You have no idea how *corporate* we've become. I haven't beaten anyone to death in simply *years*!"

"I try not to get personal," Michael admitted. "You let the personal get in the way and things can slide. Never talk to people when you're killing them, that's my rule. Of course, of late, it's been more of a guideline."

"I can hear you, you know," Bear said. "If you're trying to get information, good luck. I'm not gonna talk."

"Oh, Mr. Bear, you misunderstand the situation," Feliks said, stepping into the light and accepting a baseball bat from one of the waiting guards. "We're not here for information. We don't care about what you know. We care about what you *did*."

"You've been a bad, bad boy, Eric," Michael added, also entering the light.

"Okay," Bear said. "I have no idea why I pissed off the Russians. But the real question is: Who's the punk?"

"You or me?" Michael asked, looking to Morozov. "Age before... You first."

"Nataliya Komarova," Morozov said.

"No idea who you're—"

Morozov should have tried out for the Yankees in his prime.

"And it's going...it's going...It's over the FENCE, YAAASSS," Michael said, as Bear choked from the hit to his abdomen. "IT'S FELIKS MOROZOV WITH A *HOMER!*"

Michael lifted himself into the air so he could look the man in the eye.

"Hallo, my name is Michael Truesdale," Michael said. "You raped and murdered my mother. Prepare to die."

"Who?" Bear gasped after a moment.

"Yeah," Michael said, laughing. "I mean, there's *so many* women that could mean, right? Which *one,* for fuck's sake? Well, maybe I should use the name: Michael *Follett,*" he added, putting an emphasis on the T.

Michael grinned ferally as Bear's eyes widened.

"Ta-da!" Michael said, spinning around in the air, his arms out. He Light Shaped an aura around himself in red, white, and blue. "The missing heir!"

"Bullshit," Bear said. "She had an abortion."

"My mother was clever, asshole," Michael said, coming down to a perfect landing. "More clever than you gave her credit for; she had somebody else who was getting an abortion use her name. Hallo, my name is Michael Follett. You killed my mother. Prepare to...well, you'll die *eventually.* Oh, by the way, I'm also Stone Tactical, Junior Super Corps. *And* a member of Gondola. And...Butch Eisenberg's death, that raging pedophile, was...meeeee!" he finished, pointing at himself with both fingers.

He nodded as Bear's eyes widened again.

"If you're Gondola, you think you're the *good* guys," Bear said. "What the *fuck* are you doing with the *Russian mob?*"

Michael lifted up a ball of concrete he'd just been keeping around because he liked it and accelerated it into the security chief's abdomen.

"*Uuurup,*" Bear gasped, then vomited.

"We're not *that* kind of good guys..."

"Oh, for fuck's sake," Hinkle snarled.

"'Sup?" Starr asked.

"Eric Bear was just found in the East River," Hinkle said.

"I take it you mean 'found dead' in the East River?" Starr said, spinning around in his chair. "There goes the need for warrants." He got up to look at Hinkle's screen.

"Found dead," Hinkle replied, pointing to the crime-scene photos where the body had been unloaded from the recovery boat. The body was naked, fresh and badly bruised. It basically didn't have a face.

"Trust cleaning up loose ends?" Starr said.

"If so, they were mighty pissed," Hinkle said. "Looks as if he was beaten to death. They just ID'd him by his fingerprints."

"There goes our case," Starr said. "One dumpster dive for nothing."

"Not for nothing," Hinkle said. "I'm pretty sure that closes the Orchard Beach case. And that's something."

"Can't officially close without proving it," Starr said.

"Get his DNA from the corpse and it's proven to my satisfaction," Hinkle said. "Sometimes that's all the satisfaction you get in this job."

CHAPTER 33

"Awaken" —League of Legends
(featuring Valerie Broussard)

"God has an army," Michael said, turning onto N Street. He always got these messages on his way home.

"Update on Cannibale," Titanium said. "Diarrhea?"

"Cannibale is in Queens," Diarrhea said. "The plan is to go ahead and attack when you show up for the patrol photo op. They're willing to take the notoriety and arrests to take you down. Plan is to shoot you and the other Corps members and then chop you up with machetes."

"Powerboy?" Michael asked.

"He's brought along a super affiliated with '13," Titanium said. "Death Strong, an Invulnerable Ground like Hombre de Poder. His job is to take out Poder. Assuming that you're friends with the rest of the team, they're planning on taking out the *whole* JSC, except Ivory Wing, who'll be on air patrol. Everyone is also assuming they're going to go to prison. They're loading heavy, heavier than Baltimore."

"Plan?" Michael asked.

"Two possibilities," Diarrhea said. "With various sub-plans. Faerie Queen has authorized you to attempt to get the JSC to take him down at his safe house in Queens before your next patrol. First backup is informing FBI. They'll need Super Corps support just for the invulnerable. We have an FBI agent we owe a favor."

"He can make the arrest if we can figure out a way for him to be in the area," Michael said. "I'll talk to the team. See if they're in. Anything else?"

"We can't give you full operations support," Diarrhea said. "It would be too obvious. But we'll be up on backup. If it goes entirely sideways, we'll arrange for the Flyers to be in the general area. But it's going to require planning and contingencies. You'll have to handle that with your team."

Michael tugged his earlobe. "Just a matter of if I can keep Breeze's attention long enough. Got to get the team in. Though at this point I probably could Lone Ranger it, that's the wrong way to go."

"Good luck talking to your team," Diarrhea said. "Out."

"Thanks for coming on such short notice," Michael said.

He hadn't known when he set up the meeting place that Paphos Diner was a New York landmark. It was just fairly central to all of them, located near Broadway Junction, in Brooklyn. It might have made more sense to meet closer to Queens so Jorge wouldn't have quite such a long ride. But this was as close as he wanted to get to Cannibale.

Sasha was even in attendance, looking as radiant as ever.

"Does this place have anything that *doesn't* contain meat?" Laura asked, looking at the menu.

"Eggplant parmesan," Josh said. "Already checked."

"That's not vegan!" she said.

"Then get it without the parmesan," Josh grumbled. He pointed at the menu. "It says this one's vegan."

Laura huffed but relented.

"I was looking for a pizza place but none of them had any seating," Michael said. The diner was in full swing for dinner and crowded, which was also not optimum. But it wasn't like he could invite them all over to his house to discuss raiding a major crime kingpin. And given how loud it was it was unlikely they'd be overheard.

Besides, the more he thought about it, the more old-school this was. The Junior Super Corps getting together in a fifties-style diner to discuss a crazy operation just totally made sense. If they were in a 1960s or '70s comic book.

"So, you said this was an emergency," Josh said as the waitress arrived.

"Okay," Linda said. "Sure..."

"You guys are great," Michael said. "You're people of good heart and you're right that kids need guidance. But you don't have to worry about scary people in the dark. I *am* scary people. 'Night."

"Ho-ho-ho, Merry Christmas!" Hinkle said, looking at his computer screen. He leaned back in his chair and tapped the edge of Starr's cubicle. "DNA on Bear is back."

"And...?" Starr asked.

"We have...a positive match!" Hinkle said, grinning. "Which means he killed Annabelle Follett as well. Which makes no damned sense."

"Been looking into that," Starr said. "You know what I did before this job, right?"

"Sex crimes investigator," Hinkle said.

"Lots of CPS cases of sexual assault on minors," Starr said. "There's lots about body language. Annabelle Follett's mother set up an in-memoriam page for her, or more likely had someone set it up."

"Okay."

"A lot of it is knowing what to look for," Starr said. "Crossed arms. Drawing away. Head down. Looking into it further, grades dropped off the scale, runaway, got into drugs. All the classic signs of sexual assault by a person close to her. Then there are the tells when she's with people in photos.

"Take my word for it: Annabelle Follett was being *repeatedly* sexually assaulted. Including by Bear and her stepdad, Wesley Conn, who is now the *head* of the Trust. Not only them. There are photos of her giving exact tells for being near an assailant and some of the people pictured are *very* powerful people. Major figures in New York finance. It was an Epstein thing, and she was the cookie being passed around on a tray. Probably by Conn. What if she was going to talk? That's why she was always on the run. She was running from the Trust. From Bear. He wasn't her protector. He was her nightmare."

"Whelp," Hinkle said, "we'll need a warrant for a DNA swab. I'm going to shoot for a warrant for arrest as well. It's likely that he'll run. We've got him cold."

Starr got a curious look on his face, turned to his computer, and brought up a screen. A few taps and he swore.

"Eric Bear is scheduled for a flight to Zurich," Starr said.

"When?" Hinkle replied, angrily.

"Just took off."

"Son of a *bitch*!"

"I checked with the airline," Starr said, hanging up his phone. "Bear was *not* aboard. He never went through TSA. Apparently never made it to the airport."

"So, where is he?"

"The Vengeful One" —Disturbed

Eric Bear was hanging from the ceiling in the warehouse with his wrists manacled overhead with chains. A single light illuminated him and left dark the area where Michael and Feliks were standing.

"So, I see you decided to go the baseball bat route," Michael said.

"The healer *was* an issue with the burn ward idea," Morozov said, shrugging. "But the real reason is I just want to get personal. This job is all meetings and reports these days. You have no idea how *corporate* we've become. I haven't beaten anyone to death in simply *years*!"

"I try not to get personal," Michael admitted. "You let the personal get in the way and things can slide. Never talk to people when you're killing them, that's my rule. Of course, of late, it's been more of a guideline."

"I can hear you, you know," Bear said. "If you're trying to get information, good luck. I'm not gonna talk."

"Oh, Mr. Bear, you misunderstand the situation," Feliks said, stepping into the light and accepting a baseball bat from one of the waiting guards. "We're not here for information. We don't care about what you know. We care about what you *did*."

"You've been a bad, bad boy, Eric," Michael added, also entering the light.

"Okay," Bear said. "I have no idea why I pissed off the Russians. But the real question is: Who's the punk?"

"You or me?" Michael asked, looking to Morozov. "Age before... You first."

"Nataliya Komarova," Morozov said.

"No idea who you're—"

Morozov should have tried out for the Yankees in his prime.

"And it's going...it's going...It's over the FENCE, YAAASSS," Michael said, as Bear choked from the hit to his abdomen. "IT'S FELIKS MOROZOV WITH A *HOMER!*"

Michael lifted himself into the air so he could look the man in the eye.

"Hallo, my name is Michael Truesdale," Michael said. "You raped and murdered my mother. Prepare to die."

"Who?" Bear gasped after a moment.

"Yeah," Michael said, laughing. "I mean, there's *so many* women that could mean, right? Which *one,* for fuck's sake? Well, maybe I should use the name: Michael *Follett,*" he added, putting an emphasis on the T.

Michael grinned ferally as Bear's eyes widened.

"Ta-da!" Michael said, spinning around in the air, his arms out. He Light Shaped an aura around himself in red, white, and blue. "The missing heir!"

"Bullshit," Bear said. "She had an abortion."

"My mother was clever, asshole," Michael said, coming down to a perfect landing. "More clever than you gave her credit for; she had somebody else who was getting an abortion use her name. Hallo, my name is Michael Follett. You killed my mother. Prepare to...well, you'll die *eventually.* Oh, by the way, I'm also Stone Tactical, Junior Super Corps. *And* a member of Gondola. And...Butch Eisenberg's death, that raging pedophile, was...meeeee!" he finished, pointing at himself with both fingers.

He nodded as Bear's eyes widened again.

"If you're Gondola, you think you're the *good* guys," Bear said. "What the *fuck* are you doing with the *Russian mob?*"

Michael lifted up a ball of concrete he'd just been keeping around because he liked it and accelerated it into the security chief's abdomen.

"*Uuurup,*" Bear gasped, then vomited.

"We're not *that* kind of good guys..."

"Oh, for fuck's sake," Hinkle snarled.

"'Sup?" Starr asked.

"Eric Bear was just found in the East River," Hinkle said.

"I take it you mean 'found dead' in the East River?" Starr said, spinning around in his chair. "There goes the need for warrants." He got up to look at Hinkle's screen.

"Found dead," Hinkle replied, pointing to the crime-scene photos where the body had been unloaded from the recovery boat. The body was naked, fresh and badly bruised. It basically didn't have a face.

"Trust cleaning up loose ends?" Starr said.

"If so, they were mighty pissed," Hinkle said. "Looks as if he was beaten to death. They just ID'd him by his fingerprints."

"There goes our case," Starr said. "One dumpster dive for nothing."

"Not for nothing," Hinkle said. "I'm pretty sure that closes the Orchard Beach case. And that's something."

"Can't officially close without proving it," Starr said.

"Get his DNA from the corpse and it's proven to my satisfaction," Hinkle said. "Sometimes that's all the satisfaction you get in this job."

Cannibale from escaping and subduing the guards downstairs. Easy, you've got takedown duty."

"Why me?" Josh asked.

"Cannibale sleeps with a machete," Michael said. "What's a machete made of?"

"Oh," Josh said. "So, you want me to take this guy on hand to hand? While the guards are reacting?"

"Breeze is going to handle the guards," Michael said.

"What?" Laura said. "What?"

"Getting to that, Breeze," Michael said. "Easy, you use his machete and other metal in the room to form handcuffs and cuff him. You shouldn't even have to get to arm's length. You're a seventeen-year-old super. Even if it is hand to hand, you should have the upper hand. You do some martial arts, right?"

"Yeah," Josh said. "Brazilian jujitsu. But . . . never actually *used* it."

"He's survived a lot and he's the real deal," Michael said. "But he's also over sixty. Just don't let him have a blade and you should be good. Just get him subdued. If any of the guards make it upstairs, they may have guns. Just Metal bend, right?"

"Right," Josh said, nodding thoughtfully. "What are you and Sasha doing?"

"Handling Death Strong," Michael said. "And also hitting the guards."

"Oh," Sasha said, nodding. "That makes total sense. An Earther and a teenage Flyer taking on a hulk called Death Strong. Not to mention a bunch of armed guards. Total sense."

"I can just pick him up through the ceiling and hold him in the air 'til a regular Flyer gets there," Michael said. "He's a hulk. Get a hulk off the ground and they're helpless. I'll just pick him up like I picked up Bolt."

"'Cause that worked out so well," Laura said. "And 'hulk' is still an offensive term."

"I didn't hold Bolt at max extension," Michael said, ignoring her. "I was trying to keep it quiet, still. I could have punched him through the wall. I can pick up Death Strong and hold him overhead. The range of a hulk is his arm length. Sasha takes the door and takes down interior guards in the front room. Then there's you, Febreze."

"What am *I* supposed to do?" Breeze asked. "Blow them?"

"Yeah," Michael said. "Your job is to fill the whole main floor with tear gas. Jorge knocks down the back door and throws in the grenades. Then you just move the gas around in the interior. Guards are out of action. Think you can blow some gas around the lower floors of the house?"

"Okay," Laura said with a half-hearted shrug.

"So, front door down, back door down," Michael said. "Back glass door broken in. Just blow and blow until you blow the whole house."

Laura made a face and flipped a bird at him.

"Got the basic plan?" Michael said, pointing at the overhead of the house. "Come in together. Jorge jumps off Sasha, who continues on over the house. Sasha comes around to hit the front door. I put Josh in through the back window to take down Cannibale. Drop Breeze in the backyard. Sasha takes out the front door, Jorge takes out the back door and starts throwing in tear gas grenades. Breeze spreads it around. Wing does entry, heads to the stairs to prevent anyone from supporting Cannibale. I go over the house as that's going on, pick up Death Strong through the roof and hold him overhead, then go in behind Sasha to take out any remaining guards. Got it?"

"No," Laura said. "What was that middle bit?"

"So, I get to crash through a glass door," Josh said. "Great. You know we're not hardened yet, right?"

"You won't have to crash through the door. It's glass. That's Earth. I'll just evaporate it."

"Okay," Josh said. "You sort of skipped where we're going to get tear gas, though."

"You can make it," Michael said. "The grenades are smoke grenades. You can find those in a military surplus store. You take out the material in a smoke grenade and mix it with a particular type of heating tablet, *also* available in military supply stores. The material in the heating tablet has the same effect as CS, which is the military 'tear gas.'"

"Do I want to know how you know that?" Josh asked.

"No," Michael said.

"And it doesn't affect us?" Josh continued.

"Not really," Michael said. "Technically it does, you just recover so fast you barely notice. At worst, you'll feel itchy. We can ops-test that if you want."

"No, I'm good," Josh said with a casual wave.

"And what was that middle bit?" Laura asked. "I'm supposed to do what?"

"You land in the backyard," Michael said. "I'll put you down easy. When Jorge gets the back door open and starts throwing in grenades, you just blow the smoke around. There's a breezeway that runs from the front door to the back door. Jorge throws grenades in the back room, kitchen, you just blow down the breezeway as hard as you can. That's your *entire* task. That clear enough?"

"Yeah," Laura said, but it was hollow. Michael wasn't sure if it was doubt or disappointment.

"You're not an in-your-face fighter, Laura," Michael said. "It's something you *can* do, and it will be *extremely* helpful to the op. You're liable to disable most of the guards before Sasha can even *get* there."

"Okay," Laura said, waggling her head and glancing at Sasha.

"You can have all the guards you want," Sasha said. "Blow them *all* for all I care."

Laura glared at her and growled. Out of everyone, she still didn't seem completely sold on the plan.

"You kids ready to eat?" the waitress said, bearing a full tray of food.

"Meat!" Michael said happily.

They spent the dinner followed by milkshakes working out bugs and coming up with contingencies. Laura was going to have to enter the kitchen at the back at the very least to get the tear gas swirled in the front room. She didn't have enough range from outside. Jorge would precede her, taking out any guards who might not have succumbed to the tear gas. What if Josh couldn't take down Cannibale? Contingencies.

"Really, it comes down to if all else fails we just back off and let Sasha and Jorge handle it," Michael said. "If Cannibale gets past Josh, Sasha runs him down."

"Death Strong has me worried," Josh said. "Seriously."

"I will not show you how fast I can pluck someone up that I don't care what happens to them," Michael said. "It would damage you and damage this restaurant. But when we practice this, I'll show you how fast I can pick up Poder. Or that I can hold Sasha like a fly in amber."

"Good luck," Sasha said.

"Have you been training your powers?" Josh asked.

"Deponent sayeth not?" Michael said. "But I've got Sight and, yeah, quite a bit of power. Not sure if it's enough to take Sasha, honestly. But enough to pick Death Strong up and keep him out of action. I also can sort out supers from normals in Sight."

The diner was emptying out and he had to be careful what he said as it quieted down.

"Who pays for the damage?" the waitress asked.

"I'll..." Josh said but Michael waved his hand.

"Government credit card," Michael said, pulling it out and handing it to the waitress.

"You sure?" Josh asked.

"Positive," Michael said.

"Uh..." the waitress said, looking at him askance.

Michael pulled out his CAC card with a sigh and showed it to her.

"We're all undercover agents," Michael said. "Chosen 'cause we look so young."

"Oh," the waitress said with a laugh. "Okay. One meal on the federal government it is..."

"Mr. DiAngelo gave that to you to eat while you were on patrols," Josh pointed out.

"By the time he gets the bill we're all going to be either in very deep kimchee or heroes," Michael said, shrugging. "Either way, a meal for all of us isn't going to matter. And that brings up the other thing. We're all going to be getting some money from the federal government for what happened with Bolt. Jorge and I will probably come out best there..."

"My dad said they're stuck with our side going for something like two million for each of you and a half million for each of us and the Corps saying they want to be in the half-million versus hundred-thousand range."

"Point is, we're going to be getting something," Michael said. "But there's a reward for information leading to Cannibale's apprehension. If we inform them we've already apprehended him, that's pretty much it. And there's a reward for Death Strong. So, how would you all like to split five million dollars, equal shares?"

"*Oh*," Laura said, raising her hand. "I'm in. I'll blow the entire house for a million dollars..."

CHAPTER 34

"With a Little Help from My Friends" —The Beatles

"If you make it so I can't be a bar member, I am never going to forgive you," Josh whispered.

"Why are you whispering?" Michael asked in a normal voice. "There's *nobody* around."

They were in the process of breaking into an empty warehouse large enough to practice the raid on Cannibale's safe house. And Josh was not handling committing a felony very well.

"Besides," Michael said as he bypassed the electronic door lock, "it would be a juvie misdemeanor at best. Tell the Bar Committee you were setting up a rave. They're all gonna be Gen X. They'll pass you in a shot."

"*Could* we set up a rave?" Laura asked.

"Yeah," Michael said as the door unlocked. "But in that case, you rent the warehouse, not break into it. Wait here," he added while opening the door.

He opened up the guts of the alarm panel and connected a set of wires from his phone, then hit the app. The countdown timer had only gone down ten seconds and the alarm was shut off.

"Okay," Michael said, opening the door again. "Come on in."

"Do I want to know where you learned this?" Josh asked.

"Growing up in foster care in the ghetto, you figure you have one of three careers: drug dealer, pimp or thief," Michael said, leading the

363

way through the darkened offices to the warehouse. "The first two weren't attractive. I intended to be a thief, but one of the serious ones. Not armored cars. Jewelry heists. *Italian Job*. Cracking safes. So, I might have put a little study into it."

"Why does that not surprise me?" Josh said. "I guess I'm going to have to study criminal defense law just to keep you out of prison."

"I've already got a good attorney," Michael said as they entered the cave-dark warehouse. He lit up his aura for some light. Not full power and not extruded. The breakers for the main lights were to the left and he clicked them on. "Okay, time for some practice..."

"Okay," Michael said as they were finishing up the practice session. Jorge was getting into being dropped at speed by Sasha. He'd almost rolled into one of the I-beam supports of the ceiling, which would have taken it out.

They'd had to imagine the house. Michael had demonstrated he could pull Death Strong up fast by demonstrating it on Jorge. And as a test he'd tried grabbing Sasha with his powers.

He *could* hold her like a fly in amber. She didn't like it much.

"This week go in after school and get your costumes," Michael said.

"Costumes?" Sasha said.

"You think we're going to do this in civilian gear?" Michael asked.

"How, exactly, are we going to explain picking up our uniforms?" Josh asked.

"Easy..." Michael said.

"Hey," Michael said, opening up his locker. There was a male super changing out of workout gear in the locker room. "Uh, Mike Truesdale. Stone Tactical."

The timing of their patrols had them rarely meeting the regular Super Corps. So, Michael wasn't sure which one he was talking to.

"Hey," the guy said, nodding. "Dave Inada. Lightspeed." He looked uncomfortable for a moment then shrugged. "Heard about you and, uh, Bolt."

"I am not a transphobe," Michael said, pulling his gear out and putting it in an athletic bag. "Other than that, I can't really discuss it on advice of my attorneys."

"Got it," Lightspeed said. "And I didn't think you were—a

transphobe, that is. Though . . . Bolt gave a bad name to the whole thing. You're not clearing out, are you? We're not all . . . that way."

"Nah," Michael said, grinning at him. "Josh—Metalstorm—has an uptown friend who's having a costume party on Friday. Cosplay isn't *just* for Halloween in this generation. So, we thought it would be funny to go as *the Junior Super Corps!*"

"Okay," Lightspeed said, chuckling. "Yeah, I've been to a couple of science fiction conventions. Outreach, you know, and you get paid to sign photos," he added with a shrug. "One of them actually looked . . . a little less weird? So, I figured what the hell and put on my costume and wandered around."

"Lemme guess," Michael said. "There were better Lightspeeds."

"There *were!*" Lightspeed said, grinning. "There was a guy who did me better than *I* do me! It was weird as hell!"

"Hey, good talk," Michael said, shouldering the heavy bag. He had not realized how much stuff he carried on him.

"Good talk," Lightspeed said. "And, hey, Stone. We're really not all that way."

"Didn't think you were," Michael said, realizing that Lightspeed meant he was gay. "Not many are Bolts. Thank God."

"Glad you're okay. I was in Juniors with that asshole. He used to shock people just as a joke."

"I'm good," Michael said. "If what doesn't kill you makes you stronger, I be diamond."

"Pop the back," Michael said as Josh pulled up in an SUV with dark window tinting.

Michael had had to wait until his foster parents were asleep to fly out and meet them. Since his foster parents' recent revelation, they wouldn't have believed he was staying at Tim's, or any other story for that matter.

Everyone else had some excuse they could give for being out on a Friday night.

Josh was at a sleepover party with friends in the Hamptons. Yeah, it was winter but rich kids had to go *somewhere* to get away from their parents and far enough away from the flagpole any peccadillos wouldn't come to the attention of colleges.

Laura was at a kegger with Josh. That was actually what she'd told her mother, who was ecstatic. Josh was upper class and Laura's mom was a social climber by proxy. She didn't even seem to mind the concept of her daughter getting raped at a rich-kid party as long as she got a chance to "marry up."

Jorge had told his parents something resembling the truth: they had something they had to do as superheroes, but they weren't even telling Super Corps. His parents had told him not to get killed or have their green cards taken away, and come back with his shield or on it. Gotta love Hondurans.

Sasha hadn't had to tell her parents anything. They were in Italy. Most of the team had met up at her condo in SoHo.

Michael tossed the bag in the back, closed the hatch from the inside, and started stripping off his clothes.

"How'd it go?" Michael asked. The team had debated just wearing their costumes out of Sasha's place or changing in the car, but everyone was dressed in their costumes, including masks.

"Great, *hermanos*," Jorge replied. "The girls enjoyed changing in the back so much, they started making out."

"We did not!" Laura snapped.

"Went fine," Josh said. "Though next time I'm going to figure out how to drive the whole time."

"I'm a *good* driver!" Laura said.

Sasha snorted.

"What?"

"I've barely got my learners and I'm a better driver than you are," Sasha said.

"Maybe," Josh said. "But I don't want you ripping my dad's steering wheel off."

"It was *one time*!" Sasha said. "Freaked the hell out of my driving instructor."

"Laura," Michael said, pulling grenades, a tactical vest and commo out of his bag. "Pass the grenades and the vest up to Jorge. Everybody else take these and plug in."

"What are these?" Josh asked, not looking around.

"Commo," Michael said, tugging his earlobe. "Stuff top-line airsoft people use. Civilian frequency but they will stand up to punishment."

Michael had just had it handed to him by a courier. Though smoke grenades were, technically, available in some military supply stores, *juveniles* could not buy them. And the commo, while civilian made, was very top-of-the-line stuff.

It bothered him. There were babies to feed. Gondola didn't need to be spending money on this op. He'd intended to just use the government credit card; fully aware it was sort of a breach of trust.

He also intended to pay it back. Whether it had been Gondola or the US government. If anybody should be paying for it, it should be the feds. And it would have been if Gondola had just used the FBI.

But the Faerie Queen wanted it this way and what the Queen commanded was done.

Michael gave them some lessons on how to use the commo, not adding that they were going to be monitored the whole time.

"Main thing with commo is don't use it," Michael said.

"What do you mean, don't use it?" Laura said. "Why do you have it if you don't use it?"

"We're all on the same frequency," Michael said. "Which means that we'll be talking over each other if everybody gets excited and starts talking. You've got to keep everything you say to a minimum. Just say exactly what has to be said. Laura, what's your job?"

"Blow smoke," Laura said. "All through the downstairs of the house."

"If that's going well, you don't say anything at all," Michael said. "Jorge says 'Door down.' You say 'Blowing.' Just that word. That's all. Can you do that?"

"I guess," she said, fiddling with the headset. "This ruins the line of my costume!"

"I'm not sure I can use it with my system," Sasha said. She had her commo pack on her lap and her helmet off.

"Really?" Michael said. "Try jacking it into your commo."

She tested the jack and shook her head.

"You're serious?" she said. "This is designed for military-grade communications."

"Mil Spec isn't all it's cracked up to be," Michael said. "And this was designed off the same stuff yours was designed off of. It's why I chose it."

"Tony is going to shit a brick with you buying all this expensive hardware," Josh said. "Coming up on the parking garage."

They'd chosen a public parking garage by LaGuardia Airport as their takeoff point. It had rooftop parking, which was surprisingly rare, and since very few people would be around that time of night, they could take off unseen.

It also was secure, as Josh had been worried about his dad's SUV getting stripped or jacked.

The parking attendant gave Josh a funny look as he got his ticket. Josh just waved and proceeded through the open gate.

They parked on the roof and got out, Michael stretching his back from being in the cargo area.

"Okay," Michael said, waving everyone over. "I'd give you a pep talk but I've got something better than that."

He pulled out a large package of spearmint gum.

"Everybody take two, they're small," Michael said, pulling out two and sticking them in his mouth, then handing the package to Laura.

"Why?" Laura said, but she took a couple and passed it on.

"When you get into something real, your hands shake," Michael said, chewing the gum. "Your mouth goes dry. Chewing gum helps with the dry mouth. There's nothing that helps with the hands shaking but doing a few rodeos and this is your first one.

"Stay Zen," Michael said. "This isn't going to be much of anything. We've got a good plan, we've got backups. We're up against one super that's not going to be hard to handle and a whole bunch of normals who are going to be dealing with tear gas in their eyes courtesy of Hulke and Breeze.

"Keep off the commo," he continued. "Jorge. When you take the back door, what do you say?"

"Back door down," Jorge said.

"Laura, when you blow the back room, what do you say?"

"Back room blown," Laura said.

"Jorge, entry, what do you say?"

"Entering back," Jorge said.

"Josh, when you secure Cannibale, what do you say?"

"Target secure," Josh said.

"Sasha."

"Front door down. Entering front."

"Death Strong secure," Michael said. "Entering front. Short. Otherwise stay off comms." Michael turned toward their Invulnerable Ground. "Jorge, this is a bit of a safety issue, but we're going to straighten the cotter pins."

He pulled the grenades out and straightened all the pins.

"Don't get those caught and accidentally go off," he said. "They won't explode but it will be a hassle. But one of the big things that gets people is their hands are shaking and they have a hard time straightening the cotter pins. Don't clamp down on them. Be Zen when it's your time to toss. Don't throw them through the walls. Just light-toss into the back room, then into the breezeway. Let Breezy do the rest. Okay?"

"Okay," Jorge said seriously. "Been practicing with rocks getting a light toss."

"Just be Zen," Michael said. "In through the nose, out through the mouth. We're five very capable supers up against a sixty-year-old guy who may be called 'The Cannibal' but who isn't going to be eating anyone again, ever. We've planned this, we've rehearsed it.

"Sasha, you've got the nav," Michael said, nodding at her. "So, you're taking point. Do not lose me. We can't fly as fast as you. Right?"

"I'll be keeping an eye on you," Sasha said. "Slowpoke."

"It's going to go easy, people. Just be Zen. Okay? Josh, okay?"

"Okay," he said. "When did you take over as team leader?"

He didn't seem upset, more bemused.

"The day I arrived, Easy," Michael said, grinning. "Breezy, you easy?"

"I'm easy peasy," Laura said. "I fully intend to blow the shit out of everyone in the house. And I'd *better* get my money. I'm already spending it on shoes in my head."

She didn't look easy peasy. She looked scared to death. She'd be fine.

"Wing?" Michael asked.

"I'm Zen," Sasha said, nodding. "Honestly, what are they going to be able to do to *me*?"

"Jorge?"

"Let's go!" the diminutive IG said.

"Load up, Hulke," Michael said.

The IG clambered up the back of the female Flyer, who was taller than he was, and grabbed the straps of her support pack.

"Hulke's right," Michael said, donning goggles against the coming breeze. "Let's go fuck up some bad guys. What are we gonna do? We're gonna fuck 'em up. Say it."

"We're gonna fuck 'em up." "Hell, yeah!"

"I can't HEAR You!"

"WE'RE GONNA FUCK 'em UP!"

"Let's roll!" Michael said, picking up Josh and Laura and ascending into the night.

"I FORGOT I'M AFRAID OF *HEIIIGHTS!*" Josh whined. "AAAH..."

They assembled with the target in sight, hanging just out of the effect of the streetlights. The neighborhood wasn't exactly quiet at this late hour, and dogs barked all over, but Michael was confident the neighbors would steer clear once things got started. Flashing lights raced down the next street over and Michael briefly feared the cops were going to unwittingly blow the surprise, but it was just a single unit. It continued north without slowing and was soon out of sight. Things went back to being as quiet as they were going to get.

"Ready?" Michael said, tugging his earlobe. "Breezy, I'll put you down light. Jorge, you've got your jump to do. Keep on your feet when you land. I need to put Josh in at the same time as you hit the door. Let's go."

As agreed, Sasha kept to the same speed as Michael, coming in on his wing. He descended quickly but not so fast it was disorienting. As they reached the level of the roof, he swung Josh into the back balcony and dropped Breeze to the ground.

"Hulke," Michael said. "Drop!"

CHAPTER 35

"Honor" —Atreyu

Jorge Camejo finally felt like he was doing something superheroic. Everybody who was Latin of any Central American stripe *hated* the cartels except the ones who were in them. And of all the cartels that were most hated, MS-13 was high on the list.

This was what he was *made* for!

He jumped off Sasha's back, dropped about thirty feet through the air, and hit with a perfect superhero landing in the backyard, but then had to lean forward and catch himself with one hand.

Even better. That had to look *totally fría!* Why weren't they *filming* this?

He headed to the door, then wondered if he should wait. Josh had to get Cannibale first.

What if Michael doesn't have Death Strong yet, and he's waiting on the other side?

You're Hulke, man, knock that shit off.

He heard Josh land on the second-floor balcony of Cannibale's hideout and so he just kept going, hitting the door like a tiny battering ram.

Probably too hard—it went flying across the kitchen. He didn't know his own strength. Still, there'd been no glass to shatter, just like Michael had promised.

As he'd practiced, he stood to the side of the door and threw his first grenade into the lit interior.

"Dumbass!" Laura hissed as she ran over to stand behind him. "You've gotta *pull the pin!*"

"*¡Mierda!*" he muttered, pulling out the second grenade and yanking the pin this time. He partially bent the spoon and crushed the grenade, grabbing it too hard. Hoping it would still work, he threw that one in the room. The guards were still not reacting. He wasn't sure why. He'd better distract them.

He ran through the door at near speedster speed and the guards were just coming out of an experienced crouch. They thought that the grenade had been a flash-bang and had covered their ears and eyes as well as turning away. But now they were going in for guns. If bullets started flying, Laura might get hurt.

Jorge would never admit it to anyone, but he had a thing for Laura. Sasha was just . . . too much. She was an actual teenage supermodel and had been a child pageant queen before that. She was out of his league. Laura was a possible and he was willing to focus on the possible.

So, what was he going to possibly do to the guards to keep them from hurting Laura? If he hit them, it would kill them and while they were MS-13 and deserved it, that wasn't the plan. But he had to keep them distracted while the gas spread.

He ran up to the first one and flicked him in the crotch with his middle finger.

"*¡Mierda!*" the guard screamed, bending over and falling to the floor.

One of the other guards shot him and the bullet bounced off.

"*¡Soy invulnerable, maricón!*" he shouted, bouncing across the room like a Honduran soccer ball and striking that guard in the nuts as well.

About then the grenade went off and the room started to fill with smoke.

"Breeze!" he shouted, flicking another guard. "You're up!"

"*Hulke, more grenades, less flicking,*" Michael radioed.

"*Sí, Piedra,*" Jorge said, pulling out another grenade as the front door crashed open. "*Hale el pasador.*"

Josh put his hands over his face as it seemed he was going to be smashed through the glass door face-first. But it just melted down and away and he was suddenly in the dark room with a notorious criminal—after a brief struggle with the curtain.

El Cannibale was a veteran of hundreds of attempts to catch him. He was up and out of the bed faster than Josh could react, the machete coming fast at the teen.

Josh reacted to *that* instinctively, throwing his hand up to protect himself while grabbing the metal and pulling it to him.

Unfortunately, he forgot to bend or otherwise change the blade and it sliced the outside of his arm.

"Motherf—" he said as Cannibale bowled into him. The old man was wiry and strong. He also had a heck of a punch.

Fast, too. With one punch to distract what was obviously a super, he was out the door and over the railing of the balcony.

"Shit, shit, shit," Josh said, rushing outside while holding his bleeding arm. Cannibale was on the ground, just getting up.

He jumped off the balcony and leapt onto the old man's back, a double action that he *never* would have tried if he'd thought about it.

He brought Cannibale to the ground, then rolled off.

"¡Maricón!" Cannibale snarled, reaching down and throwing some dirt at his face. It stopped in midair and flew back into Cannibale's face.

Josh used the distraction to dart forward, grab the cartel leader's wrist, and throw a leg over his arm. In a moment, he'd taken him to the ground and had him in an arm bar.

"That actually *worked*," he muttered.

Then Cannibale bit him and he let up on instinct. People didn't bite in class, but he couldn't let the bastard get out. He kicked Cannibale in the jaw—another thing you didn't do in class—and reworked his leg tighter up against his neck. He wrenched harder on the arm bar and the ankle biter struggled uselessly.

There was a bit of metal fence just at the edge of his range. He turned it into a snake of metal, wrapped that around Cannibale's other wrist, brought it up, and had him secured. For good measure he wrapped his ankles.

About then he realized he was still bleeding. *And* he might have rabies.

He sat down on the cursing cartel leader's back and keyed his mike.

"Easy," he panted. "Target secured."

⊕ ⊕ ⊕

Laura was just getting ready to start swirling the smoke that Jorge had finally created when her ankles were taken out from under her, and she landed on her face. There was a shot and a ricochet a second after she hit the ground.

"*Breeze, stay down,*" Michael radioed. "*Gunfire. Begin blow.*"

His voice was so totally stress-free it calmed her down. She peeked around the door, then started blowing air from the kitchen straight down the breezeway.

"Blow *this*, motherfuckers!" she said as Jorge tossed another grenade.

When Jorge had jumped off her back, Sasha sped up, not too fast, and flew out over Britton Avenue. She made a hard turn and hovered for a moment.

"*Wing,*" Michael radioed. "*Door.*"

Just as she started her run, she saw a naked male, presumably Death Strong, crash through the roof of the house.

Michael was doing *his* job. Time to do hers.

She accelerated at the front door, horizontal, hands above her head, fingers spread. She'd asked Patrick—Iron Eagle—if it was fists or spread hands to do a door. Fists tended to just punch through the door, he'd said, so you spread your hands.

The metal security door smashed open with barely a crunch against her palms, and she flared out to a perfect landing in the living room.

There were four men in the room who had been watching a soccer game on TV. They were just getting up at the commotion upstairs and in the back as she flared out and landed, placing her hands on her hips and posing in proper superheroine fashion.

"*Ala de Marfil, Voladora Invulnerable,*" she said in fair high school Spanish. "*Deberías rendirte.*"

Ivory Wing, Invulnerable Flyer. You should surrender.

They went for their guns instead.

Couldn't have that. Civilians might get hurt.

She grabbed one shotgun that was brandished at her and bent the barrel. About then, the others started to have problems with their wrists. They seemed to be broken.

Then the tear gas arrived, and things got worse for them.

"Wing," Sasha radioed. "Front room secure. Nice blowing, Breeze."

Suddenly, Jorge came bounding into the front room. He tossed another grenade, then started flicking the choking guards in their nether regions. And things got still worse for them.

He held up his hands, holding down the middle finger of each hand with his thumb.

"*¡He aquí las diminutas manitas de la muerte!*" he screamed.

He looked at the TV for a moment and gasped.

"Oh, my God, is that Guatemala versus Argentina?" he yelled.

"Hey, Wing," he said, gesturing toward her with his eyes fixed on the TV. "Can you get me a drink out of the refrigerator?"

"Suuure, Hulke," Sasha said drily. "Right after I, you know, zip-tie these guys."

"Maybe Breezy can get me one," he said. "Hey, Breeze, can you grab me a drink out of the fridge . . . ?"

"She's got more important things to do," Michael replied as he walked through the door and keyed his mike. "Breeze, go help out Easy with Cannibale. He's got a cut arm."

He looked at Wing and choked a bit on the smoke.

"Ready to start zip-tying?" he asked, his eyes watering.

"Let's," Sasha said. "I'll hold 'em, you zip 'em."

Ramon Sanchez folded the stock of his sniper rifle and began putting it away. The couple who rented the ninth-story flat overlooking the corner of Britton Avenue and Ketcham Street had received an opportunity for a trip to Disney World for them and their entire family. Since that was a trip they could never afford, they took it.

Ed Carson folded the stock of the sniper rifle and started putting it away . . .

James Garvier folded the stock of his sniper rifle and started putting it away . . .

"*Situation is clear. Operation complete. Thanks for the overwatch, ladies and gentlemen.*"

Bonfire nodded at Summer Storm.

"Guess the kids did it," he said thoughtfully.

"They're not bad," she said, taking his hand. "Now let's go home and act like we're making babies."

"You're on," he said.

"*Hola, Cannibale*," Michael said, squatting down and looking at his nemesis.

NYPD had arrived along in a fleet of flashing cop cars and were in a flurry of activity cordoning the area, taking statements, and marking evidence. There was also surprisingly fast response from a couple of FBI agents who had been in the area on a stakeout. They strutted around as if this was their win and promptly took custody of the Juniors' primary captive. But before he got carted away, Michael wanted to look in his eyes just once.

There wasn't much there to see. All humanity had drained from the guy decades ago.

"*Asesinaste a una vieja puta callejera*," Michael said. "*Te puse en prisión por el resto de tu vida. Yo gano.*"

You murdered an old street whore. I put you in prison for the rest of your life. I win.

"*Te voy a follar el cráneo*," Cannibale said then spit. "*Enviaré maldición sobre ti. Morirás por mi mano.*"

I will skull-fuck you. I will send curses upon you. You will die by my hand.

"*Vas a supermax, mi amigo. Nunca nos volveremos a ver. En cuanto a las maldiciones, estoy protegido por la Reina de las Hadas. Tus maldiciones no significan nada para mí. Adiós. Vete al infierno donde perteneces.*"

You are going to supermax, my friend. We will never see each other again. As for curses, I am protected by the Fairy Queen. Your curses mean nothing to me. Goodbye. Go to hell where you belong.

Michael got up and walked back into the still slightly smoky house.

"*¡TE CAZARÁ, PIEDRA!*" Cannibale screamed. "*¡NUNCA DORMIRÁS SEGURO! ¡TE CAZARÁ, PIEDRA!*"

"What's he saying?" an NYPD officer said, coming through the door with a set of handcuffs out.

"Dunno," Michael said. "*No habla* the *Español.*"

"Hey!" the officer yelled. "How do I get this metal off his wrists . . . ?"

⊕　⊕　⊕

"Do I even want to *hear what* in the glory of *God* you were *thinking*?" Tony asked, standing in front of them with his hands on his hips.

Cannibale had been taken away under strict guard when NYPD had finally gotten through their heads who they had their hands on. The FBI agent who had taken charge, Hinkle, was pretty clear that he needed to *not* get away.

Most of the rest had had to be carted to the hospital for toxic smoke inhalation and various broken bones. Activity was dying down, and the number of cop cars was slowly dwindling.

Iron Eagle and Night Wing had carried the still struggling Death Strong off to Super Containment. He'd be stored next to Electrobolt. They could play pinochle.

When the bare necessity had been completed, Tony lined them up on the stairs of the house for a Strict Talking To.

"It was a Friday night?" Easy said, shrugging, then wincing at his still healing arm. "We were bored?"

"Did Easy just make a joke?" Michael said as the group chuckled a bit hysterically. It was sinking in that they'd won.

"This is not a joke," Tony said angrily.

"I take full responsibility," Michael said. "It's all on me. My idea. My plan."

"You *can't* take responsibility, Stone," Tony said. "You're not even *team leader*. And you're kids. I'm the one who's on the hook!"

"For more than this," Michael said. "I have violated honor in one way. All the gear we needed went on the credit card. Also, a dinner when we planned it. I'll pay it back."

"You'll pay it back..." Tony said, waving his hand in a chopping gesture. "That's not the *point*!"

"Falcon," Michael said. "We just rounded up *two* people who have Interpol *Red Notices*. The combined reward for them is around five million dollars. That's how much the federal government, and *other* governments, *hate* those guys. Any idea how many El Salvadoran police Death Strong has killed? He killed a French consulate official!

"We're not expecting a pat on the back because, yeah, we should have gone through the proper channels. But they were after *me*. And my team agreed that *we* should handle it. We're not expecting a pat on the back and we *are* expecting to be railed at and grounded. But it was our job to do. And we did it very well."

"Metalstorm got cut!" Tony said.

"We're supers," Michael said. "We super-heal. If he'd gotten *impaled*, he'd live. As it is, he's got a great story to tell at law school. He personally captured one of the most wanted criminals in the western hemisphere. Pain fades, chicks dig scars, glory lasts forever."

"You got all the answers," Tony said.

"This is the guy who ordered the killing of my Mama," Michael said tightly. "Be glad you got him *alive*, Falcon..."

"You," Secretary Harris said, staring out the expansive windows in her office, "are the biggest *headache* I have ever had in my *life*."

Frank and Linda had not appreciated being awoken by the FBI. Nor had the other parents who were planning on sleeping in Saturday morning. All the parents were livid. There had been Words. All the Words.

The news had broken on Saturday morning. Nobody paid attention to the news on Saturday morning. And nobody had ever *heard* of El Cannibale or Death Strong. It was going to be up to the news media to decide if the American public deserved to be informed.

"I am literally the reason God created pain receptors, Madame Secretary," Michael said. This was the first time he'd ever been alone with the Secretary, and it felt like he was meeting the real woman, not the politician. "I was born, bred, indeed, created in a vat programmed by mad scientists *just* to give *you* a headache, Madame Secretary."

Secretary Harris put her hand out in a throat-gripping motion, then clamped it into a fist and started to laugh.

"Okay," she said, nodding. "That's actually kind of funny. Oh, God, kid!"

"Should we have just taken the intel to the FBI? Maybe. But we chose this route. It wasn't for glory, though there is some. It was mostly because the team and I recognized that Cannibale was only in town to go after *us*. Let us take the risk."

"But you *don't have to*," Secretary Harris said, shaking her head and wistfully looking back out the window. "We have a full Corps that could have handled this. When we went after NK, all there were were kids. I was the *oldest*. Just turned nineteen and we'd been chasing him for a year. Normals couldn't take him down. He'd killed the vice president, senators, congressmen and -women, tried to get the President, twice, before we caught him.

"And we lost... too many. Black Hornet was *your* age, Michael. I watched him die, while wrapped in hardened steel I couldn't escape. Watched him torn apart by NK. I *never* want another child to die on my watch. I watched him *die*."

"When you went up against NK, Madame Secretary, you had *no* chance to plan," Michael said, tugging his earlobe. "You had to just go in there and hope for the best. And you were up against the most dangerous super-killer in history. A person who was practically a Vishnu."

She turned back toward him as he spoke but only met his eyes for a moment before dropping her gaze to the floor.

"We *planned* this," he continued. "Carefully and *well*. We had *backup* plans. And we were five well-trained albeit junior supers up against all normals except one IG who was easy enough to take off the field.

"If we'd been up against anything like NK, oh, hell yeah, I'd have pulled the emergency handle," Michael said, nodding emphatically. "If it had been somebody like Bionic or Stormsurge, we'd have pulled the emergency handle. We don't get paid enough for something like that! Although, we *are* going to be well paid."

"How so?" Secretary Harris said, looking back up at him.

"We're not federal employees," Michael said. "There's five million dollars in reward money on these two."

"I hope you didn't do it for the money!" Secretary Harris said.

"That's an improvement," Michael said, smiling whimsically.

"What is?" Harris asked.

"It used to be you'd assume I *only* did it for money," Michael said, shaking his head. "But, no. I didn't. I'm going to donate most of it. Same with whatever we enter into as a settlement. I don't do this for money. I do it 'cause it's the right thing to do."

"Madame Secretary, there have been some accusations directed at Stone Tactical of, well, transphobia. Given some of the revelations about Electrobolt, those may have been exaggerated somewhat. But can you comment on that?"

"There are some discussions going on right now as well as an ongoing investigation. And so, I cannot directly comment on that but I will, dipping a bit, into Stone Tactical's, uh, secret identity and background give you some information that may inform that question.

"Stone is a foundling who was raised in foster care in a primarily BIPOC economically disadvantaged urban area. He was found as a newborn by a black transgender street prostitute who attempted to adopt him but was rebuffed. But while he was bounced from one foster home to another, that woman remained the closest person he had to a mother growing up as he was the closest person she would ever have to her own child. The child she'd found newborn in an alleyway.

"While it was not the primary driver for this apprehension, it should be noted that she was recently killed and the organized criminal enterprise that is believed to be responsible is MS-13. Police believe that she was killed because they were targeting Stone, as previously discussed, and could not get to him immediately. So, they killed the closest person he had to a mother. The woman he called Mama.

"So, if you'd like to accuse Stone of being a transphobe, it's a free country. Or a racist. Or a white supremacist or a homophobe, what have you. But be aware that you're making those accusations about someone who called a six-foot-four African American transgender woman 'Mama.'"

EPILOGUE

When Michael got out of school, there was a text message from Frank Galloway.

Talked to the coroner. Miss Cherise body to be disposed in no more than thirty days. Sorry, I tried.

"Well," Boogie Knight muttered, "now I got me some time... *Somebody* gots to *pay...*"

Michael looked up at the bus schedule at the cash window in the New York Port Authority bus station. He was wearing a hoodie, Covid mask, and sunglasses. His cellphone was in his locker at school.

"First bus to *anywhere*," he said to the clerk.

Josh checked his phone as he was leaving school and there was an email from Michael on his official JCS account.

He opened it, paused, and muttered: "What the fuck?"

Dear All,

Writing these words are hard. In the short time I've been in New York, I've come to know so many wonderful people and you are all such good friends and parents. Even good social workers and bureaucrats, which is something I never thought I'd write.

But sometimes things have to happen that you have to do yourself. Things no one else can do for you. Things that no one can help you with. And one of those things has entered my life.

So, I am leaving. But I will be back. Think of it as a sabbatical.

There is a legend among the Chesapeake that when a person dies, they walk out across the bay and their forebearers and friends who went before greet them where the moon meets the water. It is a saying where I come from when you know you will meet again, but do not know when.

We will see each other again, where the moon meets the water.
Michael
Stone Tactical

"The clerk at the bus station wasn't sure if it was him but described a white male about his height and guess as to his age asking for 'the first bus to anywhere,'" Special Agent Smith said over the video link. "'The first bus to anywhere' was to Westchester. We observed him boarding the bus. It was scheduled to arrive after the BOLO went out and we specifically contacted the Westchester field office asking them to intercept.

"He wasn't on the bus. We're currently attempting to determine where he exited but he appears to have changed on the bus and no one that was interviewed, including the driver, remembered where he got off. We're continuing to follow leads."

"So, he's in the wind," the director said.

"Yes, sir," Smith replied.

"Family," Dr. Swanson said, respectfully standing at her desk. It had been a while since the Secretary had visited. "You should have asked me first."

"Has he ever indicated he wanted to reconnect with family?" Katherine asked.

"No," Swanson said. "He's even indicated he didn't want to. 'My Mama was a ho and to my daddy I was just a squirt.' His words. But he's also lying. Michael is very differently abled, but he is also human. And virtually every adoption child, foster care, wants to meet their parents. They may fear doing so, but they want to at the same time. Conflicted. But that's my take. He's seeking his family. Or . . ."

She paused and grimaced.

"What?" Katherine asked.

"Well . . ." Dr. Swanson said, looking thoughtful. "Even with the capture of Cannibale ... someone did *kill* the closest person he's ever had to a mother ..."

"So ..." Katherine said.

"He told me once there are only three rules on the street," Michelle said. "Big boys don't cry, never snitch, always get revenge."

"Are you saying what I think you're saying?" Katherine asked.

"Do we really wanna go there, Katherine?"

"Are we talking about MS-13?" the Secretary asked.

"Yes," Michelle answered.

Katherine thought about it for a few moments.

"I think you're probably right," Katherine said. "He's probably looking for family. Other than that ... I have discovered a sudden disinterest in his whereabouts ..."

"Line of Blood" — Ty Stone

"Thanks for the ride, man!" Mike said as he got out of the pickup.

"You gonna be okay?" the driver asked, shaking his head. The area was not the best.

"Just got to visit some friends here," Mike said. "I'll be fine and dandy."

He walked a few blocks, got on a bus, and then started switching buses along the way, checking the area around Falls Church, Virginia, and Fairfax County.

It was after dark when he found what he was looking for in a bar off Highway 7. The dive was in the center of a block covered with MS-13 tags. There were a number of people lounging around outside, and the sound of raucous Latin music spilled out of the open door.

The party was in full swing.

Using Sight, he could see that, inside the bar, about half the men were carrying and there were machetes behind the bar.

There was an office in the back, an entrance to the side of the kitchen. There were a few guys just hanging out in the hallway, couple of machetes leaning on the wall. In the office were three more men, two just lounging around, one behind a desk. There was also a safe that had money in it. Everybody was armed with guns and knives. Even the desk had a gun concealed under it.

He put on a skull Covid mask and walked over, then paused outside to surreptitiously move some dust and dirt from the floor into the barrel of the pistol under the desk. It was probably connected to a magnet, but he couldn't see it. Why couldn't he see metallic iron?

Then he walked into MS-13 Central.

He didn't say anything to anyone, just threaded his way through the patrons. A few people gave him a look, but it was just a passing glance. El Salvadorans, like Hondurans, tended to run short. Mike was big for his age. He was just a guy wearing a mask. They'd become common since Covid. He wasn't one of theirs, but they knew some people would come and go that weren't, exactly, their people. The jefe occasionally met with couriers.

If he'd stuck around at all, questions would be asked. So, he just threaded at a normal pace through the crowd and ignored the looks.

He wasn't planning on sticking around. Egress would be the real issue.

If Gondola had taught him anything, it was to have a plan and a backup plan and a backup plan for that backup plan, ad infinitum 'til you'd run out of ideas of what could go wrong. Then come up with more.

He had a plan and a backup plan and a backup for that plan.

His ultimate backup was his usual ultimate backup: Kill them all, Satan would know his own. The rest was what attorneys were for.

He pushed though the swinging door to the kitchen area behind the bar, ignoring the startled look of one of the waitresses, and headed to the back.

The two thugs outside the door picked up their machetes. They weren't expecting visitors, but it wasn't like the guy looked like a threat.

He picked both of them up by their rib bones, ripped the door open, and tossed them through the doorway. Then he flared a partial aura. Enough to give them a clue just how fucked they were.

He could see in Sight that the two thugs in the room had gone in for machetes, too. Before he reached the door, he broke both their wrists. So much for weapons. Then he tossed them on the pile with the other thugs.

When he walked through the doorway, aura flared, eyes blazing over the skull mask, the jefe was pointing his pistol at him. But the guy was shaking.

"*¡No tienes una orden de arresto!*" the jefe said.

You don't have a warrant for your arrest!

"*¿Qué parte de resplandeciente y enojado no está clara?*" Mike asked. "*Aprieta el gatillo, maricón. Mira lo bien que te hace.*"

What part of glowing and angry is unclear? Pull the trigger, faggot. See what good it does you.

Give the guy credit for guts. He pulled the trigger.

The gun blew apart in his hand.

"*Hijo de puta!*"

"Hurts, don't it?" Michael said, stepping around the pile of thugs.

"*¡Llamaré a mi abogado!*"

I will call my attorney!

"*Bueno. Entonces lo mataré a él también.*"

Good. Then I'll kill him, too.

"*¡No puedes matarnos! ¡Ustedes son los buenos!*"

You can't kill us! You're the good guys!

Mike tossed his backpack on the desk, lifted one of the guards into the air, and broke his neck accompanied by a gesture of his head. Then he tossed him in the corner of the office.

"*No soy ese tipo de chico bueno,*" Mike said.

I'm not that kind of good guy.

"You motherfuckers killed my Mama," Michael said, leaning on the desk. "I don't gots the money to bury her proper. Somebody gots to pay for the funeral. Seems like it be you. Open the safe."

When the jefe had gotten the safe opened with his off hand, Mike gazed at the stacks of cash, then looked at the men. Their arms were covered in roses and angels. Every rose was a rape, every angel a murder. He thought about all his dealings with MS-13, starting *before* the Muertos. The things he never talked about. About Mary and Marysville.

Then he stopped the earth elements in their skulls and watched their bodies drop to the floor.

"That's for all the Marys in the world," he whispered. He opened up a hole in the concrete floor, slid the bodies into it, then down deep beneath the bar. The spare dirt he moved down into the storm drain in the street.

Then he started loading the bag with cash.

"Somebody gots to pay," he whispered.

⊕ ⊕ ⊕

"Hold onto the rest?" Mike said, pulling about ten thousand dollars out of the bag.

"I'll make sure it gets where it has to go," Valerian said. The Russian contact he'd met at the Brighton Beach restaurant looked at the bag full of cash. "And we'll hold onto what's left over until you need it. You could have cleaned off the blood, *tovarisch*."

"Gimme a number for your boy in Baltimore," Mike said. "I'll tell him who to contact . . ."

"Bruno Hilyer."

"Yo, Bruno, Michael Edwards," Mike said over the phone. "What up, my man?"

Bruno Hilyer was one of the top criminal defense attorneys in Maryland and the guy who had gotten Mike out of several legal jams back in his time as Boogie Knight. The only reason he'd bother to represent a penniless street rat was the cases were so high-profile, the media attention paid for them.

Mike had gotten him onto CNN, MSNBC, *and* Fox. And from that he and his firm had gotten a slew of clients who could actually pay.

It had been a win-win proposition for them both.

"Michael!" Bruno said, in his booming voice. Mike had once asked him what his model was for being an attorney, was it Clarence Darrow or what? He'd been unsurprised to find out it was Denny Crane from *Boston Legal*. "Was wondering if I'd ever hear from my favorite client again! How's Super Corps treating you?"

"Like a runaway Brinks truck careening down a hill," Mike said. "Full of budget, no brains to be found."

"Sounds like the federal government in general," Bruno said. "To what do I owe the honor of this call I'm going to charge you for some day?"

"Take some out of what I'm sending you," Mike said. "You remember Miss Cherise. My Mama?"

"Six-four trans are hard to forget," Bruno said.

"She dead," Mike said. "Thirteen kilt her."

"I'm sorry to hear that," Bruno said, sounding actually sorry. "That's gotta be hard."

"Deal with it later," Mike said. "Some persons have generously contributed to give her a funeral. Cash. Contact Frank Galloway at Baltimore PD homicide. He'll know the details. Fellow gonna call you about the funds. May have a Slavic accent. But there's money there to get her decent buried. In a plot. Should be enough for that, too."

"Generous and entirely *legal* contribution?" Bruno asked.

"They didn't make no fuss about it when I axed nicely," Mike said. "Say you'll do it and I ain't got to axe nobody else. 'Cause I cain't exactly come down there and do it myself. Probably be some '13 show up just lookin' for me."

"I'll take care of it, Mike," Bruno said. "Yeah, coming back would be a bad idea."

"Talk at Preacher Henry at the barbershop," Mike said. "Axe can she get a church funeral. And if you could . . ." Mike stopped for a second. *Big boys don't cry.* "Axe can he get the choir to sing the 'Hallelujah.' The Leonard Cohen one. She liked that."

"I'll take care of it," Bruno said. "You take care of yourself, okay, kid?"

"See you where the moon meets the water, Bruno."

"Where the moon meets the water."

Kalispell, Montana, after 11 p.m. in January, was no place to try to sleep on the street. Mike was going to have to find some shelter. But, then again, with Earth powers he could make one.

Every sane person was home this time of night. Barely a car passed on the main drag. There was a bar and grill down the street from Smith's Foods where the bus had dropped him off, but he'd eaten before getting on the bus and shelter was more important.

He looked up at the cloud-tossed moon over the mountains to the east. In the morning, he was going to be paying a call to his biological father and seeing how that went. Whatever the outcome, he'd be going back to New York at some point. He was going after the Trust.

And Heaven was coming with him.

Vengeance is mine, sayeth the Lord. I am just how He gets it.

He tucked his hands in his pockets and, his chin low against the wind and snow, walked into the darkness. Walking to where the moon meets the water. . . .

"Hallellujah" —Pentatonix